Song of Surrender

"Perhaps we created the song together," Jason said, his words slurred as he pulled Colleen down to him. "A song as beautiful . . . as ineffably sweet and beautiful . . . as you."

For Colleen, the yearning was as great. Four years of waiting. Four years of dreaming. Four years of wanting . . .

And at last, in the pastoral quiet of the spring afternoon, she felt the soft texture of Jason's mouth, the moist fire of his tongue, the power of his loins.

There was no room for thought, only feeling, as the natural music of their ever-more insistent bodies led them inexorably into the timeless dance of love . . .

REBELS IN LOVE

Shana Carrol

A JOVE BOOK

REBELS IN LOVE

A Jove Book/published by arrangement with
Shanew Corporation

PRINTING HISTORY
Jove edition/July 1985

ISBN: 0-515-08249-X

Jove books are published by The Berkley Publishing Group,
200 Madison Avenue, New York, N.Y. 10016.
The words "A JOVE BOOK" and the "J" with sunburst
are trademarks belonging to Jove Publications, Inc.

∾ *May, 1780* ∾

Five years had passed—five heartbreaking, heroic years—
since Paul Revere had roused the New England Minutemen
and the shot heard 'round the world had ignited the American
Revolution.

For the first thirty-six months, the radical Patriots of the
North resisted the English onslaught, so much so that by 1778
Britain was forced to switch strategies: the new plan was to
conquer the far more conservative South.

The plan worked in its initial stages. Savannah fell; Augusta
fell; and in May 1780, General Benjamin Lincoln surrendered
his army of five thousand as the proud city of Charleston—
renowed for its alluring beauty, its lucrative commerce, and its
cosmopolitan culture—fell into British hands. This was the
rebels' darkest hour. The tide had turned against them. The
state of South Carolina—the great South itself—was under
the command of General Lord Charles Cornwallis.

And yet, even as Loyalists rejoiced and patriots planned
their next, desperate moves, even as intrigue and espionage
infiltrated the plantations, the battle camps, the gunsmith shops,
and the society balls, nature renewed the earth with its blissful
promise of fresh green life. Spring arrived in the fertile Carolina
countryside with balmy breezes blown sweetly from a docile
Atlantic. Wildflowers rioted over hill and vale in extravagant
yellows and blues. Lilac and magnolia filled the air with their

heady, perfumed presence. And a young woman of twenty, no matter how keen her sense of politics or deep her concern for her family's welfare, could not resist—at least not for a fleeting moment—the seductive reveries of a distant longing, the delicious daydreams of impassioned romance....

PART I

∽ *Chapter 1* ∽

Colleen Cassandra McClagan had heard the melody before, yet something had changed. The song was stronger, clearer, louder. It sounded so close, so insistent, that she could almost make out a message. There were words to the song—a poem, a promise, a melody born of the breeze, a windsong that played upon her lips, caressed her ear, and excited her heart. Its source seemed to be the sea, that vast expanse of royal blue that glistened under the brilliant mid-morning sun.

Colleen stood atop the hill, breathed in the magnificence of the landscape that stretched before her—the sweep of white below, the clusters of budding bushes and infant grass—extended her arms to the cloudless sky, closed her eyes, and silently gave thanks for the gift of her life, the miracle of the moment. When she opened her eyes, she suddenly felt foolish for whiling away her time among violets and chirping bluebirds, foolish for ignoring the danger that surrounded her, for forgetting the hour, the obligations, the harsh reality and grave responsibilities she faced as a daughter and a citizen . . . and yet . . .

The sweetness of the song stayed with her. Her eye followed the winding coastline, miles to the north and miles to the south, and beyond to the dazzling sea. What was the sea singing? What was the sea saying? Why was the ocean's endless blue so hypnotic? Like some exotic drug, it had her seeing things,

believing things, harboring hopes too bold to express. She
squinted through the peephole formed by her fist. Could she
see the tip of a sail, a tiny dot of white jutting above the horizon?
Could the distant vessel be the source of the song? She stared
ahead. There *was* a ship coming to port. It was no illusion, no
dream. The song was real and it was being sung for her. Finally,
she allowed herself the thought: *He's on the ship. He's coming
home. Home at last . . .*

The thought frightened her. She had dreamed the dream
before, and it had proven false. Instead, there had been ships
of war, ships carrying death and destruction, ships of soldiers
whom she viewed as cruel jailers, men commissioned by a
foreign despot to tax and tyrannize a people deserving of their
own freedom. These were thoughts, though, that she dared not
utter, especially not to her father, whose wild Scottish temper
would explode in fury. He already suspected her sentiments,
and his suspicion was enough to cause her anguish. Colleen
McClagan was not afraid of her patriotic convictions; quite to
the contrary. Though born in America, she, too, had the heart
and courage of a valiant Scot. It was only because she loved
her father with such tenderness and compassion that she would
rather bite her tongue than hurt him. She understood the depth
of his pain. She was all that he had in the world.

I am close. I am coming to you. We'll be together soon.

How could she deny the words to the song? The white speck
on the horizon grew and blossomed like a lily until a full set
of sails was visible. The melody set her heart racing. Was it
just another cruel hoax, another unfulfilled fantasy? He had
been gone forty-eight months, exactly fourteen hundred fifty
days. She prayed that there would be no more numbers to count,
no more surreptitious markings to hide each morning in the
secret compartment of the miniature music box which, despite
the fact that it had belonged to her mother, Colleen could never
bring herself to destroy. She cherished the box and the tiny
doll that danced atop its etched surface, just as she cherished
the daily ritual of remembering him, his wildly curly hair as
he . . .

"Colleen!" The voice of her father carried from their house
at the southern foot of the hill. "You don't want to be late now,
lass. Your Mr. Somerset won't want to be kept waiting. Come
down here this very instant!"

"Yes, Papa!" she cried, catching one last glimpse of the

ship—closer, it was coming closer—as she raced down the hill.

Dr. Roy Wallace McClagan studied the vision of loveliness running toward him. He couldn't help but see how, at age twenty, his daughter so closely resembled her mother, Sheena. At once, the thought delighted and alarmed him. It had been a decade and a half since Sheena had left him. Her desertion and the bloody battle of Cullodeen, during which, at age sixteen, he had seen his fellow Scotsmen mercilessly slaughtered at the hands of the English, had hardened his heart to wars and women. The single exception, though, was the girl who had grown into the woman who offered him the purest love he had known in his lonely lifetime. Watching Colleen—the wind playing with the long tresses of rich blond hair that danced beneath her bee-bright bonnet—he was almost frightened by her beauty.

Her face was illuminated by sparkling amber eyes that revealed a quick intelligence. Her forehead was noticeably high, her flawless skin the color of pearl. With prominent cheekbones accented by deep-set dimples, she expressed a sense of spirited motion. Her smile sang. Somewhat below average height, her slim waist and small breasts added to her youthful, fresh-faced appeal. Her lithe, limber body revealed both a daintiness and a daring. Was her beauty centered in her generous, alluring mouth or her thin, delicate neck? It was difficult to determine, for Colleen's physical appeal went beyond the elegance of her slender nose or the way in which her eyelashes fluttered and curled. In her fiery eyes, her father saw the sun rising over the Highlands of his native land. His daughter blazed with life.

How long could he keep her? When would she leave him? Her smile rivaled the radiance of summer as he watched her race toward him with the grace of a fawn. Well, now, he reminded himself, he had decided already; of course she'd marry, and marry soon, a marriage good for her and good for him. Buckley Somerset was a gentleman and, more to the point, he was wealthy. What more could a father ask for his daughter? Buckley's plantation was but a few miles from McClagan's humble farm. It would be fine indeed to watch his grandchildren grow up in such a secure and opulent setting.

"Good morning, Papa," Colleen said breathlessly, kissing him on his salt-and-pepper whiskers. His brow, normally knit in a series of nervous furrows, relaxed for the first time that day. "Don't worry," she added. "I'll be on time."

"But will you be civil to the gentleman?"

"Civil and sweet," she promised.

"And sincere," he reminded her. "'Tis a rare quality in a woman, lass. A quality far more precious than gold."

Colleen looked into her father's kind but weary eyes. At fifty, he looked at least twenty years older. He reminded her of a frail bird. His back was bent into a painful stoop. Without his customary wig, his thin strands of white hair were tossed about by the wind, making him seem especially vulnerable. He often spoke of quitting his practice, but Colleen never believed him: he would never abandon the suffering children whom he so lovingly attended, the elderly men and women, even the stray puppies and kittens, the ailing birds and horses, toward all of whom he felt a personal and compelling responsibility to nurture back to health. When his remedies failed, he was despondent for days. But when his cures took, his heart filled with gladness.

Colleen just didn't have the heart to tell her father how Buckley Somerset, for all his power and wealth, bored her to tears. Somehow, sometime later she would tell him that he was absolutely unacceptable to her as anything more than a polite escort. But not on the day of the annual Brandborough Spring Fair, a sprawling picnic that promised an afternoon and evening filled with pleasant diversions. "What a lovely spring morning," she said, taking her father's arm and heading toward the house. "You can see practically all the way across the ocean."

"What I want to see is you all prim and proper, so hurry and dress. This is no occasion for skimping, mind you. I've set Portia to heating water for your bath, so run along. And dress in your best. I'd wear that white silk headdress if I were you. Indeed, I would."

She didn't bother to answer. With no intention of wearing a headdress and veil more befitting a wedding than a picnic, she dismissed the thought and, pausing only to look over her shoulder, hurried to the house.

The house that she and her father shared stood at the base of the hill. It was a simple structure, yet spoke volumes of its master. The front rooms were for sitting and dining, and the spacious back room, which faced the great hill, was used as the doctor's study. In between were two bedrooms. Colleen's faced the open sea and her father's looked toward their farmland to the west. The entire house was dominated by Roy's profession, and smelled of an apothecary. Dozens of jars of ointments and salves stood on shelves in the hallway and along window ledges. Medical tomes lay open on every available surface— tables and stools, desks and chairs. A large variety of anatomical diagrams hung from the walls of his study, the hallways, even the small kitchen. Portia, their loquacious housekeeper, complained constantly about the macabre figures, but to no avail. Dr. McClagan was a man obsessed with his work, and his work followed him from room to room. Because he was a physician of greater instinct than organization, his surgical tools—pewter syringes, tortoiseshell tweezers, scalpels, screw tourniquets—might be found anywhere.

Colleen appreciated her father's impassioned relationship to his work. His compelling concern to broaden his knowledge, hone his skills, and cure the world's ills was the finer side of his character. It was exhilarating to live in a household where learning and healing were unending preoccupations. The overwhelming presence of medical paraphernalia, however, no matter how intriguing, could also be oppressive.

In all the house, Colleen's bedroom was her refuge, a space of her own special decor and design. The room was serene and feminine, and had been decorated largely by her paternal aunt, Rianne, who in many ways served as her friend, mother, and confidante. Rianne had come to America to care for Colleen some fifteen years earlier when Sheena McClagan had shocked everyone by abandoning her husband and young daughter. Rianne hadn't been surprised. A spinster, she'd expected the worse from the moment her brother had set sail for the colonies in 1750. She knew her brother, knew that he was of a breed that seemed to attract misfortune, so she waited. When he wrote with joyous expectations of being apprenticed to a surgeon, she waited. When he told her of his marriage to a brown-eyed beauty of Scottish descent, she waited. When word reached her, in 1760, of Colleen's birth, she tempered her joy with gloomy premonitions. Her brother was too happy, things were going too well. At last, the missive summoning her to the colonies had arrived: Sheena McClagan had run off with a wild-eyed woodsman, leaving Roy to raise a daughter alone. Six months to the day after receiving the letter, Rianne arrived in Brandborough, and in short order became Roy's housekeeper, and Colleen's friend, mother, and confidante.

The new world opened new vistas for Rianne, as it had for so many others. Always a willful, independent woman, she soon had found that domestic duties couldn't satisfy her love of worldy commerce, and within a year she had become the proprietess of a dressmaking shop in Brandborough. By the time Colleen was fifteen, even Brandborough wasn't big enough for her, and she made preparations to move to Charleston, thirty miles north along the coast. Roy had roared in protest, but Rianne was convinced that Colleen no longer required her presence, and her brother's mannerisms had become less and less to her liking. She loathed the smells of his medicines, she deplored his reclusive, studious ways, and found his temper intolerable. She respected his deep humanity and devotion to the sick and wounded, but that wasn't enough.

For Colleen, the lure of moving to Charleston was almost overwhelming, but Roy had refused her permission to accompany her aunt because the big city was too sophisticated and rife with pretense and decadence. Even more than his daughter's beauty, he treasured her natural, untarnished personality. He thought of her as a lovely country lass, an innocent farm girl who shouldn't be exposed to the sinful society of city life. What frightened him the most, however, was that Rianne had become a Patriot, and he wasn't about to let his darling daughter get involved with politics. "Mark me well," he'd warned his younger sister as her carriage, loaded with all her earthly possessions, pulled out of the yard. "Those half-crazed notions of yours will get you shot."

"Say what you will, brother," Rianne had called back, "but no dim-witted Tory will intimidate the likes of me or keep me from making a pretty pound."

She had proven to be right. Her shop was soon deemed one of Charleston's finest. Her designs were copied from the latest fashion dolls laboriously acquired from London and Paris, and her needlework was unparalleled. Even during the war years, with fabrics scarce and the value of currency uncertain, Rianne managed to prosper. She caught the attention of the most socially prominent, and within less than a year found herself an accepted member of Charleston's artistic elite. That she was a shameless but discreet gossip did her little harm. Her female customers loved her not only for her speed and craftsmanship, but for her titillating news as well. Her acquaintances numbered beyond mere society. She seemed to be on intimate terms with every artisan and artist in the city. Her passion for the arts—for music and painting, for cabinetry and poetry—was insatiable and sincere. And because she refused to return to Brandborough and its provincial ways, Roy and Colleen, at Colleen's insistence, were forced to visit her in Charleston.

The trips became the highlights of Colleen's year. On one such stay, Colleen met Ephraim Kramer, a master printer with whom she would later collaborate politically. And on another trip, Rianne arranged for Josiah Claypool, a craftsman whose skills rivaled those of the great Thomas Chippendale himself, to design for her niece a four-poster bed and secretary-wardrobe of rare beauty.

Of all Colleen's possessions, from great to small, she loved the furniture the most. Fashioned from gleaming cedar and cypress, the two pieces were perfectly matched. Neatly tied chaffs of wheat had been delicately, painstakingly sculpted along the thin posters, which sat upon carved claw feet. It was there, beneath a floral canopy, where she dreamed, but it was at her desk where she wrote and read.

And what a magnificent desk it was! With a chest of drawers below and a wardrobe above, the writing surface folded out from the furniture's center and contained a dozen tiny compartments and miniature drawers that Colleen kept filled with the deepest expressions of her secret heart. There was room for books: *Tom Jones* and *Pamela,* recently devoured with a passion that surprised even herself, had been presents from Rianne; Pope's wicked *Rape of the Lock* sat at the bottom of the pile, so that her father might not notice.

That she was reading such literature might well upset him, but, even if discovered, she was sure he would grudgingly understand because he knew that, as much as she loved the farm, she loved words, ideas, and poetic images even more. He was aware that she invented verse of her own, and though he considered such endeavors foolish and inappropriate for young ladies, he realized that there was little he could do to stop her: like his sister, his daughter had a flair for the artistic.

If Colleen could explain the presence of Alexander Pope's risqué rhymes to her father, there was also, in her possession, a small packet of tracts and broadsides for which she could not so easily account. The pamphlets had been written by people whom Roy considered dangerous, and the broadsides were political satires that Colleen had written herself, and kept hidden deep in the bottom drawer of her dresser, beneath her most intimate undergarments. Her passion for the fiery words of freedom had flowered four years earlier, when she was sixteen. Her heart had been broken because Jason Paxton had departed for Europe to study music. Without romance's golden fantasies, she was devastated. All this she had confessed to her aunt. In fact, she'd gone so far as to show her a poem she'd written about Jason. "I can see that you're an artist," Rianne had responded sympathetically, "but art won't bring him back. Art sends the soul soaring, but politics is the pudding of daily life. Have a taste of pudding, my dear. Look around and see what these English fools are foisting upon us. Wake up from your poetic fantasies!" And with that, Rianne gave her niece Thomas Paine's *Common Sense*.

Young and impressionable, Colleen read the tract in one fevered sitting, and learned in the following weeks to recite many lines by heart: "Examine the passions and feelings of mankind; bring the doctrine of reconciliation to the touchstone of nature, and then tell me whether you can hereafter love, honor, and faithfully serve the power that hath carried fire and sword into your land." No, she decided; she could not serve that power. It was plain and simple, it was common sense as the title itself said. The British were tyrants who robbed the colonists of what was rightfully theirs—their fair share of commerce and trade, and, most precious of all, their personal freedom.

In the months that followed, and as America's armies of the North were beaten and ran and were beaten again, she became convinced that duty demanded she contribute to the cause so eloquently expressed and in such great danger. In a style at first strained and turgid, then more and more cutting and eloquent, she wielded the only weapon she had—her pen. For the last year, the name Sandpiper, the songbird of the coast and a natural pseudonym, had begun showing up on an occasional broadside displayed aroud the countryside and in Charleston, whose recent surrender to the hated British sword chilled Colleen's heart and redoubled her patriotic convictions.

Checking to make certain her bedroom door was closed, she quickly opened the drawer and there, beneath hosiery and chemises, found the well-worn broadsides—sheets of paper containing revolutionary lyrics—and pamphlets that reflected the passion of the patriots. And among them, there was another sheet that meant nearly as much to her as all the others combined—a letter from Jason Paxton.

The paper he had touched, the words that his hands had penned! Whenever she held it, he seemed close to her, so close that she could imagine the sound of his voice and picture his soft lips as he might have said the words himself.

Emilia, Italy
January 8, 1780

My dear friend,

I trust this finds you in robust health. I'm deeply grateful for your several letters, the last of which I received before leaving England for the Continent. News of the war distresses me, as always, and were it not for my music, my mood would be exceedingly melancholy. I suppose it fair to say that music enables me to escape the pressing reality of worldy affairs—at least for a while.

After three years in England, I'm finally seeing the rest of Europe, andfor the last several months have been traveling and absorbing the sights. Autumn here is incredibly beautiful. The colors are magnificent, and as one sits a fine horse alone at the crack of day and watches the sun sparkle on the frost and bring the rainbow palette of the landscape to flaming life, one can only revel in life. For one glorious week, my companions and I stalked the nimble chamois, a deerlike creature of the mountains here. How good it felt to be outdoors and at one with nature again! As important and as glorious as music is, I must never forget that part of me that loved to tramp the woods, to scale cliffs and swing from ropes, to ride and hunt and shoot. Before art, there was the struggle to survive, and though I believe art to be the crowning glory of mankind, I also believe that the man who lives for art and art alone, and expects the harsh realities of life to somehow take care of themselves, is, no matter what his achievements, only half a man.

Philosophy aside, I must report that the art is glorious. There is a whole universe of painting and sculpture here that Americans can only imagine. And the music? Ah, the music! In Salzburg, I sat in a chamber surrounded by cherubim of glittering gold and listened to *concerti* written and performed on pianoforte, that most marvelous of modern inventions, by a man, I'm ashamed to say, younger than myself. His name is Wolfgang Amadeus Mozart, and if I tell you that his genius for technical perfection and lofty elevation of sentiment exceeds even the great Bach, I exaggerate not in the least.

In Vienna, I was privileged to hear the *divertimenti* os Josef Haydn, Mozart's teacher, a strangely introverted man whose work rivals the ethereal joys of his extraordinary student.

I've now reached my destination. I write you from Emilia, a section of the Italian peninsula wedged between Bologna and Milan. I'm in the city of Parma, at the Conservatorio di Musica, where, with the gracious help of my Charleston patrons Robin Courtenay and Piero Sebastiano Ponti, doors and opportunities have been opened to me. I'm studying composition with the masters of *opera seria* and *opera buffa* while also spending much time in the nearby city of Cremona, where the sons of Antonio Stradavari craft violins, the sweet sounds of which fill my eyes with tears.

Yet amid such lovely and lofty strands, why is my heart so heavy? For days a fog has covered this mysterious city. This morning is bitterly cold and uncomfortably humid, and how I long for the fragrance of magnolia! These years away from home seem an eternity. I've been living a long, beautiful dream, but one that soon must come to an end. I can escape no longer. I've arranged passage back to America. Look for me in the spring, Colleen.

My various motives can and will be explained later. Suffice it to say that I'm not unaware of the terrible ways in which my homeland has suffered. From afar, I've felt the pain inflicted from every quarter. Even the sublime genius of Herr Mozart cannot assuage my pain. I've learned that though I dearly love the music of this ancient continent, there is an even deeper love within my soul . . . for the place of my birth.

Your letters and lines of poesy, my loyal friend, have been of comfort to me, and I only wish I could have found the time to write more often. This will have to be my final word to you before we see one another again in Brandborough. Please convey my regards to your distinguished father and your kind aunt.

> With sincere affection, I am your friend,
> Jason Behan Paxton

Sincere affection! Loyal friend! Why not *love?* she wondered. Why not *passion?* Of course he couldn't be expected to include such words. She was glad that he had responded at all. And naturally she was overjoyed that he was actually coming home. She thought back over their long separation. He had written only three letters in four years, and each with the same friendly but distant tone. Had he fallen in love? Would he return with a wife? Surely he would have mentioned a marriage. But, just as surely, the women in the courts of London, Salzburg, and Paris were devastatingly beautiful and irresistibly enchanting. What would he say when he saw her? Certainly he'd consider her provincial, and yet he'd taken the time to write, which meant he cared—at least a little. He must have been impressed with the European writers she told him she'd read, in French as well as English. She'd mentioned her favorite poets, and surely he realized that she was no fool. In her long letters, hadn't she displayed an understanding of the political turmoil that South Carolina faced? Yet, strangely enough, when it came to politics, he had been mysteriously silent, except to indicate his sympathy to the plight of his own people.

But how could he not be sympathetic? He was an artist, and artists were sensitive people, and together they would be artists dedicated to the cause of the revolution. If only she had sent him the poems that expressed her true feelings for him instead of those celebrating the Carolinian countryside in rhyming couplets! Yet, how could she—yet a child, no doubt, in his memories—have told him the truth? How she wished she could send him a portrait of the woman she'd become!

Colleen's eyes went from the letter to the open window. The breeze was blowing stronger, the ship was in full view and nearing port. She found herself trembling ever so slightly. Even in a letter so brief, his words had intoxicated her. She could feel the sincerity of his emotions, the depths of his very being. How lonely he must have been! How lonely she had been without him!

"You'll not insult your Mr. Somerset by making him wait.

Do you hear me, lass, or shall I say it again?" her father's voice rang through the house.

"I'm going to my bath, Papa. I won't be long."

"Don't do no good fo' me to heat water, girl, ya lollygag aroun' an' let it git col'." As thin, tall, and gnarled as a split-rail stuck upright in the ground, Portia stood with arms on hips and glowered as her mistress ran up the steps of the bathhouse.

"Don't be such an ogre, Portia." Colleen laughed, hurrying inside and testing the water with her foot. "Mmm. Just right. The day's warm enough. Slightly cool is fine, thank you."

"Yo' backside be slightly warm, was ya my chile," Portia grumbled. "Make a soul stan' aroun' when they's work to be done. Give me that robe now, and git yo'self in an' washed."

The light inside the bathhouse was dim and soft, the great sweetgum tub filled with inviting water. Colleen handed Portia her robe and stepped in, sank into the water with a sigh. Slowly, neck, back, knees, calves, and thighs relaxed in the soothing liquid. Outside, a cardinal sang its repetitious song, and some wrens that made their home in the tree that shaded the bathhouse chirped softly. Inside, the stillness was a balm that, with the water, calmed Colleen's anxious thoughts. The fragrance of the rich wood, like some exotic perfume, transported her to a magic forest where, with closed eyes, she envisioned lovely maples, pines, and long-leaf poplars, and thought of Jason's slender face, the softness of his chestnut-brown eyes, which had always appeared half closed to her, far away, lost in a misty dream. It had been that very expression—she still saw it so clearly—that had rendered her helpless on the day of his departure. The day had been warm and blustery, tinged with an air of excitement, as there always was when a ship sailed. His father standing gruffly by, and flanked by his twin sisters, Jason had been bright-eyed and animated as the hour for his departure approached. The dock was crowded and chaotic as the final provisions were loaded and the crew hurried about its tasks. Horses whinnied, winches and blocks squealed, children ran about shouting and getting underfoot. And in the midst of the madness, Colleen had arrived at virtually the last minute. She hadn't planned to go to the dock—had feared she would cry or otherwise make a fool of herself—but the thought of not seeing him one more time had been too much to bear.

Had she been, then, after all, as silly as she'd feared? Stumbling, hurrying through the crowd, she'd run up to him and, her tongue leaden, had uttered a single, pathetic "Good-bye."

"Good-bye, Colleen," he'd said. "You'll write me, won't you?"

"Of course. I—"

But he'd turned away from her at the boatswain's call. Quickly, he embraced his father and shook his hand, then, Colleen forgotten, bent to kiss his sisters and started up the gangplank.

The sight almost broke her heart. Unable to control herself, Colleen had run after him and had thrown her arms around his neck, pressed herself against him, and, standing on tiptoes, found his mouth with hers. His lips were soft. She had kissed him only once before, and she remembered the sensation as though it had been the day before—the sharp, manly taste of his skin, the moistness of his tongue. Her head whirled with the intimacy of the moment, her heart beat madly as his eyes, his beautiful, sleepy eyes, registered pleasure. She backed off as he smiled. Had he felt the heat of her passion? Had he considered her silly? Had he considered her at all? But there'd been no time to know, no time to ask, because he'd turned and bade his father and sisters a final farewell and walked up the gangplank and out of her life.

Four years, she reflected as the mysterious melody from the sea returned and stirred her to life. Four years and nothing less than a revolution, a transformation from girl to woman. Four years and still, even as she soaked in the cooling water, the song whose source was the white sails moving slowly, steadily over the blue-green sea, came closer and closer.

~ *Chapter 2* ~

Jason Behan Paxton stood on deck listening to a strange, silent song, his eyes fixed on the distant shore he had left four long years earlier. Next to him was his good friend Captain Peter Tregoning of His Majesty's military command. The two were a study in contrast.

Both men were the same age, twenty-five, and of the same height, but while Peter was big-boned, Jason was thinly built. The musician's soft, sensitive face and sloped, smoky brown eyes gave him the profile of a poet as he leaned over the railing and pondered the deep. Draped over his shoulders was a charcoal gray woolen cape, simply but elegantly cut, that he'd purchased in Parma. The wind blew freely through the mass of springy brown curls that crowned his head, giving him an angelic look of disorderly charm. His eyes, deep-set and distant, were accented above by thick, angular brows. Inadvertently, he felt inside his cape and shirt for the gold amulet that hung on a chain around his neck. The family heirloom, passed down from his grandmother, Marie Ravenne, displayed a spreading oak tree entwined with brambles, its design a reminder of all he'd left and all that awaited him.

Standing next to Jason, Peter, the solider, maintained an unflinchingly correct and straight-backed posture. His chiseled chin and clear green eyes spoke of discipline and determination. Flaming orange hair peeked out from beneath his wig. His face

was covered with freckles, giving him a strangely boyish quality further contrasted by his uniform, a blood-red coat decorated
with silver lace, and tight white breeches tucked into jet-black
boots. He was wrapped in a campaign cloak of Mazarine blue
whose deep rich exterior added to the somber effect. His leather
helmet sported a scarlet plume from its brass crest. The helmet's
black facing provided a distinct background for the skull-and-
crossbones insignia worn by all members of the Seventeenth
Light Dragoons.

From Jason's lips emerged a simple melody that broke the
silence between him and his English friend.

"Writing something new?" Peter asked.

"Not really. I'm not sure where it comes from." Perplexed,
he tried to shrug it off. "One of those melodies that comes
from . . . somewhere . . . and then sticks with you."

"Jase, I swear that your tombstone will carry the inscription:
'He died in the middle of a new melody!' Back home, when
I had one of the loveliest ladies in all Londontown awaiting
your company, you were holed up in your room with your
bloody flutes and lutes—composing!"

"But I'm not composing, Peter. Just listening. Remembering, perhaps, but if I have heard it before, I can't figure out
where." Poignant and evocative, the seductive lilt carried him
back to the hot summer evening when he'd brought Casey, one
of his father's favorite hounds, to Dr. Roy McClagan's farm
beneath the high hill overlooking the Atlantic. Casey had been
inexplicably dragging one hind foot for days, and while
McClagan examined the dog in his study, Jase happened to
glance into one of the side rooms and see Colleen.

He'd known her, of course, as everyone in Brandborough
knew each other, and though the brightness of her eyes had
attracted him he'd never seen her as more than an alert, in-
quisitive child who was forever asking questions about his
music. Suddenly, though, his perception of her changed radically. Sitting before an oval-shaped mirror no larger than her
hand and silently brushing her silken blond hair ever so slowly,
ever so deliberately, her head fell back and dipped forward with
each elongated stroke. Candlelight gave her skin the color of
rich gold, soft and pure, and accented the amber color of her
eyes. He was fascinated by her beauty, and though he knew
he should turn away, he couldn't.

That she had seen him, too, was obvious, for the soft sway

of her body was clearly calculated. Her calculations worked. When she rose from her chair to acknowledge his presence with a greeting and invite him to the porch, where they might view the star-filled summer sky, he was unable to refuse. Nor could he, minutes later, refuse her advance—or was it his?—when, under the silver light of a crescent moon, he felt her heart beating madly against his, felt her lips, moist and warm, felt . . . But her father's jubilant announcement that a long, sharp thorn embedded near Casey's spine, and undoubtedly pressing against a nerve, had been successfully removed, separated them with a start.

In the months that followed, they became friends. Five years younger than he, only fourteen at the time, she was amazingly well read for a country girl and could discuss William Shakespeare or Roger Bacon, Dante and Molière, and even Jason's favorite—a secret they shared between themselves—the French essayist Montaigne. Her interest in his music was gratifying, and she learned quickly the names of composers and, with his tutelage, the rudiments of reading music. If he had deeper feelings for her, he wasn't inclined to explore them. Rather, being careful to maintain their friendship on a strictly platonic plane, he looked upon her as a companion, and a younger companion at that. And it wasn't until the day of his departure for Europe that he'd tasted her lips again. Yet, suddenly, four years later, that final kiss, along with the first one, had come back to haunt him.

For Peter, the music led not to the past, but to the future. Two years earlier—already they were close friends—Jason had shown him a pair of miniature portraits he had received from his home. "My sisters," he'd said, laying them on the table. "Were my descriptions apt?"

Why, he could not say, but Peter's heart had raced even as he effected a nonchalance he didn't feel. "Not at all. They're far prettier than your words indicated. Far prettier," he drawled, indicating the first. "This would be, what's her name? Hope?"

"Aye. Hope Elaine. And the other's Joy Exceeding."

Jason had spoken at length about his sisters, but nothing had prepared Peter for seeing the portrait of Joy Exceeding. She was, in a word, beautiful. Her face was thin and of a patrician cast, with a slight upturn to her nose. Her hair was similar to Jason's, light brown in color and gently waving. She was the second born, he remembered, and got her name from her mother's exceeding joy at the sight of a second girl. It made no sense whatsoever to him, for she was certainly no more beautiful than many women he had known, but he was stricken, and from that moment on, though keeping his true feelings hidden for over a year, found it impossible to keep her from his thoughts.

And finally, he would meet her, see her in person, hear the sound of her voice. Each spin of the taffrail log brought him closer. How ironic that his first trip to the new world was to land him at Brandborough, the very home of his friend, and of Joy Exceeding. And how ironic, too, that the reinforcements he led were being sent to help subdue and secure the Carolinas, in direct contravention to everything Joy Exceeding's father, Ethan, believed. "You haven't forgotten your promise to introduce her to me," Peter said aloud, suddenly breaking the silence between him and Jason.

"What?" Jason asked. "Oh, Joy. No. Of course not."

"And your father . . . Damn it all! I can see it now. The English captain calls on the patriot's daughter. What a fine mess!"

"Perhaps you're right," Jason said, tongue in cheek. "It might not be a very good idea—"

"Now wait a minute." Peter laughed. "I've looked at her picture until I'm blue in the face, and read every word of her letters until I'm sure I know her. You can't go back on me now, old friend."

"And so I shan't," Jason said. His eyes met Peter's, and his hand gripped his arm in a firm clasp. "You have my word," he promised solemnly. "And beyond that, you have my friendship."

The sincerity in Jason's resonant, baritone voice was unquestionable. For the three and half years Peter had known him, he had proven to be a man of easy humor, gentle manners, and uncompromising honor. They had met at the home of Peter's maternal uncle, Sir Walpole Gatley, a distinguished harpsichordist, and, as Peter was an amateur violinist himself, they had struck up an immediate friendship.

The friendship had ripened with each passing day. Peter stood in awe of Jason's talent: Jason was Peter's apt pupil in the ways of a society new to him. Together often, their favorite hours were those they shared strolling along the Thames. On one such stroll, on the day after Jason had conducted his concerto for two violins at the Court of St. James—astoundingly, the king had stayed awake for the entire performance—Peter had seemed disturbed. "Doesn't it bother you at all," he'd finally blurted out, "that your father can't be here to witness your success?"

Jason had laughed. "Father? My God, no. He's the last one I'd want here. The very notion that I'd conducted before the English monarch would appall him."

"But he's the king!"

"You have to understand," Jason had said gently. "My grandmother was a pirate—an incredible woman who any one of three kings tried, in vain, to hang. My grandfather, her husband, and for whom I was named, was a renegade Scottish nobleman who was outlawed and whose properties were confiscated by a king. With a father and mother like that, you can understand why my father doesn't hold much with kings."

"But what's that have to do with music?"

"Your brother manages your family's estates and is a member of Parliament. What would your father have said if Charles had given up all that for music?" Jason had asked in return.

It was Peter's turn to laugh. "He wouldn't have said anything," he chuckled. "He'd've either choked Charles—or choked on his own bile."

The chimes of St. Paul's rang out over the London landscape. "Father enjoy's music," Jason had gone on in the relative silence that followed, "but he considers my talent somewhat of a curse. Music might be tolerated as an avocation, but when it interferes with work, he becomes furious. Of more importance are cotton and tobacco—and shipbuilding these past few years. He's a businessman, you see, and Paxton business—and profits—comes before all else."

"I've noticed that the colonists tend to be a wee bit tight-fisted when it comes to money," Peter had replied dryly.

"That's not the point. Father feels that our holdings have been earned through the sweat of our brows, and must be protected. Against everyone, including kings."

"I'll drink to that," Jason had replied, just as relieved as his friend to quit the subject. "And the one best able to walk a straight line two hours from now pays for dinner after next Sunday's hunt."

* * *

For all the satisfaction that their friendship brought, however, the sticky issue of politics and the American revolt could not be avoided entirely. One winter night, shortly after they'd met, Jason seemed unusually glum.

"You're acting distracted, old chap," Peter had said, pulling up his collar against a freezing wind that nipped at his ears. "Something bothering you?"

"A letter from Father. This time he's irritated about the corn."

"The corn?" Peter had asked, not understanding.

"Aye. They had a wet fall, there was mildew, and they didn't get the crop in on time. It's my fault, of course, since I wasn't there to help."

Incredulous, Peter had stopped short. "Surely, old boy, you don't actually work in the fields yourself."

"But of course I do. Or did," Jason had said.

The very thought was appalling for one of an aristocractic family, and Peter said so. "I should've thought he'd have simply gone out and bought another slave or two. Surely—"

"Slave?" Jason had snapped with surprising anger. "No Paxton has *ever* owned another human being."

"I only thought—"

"It's the freedom of the colored people who work our lands that enables us to compete so successfully. Free men work harder—that's one of the Paxton creeds."

"So you're a proud Paxton, after all," Peter had said, stepping back to regard this new aspect of his friend.

"I'm proud of the accomplishments of my forebears, if that's what you mean. I'm equally proud of our colony. You'd like Brandborough, Peter, and you'd be impressed with the cultural life of Charleston."

"Charleston or Charles Town?" Peter had asked. "I was under the impression that the city was named for one of our illustrious sovereigns."

"And so it was. But the locals pronounce it Charleston nonetheless."

"Locals?" Peter had inquired with a raised eyebrow. "Or rebels?"

"Names change, Peter. Just like everything else."

In the months that followed, though there were differences of opinion, the friendship grew. Jason studied hard, learned his way around the music world of London, and increased his reputation. Peter's father, under pressure from the crown, bought him a captaincy and outfitted a company for him to lead. Both men enjoyed the hunt, and they were superb riders and marksmen. Both, in the manner of their time for gentlemen, were avid readers and conversationalists, and they educated themselves in a wide range of disciplines. Each learned to respect, as well as like, the other. And when, after Jason's return from Italy, they learned that they were to sail on the same ship, both were intrigued as well as delighted: Peter because he had seen Jason live and work as a foreigner in England, and was curious to see what would become of his friend once he returned to his native soil; and Jason for exactly the opposite reasons.

Excitement rippled through the ship as the call came from the masthead, and a quarter-hour later America became a thin line of blue-green on the horizon. Word was sent below to Peter's men to prepare to disembark. Sailors rushed about polishing brightwork and greasing the anchor chair and capstan. Alert, the pungent smell of salt water assaulting their senses and the sea's fine spray refreshing them with a cool, pleasant mist, Jason and Peter stood at the rail and stared hungrily at the growing line of land.

"A hot day ashore," Jason said finally, breaking the hypnotic melody that he couldn't get out of his mind. "Not too muggy, though, I shouldn't think."

"Mosquitoes?" Peter asked, having heard too many exaggerated stories about the American variety.

"Shouldn't be too bad during the day, as long as the shore breeze keeps them in the swamps. Tonight, though . . ." Jason shrugged. "Who knows? You'd best be ready to sleep under your netting."

The conversation seemed inane to both, but perfectly suited to relieve the growing tension that gripped them. "An American song, I gather?" Peter commented waspishly, tiring of it.

"I suppose so."

"Based, of course, on your long-standing conviction that there really is some musical tradition in your homeland."

The best of friends could argue when nerves were strung too tightly. "Why you insist on maintaining this skepticism, I'll never know, Peter. We'll see it shattered soon enough, though, mark my word. Tomorrow I'll take you on a tour of

Brandborough, where you'll hear flower vendors selling their
wares with charming songs. On the plantations, you'll hear
workers sing of their toil and sorrow with—"

"Must I hear again your veneration of the musical genius
of the American coloreds? Spare me, please, the—"

"All I ask is that you accompany me through the fields just
once. When you hear those extraordinarily talented people sing,
you'll understand that God has blessed them with a gift—"

"Really, Jase—"

"A gift that even the greatest European musician would
envy. They sing neither from scores nor notations, but from
the depths of their souls."

Peter shook his head. "The same old argument. You've come
home to write American music, to move out of the shadow of
Vivaldi and recast yourself as native son! And I still say
balderdash!"

"Say what you will," Jason countered. "You'll know what
I mean about missing things after you've been away from home
for a couple of years. With me, it's music—the music I heard
as a boy—the spicy rhythms, the bawdy ballads, the enchanting
songs sung by the Irish and French and Dutch."

"You're the only person I know who stoops to exalt a hodgepodge," Peter said with a derisive snort.

"As music, and as a country, yes. You might say that America is a hodgepodge, but a delicious one at that."

"A country? Please, Jase. I wish you'd get it right for once.
A collection of British colonies."

"Call us what you will. Our music is primitive, I'll grant
you. But it has a fascination and beauty all its own."

"Damn it, Jase! You're infuriating. You've the heart and
soul of a European, and a cultivated European at that. You said
so yourself. The Viennese swore you were born in Vienna,
and the Italians were convinced you were one of their own."

"When I write, I tend to take on the artistic characteristics
of my surroundings. That seems perfectly natural."

"You can explain it any way you see fit, but I doubt very
much that you'll abandon the musical culture of Europe. Not
for a minute."

"You do, eh?" Jason snapped, his homecoming forgotten in
the heat of the moment. "Well, perhaps you don't know me as
well as you think you do."

"Perhaps you're right," Peter said, equally miffed. "And now if you'll excuse me," he added, spinning on his heels and stalking away, "I have a great deal to do before we land."

Not perhaps, Jason thought, dejectedly turning back to the rail and staring down into the water. Deception was difficult for one who'd made honesty a point of personal honor. His anguish had begun one night in Emilia, shortly after his arrival there. The night was balmy, with a soft breeze wafting the scent of flowers to him through the open window, and it had reminded him of home. As his fingers wandered over the keys, he realized he was playing the songs of his childhood and of his native land, and suddenly he was filled with a great sadness, out of which had grown a determination, in the months that followed, that he could no longer sit idly by. Sooner or later, he had to return, and do his part in the struggle to bring freedom to America. *What,* however, had taken him many months more to determine: not until two weeks earlier had he known. As usual he and Peter had been dining with the ship's captain, Henley Boswell, and, as usual he had been forced to be a deft diplomat when the conversation had turned to politics. That night, however, whether because the captain had consumed a large quantity of plum brandy, or perhaps because of the suspicion he bore of all native-born colonists, he dropped a shocker.

"Pardon me for saying this, Paxton, but wouldn't you just make the perfect spy for the bloody Patriots?" he ruminated as he drew on a long cigar. "With all your aristocratic British friends, with this image you choose to cultivate of yourself as an artist above the political fray, you've invented the perfect camouflage. Who'd ever suspect Jason Paxton, composer *extraordinaire,* as a fiendish worker for the revolution?"

The perfect camouflage. A fiendish worker for the revolution. That was it! But how? His heart racing wildly, a great exultation filling his very being, he'd smiled as he leaned forward to replenish his glass. "No one but you, Captain," he'd drawled, even then aware that he'd have to be very, very careful around Peter. "And even you, if you think about it, have no more reason to suspect my motives than my fugues."

It had been an awkward moment, but he'd gotten through it well, and Peter had had the good grace never to mention it. The suggestion was there, though, and grew as an acorn grows into a great oak. Whatever form his actions took, the broad outline was clearly set in his mind. Even if it meant deceiving his best friend, he would fight for freedom.

Freedom for my country, for the land and people I love.

Love? The lilting song grew within him, the love song which, despite the hundreds of thoughts tumbling chaotically through his mind, sang so seductively to, and in, his heart.

And with every minute, the land, and home, came closer.

≈ *Chapter 3* ≈

"'Bout time ya git out of that bath 'fore ya turn into a prune, Miss Colleen."

Portia's voice shocked Colleen from her reverie, in which she'd floated off and washed herself in a dream of memories, reliving that farewell kiss that had stretched from a few seconds to a few years. How long could such kisses last? How long could a dream endure?

The water was decidedly cool; the sun had crept far enough across the sky to slant through the lower corner of the single ventilation window high in the wall. Colleen stepped from the tub into the waiting sun-warmed towels Portia had prepared. She put on a long, comforting robe of green satin, a Christmas gift from Rianne, and walked to the east side of the house, where she stole another glimpse of the shimmering sea. The ship was still there, much, much closer. As she stood and stared, shivering slightly in the cool sea breeze, she heard the song, and though she wanted to stay, to look and listen, she turned away and hurried to the house.

When she opened her bedroom door, her father, his eyes filled with rage, was waiting for her. In his hands was her copy of *Common Sense*—and Jason's letter.

"How dare you?" Colleen flared, instinctively taking the offensive. "Not even a father has the right to rummage through a woman's private possessions."

"Private!" His voice quivered with anger, pain, and shock. His eyes were red, his hands shook. "This *Common Sense* is the most public nonsense I've ever laid eyes upon! It's rubbish, I say. My sister and her scatterbrained ideas be damned, but you, you'll have none of this, do you hear? None of this!" he swore, ripping the book and the letter with one quick movement.

Colleen ran to collect the torn papers from the floor. "You have no right!" she cried, tears springing from her eyes. "No right at all!"

"In heaven's name, daughter, can't you see that you're endangering our very lives? This is no childish game, as your aunt would have you believe. This is war, child. Have I not told you often enough of the Battle of Culloden? Need I paint more pictures of the maiming and murdering? The English think themselves cultivated gentlemen, but I've seen them on the field of war and they're animals, raving beasts without mercy or sense. When it's territory they want, no barbarian has ever slaughtered with more vengeance. And this is their territory, lass. They wanted Charles Town, and, by God, they took Charles Town. Wasn't that enough to convince you and that daft aunt of yours? They'll keep these colonies, and there's nothing we can do, nothing we should do, to stop them. Try and we'll be trampled like helpless kittens."

"I know how you feel." Her back to her father, Colleen stood in front of her desk as she struggled for composure. At the very least, she was relieved that he hadn't discovered the revolutionary poetry written by her own hand. "I understand, I do, Father, but I was born in this country, not in Scotland, and I see it all differently. My own attitude . . ."

"Attitude? You're a woman, and women need not have attitudes when it comes to matters of the world."

"I read, I think. I can't help but form opinions. Did not God give women brains?"

"God gave women obedience, that's what, missy. You'll forget your Mr. Paine and you'll also forget your Jason Paxton. His return to Brandborough is of no concern to you. Why, his own father will have naught to do with him. He's a man without station or hope of prosperity, and politically dangerous to boot. The farther you stay away from him or any of the Paxtons, the better off you'll be."

Colleen turned to face her father. She wanted to show him

the patriotic verses she had written—not to spite him, but to make him proud. Yet she knew it was impossible to change his views. He was convinced the Paxtons were political poison, and he was inflicted with an irrationally unassuageable fear of the English. No matter what she said, he wouldn't in a thousand years understand the frustration she felt as a woman committed to a cause in which she believed so fervently. Instead, she remembered the way he'd stayed awake all night a week earlier to save the life of a baby lamb. She remembered how he'd cried when, at daybreak, the tiny creature had died. As she looked at her father, a wave of compassion crossed her face.

Roy saw her concern and responded by lowering his voice as he sat on the edge of her bed. "You're a bonnie lass, Colleen, and I want you to enjoy a long, healthy life filled with peace and joy. The thought of you in grave peril is enough to make my heart stop beating. I wish nothing more than for this war to leave us alone. I profess nothing but neutrality, though it's clear that the advantage rests with the Crown. If that be the case, why fight the advantage? Am I wrong when I say that my fondest wish is to see you a great lady? The Somersets are aristocracy, my love. One of the most eminent, strong, and powerful families in the colony. Their holdings vastly exceed those of the Paxtons, and they're more sensible people, more practical. They understand who governs here and are content to work with the Crown. Young Buckley is the heir to the fortune and he, too, is a practical man. His feelings for you are strong, Colleen. Strong enough"—he hesitated, then plunged on as he knew he should have days earlier—"to ask for your hand. I—"

"What?" Colleen asked, shocked. "What?"

He had anticipated her reaction, but was determined to press ahead boldly. "You heard me, lass. He asked for your hand. Last week on the Commons in Brandborough."

"Surely you—"

"I told him he has my blessing."

"Father!"

"As long as you agree, of course," he amended hastily.

"I'd never—"

"Listen to me, Colleen. Just once, listen to me. You don't have to say yes this instant, but I beg you not to say no, either. Think about it, lass. Think about it and ask yourself if you want to deny me the pleasure of seeing my grandchildren grow

up on a fine plantation so I might visit them in the evenings
and kiss their sweet brows. Is that asking too much? Is it wrong
for me to seek that solace for my old age?"

Collen chose her words carefully. "I understand what you're
saying, Father, but I also must be true to what I feel in my
own heart."

"Poetry! Drivel! Nonsense!" He was off the bed again, his
hands shaking, his voice exploding with renewed anger. "Words
your mother might have spoken before she ran off with that
wild, drunken woodsman. How in the name of a merciful God
she could have left a five-year-old child, and why"—he eyed
the miniature music box that rested on her desk—"why you
keep anything of hers is something I'll never fathom."

"It's all I have of her," Colleen said in a whisper.

"A wanton—that's what she was. A wanton and a witch."

Every time this discussion occurred—and it had come up
dozens of times over the years—Colleen felt inexplicably moved
to defend her mother, even though there was no reasonable
defense to be made. Once again, she wanted to argue, but this
time she stopped herself because his face had turned beet red
and she feared for his health. "Yes, Father," she said at last,
knowing her subdued tone would calm him.

"There. You see?" Mercurial as ever, Roy's mood changed
rapidly, and his rage was soon replaced by a kindly smile. "A
little loyalty isn't so difficult after all, eh?" His shaking having
stopped, he walked to Colleen and embraced her warmly. "Now
get dressed, child, and behave yourself. Trust your old papa.
Believe him when he says he loves you. Believe him when he
says he wants no harm to come to you. Only happiness for the
rest of your days."

More than anything, Colleen wished she could reassure him
that she would respect his wishes and obey his commands, but
her tongue choked on the words.

"Eh?" Roy asked, his hands on her shoulders. "Eh?"

Nothing had changed, and it never would. Tired of the
argument, Colleen found a smile. "I understand, Papa," she
said noncommittally. "I believe you."

"Good. Good! Now, where's Portia?" Enlivened, he hurried
to the door. "Portia!"

"Right here, suh," came the maid's voice from the kitchen.

"My daughter needs dressing," he bellowed, winking at
Colleen as he left. "Must she wait all day?"

Portia entered and, sensing the terrible tension, said nothing as she helped Colleen dress. A long gown of yellow gauze—a scarce commodity since the beginning of the war—had been embroidered by Rianne with whirls of lavender and green. It was Colleen's happiest gown; and yet, looking at it, her mood remained melancholy. The sadness she felt thinking of her father—his narrow-mindedness, his intolerance, his warped view of the war and women—couldn't be expressed. One way or another, she had to live with him. To abandon him in any form or fashion would be to repeat the act of her mother, and she was afraid he wouldn't survive another blow like that.

She stood perfectly still as Portia placed the gown over her head, then closed her eyes as the maid combed and collected her hair in two long rolls that fell symmetrically on either side of her head and covered her small, delicate ears. Since pins were scarce, the coiffure was secured by long, slender thorns that, in Colleen's eyes, became symbols of her own pain.

"I's hearin' horses," Portia said. "That's a sure 'nough carriage comin' for ya. Now, girl, ya mind yo' papa an' be nice to that man," she urged, understanding her mistress's independent ways.

Gazing out her bedroom window, Colleen could no longer see the ship. Perhaps it was so close it had already slipped into the far side of Brandborough Bay and out of view. But how could she know that Jason was aboard? She began to doubt. Where was the melody? The thundering sound of hooves had muffled the song. The music was lost, and Colleen sat there, angry at herself, confused by her ties of sentiment and loyalty, irritated at the fact that her escort-to-be was a preposterous prig and profoundly boring. For a while, a note of defiance rang through her head. Instead of completing her preparations and tending to the application of her perfumes and modest jewelry, she excused Portia and thanked her for the help. For the next several moments, Colleen sat motionless, all the while knowing that Buckley Somerset was waiting, all the while wishing that the lost melody would somehow return.

Buckley Somerset's wig, snow white in contrast to his deep olive complexion, had been fashioned in London. He sat in his ornate carriage—crafted in Paris and assembled in Charleston—and inspected the lay of the land rolling by. Much of the land he'd driven through was his, even though, of the three

Somerset holdings in South Carolina, his four-section plantation was the most modest. Marble Manor, overseen by his father
and lying halfway between Brandborough and Charleston, was
considerably larger, and Somerset itself, certainly one of the
half dozen or so most grandiose plantations in the South, belonged to his grandparents and sat just outside Charleston. Yet
Buckley couldn't complain. The time was rapidly approaching
when he'd control all three.

Buckley rode at peace with himself and with his place in a
world that had been made for him and men of his class and
station. As if God himself had planned it, the usually drab drive
was actually pleasant. The horses moved swiftly and easily
along the path. High above him, hanging on the thermals over
the coastline, an eagle soared majestically to remind him of
his own aristocratic heritage. Even the swamp itself, which for
much of the year exuded an odor of putrid humidity, had been
turned sweet-smelling by the grace of spring.

Buckley was a handsome man, in his own demanding way.
His eyes were a fierce gun-metal gray, his face unusually,
aggressively masculine. His strong features—large lips, even
teeth, jutting chin, and sweeping eyebrows were contradicted
only by a noticeable, badly healed break in the bridge of his
nose, which, from time to time, he touched out of nervous
habit.

It was a strange passion he felt for the simple country girl,
Colleen, Buckley reflected, and one he was hard put to explain.
There were other women, dozens, in fact, who flirted freely
with him and offered him their most succulent treasures for the
mere asking. His appetite was large and he'd indulged himself
freely. At twenty-six, he'd tasted a wide variety of female fare,
from ladies of breeding to bawdy beauties in houses of ill
repute. Why, then, was he obsessed with this daughter of a
Scottish doctor? Why Colleen McClagan? Her breasts weren't
large. She eschewed the fashions of the day and dressed rather
modestly. She spoke plainly and simply, with no attempt at wit
or conversational brilliance. And yet...

And yet. Buckley had but to close his eyes in order to see
her standing before him like a recurring dream he couldn't
shake no matter how many other women he took. Her long,
shining blond hair and bright, amber eyes were alluring in the
extreme. Her chasteness—and, he was sure, underlying sen-
suality—fascinated him and provoked him to wild fantasies.

She moved with the sudden, enticing energy and fluid motion of a colt as yet unbroken. Neither frivolous nor cloying, as opposed to the silly women who threw themselves at him with their fawning flattery, she was mysteriously and deeply private, and no matter what presents he had given her or to what balls and outings he had escorted her, she held herself aloof from him. His pursuit of a woman he had yet to kiss was ironic, but his mind was set: he had to have her. Of all the women in the colony, it was his fate to want the one who showed the least interest in him.

The father was waiting on the porch as usual when the carriage pulled to a stop and the black coachman jumped down to open the door. "Wait here," Buckley commanded, stepping down. "Good to see you again, McClagan. Colleen's ready, I trust?"

Roy glanced nervously behind him. "Almost, sir. Almost." He gestured for his guest to enter, and followed hard on his heels. "No more than a minute. If you'd be so good as to come in, I assure you that my daughter will be ready in no time. Meanwhile, I trust you'll join me for a spot of sherry."

There was nothing Buckley wanted less than to spend time drinking with McClagan. "I think not, than you," he replied shortly.

"Of course. Of course," Roy stammered. Flustered, he pushed a chair forward. "Perhaps you'll sit? I'm sure your trip—"

"I'll stand, thank you."

"Of course. Exactly. Well!"

Spring had renewed the countryside, but not the interior of McClagan's house. Everywhere Buckley looked there was the usual dust and clutter, books strewn about, and, God save his soul, collections of bones and bottles filled with obscene-looking pieces of flesh. The place was quite simply appalling, and why the poor girl had chosen to remain there so long escaped him. Loyalty to her poor, cringing, cowering fool of a father, no doubt, as well as a lack of adequate contact with the better things of life. A faint smile played over his face. How much more loyal would she be to him, who could remove her from her distressing circumstances! How much more—

"Something . . . amusing, sir?" Roy ventured cautiously.

Buckley didn't like people interrupting his thoughts. "I beg your pardon?" he asked archly.

Roy blushed furiously, wished he'd had Portia clean up

better, wished Colleen would appear, wished that he could think of something, anything, to say. "Well!" he virtually exploded, blurting out with false joviality the first thing that came to mind. "I understand that General Cornwallis himself was a guest at your house last week."

Buckley smiled condescendingly. His black velvet suit and plum-colored crepe blouse spoke of wealth and impeccable taste. Standing several inches over six feet, he towered above the stoop-shouldered doctor. "Yes," he drawled, "I'm afraid I trounced him rather severely at whist. But that's another story. Do you think you might suggest that she hurry along?"

"And may I suggest that that won't be necessary?"

Startled, both men looked around to see the very picture of beauty itself standing in the open door to her bedroom. Roy beamed with pride and heaved a sigh of relief. "Dear God!" Buckley exclaimed, inhaling sharply.

"Mr. Somerset," Colleen said, curtseying shallowly, "welcome again to our humble home."

Her walk was exquisite, her simplicity dazzling. The sight of her slender, graceful neck, the shape of her sensuous mouth, and the incredible amber of her eyes filled Buckley with wonder. His heart beating wildly, feeling as clumsy and awkward as a country bumpkin, he went to her and kissed her hand. "No house graced by your presence," he murmured, "could ever be called humble."

All was ready. Portia handed Colleen a veiled bonnet in case, later, the mosquitoes swarmed, then fetched a basket of fried chicken, cucumber-and-onion salad, and cinnamon rolls from the kitchen.

"You shouldn't have bothered," Buckley said as Colleen passed it to him. "My servants have prepared a feast of pheasant for us."

"But I prefer chicken, thank you," Colleen said, knowing that her modest meal would irritate him. "Besides," she added with a coquettish smile, "I must have a basket to be auctioned off."

The prospect of being forced to participate in the rustic custom of luncheon auctions bored Buckley nearly to distraction, but he smiled gallantly and took her arm. "I can assure you," he promised, "that I shan't be outbid. Good day, Doctor," he added with a hint of a nod in Roy's direction.

"Papa," Colleen murmured, kissing him good-bye.

"Be gracious," Roy whispered in her ear. "And dare ye not discuss a word of politics," he added as Buckley whisked her out the door.

The ship. Where is the ship? Where is the song?

Colleen sat well to her side of the carriage, listened without paying attention to what Buckley said, and made what she trusted were appropriate, if noncommittal, answers. The winding road took them from the McClagan property to the coast, where the rolling, bud-green farmland gave way to a series of flat, reedy marshes. For the mile south to the village of Brandborough, the well-worn dirt coastal road, barely wide enough to hold the carriage, separated the marshes from the beach. Colleen breathed in the clean, tangly smell of salt water and looked beyond the sand dunes that rose out of the ocean like miniature islands. Her eyes swept the seascape for a sign of the ship, but it wasn't to be found. She struggled to bring herself back to reality, and to Buckley.

The picnic, to be held in a meadow a little over a mile south of Brandborough, would be amusing, she tried to convince herself as Buckley told her how his father's latest stroke meant that control of more than half of one of the South's mightiest business empires had effectively been passed on to him. His growing domain, however, was of no interest to Colleen. She was unimpressed by his fine clothes and his expensive, powdered, perfumed wig. She ignored his declarations of self-importance, and when he spoke of his ties to the British command and the signficance the Crown placed on Somerset loyalty, she held her tongue. And though she feigned interest, she couldn't keep her eyes from the great expanse of the ocean, nor could she stop searching for the long-awaited ship that she hoped bore Jason home to her.

"Drab business, these matters of property and state," Buckley said laconically, "but necessary under the circumstances, for they concern another issue of great importance to me and, I trust, to you. Of course," he said, sliding toward her and taking her hand, "tradition has it that the matter take the form of a question."

He certainly hadn't wasted any time, Colleen thought. The question for her was: Should she tell him no immediately, or attempt to humor her father by telling him she'd consider it, and then turn him down later? Whichever she did, she hoped he'd get it over with quickly and move away from her, because his touch annoyed her as much as the political opinions he espoused.

"The question," Buckley continued, absolutely certain that no woman, not even Colleen McClagan, could refuse his proposal, "has already been posed to your father, who was quite pleased by the prospect."

Or, Colleen thought, grasping at straws, *I could simply evade the question for as long as possible.* "When we arrive in town," she said, flashing him her warmest smile, "do you think it would be possible to take a small detour and ride by the docks?"

"What?" Buckley asked, taken aback.

"I said, when—"

"I know what you said," he snapped, irritated by the abrupt change of subject. "But for what purpose?"

"I spotted a ship approaching this morning, and since I've been expecting something important from London, I thought we could ride by to see if it's arrived."

Buckley fumed inwardly, but forced himself to smile. She was such a child. A beautiful, willful, naïve child, totally beyond the temptation of property and station. How utterly refreshing! His heart filled and his head whirled. To think that one day, and soon, he would win her, carry her away as his bride... "Of course," he acceded, patting her hand and then moving to sit across from her so he could see her face better. "It won't do any harm to pass by. But remember," he added playfully, wagging a finger at her, "there's still that question..."

Dear God, but what kind of an idiot does he take me for? How is it possible for such preposterous buffoons to hold the high positions they do? Very well, fool. We shall see who plays this game best.

"... and I don't intend to let the day get by without asking it."

"Can't the questions wait, Buckley? Can't we just enjoy the ride along the sea? Don't you love the way the sandbars form such graceful designs, the way the sea oats bend in the breeze?"

Buckley couldn't have cared less about sandbars and sea

oats, but the look on Colleen's face was another matter entirely.
Content for the moment to feast on her beauty—his time would
come, his time would come—he sat back and dreamed, as he
so often had, of what their first night together would be like.

*Home. Can it be true? My God, but I'd forgotten how
beautiful this corner of the world is.*

The water was incredibly blue, the shoreline green beyond
green. Brandborough had grown in the four years Jason had
been gone. Six new buildings stretched the main street farther
inland, and new houses had been added at either side. Horses
and buggies and draymen's wagons clotted the waterfront, where
his heart leaped in his throat—*No! No! It can't be!*—the British
flag flew over the customs house.

The boatswain's pipe shrieked, a command rang through
the air, and the anchor chain rumbled through the hawsehole.
Aloft, the crew was busy reefing sails; below, a profusion of
lighters nudged the *Shropshire.* Behind him, unheeded as he
stared at the shore and waited for a ladder to be rigged, a fife
and drum accompanied the measured tread of soldiers lining
up in ranks preparatory to disembarkation.

"Jason Paxton! Down here, damn your eyes!"

Jason searched through the clot of small boats and spotted
a barrel-chested man with one leg waving his hat at him. "Elton!"
he called back. "How long does it take a fellow to get ashore
around here? I've been on this tub for eight weeks. Must I wait
eight more?"

Forward, a ladder snaked down through the air. Elton caught
it, made it fast to his lighter. A minute later, after hurried
instructions to send his trunks ashore at the earliest possible
moment, Jason was scrambling down the ladder and into the
embrace of the man who had taught him more about ships and
the sea than his own father had.

"Damn me, but you're looking good, lad," Elton said moments later as the lighter made its way toward shore. "Filled
out. Put on a little weight," he added, poking Jason in the
midriff.

"Which will be shed soon enough, I warrant," Jason said
with a grin. "A week or two under father's tutelage, and I'll
be fit as a fiddle again." He gazed fondly at the older man
facing him, remembered the hours they'd spent together as

he'd learned how to tie knots and handle a small boat. "You haven't changed by so much as a wrinkle. Still the scourge of Brandborough?"

Elton winked. "The lassies like to think so. It's by God still as hard as my peg when I wake up in the morning."

"Good for you. But where is everybody?" he asked, searching the dock for familiar faces.

"Where else on a beautiful Saturday in May? At the fair, lad. A fine day you've picked to come home."

Moments later, Jason stepped onto the dock and, as Elton returned to the *Shropshire,* stood alone, his mind churning with a thousand thoughts. His ear was alive with sounds, old and familiar, new and wonderful—wavelets slapping rhythmically against pilings; a blind piper tooting a jocular ditty as he sat on a keg of rum; the deep, rich voices of slaves singing melodiously as they hauled and carried great weights of cargo. The sounds of the music of his home, long lost but never forgotten—birds singing merrily, mothers calling after children in decidedly American accents—swelled his heart and filled his head with wonder. And questions, he realized, sobering quickly. The British flag flying in Brandborough! What did that portend? And how, after the bitter letters he'd received, would his father greet him? And what of the strange, haunting song? What of Colleen? How had she changed in the four years he'd been gone? Would she...

Her eyes told him that it was she. Amber and piercing, those remarkably radiant eyes glowed with warmth and life. She stood only yards away, poised and regal, more beautiful than he could have possibly imagined. She had filled out and matured: she had blossomed into a desirable woman. And suddenly, he realized that all his other reasons for coming home—noble, well-intentioned reasons—paled in comparison to the sweetness of her face.

Massively sculpted in dark-hewn woods, its masts, booms, and rigging jutting high above the water, the *Shropshire* had been a distraction, and its imposing presence gave proof to the power of the mighty British empire. And yet, once she saw him and moved toward him, all the world's weapons of war seemed weak beside the wave of passion that washed over her. Her breath catching in her throat, she stopped, only yards away, and waited for his eyes to meet hers. He was so beautiful! His face was softer than she remembered, gentler, wiser than when he had left. He had put on weight, but his body was still lean and elegant with the grace of a tiger. His charcoal gray cape was dashing, and the marvelous curls that covered his head glistened in the sunlight. His sleepy, half-closed eyes appeared more romantic than ever. And finally, when his head turned and his eyes found hers, the song returned and swelled to majestic proportions.

Her heart hammered, his chest heaved. He felt his pulse quicken. She struggled for control, but it was no use. Suddenly losing her last link with self-restraint, she found herself running to him, throwing her arms around him and kissing him, tasting his lips, igniting memories and music . . .

"Colleen."

His first word was her name. He remembered! He actually remembered!

"You're more beautiful than I remembered. More beautiful by far."

"Oh, Jase," Colleen whispered with a sigh.

"So this is the package you were expecting from London," Buckley said, bulling his way through the crowd to their sides. The kiss had infuriated him, but he covered his fury with sarcasm. "I didn't realize you and Paxton were such good friends. Welcome home, Jase. Everyone will be most glad to see you've returned. We've been needing a reliable piano tuner around here. A most vital job in these troubled times. In fact, you've arrived just in time to play at our wedding."

"Oh?" Jason asked, taken aback momentarily until he caught the slight shake of Colleen's head and read the look of denial in her eyes. A wry smile twisted his lips. Buckley was up to his old tricks, barging ahead as if he were royalty, making a fool of himself. "It appears I arrived in the nick of time, eh?" he said, extending his hand.

Buckley's fingers touched the dramatic break in his nose as his hand moved to accept Jason's. The automatic, nervous gesture provoked both men to memories of a dark, narrow alleyway in Charleston, where, ten years earlier and beneath a wrought-iron balcony twisted into the shape of twin peacocks, Buckley had slurred Jason's name by calling the Paxtons a pack of half-breeds and bastards spawned by renegades and whores. He had been shocked by Jason's sudden response. Never for a moment had he guessed that the farmer turned musician was a fighter—and a ferocious one at that. The two men had fought viciously—fought with bloody fists, fought until their knuckles were red with blood, fought until one final blow found its target, until Buckley felt the savage pain in his shattered, ruined nose, and fell to his knees before Jason, the surprising victor. A decade had passed, but the ill will hadn't.

"Well, then," Jason said heartily, looking over his old antagonist, "I see you're prospering."

"Better than even I had hoped," Buckley said, his chest swelling. Impressed with himself, he put one arm around Colleen, whose eyes spoke only to Jason. "My fortune is on the rise. And yours?" he asked with a sarcastic bark of a laugh.

"That depends, I suppose," Jason said, deflating Buckley's puffery, "on how many weddings I'm asked to play at. Ah, Peter!" he said, noticing his friend, who'd appeared at his side and was debating in light of their earlier tiff, whether to interrupt. "May I present Miss Colleen McClagan and Mr. Buckley Somerset. This is my good friend and companion, Peter Tregoning."

Relieved that all was apparently forgiven, Peter smiled and clapped Jason on the shoulder. "So this is the 'young girl' you spoke of. My great honor," he said, kissing Colleen's hand. "Mr. Somerset. My pleasure."

"And mine, too, sir," Buckley said, shaking his hand. "And a double pleasure to see such a strong display of our sovereign's commitment to his grateful colony. I suppose you've heard already that Charles Town is safely under the Crown's control?"

Peter nodded. "A felicitous piece of news, sir. Given to me but moments after our arrival."

"Charleston?" Jason asked, his heart sinking. "Taken by the British?"

"Much to the chagrin of the so-called Patriots, of course," Buckley said, enjoying Jason's discomfiture. "You'll be undoubtedly pleased to learn that Brandborough is just as securely under the Crown's control. And your presence here can only reassure those whose long loyalty has been so bountifully rewarded."

"We are duty-bound," Peter said simply.

"And we're bound for a splendid picnic," Colleen broke in. "Did you know, Jase, that today is the Brandborough Spring Fair?"

Charleston taken! My God, is it possible? And Brand-

borough? The whole colony, too? "Eh?" Jason asked aloud. "Oh, yes. I was told." He manufactured a smile. "What a happy coincidence."

"Your arrival couldn't have come at a more appropriate time," Colleen went on. "I'm certain Mr. Somerset would be honored to have you and Captain Tregoning join us in his carriage. Your family will all be there. Do say you'll accompany us."

Jason looked at Colleen with wonder. She was almost enough to make him forget the bad news about Charleston. There was a vibrancy to her voice, a vivaciousness he found irresistible. Her transformation from child to woman was nothing less than astounding. "You'll meet Joy," Jason told Peter. "That is, if Buckley doesn't mind our intruding upon him and his fiancée..."

"I'm not his fiancée..." Colleen began to explain before Buckley cut in.

"Mind? Why, it would be an honor to introduce the captain to our distinguished citizenry."

"I've only to place my lieutenant in charge of the men," Peter said, intrigued by the idea of an American picnic.

A few moments later, after Jason made arrangements for his trunks, the quartet climbed into the carriage. Buckley faced Peter and began to expound on the current local military situation. Jason faced Colleen, and though they spoke not a word, their eyes embraced as their souls sang the same sweet song of longing.

⤳ *Chapter 4* ⤳

Jason felt rather than saw the passing countryside. In spite of the fact that he hadn't been on American soil in four years, he was unable to look out of the carriage, unable to keep his eyes off Colleen. In her, he saw all the beauty that he associated with home, that spark of aesthetic energy that he'd missed so deeply. Her smile seemed to symbolize the vibrant innocence that old-world Europe, for all its great cultural riches, sorely lacked. Looking at her, he realized how accustomed he'd become to the world-weary attitude of the English, French, and Italians. In her fresh eyes, he felt renewed, and his heart stirred when he realized that the tune she was humming was the very same that he had heard on the *Shropshire*.

The short ride passed quickly for everyone, and soon enough the sound of boisterous, happy music signaled their arrival at the picnic grounds. The sound, yes, and the scent of spitted beefs and fresh bread and piping-hot berry cobblers. Simple, hardy fare, blending with the music of a people at play.

"I say," Peter exclaimed as they stepped from the carriage, "these hardly seem the sounds of a people at war."

"This is our day, good Captain," Colleen volunteered, "to forget all that has been so harshly imposed on us. It'd be a mistake to interpret this as our customary mood."

"Yours is a most peculiar interpretation, Colleen. One hardly fitting to be expressed in front of our honored guest, who—"

But noise from the picnic diverted everyone's attention, and Buckley's reprimand was cut short.

Away for so long, hearing voices so familiar and, after his absence, so strange, Jason could barely contain his excitement. Right before his eyes, it seemed as if everything and everyone he'd forgotten were returning with a rush of fond recognition. Even the sound of the untutored band filled his heart with pleasure.

"Is this the American music of which you spoke so lovingly?" Peter asked, mopping the sweat from his forehead.

The light sarcasm didn't ruffle Jason in the least. His head was whirling with the crude, shrill notes of the piccolos and fifes, and the harsh bravado of brass. The execution was amateurish, but the feeling intoxicating. The music was utterly free-spirited, lacking in self-consciousness or pretense. This was a picnic, and here was picnic music, brash and wild as the wind, and here were well over a hundred people, most of whom he'd known since he was a child.

As word of Jason's presence spread, it seemed as if the entire picnic began to move away from its sundry activities—games and gossip, singing and dancing, and the preparation of enormous quantities of food—to greet him and separate him from Peter, Buckley, and Colleen. Farmers and artisans, school chums and teachers and friends of the family questioned him about his travels, and he asked after their welfare. The attention both delighted and embarrassed him. He grew alarmed only when old Chester Wills, a man who had worked for his father for decades, whispered in his ear, "You've come back in the nick of time, my boy. These Redcoats are running us over. If we don't strike back, and strike hard and now, we're doomed."

Left alone, Peter was touched by the warmth of the reception given Jason, but even more by what to him was the bizarre nature of the gathering. Such an assembly, such a mixing of classes and styles, he reflected, would not be possible in England. Manual laborers in rough working clothes joked among themselves under a great weeping willow tree while, nearby, refined ladies in perfumed wigs strolled beneath dainty parasols. There were dandies and fishermen, wealthy landowners and struggling merchants, all moving about with a gaiety Peter concluded was amusingly and uniquely colonial.

And then . . . he saw her. Not clearly, for she was racing—now visible, now hidden—through the crowd toward Jason.

Not clearly, for her features were obscured by the angle and the distance that separated them. Not clearly, for the sun was in his eyes. But clearly enough . . . clearly enough after months of waiting to know that her portrait hadn't misled him, and that his instincts had been right. His breath shallow and his steps so light that his feet seemed to float above the ground, he started toward her.

"Jase! Jase!"

Jason turned and was almost knocked over backward as Joy flew into his arms. "Oh, Jase, I've been so worried—afraid you'd change your mind and never come home." Ecstatic, her eyes brimming, she wrapped her arms around him and pressed her cheek against his chest. "It is you, isn't it? Isn't it?"

Laughing, Jason moved her away, held her at arm's length and tilted her chin up. "Joy Exceeding," he said, the rest of the crowd forgotten. "You look wonderful. You're different, and yet you seem the same."

They both laughed at his inconsistency, the sort of easy, familiar laugh possible only between brother and sister.

Suddenly, a pair of hands covered Jason's eyes. "Have you been gone too long to recognize me?" asked a disguised voice.

"Hope Ellen!" he exclaimed as the hands dropped and he turned to face his sister.

Reluctant to interrupt their reunion, Peter stopped a few yards away. There were tears in Jason's eyes, tears he'd observed only once before, when, on a misty night in London, Jason had stood silently and listened reverently to an urchin street flautist, and then dropped sixpence into the lad's hat that lay on the pavement in front of him. The differences between his twin sisters, obviously not identical, were dramatic. Hope was the taller of the two, and there was a hardness to her dark brown eyes and plump beauty that her portrait hadn't revealed. Her hair was blond, a fact revealed by a stray wisp poking out from under her wig at the back of her neck. Her voice was strong and self-assured, the voice of a woman who knew exactly where she was going and what she was about.

But Joy! How insipid was her portrait in comparison to reality! Like a man dying of thirst, Peter drank her in. Everything about her was softly elegant. Her light green, laughing eyes set off a smile that would warm the heart of a stone. She was thin but delightfully curvaceous in a crepe gown the color of robin's egg blue. Her light brown hair—she was unwigged, curiously enough—curled about and framed her face in much the same manner as Jason's did. Her voice was tinged with a sweet, soft accent that was quietly but decidedly Southern. If he hadn't fallen in love with her as represented by her portrait, he decided, he surely should have when he saw her first in real life.

"Peter!" Jason called, noticing him and beckoning him to join them. "At long last you meet them. These are my sisters I've spoken of so often. Hope Ellen and Joy Exceeding"—his eyes flicked back and forth between Joy and Peter—"my good friend, Captain Peter Tregoning."

"Friend?" Hope remarked with surprising sharpness as she stared at Peter's uniform.

"Yes. Peter and I were together in London for some time. He's a violinist himself and . . ."

"Here in the service of your king, are you, Captain?" Hope asked.

"Really, Hope," Joy chided, compelled by some reason she didn't understand to defend him. "If he's Jase's friend, and a musician as well, he should be more than welcome to join our festivities."

"You're kind to say so," offered Peter, allowing his eyes to rest briefly on Joy's, "but I could scarcely call myself a musician, especially in the company of your distinguished brother. Now, *there's* a musician. He must tell you how he single-handedly conquered Europe's greatest concert halls."

"That's a wild and irresponsible exaggeration, Peter," Jason protested with a self-conscious laugh.

"My dear brother, you've always been far too modest. We want to hear about all your successes—every one of them," Joy insisted, pleased that Peter seemed to admire her brother as much as she did. "Have you seen Father? He's here, you know."

"No, I didn't know," Jason said, a look of concern crossing his face. "That is, I assumed he would be, but—"

"Before we fetch him, Jase, there's something I'd like to tell you. Alone, if Joy and the captain won't be offended."

Peter and Joy were pleased to be left to themselves as Hope took Jason by the arm and led him away. "So what is this?" Jason asked, in between greetings to those they passed. "A deep dark secret only half an hour after my arrival?"

Hope's stride lengthened as they broke free from the crowd. "Not really. I want you to meet my husband."

"Husband? That's marvelous, Hope! Who is he? That Coleridge fellow you wrote me about?"

"Yes. Now hush."

They stopped a few feet inside the shade at the edge of the forest bordering the meadow. "Allan?" Hope called in a loud whisper. "It's me. I've brought my brother, Jason, with me. He wants to meet you."

"Over here," a voice called in answer.

Jason followed as Hope bent aside a dogwood branch and ducked under a low redbud tree limb. "Why so mysterious?" he asked.

Hope stopped again, looked around. "Allan? Where are . . . Aii!" she yelped as a figure stepped out from behind a huge old hickory nut tree. "Don't do that! You want to give me an attack?"

Allan Coleridge was shorter than either Jason or Hope. Stoutly built with broad shoulders, chunky hands, arms, and legs, he had the look of a man hewn from logs. Piercing, slate-gray eyes and a shock of prematurely graying hair gave him a look of fierce determination. His clothes were of deer hide, making him blend in with the colors of the forest. "So you're Jason, eh?" he said.

"Most pleased to meet you," Jason said, nodding in acknowledgment and shaking Allan's hand. "Hope's written me many good things about you. I'm honored to call you brother."

When Allan spoke, he did so in spurts. "You've returned not a second too soon," he said in an unschooled accent. "We're desperate for good men. Have you heard that Charleston's been taken?"

"I have," Jason answered solemnly. "But not of the particulars."

"The Green Dragoons, that's who they were. Traitors to our cause. Bloody Americans fighting on the side of Tarleton. Tarleton's a vicious son-of-a-witch who loves nothing more than murderin' his prisoners. Now he'd put Randall Embleton in charge of the city and everything to the south. Embleton! The bastard makes Tarleton look like a schoolmarm. He'd sooner skin a farmer than a cat. Well, this is one farmer he'll never catch! You see, there's the Continental Army, and bless them, 'cause they're brave boys dying for us every day, but there's also hundreds of us working alone or in small groups doing whatever damage we can by the dark of night when they least expect us, because, you see, no one knows these territories like the men who live in 'em."

"For God's sake, Allan, keep your voice down," Hope pleaded. "There's danger enough in your being here."

"That's your fear, not mine," Allan snapped peevishly. "Since I came to this colony from North Carolina some three years ago," he went on, turning back to Jason, "I've lived my life openly, with nothing to hide. I staked out my own farm, made my own way, and if I fancy, I'll walk about this picnic area with my head as high as any man's."

Hope paled. "You promised, Allan. Not until dark—"

"Any time I wish, woman. Any time."

"Allan led a raid on the Crown's arsenal just outside Brandborough two nights ago," Hope whispered to Jason. "The arsenal's new, so the supply of guns and powder was small, but they got them all. What worries me is that we've reason to fear that Allan was spotted and recognized."

"What reason? It's nothing but that womanly imagination of yours. We got clean away and we're going back as soon as the thievin' English resupply. What I want to know right off is," he added, his eyes boring into Jason's and his voice as blunt as a cudgel, "are you with us?"

Caught off guard, Jason's hesitation alarmed his sister. "I . . . I'm a musician," he explained lamely, "not a warrior."

"I'm a farmer, but it's either fight or die, fight or give up all we've been working for. You can understand that, can't you?"

Seconds of silence passed. Jason's eyes fell to the soft, leaf-spongy earth underfoot. He could appreciate Allan's position, and in many ways was in complete sympathy. But their means to the same end must be different, for they themselves were cut from different bolts of cloth.

"Father said this would happen," Hope said, disappointed. "He said they'd turn you into a Tory over there. Is it true, Jase? Tell me it isn't true."

The urgent plea in her voice broke Jason's heart and compelled a reply. He wanted to reassure Hope and Allan that he was indeed on their side. But because his plans were still only half-formulated, and because, even in their formative stages, he knew they would require absolute secrecy, he couldn't speak his heart. Instead, he answered in what he himself knew to be silly-sounding clichés. "Music's become my whole life, Hope. The pain that you've suffered wounds me as well, but I've come home to be with my family, and to compose and play music. Isn't that enough?"

"No, it's not!" Allan hissed. "This is a time when every man jack has to choose sides. There's no in-betweens. Anyone caught sitting on the fence will be shot by both sides, I guarantee you, 'cause I'll be one of those doing the shooting—brother or no brother."

"Allan!" Hope gasped. "What are you saying?"

"It's all right," Jason assured her. "I understand how he feels."

"Understand all you want," Allan shot back, his eyes flashing, "but remember. If you ain't with us, you're agin' us. Come along, darlin'."

"No!" Hope gasped, plucking at his sleeve. "You can't, Allan. Any one of a dozen men out there—"

"Let cowards stand in the shade," Allan spat.

"Now look here!" Jason protested. "You have no—"

"I've looked," Allan said, cutting him off. "And my eyes have seen what there is to see. Now you look, and see how bold men dare stand in God's light!"

"Allan, please!" Hope pleaded, and then, as her husband strode out of the forest and into the open of the meadow, she whirled on Jason. "This is your fault!" she hissed. "And if he's turned in . . ."

The sentence hung ominously on the air. Left alone when Hope raced off, Jason sighed and leaned against the hickory tree. Everything had happened too fast, he thought, closing his eyes and smelling the deep green of the Carolina forest, a fragrance he'd dreamed of for so long. Too fast . . .

The setting was peaceful, but his mind was troubled. Should he have taken Coleridge into his confidence? But how, when he'd only just met the man? And how, when he himself didn't know what he was going to do? Did they truly expect him— or any man—to give himself over to them without question, and if he didn't, to cast him out like so much rotten fish? Who gave them the right to decide he was against them simply because he didn't march in with rifle in hand and immediately beard the British lion in its den?

It was too much. Too much for a day or a week, much less

an hour. What a homecoming! Buckley, as much the fool as ever, pompously throwing his weight and fortune around. Coleridge, with his brittle temper and quick accusations. Colleen... Ah, Colleen. Colleen on the dock, her amber eyes burning as they stared into his. Colleen in the carriage, the song on her lips, which had tasted sweet as clover, or honeysuckle. Colleen, whose beauty, whose smile, whose touch was enough to drive away demons and—

"There you are!" Joy's soft, lilting voice interrupted his meditation as, with Peter at her side, she approached him. "We've been looking everywhere for you." She glanced back at the picnic. "You've met Allan?"

Jason nodded. "Yes."

"A hard man to like. He's very..."

"Opinionated?" Jason asked. "Quick to judge? Sure of himself? Hard-headed?"

Joy smiled wanly. "All of those. But he's a good man. Father thinks the world of him." Knowing something was wrong, but not sure what, she hesitated before she went on. "Father knows you're here," she finally said. "It might be best if you saw him now. If you like," she added as a measure of comfort, "I'll go with you."

With no reason to refuse, Jason followed her back to the picnic through the crowd, which was busy quaffing tankards of ale and flying brightly colored kites while children chased after pet puppies and mothers chased after children. A merry confusion was the order of the day. The meadow in which the picnic was held was a huge circle, in the middle of which a section had been set aside for a horseshoe-throwing contest. Stakes had been hammered into the ground, shallow pits dug, and teams organized. Jason's first view of Ethan Edward Paxton, his father, whom he hadn't seen in four years, was of a man, his small teeth clenched and his dark eyes squinted, heaving a rusty horseshoe through the air. The pitch was magnificent. It cut a long, lovely arch and landed with a satisfying thump before neatly surrounding and clanging against the stake.

"Fifty points clean!" someone shouted as a cheer went up from the spectators.

Money and goods changed hands as bets were paid off. Ethan's teammates crowded around him and slapped his back, finally letting him go to retrieve his tankard of ale from a nearby table.

"Now's as good a time as any," Joy suggested.

Ethan Edward Paxton was one of those men who never seemed to age. At fifty, he looked fit and stronger than ever. His hair was thick and wavy and only slightly gray at the temples. His eyes were the same deep brown as Hope's and they shone with the same determination Jason had seen in Allan's. His rolled-up sleeves revealed great bulges of hardened muscle, and it was said he could still, when occasion demanded, fell a mule with one blow of his fist, an impressive feat for a man of any age. No matter how important his position as a landowner and merchant, it was obvious that he hadn't forgotten that he came from a sturdy, stubborn stock of pirates and pioneers.

It seemed an eternity, but no more than ten seconds passed as the two men looked at each other. "Good afternoon, Father," Jason finally said in a measured voice.

Ethan slapped the dust from his hands, then took a long drink of ale. Was there tenderness in his eyes as he gazed at his son? Was there a longing to embrace him? For a fleeting second, Jason thought his father would extend his hands, his arms, and that he might actually take him to his bosom. But he didn't, and when he spoke, his voice was dry and harsh, and his words were free of sentiment. "Did you come back to fool with your music," he asked, "or to fight for your land?"

As he had been with Allan, and as he could see he would be more than once again before the afternoon was over, Jason was trapped. Unbidden, anger surged through him, and it was only with effort that he kept his voice neutral. "I came back because I missed my home," he said noncommittally.

Ethan peered at his son, then shifted his eyes toward Peter Tregoning. "A British officer." He wiped the foam from his lips with his forearm. "A friend of yours?"

Accused, tried, and hanged. No questions asked, no defense allowed. What has the war done? Is my own father, my own flesh and blood, as obdurate and quick to judge as Allan? Can he have so little faith in me? Can he truly think, even for a second, that I would sell out all I love so dearly? Father, Father . . .

"Yes," Jason said stubbornly.

Ethan's eyes narrowed and his hand balled into a fist. "You'd best entertain him, then," he finally said, getting control of himself. He drank, then spit a stream of ale into the dust. "I know you want to make him feel right at home," he finished, and without looking back he turned and stalked away.

"Father is sometimes . . . blunt to a fault," Joy awkwardly tried to explain to Peter and Jason. "He means no harm."

"I'm terribly sorry if I've bungled your reunion, old man," Peter apologized with genuine regret. "Perhaps it would be best if I—"

"It has nothing to do with you," Jason consoled his friend. "It's an old matter between my father and myself."

"He'll feel different tomorrow," Joy promised. "The excitement of the picnic has everyone overwrought. He's glad to see you, Jase. I know he is."

Shaken by the exchange between father and son, Colleen found herself questioning Jason's politics. There had been so little time—virtually none—for them to talk. Could his father be right? There was the matter of Peter Tregoning, after all. Was it possible that Jason harbored Tory sentiments or was, God forbid, an out-and-out Tory? The possibility stunned her and left her knees weak, but there was no time to question him because Buckley and a large group of his friends, their mugs raised in fellowship, had begun to sing an altered version of the spirited "Liberty Song," one of the most popular songs of the day. Their voices were directed at the rebel sympathizers at the picnic who, with Hope and Allan in their midst, stood defiantly and listened.

> Come shake your dull noodles, ye rebels, and bawl,
> And own that you're fools at fair Liberty's call;
> No scandalous conduct can add to your fame,
> Condemned to dishonor, inherit the shame.
> In folly you're born and in folly you'll live.
> To madness still ready
> And stupidly steady,
> Not as men but as monkeys the token you give.

The challenge was not to go unanswered. With Ethan—and Colleen, Jason noted with alarm—at his side, Allan lifted his arms and conducted the Patriots in their own original, and louder and lustier, version of the same song:

> Come swallow your ale, ye Tories, and roar
> That sons of fair freedom are hampered once more.

But know that no cutthroats our spirits can tame,
Nor a host of oppressors shall smother the flame.
In freedom we're born, like the sons of the brave,
    We'll never surrender
    But swear to defend her,
And scorn to survive, if unable to save.

The Tories retorted by repeating their version, only to be drowned out by still another rebel rendering, this time with Colleen's voice and defiance growing even angrier. At one point, she looked to Jason, who could only shrug as if to say, "I don't know the words."

The rebels gathered to the west of the horseshoe pits and the Tories to the east, splitting the picnic virtually in half. With other members of the community who, for a variety of reasons, were reluctant to commit themselves, Jason, Peter, and Joy stood off to one side. Louder and louder, more a brawl of voices, the words mixed in a grand cacophony of shouting that bore, with flat notes, off key and sour, little relationship to singing.

"Beautiful voices," Peter said, wincing at one particularly sour note. "A veritable choir of angels."

There were hints of violence in the voices, and daring, taunting looks in the eyes of the singers. "You'll have to admit it's lively," Jason quipped, trying to maintain his humor even as he worried that the musical struggle would soon turn physical. All semblance of patience vanished as the warring versions of "Liberty Song" clashed disonantly. Louder and louder, angrier and angrier, until it seemed as if all the sounds of the natural world—children's cries, chirping birds, whining puppies, croaking frogs—had been drowned out by voices intent on victory until the explosion of a single musket shot broke the spell and turned the heads of the feverish singers.

There, where the carriages had been left and attended to by servants and slaves, stood Major Randall Embleton, accompanied by a dozen red-coated English soldiers, one of whom lowered the Brown Bess that had just announced the Crown's military presence. Not yet forty, Embleton was a man whose ambition shone in his enormous jet-black eyes. His reputation as a ruthless warrior had been won in Scotland and was being hardened during his tour of duty in the colonies. The son of a wealthy London banker, Embleton was not an attractive man.

His bug eyes and floppy ears were too large, his neck too thick, his lips far too protruding. He nonetheless looked formidable as he sat firmly upon a black steed. His uniform was graced with fringed epaulets the color of gold, and an impressive array of medals. His highly polished boots matched his eyes and his horse. He removed his tricorn to reveal a short white compaign wig that was braided in the back into a ponytail secured on top and bottom by black velvet bows. On his appearance, and without causing notice, Hope and Ethan quietly moved Allan to the back of the crowd and into the dense woods.

"I mean not to disturb the festivities," the major announced in a voice laden with murderous restraint. "I've recently arrived from Charles Town"—he was careful to separate the two words—"where I'm most happy to report that the king's forces, as you might well expect, continue to be handily in control. Furthermore, I've been asked by Colonel Tarleton to ensure the peace and political tranquility that the Crown has brought to this colony. We've had, however, some reports of trouble in your fair community of Brandborough, and therefore I think it appropriate that I take this festive occasion to state that under no circumstances will insurrection be treated with anything less than swift and severe rebuke."

The Tories cheered, the Patriots jeered, and Embleton raised his hand to still the crowd. The thin veneer of civility peeled away from his voice, revealing a harsh, strident undertone. "If I must set an example, mark me well, I'll welcome the opportunity. It should be clear to all that these colonies are the king's. To think or, more foolishly yet, to act otherwise is a hopeless endeavor. My mandate is to keep this great colony secure and, no matter the cost, I do not intend to fail. If any of you has any questions in this matter"—his smile resembled a shark's open-mouthed gaze—"I shall be glad to answer them—in the more . . . felicitous surroundings of the Old Customs-Exchange building in Charles Town."

There was a great stir from the crowd, a mumbling of more muffled jeers from the Patriots and a swell of hearty cheers from the Loyalists. "I've got a question I want answered right now," an unidentified voice shouted. "Why don't you pack up and go home?"

The corner of Embleton's mouth twitched and his hand tightened around his reins, but he maintained control of his temper. His eyes swept over the crowd and, one eyebrow raised, stopped on Peter. "You're Tregoning?" he asked.

"Yes, sir! Captain Peter Alfred Tregoning, commanding, New Dunston—"

Embleton silenced him with an imperious wave, and with the same gesture commanded him to approach.

"Damn!" Peter whispered to Jason. "What a pickle. Just arrived, and already partying. He'll be furious. Walk with me, will you?"

There was no way out of it. Made to walk the gauntlet between the two opposing groups of colonists, Jason wished he could become invisible.

"Lost no time, eh, Captain?" Embleton asked, returning Peter's salute.

"Sir, I—"

"Your troops looked good, considering they'd just landed, and your lieutenant was suitably impressive. On top of which, you're making yourself known with an alacrity I find commendable." His face breaking into a smile, he dismounted, removed his glove, and extended his hand. "Well done, Captain Tregoning. And welcome to South Carolina. It's the arsehole of the world, but we've a job to do, eh?"

"Thank you, sir," Peter replied, inwardly wincing. "May I present my friend, Jason Paxton. He's a—"

"Paxton." Embleton frowned, tugged at his earlobe. "Something about a Paxton in the dispatches on last week's packet ship." He peered at Jason. "Ah, yes. You the musician?"

"It's my honor, sir, to call myself—"

"Don't care much for music, myself. Damned infernal noise if you ask me. But the colonel does, and he's expressed some interest in you."

Jason tensed, and he imagined the reaction that would elicit from his Patriot friends. "I'm flattered, sir," he answered in a carefully uninflected tone.

"Be coming to Charles Town soon?"

"I have no idea, sir. I've only just now arrived."

"When you do, look me up. Be a feather in my cap if I can introduce you to Tarleton. Well, then!" Pleased with himself, Embleton remounted. "I'm due at the Martin estate shortly. Tregoning? I'll be staying the night here and will see you tomorrow morning at the Customs House in Brandborough. We'll have a cup of tea, get acquainted, and discuss your duties."

"It'll be my pleasure, sir," Peter answered, saluting.

"Your servant, Paxton."

"And yours, sir," Jason said.

Thankful that the encounter was over with, Jason heaved a sigh of relief. And then, as he turned and saw his father's eyes boring into his and felt the ominous silence directed toward him, he realized that the real encounter had only then, perhaps, begun.

~ *Chapter 5* ~

It was too hot to dance, but dance they did, and with abandon. From seven to seventy, barefoot and booted, they shouted and kicked, wore away the grass to stubble, and raised a great cloud of dust. Skirts flew, coattails jounced, and wigs skid askew as the musicians, already a bit tipsy, played something that sounded like a mixture of an Irish jig and a Viennese sonata. No less comical than the musicians' inept attempt at harmonic and rhythmic unity was Buckley's attempt to follow them. Everything went wrong for him. No matter how hard he tried or how fast he danced, he couldn't keep up with Colleen. He'd taken the time to return to his carriage, where his slave, a black liveried in black and gold, had attended him, but even with a repowdered wig, fresh perfumes, and ointments, he felt woefully out of control.

Buckley had benefited from years of practice at society balls, but makeshift musical aggregations of the rustic sort left him flustered. At last, his temper fraying, he dismissed the musicians' incompetence with a curse, quit the field, and led Colleen to the line of shade on the western edge of the meadow, where on his earlier instructions his slave had laid out a blanket.

The wine he'd brought, and kept wrapped in damp towels, was refreshingly cool. "Barbarians!" he snorted, wiping his brow and leaning back against a pillow. "They want to govern themselves, they say. Yet how can any such mad rabble have such pretensions? There is a parallel, you know, my dear. The essence of government is order, and if this is an example—"

"I rather enjoy it myself," Colleen said, the very voice of moderation in comparison to the way she felt.

"Because you've had so little chance to experience the more civilized aspects of society." His gesture was grand and all-inclusive. "What is this, I ask you? A mob of unschooled rustics bouncing about in a field. No, my dear." He leaned toward Colleen in his own inimitably pompous manner. "You deserve better. Far better. And only I, and my family, can place you in the position that a woman of your intelligence and beauty—"

"There you are! Given up already?"

Buckley's eyes narrowed as he looked up and saw Jason standing over him. "Just resting for a moment, old boy," he said between clenched teeth. "Why don't you run along and—"

"Run along?" Jason asked. "When there's dancing to be done? After eight weeks aboard a ship, the muscles in my legs are about to atrophy if I don't give them a good exercise." He held out a hand to Colleen. "What do you say, Colleen? One dance, to get a poor seafarer's blood moving?"

"I'd love to. Be a dear and hold this for me, will you, Buckley?" she asked, handing him her glass and jumping to her feet.

"Now, look here!..."

"Terribly kind of you...old boy," Jason said, tongue in cheek. "I promise to return her to you unharmed in just a few moments."

"I wish you hadn't said that," Colleen complained as they moved to the center of the meadow, where dozens of couples were whirling around.

"Why?"

"Because I don't want to be returned to him, thank you."

Jason smiled, appreciative of her spirit, and found himself leading her in an improvised dance that seemed to have been building within him for hours, even years. Not even the angry scowl of his father stopped him. Unlike Buckley, he loved the hybrid music. Its rawness and confusion seemed to match his own, making him feel carefree and loose. Entering in the spirit of the afternoon, he and Colleen linked hands with the other dancers in a moving, swirling circle, his old neighbors in their finery and their plain work clothes, his newfound friend in her gown of yellow, lavender, and green, her eyes catching the afternoon sun. They danced in a square, danced in a circle, changing partners and flying with the breeze, over and under, arms and hands, kicking up dust and singing out, squealing and hollering and not caring whether the steps were wrong or right, Jason finally shedding the tension that had crept under his skin, Jason reveling in the freedom, the wild-spirited freedom of the bastardized concoction of minuet, cotillion, quadrille, reele, allemande, rigadoon, and hornpipe. It was as if the melody of the morning—from Jason's ship and Colleen's bedroom—had been refashioned into an exuberantly shapeless form. Jason laughed out loud as he thought of the dance masters he'd met in Europe, and what they would think of the improbable, confusing extravaganza.

I am with him. He asked me to dance. He sought me out, saved me from the terrible boredom of Buckley Somerset. He's everything I've ever dreamed of.... Colleen's head bounced from side to side and her feet flew. Not caring if she appeared giddy or undignified, her doubts about Jason's political persuasion forgotten, she abandoned herself to the whirlwind dance, threw herself into the crazy jig. When the dance ended, the spell lingered. Colleen and Jason stood facing one another, the heat of the rhythm and their impassioned movements still passing through them, their eyes expressing thoughts and feelings that their tongues dared not utter. Only the announcement of the basket auction interrupted their hypnotic stares.

"You brought a basket?" Jason asked.

"A beige wicker hamper tied with a light green bow," Colleen answered as if in a dream. Shyly, she looked down at the ground, then back into his eyes. "I'd be ... pleased ... if we could share it."

"And Buckley?"

Colleen's eyes flared. "If you think for one minute, Jason Paxton, that—"

Jason grinned, then touched one finger to her lips to stop her. "You're looking at a hungry man," he said. "Don't worry. I'll think of something."

"I know it ain't the best time to eat," Chester Wills, the auctioneer, announced, "but seein' as the supply of spirits is gettin' low, and that of tempers is startin' to rise—not to speak of the mosquitoes that'll move in in another few hours—the committee's decided we'd best get on with it. Now, this basket here . . ."

Off to one side, where the grass was still green and the dust was at a minimum, the women stood arrayed behind a line of blankets on which sat their baskets. In front of them, in a tightly packed group, stood the anxious men. Since money, like everything else, had grown scarcer as the war wore on, the bids were low—the orphans' fund would suffer—but Chester, with his salty humor and impish grin, did the best he could. "This woman's strawberry jam," he said of Becky Siswell, who blushed the color of strawberries, "has been tasted by many a starving man—and ne'er a one of 'em left her table unsatisfied." No spring chicken, Becky was secretly glad for the strong endorsement. James Gaffin, a lusty carpenter whose wife had died of scarlet fever six months earlier, beat back the other bidders and, with a merry gleam in his eyes, escorted Becky and her basket away.

Peter Tregoning would not be outbid for Joy's basket, much to the delight of Joy and the obvious annoyance of Ethan, Hope, and Allan, who had slipped back to join the crowd. Colleen remained calm until Chester picked up her basket and asked for an opening bid. She desperately didn't want to share her lunch with Buckley, who was standing directly next to Jason, but didn't know how to stop him if he was determined enough. Jason participated in the early bidding, as did several others who fancied Colleen. For several minutes, Buckley laughed to himself as the meager bids built, and then calmly, almost casually, he raised his hand and called out, "Five pounds!"

The crowd gasped. It was as though he were buying much more than a basket of simple luncheon fare. With such a sum, in silver, the average citizen of Brandborough could feed himself and his family for months. Colleen, whose face fell with the realization that no one could match a bid so ridiculously inflated, looked fleetingly at Jason, who could only offer his customary shrug and shy, little-boy-lost smile before ducking out of sight and disappearing.

Five pounds was more than all the rest of the baskets put together would bring in, so no matter how much he disliked Buckley or how sorry he felt for Colleen, Chester didn't bat an eye. "Well, you won it, so come an' get it—and the lucky young lady," he called.

Enjoying himself and his victory over Jason, Buckley stepped forward and reached into his waistcoat pocket for his purse. "That's strange," he said. He patted his coat pockets. Nothing. His trousers pockets. Nothing. "I had it right here," he muttered, his face turning red as, once again, he searched each pocket and even looked around on the ground.

"Lose something, Bucky boy?" someone shouted.

"Oh, my!" someone else groaned comically. "Daddy forgot to give him his purse this morning."

"Thief!" Buckley roared, whirling to confront the chorus of guffaws, catcalls, and whistles. "Thief, I say! I've been robbed!"

Chester held out his hand. "That'll be five pounds, Mr. Somerset."

Furious, Buckley turned his back on the crowd and reached for the basket. "You'll get your five pounds tomorrow, damn your hide!" he spat.

"Sorry." Five pounds was a fortune, but the spectacle of Buckley Somerset being caught out was of inestimably greater worth. "This is cash and carry, Somerset. You knew that when you bid. Now quiet down, all of you!" he yelled, stilling the crowd. "Accordin' to my best recollection, Jase Paxton, who's just got home, made the next highest bid, and accordin' to the rules"—which he'd made up on the spur of the moment—"he gets the basket and the girl. Jase? Where'd you get to?"

"Right here, Chester. What did I bid?"

"A pound, two pence."

Jason pulled out his purse and made a show of counting out the money. "That much, eh? Lucky for me," he added with a broad wink to the crowd, "that I have that much right here."

The crowd applauded. Colleen, making no attempt to hide her happiness, kissed him on his cheek. "Sorry, Buckley," Jason said, pausing as he and Colleen started to leave.

His eyes burning with hatred, Buckley stared back. "You stole my purse," he said flatly. "You—"

"It's a dangerous thing, to accuse a man of being a thief," Jason said, cutting him off, "especially when I distinctly remember seeing your purse on the floor of your carriage." Again, he winked, but this time for Buckley alone. "That's where you must have dropped it earlier. I meant to mention it before, but it somehow slipped my mind."

Enraged by the knowledge that he'd been bested and publicly humiliated, Buckley toyed with the idea of slugging Jason flush in the face, but then, instinctively touching the break in his nose, he decided that both time and place were wrong. Instead, he stood stock still as Jason and Colleen walked off together, and only then, swearing to see Jason suffer before the day was over, did he stalk through the derisive laughter toward his carriage.

It was never said or even suggested that they walk through the woods, and yet they found themselves unable to stop, traveling deeper and deeper into the hushed silence of the forest. They were relieved to be free of the crowd, free of Ethan's scrutiny and Buckley's watchful, jealous gaze. Mostly, though, they were grateful for the privacy and for one another's company in a setting whose lush scent of fresh green growth made them heady. The smell of pinecone and sweet wildflower mingled in a sensual, pungent perfume. Shafts of golden sunlight darted through the trees while, from above, birds exotic and plain cooed and wooed one another with lilting spring mating songs.

"The sunbeams remind me of the cathedral at Chartres," Jason reflected, breaking the easy silence between them. "The first time I was there, the sun danced through the magnificent stained-glass windows and suffused the whole incredible interior with the eeriest and most heavenly light you can imagine."

"I can see how the forest resembles a cathedral." Colleen looked at him with admiration—for his worldliness, his sense of beauty, the way his long, delicate fingers gripped her basket lightly, as if he were holding a violin. "The trees are so majestic and the presence of God can be felt everywhere. But please, Jase, tell me more about France. Are the women very beautiful?"

He laughed. "I hardly noticed."

"You did," she protested good-naturedly. "Of course you did."

"I was far too busy reading your poems," he continued in jest.

"You're making fun of me. There were only four of them, and you thought them childish to boot, didn't you?"

"On the contrary. I thought them quite accomplished. The

keen observation of nature—"

"I'd have sent you the love poems I wrote you, if I'd been more courageous."

Love poems? It's too soon to talk of love. It takes time for these things. It takes thoughtful consideration. . . . Nervous, Jason found himself walking faster. "You flatter me," he finally managed to say. "And yet you hardly know me."

"I know you well enough. Long before you left, I knew I loved you."

Jason was taken aback. Her candor surprised and confused him. Her kiss had stunned him; her touch set him afire. Every time he so much as looked at her he wanted to shout and sing and dance. But love? Did he dare to call it love? They'd been together only a few hours. His homecoming had thrown him into a state of emotional upheaval, and it would be irresponsible to tell her how deeply she'd touched him. As if trying to escape his thoughts, he began walking even faster, until Colleen could hardly keep up the pace. "Are we to walk together, or am I to chase you?" she asked.

Her easy sense of humor saved the moment. Laughing, Jason slowed the pace to a more relaxing stroll. "You aren't afraid of saying what you think," he said. "I'll grant you that."

"Or writing it either," she announced.

"May I see the poems you wrote about me?"

"I'm afraid they're too overwrought to show anyone. Aunt Rianne had given me the love verses of John Donne and Andrew Marvell, and I was convinced I could emulate the style."

"Your aunt's taste for poetry covers a wide range."

"She's been wonderful to me, Jase. She's the one who encouraged me to write my broadsides."

"Your what?"

"Broadsides. Printed sheets that one posts up about town."

"I know what broadsides are, but what's written on yours?"

"That's the most glorious part. My words! Words to songs that everyone knows. Like today at the picnic? Those words were mine. Didn't you see the fury on those greedy Tory faces? They hate our version of that song. It's such a wonderful invention! Not that I've perfected the art, but I work at it every day. I'm thankful to be able to be doing something to help push the brutes out of here. It was Thomas Paine who inspired me. His words sing so! And Alexander Pope and John Dryden.

They're masters of satire, aren't they? And, of course, Shakespeare, but he's too great a genius to emulate, even though I adore his sonnets. I read them all the time. Do you know them? Have you read them?"

Who *was* this woman by his side? Jason wondered, feeling a bit overwhelmed. Her spontaneity and exuberance were contagious, and utterly charming. Her intelligence sparkled as enchantingly as her luminous amber eyes. But revolutionary verse? Published in broadsides? "Do you have any idea of how dangerous that sort of thing can be?" he asked.

"We live in dangerous times," she replied, dismissing his concern, "and must use whatever gifts God has given us to ensure our own freedom. Besides, they'd never suspect a woman, nor would they harm me even if they did."

"I wouldn't be so certain," Jason warned. "As far as the English are concerned, sedition is sedition, no matter what the sex of the offender. And jailors are by nature an ill-sighted lot, blind to the contents of their cells, however wretched the poor prisoners within."

"I'm not afraid. I do what I please, and what I think is right. I may be just a beginner, but I'm determined to become unmatched at the form."

Her spirit excited him, and yet he felt obliged to voice his skepticism. "Who knows about these . . . activities of yours?"

"Only Aunt Rianne. And Ephraim Kramer. He's a master printer. He—"

"Ephraim Kramer?" Jason asked. "In Brandborough? I know of no—"

"In Charleston. He has a shop on Legare Street. He grumbles every time I ask him to set type for me, but he gives in eventually. He's a brave man, courageous and true. I admire him greatly."

"He is, I take it, a Patriot?"

"All men of good conscience are Patriots."

Jason had been gone for four years, and for almost every day of those years, war had raged in the colonies. Family and friends had written him, and he'd read accounts and commentaries in the British and foreign press, but to experience the reality of friend opposed to friend, of brother to brother, of father to son, had shocked him to the core. It was, he thought, as if everyone he'd ever known had become strangers to whom he hardly dared speak without first ascertaining where his loyalties laid. Suddenly tired, he shifted Colleen's basket and his coat to his other arm, and massaged his eyes. "And that includes your father, too, I assume?"

"My father . . ." Her face reddened, and she appeared near tears.

"I've been gone, Colleen," he gently reminded her. "I don't know who's on whose side. I honestly didn't mean to offend you if . . . that is, if . . ."

"It's all right. I understand." She took a deep breath and smiled bravely. "Father's suffered greatly in his life and wants nothing to do with either side. He has a good heart, and I shouldn't expect him to be something he's not."

Jason thought of the great gulf that separated him from his own father, and he nodded sympathetically. Several long minutes passed before Colleen could abandon thoughts of her father and return her attention to Jason. "So what are your plans?" she asked, as they ambled on. "I know you've come back to help the revolution. You must have. Living abroad for all those years, hearing of our bravery and our fortunes—often losing, but never surrendering. That's what inspired you to come back didn't it? We could work together, Jase. And we shall! I'm certain of it. With your music and my words, we'll help spread the message from colony to colony, from—"

"I think we should stop and enjoy this lovely luncheon you've prepared," Jason interrupted.

She looked at him quizzically. "You can't be . . . you aren't . . . I won't even say it. Tell me, Jase. Swear you're not a—"

"Tory?" He finished the sentence for her. "No, I'm not. But neither am I about to declare myself for one side or another."

Her face turned scarlet, her voice jumped a whole octave. "You sound like Papa, like a man completely devoid of—"

"Food," he interrupted again. "I'm famished. Haven't eaten a thing all day. Can't you find enough mercy in that hard revolutionary heart of yours to feed a hungry man?"

"No. I—"

"Listen to me, Colleen!" He dropped both basket and coat, grabbed her arms more roughly than he'd meant to, and turned her to him. "I've been gone four years. I just spent eight weeks at sea, and only three hours ago stepped off the ship and into a world that's upside down. My father treats me with contempt.

Half the people I know seem to be at each other's throats. The town I was born in and raised in is occupied. What do you expect of me?"

"I expect—"

"No. Don't say it, whatever it is." His voice gentled. He let go of her arms and, his fingers light as feathers, brushed the hair back from her face. "I won't stand on a commons and shout songs at the top of my lungs, nor will I remake myself in Allan Coleridge's image, but I'm not a Tory. But that's something you'll have to take on faith, because there's no way to prove it to you—at least for the time being."

Colleen closed her eyes, breathed deeply in and out, and shuddered. "I'm sorry," she whispered. "I shouldn't have—"

"Don't be. You had every right. And now?" Smiling, he touched the corners of her mouth to make her smile. "Enough of politics. It's time to laugh and to eat." He drew himself up in a comic declamatory posture and spoke in a deep, booming voice. "Speak to me, woman, of food!"

Colleen melted. His sloped, hooded eyes, gleaming merrily, were impossible to resist, and his humor was infectious. "I trust you like fried chicken, sir?" she asked with a coquettish curtsey.

"Fried chicken!" Jason exclaimed. "Four years and not even the suggestion, the slightest hint, of that delicacy. How many were the times I'd have traded an arm for a single morsel of real Carolina fried chicken! Fried chicken! The very words are music to my ears."

"What about cinnamon rolls and a cucumber-and-onion salad?" Colleen asked, laughing.

Jason ducked under a branch, held it high so Colleen could pass without snagging her hair. "There is, *mademoiselle,*" he said with mock seriousness, "no question that the three go together as naturally as Aristotle's unities. Philosophers, as well as men of action, agree that . . . Let me see. . . . Is this it?" he asked, stopping and searching about to left and right.

"What?" Colleen asked, confused.

"Yes! Right there by that tulipwood tree, if I'm not mistaken."

Colleen took his hand and hurried along at his side, only to stop, seconds later, at the edge of a narrow, brush-choked ravine.

"Damnation!" Jason cursed in obvious disappointment. "See

how time can plot against a man? Well, let's not give up yet. C'mon."

"Where in heaven's name are you?"

"Aha! I was right. There! Can you think of a prettier spot for a picnic?"

It was beautiful. Some eight to ten feet below the level of the forest floor, the small, choked ravine had broadened out and silted in. Perhaps twenty feet wide and carpeted with a lush grass, the floor was cut by a tiny brook no more than a foot across. "It's exquisite!" Colleen exclaimed as Jason helped her down the steep bank. "But how did you know about it?" Laughing, she spun about, ran to the brook, and dipped her fingers in the clear, cool water.

"Like it?" Jason asked, looking for a level spot.

"You were bringing us here all the time, weren't you? You had me believing that there was no plan to our walk, but you're a schemer, Jason Paxton. Indeed you are. You robbed Buckley of his purse, and now you've lured me into your secret den."

Jason set the basket down and dropped his coat next to it. "You're right. It is mine. I discovered it when I was a boy and used to explore these woods with a vengeance. Did you know that I've been over every inch of the land inside and outside Brandborough, halfway to Charleston? I'd go hunting with my father, and then I'd hunt by myself. You might not know it by looking at me, but I was a wild child. I'd get carried away making up all sorts of ridiculous games, pretending I was chasing or being chased." He laughed softly in recollection. "I was convinced that I'd be a pirate, like Grandmother and Grandfather had been. I even drew elaborate maps of the entire territory."

"You? A pirate?" Colleen laughed.

"Ruthless and cunning, fearless and wild. Yes, this is the region of my youth, when I'd memorize every last detail of forest and swamp, hill and valley, with the precision of a mathematician."

"Musicians, they say, are also said to have an aptitude for mathematics."

"Music was the furthest thought from my mind. I wanted only to please my father by showing him my mastery of the land and my undying bravery."

"Then how did you come to music?"

"By sitting alone in this ravine, among other places. Here

and in a hundred other secret dells and sheltered meadows. Listen! Is there a more enchanting song than the one sung by sparrows and blue jays? Is the lazy buzz of the bumblebee not an enticing sound? Are the bass-voiced frogs not figures of deep percussive delight? And is the cool rustle of leaves kissed by the breeze any less thrilling than a viola kissed by a bow? I considered this delightfully noisy silence for hours, as a boy. For the first time I listened to the thump of my own heartbeat. It was then that I knew the essential rhythm was within us all, and that to create music was my real destiny."

"You understood that at so young an age?" asked Colleen, intoxicated by the manner of his speech and sound of his melodious voice.

"I heard music then—here, for the first time. Just as I'm hearing music now...with you."

Nervously, she spread a white cloth on which she placed the food while the morning's melody began replaying within her head, thrilling her wildly beating heart. Jason ate and hummed at the same time. He made small, gracious sounds of satisfaction and complimented her on the succulent chicken. He noted the way a single beam of light crossed her face and fell upon her breast. For a hungry man, he didn't eat ravenously, but rather delicately, patiently, savoring each morsel. Unable to take her eyes from his, experiencing strange and new sensations along the most sensitive sections of her body—her back, legs, thighs—Colleen barely ate at all.

"Wonderful." Jason finally sighed. "Never have I tasted anything...Your cooking?" he asked.

Colleen blushed. "The chicken, aye. Portia made the rolls and the salad."

"Portia? Old Portia? Tall and thin as a rail?"

"Still with us." Colleen laughed.

"Well, you make a fine pair of cooks." Satiated, he lay back on the grass and stared up into the trees arching over the secluded ravine. "Maiden and maid...but only the maiden at my side. What man could ask for a better...better...What rhymes with side?"

"Bride?" Colleen blurted out before she could stop herself.

"It does rhyme," Jason said after a long pause. The hum of insects. Somewhere the strident call of a woodpecker, followed by a rat-a-tat-tat on a hollow log. Peace. The morning's song swelling in his mind, he began to hum, and seconds later he realized that Colleen had joined him. "You have an exquisite voice. But tell me," he said, propping himself up on one elbow, "where did you learn that melody?"

"I don't know," Colleen admitted. After she had repacked the basket, she sat next to him and stared down the ravine. "It came to me this morning. At least I think it did. Or are you teaching it to me now?"

Colleen Cassandra McClagan. As beautiful as any woman he'd seen in four years of travel. Intelligent, sensitive . . . Looking up at her, her eyelashes, long and dark, peeked out above the softness of her cheeks. Her arms were as white as fine linen, and the swell of her breast, tantalizingly close, set his blood racing.

But it was insane. He'd been gone so long, had barely known her. They'd kissed twice—three times, he amended, recalling that night in the dim past on her porch. He hadn't thought of her that much. Oh, now and again—when he'd received a letter—when his mind wandered homeward—sometimes for no reason that he could think of. And yet, that song, and the rush of emotion that had surged through him when he'd seen her that morning. Each moment they'd been together since then had sparkled like the finest of jewels. Never had he felt more alive. Never had he been so intensely aware, so attracted to a woman.

"Perhaps," he said, his words slurred as he pulled her down to him, "we created it together. A song as beautiful . . . as ineffably sweet and beautiful . . . as you . . ."

For Colleen, the yearning was as great. Four years of waiting, four years of dreaming, four years of wanting. And at last, in the pastoral quiet of the spring afternoon, she felt the soft texture of his mouth, the moist fire of his tongue, the power of his loins. There was no room for thought, no analysis or abstract consideration. There was only feeling as the natural music of their insistent bodies led them to peel away their clothing and discover one another's secret passages. For a fleeting second, she led, then he, as the dance of love unfolded with a choreographic majesty that no master of ballet could have planned.

She dug her fingers into his long, lean back as he buried his face in her sweet-scented neck. He caressed the lobe of her ear, brushed the softness of her low-moaning throat with his lips. Kneeling, cupping her buttocks with his strong, steady hands, he raised her higher, entering her slowly and tenderly so that she felt the full length of his love. For it was love, he knew in his heart. No woman had ever felt this way, no woman had ever drawn from him such wild, yet gentle, passion. Her sharp cries of piercing pleasure provoked his deep, insistent penetrations.

Their rhythms ran identical courses. The melody expanded, and a suite blossomed, a sonata, a swelling concerto, building—patiently, proudly building—soaring, and then spilling into swoons of ecstasy. For minutes, for what seemed an eternity, they lost control. Their legs and arms shook and swayed like graceful branches blown wild in the midst of a raging storm, all the time moving to the majestic motion of the swelling music. They soaked themselves in the long, liquid melody—he astride her, she below, rising and falling, falling and rising, higher and harder, harder and faster—until the frenzied crescendo exploded with the power of a thousand flutes, a thousand violins, a thousand brilliant trumpets. As their opened mouths met, as their limbs locked together, they became the music, falling into thin air like vanishing notes or fluttering leaves from the ancient birch trees that protected their exhausted, glowing bodies. They faced one another with tears of unspoken joy as a single yellow butterfly, its wings etched in glittering gold and black, danced above their heads.

Still wrapped tightly in her arms, he whispered, "I love you, Colleen McClagan."

And she whispered back. "And I love you, Jason Paxton. I always have, and I always will."

∽ *Chapter 6* ∾

Hand in hand, lost in thoughts and feelings too exquisite to express, Colleen and Jason walked slowly back through the woods as the sky slid from blue to pink to blazing purple. Colleen's whole body tingled after the long-awaited rite of passage from girl to woman, and she knew that her life would never be the same again, that the consummation of her passion had been an awesome awakening of senses that she'd only imagined had existed, but had never dared explore. Until then. Until that afternoon. Just as, earlier, she'd dared to write her love verses and political broadsides, she had at last dared to love a man fully and to throw caution to the wind without thought of the consequences. For love knew no consequences, she told herself. In her secret soul, she had always known, given the opportunity, that she would give herself to Jason Behan Paxton. She was convinced that it was their destiny always to be together, loving and creating.

Jason was confused. He had anticpated a great deal about his return, but not, within the first hours, a romantic entanglement. In his heart, his love for his home and all it represented—a freedom from tired traditions, a vigorous spirit of independence—had somehow mingled with the explosion of love for Colleen. Her enthusiastic spirit was more than attractive; it was contagious. How could he separate duty from desire? How could he resist the remarkable woman at his side?

How could he balance the calling of his spirit with that of his heart? For the past four years, he'd spent his days and nights in fashionable parlors and salons, in close proximity to some of the Old World's most charming women. They'd been drawn to him, as many women were drawn to musicians, for his heightened sense of beauty and his subtle physical appeal. It was widely rumored that a frigid spinster could be reduced to a swooning lovestruck girl at the sight of his swaying body caught in the music of his own creation, his fingers darting over delicate clavichord and pianoforte. But no woman had succeeded in distracting him from his calling—at least not for more than an hour or two. Colleen, however, in one dazzling afternoon, had melted into his art, and worse, unless he wanted to jeopardize their love, was making him wonder if his as yet murkily formulated plan to play the part of a Loyalist was a very good idea.

"I wish we could turn back to your secret ravine right now," Colleen said as the pungent aroma of roast beef and the sound of music and voices reminded them that they were returning to civilization.

"No longer mine alone," Jason reminded her. "Ours."

They stopped to embrace, neither wanting to let go of one kiss, then another, and still another. But night hastened, drawing its deep purple coverlet across the sky. Ahead, they could see torches being lit. Flickering lanterns looked like so many hovering fireflies. Jason worried that their prolonged absence would cause talk and concern, but the sudden explosion of gunfire interrupted his thought. He and Colleen glanced at one another, then ran the final few yards to the edge of the meadow, where fate and poor timing placed them directly in the path of trouble.

Men shouted and women screamed, grabbed their children, and fell on them to protect them. Nearby, a group of six little girls playing ring-around-the-rosy stopped and looked up in alarm. A torch flew through the the the air, another gunshot sounded. In the midst of total confusion, the crowd parted and a half dozen figures emerged from the clot and ran toward the safety of the forest—directly toward Jason and Colleen. At the leading edge, Jason saw as they drew closer, were Hope, Ethan, and Allan. Behind them by twenty good paces, a band of Embleton's soldiers, their muskets at the ready, followed hard on their heels.

"Hold!" one of the soldiers shouted. "Hold in the name of the king!"

"Keep going!" Ethan roared, giving Allan a push. "The rest of you, stop!"

Allan kept on toward the forest at breakneck speed. Ethan, Hope, and the others stopped and began to mill about in an attempt to obscure Allan's escape and slow the British. None of them noticed the band of little girls who, frightened, ran first toward the center of the meadow and then, as Allan raced past them, turned and tried to follow him toward what, in their terror, they assumed to be safety.

The soldiers collided with the Patriots, beat them aside with their musket butts, and broke through just as Allan gained the edge of the woods, turned, and, oblivious of Jason, pulled a handgun hidden under his coat. "Stop yourselves," he yelled, "in the name of freedom!"

Terrified, like sheep caught between two wolves, the children stopped and stood halfway between Allan and the soldiers. At that moment, Jason, seeing the danger to them, stepped forward, snatched the gun from Allan's hand, and moved to one side.

"Damn!" Allan roared, leaping to retrieve his gun.

"Don't try," Jason warned, aiming at him and putting the gun on cock. "Just run! Get out of here while you can!"

Allan blanched, stared into the .52-caliber maw. "What in God's name are you doing, man?" he pleaded.

"Run, damn it! Don't you see I can't let you fire into—"

"The children," he was going to say, but it was too late, for Embleton's men were upon them. With half a dozen muskets leveled at Allan's chest, there was no escape. Seconds later, Embleton himself, with a dozen angry Patriots close behind, caught up. With a flourish, he raised what, in the excitement, he had taken to be his pistol, but was instead a turkey leg he'd impetuously picked up while his men searched for Allan. Ignoring the Patriots' jeers and derisive laughter, he carefully drew his flintlock with his free hand, cleared his throat, and histrionically announced his intentions. "In the name of his Majesty, King George the Third, you, Allan Coleridge, are hereby arrested for the unwarranted and altogether heinous assault on the Crown's arsenal at Brandborough. You'll be brought to the Old Customs Exchange in Charles Town tomorrow, there to await sentencing." He started to take a bite of turkey, almost bit the pistol instead, endured another ripple of derision at his expense, holstered the pistol, bit off a chunk of meat, and dropped what was left at Allan's feet.

The quickness with which events had unfolded left those who witnessed the arrest shaken and confused. The shock was tremendous. That Allan had been captured was one thing: that Jason had helped in his apprehension was a tragedy of immense proportions. Not having noticed the children, who by then had been snatched up by their parents, the Patriots' initial reaction was that Jason had most certainly worked against them. If there were any doubts, they were dispelled when, before leaving to escort Allan away, Embleton turned to Jason and said, "We're most grateful for your help in this matter. We received your message alerting us to Coleridge's presence, and we're pleased to note your prodigious loyalty to the Crown. I hope to renew your acquaintance in Charles Town, where, once again, I trust you'll see fit to favor us with a visit." Then, to make matters worse, the major saluted the slack-jawed musician before leading away his soldiers and prisoner.

Allan could be heard shouting profanities, both against the monarch and his brother-in-law. Rigid with fury, Hope and Ethan stared at Jason as if he were a corpse, for in truth, in that instant, he was dead to them. The expression on their faces as they turned their backs on him cut deeper than any sword.

As for Colleen, the magic of the secret ravine had been shattered in one swift, brutally revealing moment. Jason had lied to her: unthinkably, he was a Tory after all. Hadn't he betrayed his own brother-in-law? Hadn't the major said as much? How was it possible? Unable to meet his eyes, she turned away from him—and found herself face to face with a smug and apparently most self-satisfied Buckley Somerset. "Oh, God," she sighed, no more anxious to see him than Jason.

Freshly powdered and perfumed, Buckley took her arm possessively. "It's a terrible lesson in life, my dear, but you never can tell what some people will do," he said, as much for Jason's benefit as Colleen's. "I think, perhaps, it's best I take you home."

Jason's face creased in pain. "Go on," he whispered in her ear. "I'll come to your house later tonight. Everything will be explained. I give you my word."

Colleen desperately wanted to believe him, but couldn't.

And when she and Buckley rode off into the star-filled night, it seemed as if the morning's melody might never return.

The elimination of a rival, Buckley thought as his carriage rolled through the night, was an art. The forged note to Embleton informing on Coleridge, sent in Paxton's name, had been a stroke of genius. Nothing could please him more than to reflect on the deft killing of two birds with a single stone: not only had Paxton been publicly humiliated and alienated from his family and friends, but his arrogant brother-in-law had been dragged away to prison. How delightful!

Of far greater importance was the effect on Colleen. Buckley wasn't a complete fool. He as well as anyone else knew that her sympathy lay with the Patriots, and he suspected that his identification with the Tories had long been the main reason for her antipathy toward him. Women were strange creatures. How she'd known Paxton had been on the ship was a puzzle, but she had. And it also seemed obvious that she, in the past, had been childishly infatuated with Paxton. All that, however, had been undone with his apparent perfidy: the look in her eyes when Embleton gave him the credit for Coleridge's arrest told the story of her disillusionment. There was no reason not to be optimistic. With Paxton out of the way, Buckley's suit was very much alive. Colleen would come to her senses soon enough. Politics aside, she was too intelligent not to accept his proposal—and the wealth and prestige that he offered her.

Colleen was totally absorbed in thoughts of her own. Her eyes fixed on the black of night, she sat on the opposite side of the carriage from Buckley. As the horses trotted through Brandborough, she recalled the moment she'd first seen Jason. Only hours earlier, it seemed a decade. What had happened? He was everything—even more, so much more—that she'd imagined. He was kind, compassionate, tender, and sensitive. He'd told her about picking Buckley's pocket, and at the time she'd laughed. But perhaps it wasn't so funny. Perhaps it was an indication of his real self—a schemer who could just as readily deliver his own sister's husband to the British. She didn't dare trust him. Not ever again. But she *did* trust him. Her mind might be riddled with doubts, but her heart trusted him. She tried arguing with her heart, but her heart wouldn't listen: her heart remembered only the mystery of the secret

ravine, the roaring thunder, and the gentle music of love that
had washed over them. Yet, with her own eyes and ears she
had witnessed the cruel betrayal. She was torn; her head throbbed
with pain, her heart felt listless and beaten. The cool Carolina
night did nothing to revive her. The questions would not stop.
Her thoughts chased themselves into the corners of her mind.
And when the ornate carriage finally arrived at her father's
farm and began climbing the hill to her front door, she barely
heard Buckley as, once again, he brought up the question of
his proposal.

"I'm . . . I'm not able to think clearly right now," she said,
knowing that a flat refusal would only cause him to extend his
arguments.

"Ah, but it's so obviously the wise decision," he urged.
"Why delay the inevitable answer any longer?"

"Tomorrow . . ." she said.

"What of tomorrow?" he asked.

"Tomorrow," she suddenly remembered, "my father is escorting me to Charleston, where I'll be staying with Aunt Rianne
for some time. Perhaps there'll be a chance for us to talk there.
Right now I'm frightfully tired."

The thought of courting Colleen in Charleston, a city where
Buckley was known and accepted in the highest circles of
society, was not unappealing, for there he would be seen in
the best light. Willing to bide his time, he bade her a reluctant
good-night, then gave his driver the order to take him home.

The house was dark. Colleen lit a lantern and, above the
fireplace in its accustomed spot, saw a note from her father
informing her that he'd rushed to Brandborough to attend a
gravely ill patient and wasn't sure when he'd return. Portia was
asleep in her quarters in the back. Colleen let the note fall from
her hand. She was alone, for which she felt gratitude and
sadness at the same time. She was tired. She wanted to believe
Jason would keep his promise and come to explain what had
happened. But would he arrive before her father? Or would
they arrive simultaneously in the middle of the night? Why
couldn't she simply luxuriate in the memory of their lovemak-
ing? Why did the melody have to cease? Slowly, she walked
to her bedroom, where for a long while she stared at her mother's music box. In spite of the fatigue flowing to every part of
her body, her overly stimulated mind wouldn't let her sleep.
She would wait for him, she decided, just as she had waited

for four long years. He'd promised he'd come, and so he would. At last, with a sigh, she bestirred herself and, after changing into simpler clothes, began to pack for the next day's journey.

Not entirely comfortable with the idea of giving Jason a ride and thereby incurring Ethan's wrath, Chester Wills nonetheless agreed to allow him to share his and his wife's tiny one-horse buggy. For Jason, the ride was filled with trepidation. There had been no mistaking the look on his father's face as Allan had been led away. Whether he would listen to reason—perhaps, Jason dared hope, he'd calmed down during the past hour—was a question that could be answered in one way only: by facing him.

The Paxton house sat a half mile inland on a promontory that overlooked Brandborough and, beyond, the Atlantic. "I appreciate it," Jason said as the buggy stopped to let him out. "Chester. Merriwether."

"Good luck," Chester said.

Jason chuckled. "I'll need it is what you mean, right?"

"I seen them children. You done right, no matter what anyone says," Merriwether said. "And don't you let Ethan tell you otherwise. If he does—"

"Hold your tongue, wife," Chester snapped.

Merriwether's look would have frozen water in August. "If he does, you tell him to come see me, and I'll set him straight."

"Yes, ma'am. I surely will," Jason assured her. "And thank you."

Freshly painted, the house gleamed starkly white in the moonlight. Jason stood alone, looked at the trees he'd climbed so often as a boy, and breathed in the fragrances of his childhood: the chilled, ocean-fresh night air, the essence of rich, black earth, the light perfume of wisteria. The house itself was unchanged, plain and simple, just the way Ethan, a man with little patience for grandiosity, wanted it. The leather-hinged gate opened easily, and the oyster shells filling the curved drive crunched underfoot. The porch was empty save for a pair of rocking chairs and a chain-hung swing that swayed slightly in the breeze. The door was closed, but not yet barred. Taking a deep breath, he pushed it open and entered.

The foyer was dark. Wondering where Ethan was, Jason took the four well-remembered steps—*How many times during the past four years have I, in my dreams, stood here?*— and entered the lantern-lit living room, where over the massive fireplace hung the rapier and scabbard of Marie Ravenne, the lady pirate and grandmother he'd known as a small boy and whose spirit had loomed so large over his formative years. How strange it seemed to be home! Strange but comforting. He'd missed—

"What do you want here?"

Jason turned, saw his father, his eyes cold as winter wind, enter from the kitchen. "I said it before, Father. I've come home."

"And I've said you no longer have a home here, especially after your conduct today. I mean it, boy. You're to get out of here, and get out now. Or have you brought a regiment of bloodthirsty soldiers to lay claim to this house and drive out the rest of your family?"

Hearing voices, Hope and Joy entered and saw the two men face to face—the muscular, strong-willed father, and the curly-haired, soft-spoken son. "Have you no shame?" Hope asked. "Coming here after this afternoon? Allan is in chains this very moment all because—"

"There were children who would have been caught in the crossfire if not for Jason," Joy interrupted. "Didn't you see? Why won't you believe me?"

Ethan swiveled to his right and, shoulders hunched, glared at his daughter. "I saw him aid the English dogs—and nothing more," he answered.

"You've always protected him," Hope protested, her clear brown eyes flecked with firelight, her voice as strong and authoritative as Ethan's. "Father's right. We don't need him, and we don't want him."

Still controlled, Jason spoke slowly and deliberately. "I had nothing to do with Allan's capture. I sent no message, for heaven's sake. I suspect it was—"

"Your English soldier friend?" Ethan interrupted. "Or is he not really your friend? Was that also a case of our mistaken perception?"

"You're in no mood to listen to reason," Jason said.

"I'm in no mood to entertain a son of mine who, for years now, has wantonly neglected his birthright and duty. Allan Coleridge has done more in a few months to help us in our enterprise than you've done in the past decade. Did it ever occur to you while you were playing kingly music for your

English aristocrats that we've been fighting a war? That the Paxton businesses were going through a crisis, the likes of which this family has never before known? Did it bother you in the least that the taxes imposed by the very perfumed lords and ladies whom you so graciously entertained were choking us to death?" He paused to catch his composure, then continued, his voice still cracking with emotion.

"You're my flesh and blood, Jason, my only son. May God be my witness that I loved you as a little boy. I loved you as a young man. I taught you whatever I knew about this land, and taught you, too, as our fortunes grew and I learned. You were bright, there could be no doubt. You learned twice— thrice—as quickly as I had learned. In the swamps and woods, you displayed all the qualities of a fine hunter. You were a crack shot, a fearless rider. You had strength and courage. In the fields, you proved to be a fine farmer. You had good judgment. You showed a keen sense for commerce. Nothing went unnoticed by your curious and nimble mind. Oh, the pride I took in you! And in the darkest hours of your mother's sickness, it was you and your loving sisters who comforted me and saved me from despair. Many were the times I told my men that this life of endless toil seemed worthwhile only because I knew that someday you'd benefit from my labor. This was all to be yours. And yet you've chosen not simply to throw it away for a fiddle and a flute, but to conspire with the same blood-sucking scoundrels who'd destroy the very things I hold precious—our ships, our land, and our home."

Rarely had Jason heard his father speak with such passion. "You misjudge me, Father," he said finally. "I love you, and I love this land with all my heart. There are ways I'll help the high cause of freedom, but you must trust my judgment. Trust me to act—"

"Do you expect me to believe that? When I see you throwing off your Tory friends and joining up with us—that's when I'll believe you. Tell me, are you prepared to do that?"

"No, because it's impractical. I must work in my own way, according to my own skills and—"

"Hah! Just as I thought! An excuse for cowardice!" Ethan yelled. "You may deceive yourself, but you don't me. Hiding behind your pianoforte—is that your way?"

"Please," Jason implored. "Listen to me."

"Listen to what? The words of a traitor?"

"Traitor?" Jason flushed. "You dare to call your own son a traitor?"

"When treason is what I see—"

"And faith?" Jason asked. "Have you so little faith in me that—"

"Don't speak to me of faith," Ethan roared, striking the sideboard so hard that it almost broke. "Not when for four long years you've not lifted a finger for your family or friends or freedom. Why should I believe you now? You disgrace yourself with hypocrisy. I'll not be moved by sentiment. You're not welcome here, Jason. Return to England. Go elsewhere to compose your ditties, or whatever it is you write, and leave us alone. I pray only that the day doesn't come when I find myself facing you, along with your Tory compatriots, on a battlefield."

The blood of pirates, of men and women of great pride and no little temper, flowed in Jason's veins. To be misunderstood was one thing, but to hear his honor impugned even by— especially by—his father was beyond endurance. As if a plug had been pulled, the blood drained from Jason's face and, ready to fight, he balled his hands into fists.

"You want to try?" Ethan asked, a death's-head grin splitting his face. "Look at you. You're soft as a pillow. Get out of my sight before I thrash you within an inch of your life."

There was nothing more to say. Even if Ethan, beyond all reason, asked for Jason's thoughts, it would have been too late. Spinning on his heels, Jason stalked silently past his sisters, out of the room, through the front door, and onto the porch.

Only Joy followed him. "What will you do now, Jason?"

He put his arm around her and sighed. "I don't know. But one way or another, I'll manage." He leaned over and kissed her on the cheek.

"Where will you go?"

"Charleston, I imagine. Robin and Piero are there, and I shall be most glad to see them."

"Then we'll contact each other through them. But what of Peter?"

"He's in Brandborough, setting up his headquarters and getting things in order."

"Did he mention me after I left?"

"Oh, yes, Joy, indeed he did," Jason said with a smile.

"And how will I be able to see him? I *must* see him."

"Nothing will be easy, and yet nothing's impossible."

"Where will you sleep tonight?"

"I'll find accommodations, mother hen," Jason chuckled.

"Please, Jason, take my horse. You remember Cinder. He's stronger than ever. He'll serve you well."

A horse would be handy. "Just for tonight," he grudgingly accepted.

"No. You gave him to me when you left. Now I'm returning him. I'll feel better knowing he's with you."

"But Father . . ."

"Daughters have powers over fathers that sons lack. Leave Father to me."

Together they walked to the stable, where Joy helped saddle the great dun-colored stallion with the black mane. The brother and sister embraced before Jason rode off into the night, each uncertain of the fate that awaited them, each filled with the thrill and promise of the days to come. For Jason, his troubled spirit torn by his family's alienation, his heart thrown into turmoil by an unexpected love, what did the future hold? There was only one answer . . . ride, ride boldly into the night.

～ *Chapter 7* ～

He rode heedlessly, knowing only that Cinder carried him north along the hard-packed sand, away from Brandborough and his father. At last, his mind crowded and confused by the long day's events, he reined to a halt, dismounted, dropped Cinder's reins so he wouldn't wander, and threw himself down on the soft, still-warm sand. When he awoke, moonlight danced on the dark Atlantic and picked out the breakers as they crashed ashore. The air was cool, fresh, and fragrant with the tangy smell of salt. With the easterly trades to keep the mosquitoes at bay, there was only the hiss of wind in the sea oats and the dull roar of the surf.

Sleep is the mind's balm. Lazy, relaxed for the first time in hours, Jason stared into the sky, picked out the skewed W of Cassiopeia, and, below it, the parallelogram of Ursus Major, the Great Bear, pointing the way to the pole star. In the west, Orion the Hunter hung over the horizon. The stars, the constellations, ever constant in their annual rounds, brought a sense of order to a troubled mind. What had been muddled became clear.

Ethan was an impetuous man given to making snap judgments and harsh decisions. He was strong-willed, tenacious, and single-minded. He not only misunderstood Jason—couldn't appreciate the fact that his acceptance by the British was the strongest tool at his hand—but was incapable of accepting him for who he was. That truth, so painful earlier in the night, Jason suddenly saw, was an even stronger tool. The war had changed Ethan. From a taciturn man, he'd become dangerously outspoken. If he had accepted Jason's word, if Jason had convinced him, his very silence would alert the British. And if he was privy to Jason's plans, he'd undoubtedly tell friends who'd tell friends until, eventually, the wrong person heard and informed on him. It was cruelly ironic, but Ethan's hatred and ignorance were Jason's best protection.

Cruelly ironic . . . hatred his best protection. But what other course was there? None, if he wanted to be effective. Alone, he would call on the courage and skill learned at his father's feet, and accept the scorn of those he loved the most. Including, if necessary, Colleen.

Colleen, Colleen, Colleen. She'd cast a spell on him, the sort of enchanting spell cast by the seductive strains of a sonata or sensuous string quartet. Her music had reached him when he was dangerously vulnerable, and it was understandable that he'd found her so hard to resist. Never before Colleen had he thought himself capable of loving a woman deeply and without restraint. But she was as dangerous as Ethan. She wore her patriotism like a placard, and sooner or later, if they were known to be friends and lovers, the British would suspect him to be the imposter he was.

Thank God, he thought, he was bound for Charleston. With him there or wherever he ended up, and her safely distant in Brandborough, their love had a chance of surviving the war. Until then . . . He had to see her at least one more time, had to feel her lips on his, to feel her heart beating wildly against his own. "I'll come to you later," he'd said. "I give you my word." But later had been what? Six, eight hours earlier? Her disappointment in him when they'd arrested Allan told him well enough what she'd think of his word if he didn't go to her, and he didn't think he could stand that. Not during the long, difficult time that lay ahead. Hastily, he rose, mounted Cinder, and turned the dun's head back toward Brandborough. And as he rode, he saw Colleen as she'd appeared on the dock, as she danced with him, as she lay in his arms in their secret ravine, her bright, golden eyes shining as she'd led him deeper and deeper into the warm center of her bountiful love.

* * *

Colleen awoke from a startling dream. She couldn't remember the details, but there'd been gunfire, cannons, charging soldiers, wild horses . . . and Jason. Had someone tried to kill him, or had he done the killing? And where was she? What was real? Her packing completed, she'd sat down to work on a poem and, overtaken by exhaustion, had fallen asleep at her desk. Black night was turning gray. Suddenly, she remembered Jason's promise and, anger coursing through her veins and reddening her cheeks, realized he'd broken it. Furious, she stormed about the house. Her father had yet to return. Alone— never in her life had she felt more alone. Jason had lied, he had schemed, he had taken her and left her and damn his face! Damn his flowery talk! Damn his soul! Back in her bedroom, she quickly began to strip off her clothes and was down to her chemise when she heard a faint tapping at her window. Jason! Anger tamed to embarrassment and shame for misjudging him. Too excited to be concerned with her semi-nudity, she opened the shutter and looked out at her lover, standing alone in the graying dawn. "Why did you tarry so?" she asked. "Where have you been? Are you all right?"

Jason put his finger to his lips. "I don't want to wake your father."

"He isn't here," she said, pursing her wine-red lips. "Jason Paxton, just for a moment forget you're a gentleman and climb through the window."

The window was low and wide. Once inside, Jason found himself unable to stop staring at her and, against all his well-reasoned plans, took her in his arms and brought her to him in a fierce embrace.

Untamed memories of their afternoon tryst—recalled by mind, heart, and flesh—inflamed Colleen's desire as she felt the lean, hard strength of his body against hers. Her imagination had so often conjured up that very scene—in the middle of the night, he had returned from London, opened her shutters, sneaked inside, and made mad love to her in her own canopied bed, soft arena of longing and frustration, after which, joined in flesh and spirit, they cast their fates to the glorious cause of the revolution and become one in the noble struggle.

She couldn't quite believe that it was Jason, ardent and loving, the sweet Jason of her youth lying next to her, his lips enticing her, his long legs entwined with hers, his eyes pleading with hers, his insistent manhood, yearning, seeking, his muffled cries mingling with hers. Again and again, deeper, higher, stronger, and faster, he drove himself into her. Again and again, she met his thrusts and his sweet length, opening her very being to his every need, giving all she could, and, oh, the sweetness of the sweat along his long, lovely back, the power of his thighs and his buttocks, the steadily rising rhythm, carrying her to a place beyond her bed, beyond her dreams, beyond her room to the sound of singing, soaring stars, rising to a silver peak of blinding moonlight, white and silver snowflakes falling from a frozen heaven, easily, lazily, blissfully back to earth.

Afterward, turned on their sides and facing one another, Jason punctuated his explanation with a string of kisses on her mouth, neck, breasts, and eyes. He told of the long-smoldering rivalry between him and Buckley, and how Buckley, fraudently using Jason's name, had surely alerted Embleton. He narrated the events at his father's house, and explained how he had ridden, slept, and searched his thoughts for what he must do.

"For a moment," Colleen confessed, "I thought you were surely a Tory, and that love had blinded me to your true color."

"Whatever may happen," he warned her, "you mustn't believe that. These are difficult times, and often things aren't what they seem, but I tell you that my love for my home and my people is strong, as strong as my father's. Yet my way of expressing that love may be different."

"You speak in mysteries, Jase. You must tell me exactly what you mean."

"I can't. I myself am not sure," he hedged. "I only know that the point of this struggle is victory, and victory is won by intelligence, not necessarily brashness. You must remember that. Those broadsides of yours may ultimately do you more harm than good."

"You're wrong!" Colleen sat up in bed. A wayward golden strand of hair fell across her shoulder and lay enticingly across her naked breast. "The broadsides must be written. The word has to go out. If I don't compose them, who will? It's my sacred duty. Can't you see that?"

"I can see you in terrible peril," Jason replied, frowning, "and the thought plagues me."

"Why? Because I'm a woman?" she asked indignantly.

"No, because I . . ." His voice faded. *My God in heaven, I've come home to join a fight for freedom and here I sit about to declare . . . oh, no, what madness!* "Well, yes, partly because you are a woman," he stammered lamely.

"Oh, Jase," she said, "it's our destiny to work together, and to be together. Don't you see? I know that with all my heart."

"We're together now, but in a few moments I'll be leaving," he told her, preparing himself to explain how, in spite of his feelings for her, he could no longer see her.

"For where?"

"Charleston. Robin and Piero will be able to help me there."

"Charleston! That's where father and I are going. He's to take me to Aunt Rianne's today, if he returns in time. Don't you see, dear Jason, we *are* meant to be together!"

"But that's impossible!" Jason protested, casting wildly about for an excuse, any excuse, to justify their separation. "I can't—"

"Hush! Do you hear?"

He did. Hoofbeats, and the creak of carriage wheels. "Good God!" he croaked, and without time for further thought, he leaped up and scrambled for his breeches.

Dr. Roy McClagan was too tired and far away to notice the world around him. Behind him, the great Atlantic lost its grayness to the pink, gold, and crimson of morning as the sun spread its molten glow on the peaceful Carolina morning. But Roy was too distraught to be comforted by the natural wonder of daybreak. His patient, a frail boy not yet nine years of age, had died. Only two weeks before, the boy's father had been killed defending Charleston with the Continental Army. Roy was saddened beyond reason: part of him had died with the child.

Slowly, he rode into the barn, unhitched his horse, led her to her stall, and gave her water, oats, and a pitchfork of hay. On the way to the house, he tried to remember to whom the dun-colored stallion grazing in the front yard belonged and then, his mind too muddled, gave up with a shrug. By the time he entered, Colleen and Jason were properly seated in the straight-backed, thinly cushioned chairs placed on either side of the fireplace.

"Ah, well, then," he said, pausing in the doorway. "Don't know how I could forget that dun. Someone in town said you were back, but I didn't expect to see you this soon."

Jason rose and extended his hand. "It's been a long time, Doctor. I trust you're well."

"Well? Well?" He blinked and shook his head in order to keep awake. "Well enough, I suppose. Just extremely tired."

Colleen took his arm and led him to his favorite chair. "The boy? . . ."

"I'd rather not discuss him right now," Roy said.

"I'm sorry, Papa," Colleen said, understanding from his behavior full well what had happened. "I'm so sorry."

"It's the way of the world," Roy said harshly, looking up at Jason. "So what are you doing here?"

"He's come to take me to Charleston," Colleen answered, to Jason's surprise.

"Now, see here!" Roy exploded. He glared at Jason. "What the devil is this all about? I'll be damned if I'll have you coming in here and—"

"I asked him to," Colleen interrupted. She knelt at her father's side and took his hand. "I knew you'd be too tired after working all night. It's such a long journey."

"I'll take you next week," Roy snapped, throwing off her hand. Agitated, he lurched to his feet, went to the sideboard, and poured himself a mug of cider. "That's plenty time enough. If ever. Charleston's too dangerous."

"Less dangerous than Brandborough," Colleen argued, "if for no other reason than that the British are there in force, and here anything can happen. Besides, you know Aunt Rianne expects me today and will die of worry if I don't arrive."

"She'll expect I told you you couldn't go," Roy said, not giving in. "She knows me, and knows I argued against this trip in the first place. Let her find someone else to sew for her."

Colleen pressed on determinedly. "The Somerset Ball costumes account for half her year's income, Papa. She's lost three of her best seamstresses. I promised her—"

"No." He finished the cider, then poured himself a second mugful. "No and no again."

"Buckley Somerset will be there, and we've agreed to meet."

"Oh, did you, now?" Roy asked suspiciously, knowing his daughter's manipulative ways. The cider going to his head, he peered at Colleen over his cup, then swung toward Jason. "And what'll our young Mr. Somerset say about you?" he asked sarcastically. "Seems to me I remember you boys aren't the best of friends. And from the look on your face, I'm not so sure you think this is such a good idea either."

Jason was trapped. He didn't want to accompany Colleen to Charleston, and yet he wanted to. Making love to her the day before had been excusable, but that morning's episode had been a lapse of good sense. What had come over him? A relationship with Colleen was impossible if he was to play his game well, and he in turn could be highly dangerous for Colleen. He couldn't afford to be seen escorting her to Charleston, and yet the temptation to spend that day with her—that last day—was irresistible. "She'll be safe with me," he said, evading the issue. "Nobody can find fault with that. Not even Buckley. I'll need to borrow a conveyance, though."

Roy laughed. "A Paxton borrowing a buggy from a McClagan? I find the idea a wee bit ludicrous. Ethan has several of his own, I believe."

"I'm afraid Jason and his father don't see eye to eye," Colleen explained.

"So you're not a bloody Patriot like old man Ethan, eh?"

"I'm a musician, Dr. McClagan."

"A Tory musician?" asked the Scotsman.

"A simple musician," answered Jason.

"I *am* tired," Roy admitted, letting the bulk of his body sink into a rocking chair. "And the idea of going to Charleston next week is no more inviting than this week. Will you be careful, lad? Will you guard my daughter with your very life?"

"I shall."

Smiling, Colleen ran from the room to finish her packing. By then, Portia had emerged from her servant's house out back and was hard at work on breakfast. A few minutes later, Roy and Jason faced one another in the living room as they drank tea brought to them by Portia. The older man, fighting fatigue, quenching his thirst with a sip from the teacup followed by a swallow of hard cider, spoke vigorously. "I care not a whit for your family," he told Jason. "You know that. But I also know that my Colleen favors you, and it's only fair to warn you that I'll have none of it. You're a musician and you're a wanderer, and you're no match, not in my eyes, for young Somerset. He and his family . . ."

Jason let Roy amble on without rebuttal, for even as he spoke, his eyelids grew heavier with each passing second and his voice began to lose its clarity. At last, the night's tragic business took its toll and Roy's eyes fell shut and his head dropped to his chest. Gently, Jason took the cups from his hands and carried them to the kitchen. When he returned, the weary doctor was deep in sleep, his snoring creating a tension and release that rocked him back and forth, back and forth.

∽ *Chapter 8* ∽

Cinder maintained a brisk pace along the winding path that led downhill and away from the farm. It was another splendid spring Sunday morning, and the enormous fatigue that Jason felt in his eyes, along his neck and his aching loins, added strangely to his exhilaration. Beside him in the buggy, Colleen felt alive, vibrant, and full of energy. Everything had happened so quickly. Her trunk was packed and loaded, and in her heart she knew that her life was changing forever, and though the feeling was frightening, it was also exciting. Events spun her in a dozen different directions. Less than thirty-six hours earlier, she never would have dreamed that she and Jason would be escaping from her father's home alone and together. Yet the incident with Allan Coleridge added another, more confusing, dimension. She had listened closely to Jason's explanation. She wanted to believe—she had seen the children, after all, so she did believe, at least on one level—that he was sincere, but Rianne's warning continued to haunt her. "In times like these, dearie," she'd said one day, "you're to judge men by actions, not mere words."

They rode first to Brandborough to pick up Jason's trunk and bags, and Colleen, not knowing how she buttressed his resolve not to include her in his plans, rattled on about the war and what it meant to her. "Surely you can see the desperate straits we're in," she said, pointing to a burned-out house for

93

emphasis. "The English couldn't defeat us in the North, so they've swarmed over us down here. That's why it's absolutely critical that—"

"I know the situation, Colleen. There's little doubt that the fall of Charleston is the colonies' greatest defeat of the war."

His faint sarcasm—what of Québec and Manhattan and Brandywine, to name only three of many devastating setbacks?—fell on deaf ears. "But what will you do about it?"

"Ride to Charleston to see for myself."

"And then?"

He laughed at her impatience. "And then . . . we'll see what we see."

Sunlight highlighted Colleen's hair with streaks of gold—the color of her gown, the color of her eyes. "We should put out a broadside, that's what we should do," she argued, exasperated by his aloofness. "We should tell the people just what a damned fool this Embleton is, how pompous and how—"

"He's no one I'd want to antagonize right now."

"But he's precisely the sort of—"

"Man who fancies himself in complete control, which, I might suggest, he is."

Trying not to be distracted by the sight of his wild curls blowing in the breeze, Colleen thought for a few seconds. "You wouldn't for a second entertain the notion of accepting his invitation to perform your music for the English warlords who rule Charleston, would you?" she finally asked.

"I don't know what I might or might not do," Jason answered, finally becoming peeved by her ceaseless questioning.

"You're maddeningly circuitous, Jason Paxton, and I wish for once you'd simply and plainly state your intentions."

"I intend to praise beauty." He took a deep breath of the cool, fresh ocean air. "And that means praising you."

"You're avoiding an honest reply. I therefore will not accept your praise."

"I therefore will not withdraw my praise," he answered, teasing her with a smile.

Determined not to be undermined by his charm, she sat silently, defiantly, her arms folded, her eyes gazing out toward the immense ocean. He was infuriating, but he was also irresistible as he hummed a soft, rhythmic melody to accompany the surf's great roar. Colleen wanted to tell him to be quiet, but the sound of his voice was both soothing and hypnotic, and it left her content to let the argument end as they pulled up in front of the Paxton warehouse where he'd had his things taken. "It won't take but a few minutes," he assured her and, leaping down and tying Cinder to a hitching post, he disappeared inside.

Less than fifty feet down Market Street, a crowd of church-goers was gathered around the commons, where, in full dress uniform, the newly arrived company of British soldiers led by Peter Tregoning was arrayed on parade. A snare drum rattled a slow beat. "Present . . . arms!" came the sergeant's crisp command, followed by the crack of almost a hundred hands simultaneously slapping their musket stocks.

Colleen watched with rising anger. The taking of Charleston had been a grievous blow, but distance had mitigated the effect and the local rebels had been free to act with relative impunity. The picture changed radically, however, with a whole company of British regulars on hand. Would, for example, Embleton have dared to arrest Allan Coleridge without ready resort to such a force?

"Miss Colleen?"

Colleen jumped, twisted about to see a disheveled old man dressed in sailor's canvas standing at her side. His left cheek was horribly scarred, and his left eye was covered by a black patch. "Jeth! You gave me a fright!"

Jeth's grin was toothless. His good right eye twinkled merrily as he reached up to touch her hand. "Like ticks in springtime, ain't they?" he said, nodding in the direction of the commons. "Everywhere you look. How's your daddy?"

"Well enough. But you must go see him. He'll be—"

"Don't have the time," Jeth said, raising his hand to stop her. "We're in a cove down the beach. Put in long enough to fill our water barrels, and then it's back to playing fox and hare with the British Navy soon as the sun goes down. Bloody business, this blockade-runnin'. I just come into town for news."

"And brought some, too, I hope."

"Aye, as always, but I've little time. The bare bones, though, is . . ."

Gone longer than he'd expected, Jason emerged in time to see Colleen squeeze Jeth's hand in farewell, after which the old sea dog slipped around the corner and out of sight. His trunk and bags safely tied down in back, and the warehouseman paid off with a coin, he climbed aboard and took the reins. "Who was that?" he asked as Cinder headed away from the commons and back to the coastal road heading north.

"Jeth Darney, a friend who sailed out of New York harbor on a blockade runner only a fortnight ago with news of the war."

"He doesn't look like a sailor."

"He's a cook and a surgeon, and a good one. He's sailed on merchant ships under a dozen flags and a dozen names."

"How does a young lady of good breeding happen upon such an unsavory character?" Jason asked with a combination of concern and amusement.

"My father saved his life three years ago. He'd been in a bloody knife fight and stayed with us a month after he'd healed to show his appreciation by cooking all our meals. Portia was upset, but she learned to love his beef stew. Father was amazed to discover that in spite of his wild manner, he had a good working knowledge of surgical methods—and anything else he set his mind to. In some ways, he reminds me of Aunt Rianne. He despises the English and has a hundred tales to tell of their unfair tariffs. Whenever he moves in and out of the colony, he carries news. Just now he told me that two regiments of General Washington in Connecticut have protested to the point of near mutiny. They've complained of insufficient food and the fact that they've not been paid for months. Pennsylvania troops sympathetic to him disarmed the malcontents, and the last word is that the situation is under control, but how long can we go on like this?" Colleen sighed and stared at the passing scene, fields newly plowed, cleared ground, patches of forest offering shade to the weary. "How can we continue fighting the Crown and ourselves at the same time? If we could only write a song, Jason, telling the men to be patient—that food and compensation will soon be coming—I know we'd reach their hearts and . . ."

"Spend the rest of the war in a British jail—or be hanged for our troubles."

"Is that your fear?"

"It's a thought that's crossed my mind, yes."

"I don't believe you," she said, taking his hand and bringing it to her lips. "I believe you to be a brave and fearless artist who will use your art toward the cause of freedom. That's why God has brought us together."

"Please don't blame God"—he smiled—"for any imbalance in my character."

"What do you mean by that?"

"I mean," he said, playfully nipping her fingertips, "that when I'm with you, all semblance of common sense seems to vanish into thin air."

"Are you scolding or complimenting me?"

"I'm merely confessing to a beguiling affection I feel for you."

"Would you call such affection love?" she wondered. "You did at the ravine. You spoke the words. You said, 'I love you, Colleen.' Why do you hesitate to repeat yourself?"

"Perhaps I shall compose something to describe exactly what I feel. I will perform it for you alone, and you will hear, and know."

"Jason," she said, turning, offering him a smile as radiant as the mid-morning sun, "I don't mind saying it at all. I love you."

The sun was hot, the sea breeze cool. Jason was full of questions and listened avidly as Colleen regaled him with four years of accumulated news of births and deaths and marriages and the myriad of trivia that made up life in a small town anywhere in the world. They stopped for a leisurely lunch that Portia had prepared, and when they resumed their journey, it was Colleen's turn to ask questions, and Jason's to talk.

They bore inland to skirt the great marshes on Charleston's southern flank. Jason related tales of his European sojourn: of stag and boar hunts in England; of wild rides on horseback through French forests; of the precarious journey over the Alps to Italy; and the incredible sights he had seen. Most of all, though, he talked of the great composers he'd met and how they had inspired him and filled him with awe. He couched his narrative in modest terms, but Colleen knew him well enough to realize the importance of his triumphs, and while he spoke of the work of others, she urged him to speak of and even sing some of his own. Much to his delight, Colleen learned his motifs quickly and, her arm through his, her breast pressed against his arm, she harmonized with him to the rhythm of Cinder's smooth, easy pace.

"Marvelous!" Jason laughed when they finished an occasional piece he'd called "Dawn's Hush!" "You're a fast learner. Have you thought of becoming a musician?"

"Heaven forbid! I should be as clumsy as a carp on land.

Words are my forte. Listen." Inspired, she recited an Italian poem, "La Libertà," which Rianne had given her in translation some months earlier. "Well?" she asked as the first spire of Charleston appeared above a line of trees. "What do you think? Isn't it beautiful?"

Not wanting to seem pretentious, Jason hesitated, but then confessed that he not only knew the poem, but the poet as well. He had met Pietro Metastasio, a wonderful old man, in Cremona, and had promised to put the stanzas of his great poem to music.

"Will you so honor me, Jason, by writing music for my poems?"

"In London, I heard talk of a young Scottish poet by the name of Burns who has a great gift for setting words to music. Does that interest you?"

"Yes, of course. You know it does. But certain feelings of my own, already set down on paper, naturally seek musical expression that only you could give. Tell me you will."

"Only if I can find notes sweet enough," he replied as, in the far distance, the chimes of St. Michael's Cathedral rang out the hour to the citizens of Charleston, the Queen City of the elegant South.

Chapter 9

Nearly five years had passed since Jason had been in Charleston, and his first impression was one of shock. Soldiers were everywhere. The red-coated English were constant and irritable reminders of their recent victory, just as the numerous green-coated colonials served to illustrate painfully how many American men were willing to fight for a foreign king. To see both factions patrolling the narrow cobblestoned streets and pathways caused Colleen and Jason considerable pain. And yet the quiet charm of the city could not be destroyed, not even by the presence of an occupying power.

Charleston was a miracle of natural and man-made detail: intricate ironwork on doorways and gates, pastel-painted town homes, high-walled gardens, the rotund, exotic presence of palmetto trees, bright sunshine playing with heavy shadows in alleyways green with fern, yellow with bignonia, air fragrant with a hundred breeds of blossoms cultivated and wild, wisteria and velvety violets, red-flowered pomegranate trees, brilliant splashes of azaleas and pure pink roses—and everywhere the strong scent of the open sea. A Huguenot church sat next to a small Jewish synagogue. Dozens of miniature verandas and piazzas dotting the city gave it a decidedly European flavor that clashed with a climate and ambience more akin to the West Indies. There was something tropical about Charleston, something cultivated and refined.

The buggy bounced down South Battery and came to a halt at the foot of East Battery, facing the Charleston harbor. A low red brick wall separated the narrow thoroughfare, lined with two- and three-story homes that were among the city's most stately, from the water. Jason took in the magnificent view of the harbor, the open water where the great Cooper and Ashley rivers met. The crystal-clear day had turned quietly misty, and as Colleen and Jason left the buggy to stand before the panorama, the bells of St. Michael's rang six o'clock. The ride from the McClagan farm, with the stop at Brandborough and the rest for lunch, had taken nearly all day. For all their disagreements and doubts, they had moved closer together, and momentarily forgetting his resolve to terminate their relationship, Jason took Colleen's hand in his as their spirits soared above the fleet of massive English warships that might have otherwise marred the beauty of the moment.

The harbor was protected by two bodies of land—James Island to the south, Sullivan's Island to the north. In 1776, in that proud, hopeful period during which Jason had set sail for Europe, no more than four hundred South Carolinians had stood firm at Fort Sullivan against the fire of over one hundred British naval guns, even though the fort, half built, consisted of little more than piles of palmetto logs and sand. There were those who claimed that if the Crown had succeeded in taking Charleston so early in the conflict, the colonial rebellion would have fizzled and failed to grow into a full-fledged revolution. Yet this was the same scene where, only weeks before, the Royal Navy had ultimately triumphed by taking advantage of General Lincoln's tactical mistake: reasoning that the populace would be best protected by committing all his troops to the city itself, he had allowed the forts to deteriorate. As a result, Major General Henry Clinton's fiery siege could not be withstood, and the gracious Queen of the South had fallen into foreign hands. The obviousness of the current situation—English ships, English soldiers, English flags flying wherever the eye turned— was reason enough for Colleen and Jason to fall into a mood of quiet melancholy.

They returned to the buggy and rode the short distance up South Battery to 32 Meeting Street, which served as both domicile and business establishment of Miss Rianne Mary Mc-Clagan. The hand-painted sign that swung from a metal bar extending from the rose-colored building was decorated with graceful needles and swirling threads announcing Rianne's handicraft. Colleen walked ahead into the shop as a bell above the door tinkled softly. Following half a minute later with her trunk, Jason entered in time to see Colleen enveloped in an embrace by a woman who, at six feet, was as tall as he.

It had been five years since he'd seen Rianne, and he'd forgotten what a startling appearance she made. Her eyes were her most remarkable feature: slightly darker than Colleen's, they were more burnt gold than pure amber, but piercing nonetheless. Her small unsmiling mouth was but a short line beneath a long, thin, sloped nose. Her face was lean and angular and revealed a certain hard beauty. Her arms and neck were especially long, giving her the impression of being somewhat thinner than she actually was. Her crowning glory was a fantastic wig that rose above her head like a proud bird with an independent life of its own. The section over her forehead, a combination of human and horse hair, was embellished with a network of jewel-strung wires that gave the whole affair the look of a crown. In the back, cascading rows of elaborate curls were decorated with long strings of pearls, multicolored feathers, and bunches of silk violets and lilies of the valley.

"I'm happy to see you again, Miss McClagan," Jason said, bowing politely.

"And I'm delighted to see you, Jason. But I thought you were in Europe."

"I was, and—"

"Just returned yesterday," Colleen broke in. "Isn't it wonderful?"

"And so soon in Charleston," Rianne murmured, wondering what could have prompted him to leave Brandborough after so short a reunion with his family. "Roy? . . ."

"He was exhausted. He'd worked all night, only to lose his patient. You know how he is."

"I do indeed," Rianne said dryly. She shook her head. "Every time is like the first for that man, bless his soul. But enough of your father's eccentricities. I'm pleased, if somewhat astonished, that he allowed you to escort my niece here, Mr. Paxton."

"What?" Caught off guard because he'd been staring at her wig and hadn't paid attention to a word she'd said, Jason answered as best he could. "Oh, yes. My pleasure, ma'am. My—"

"My wig . . . alarms you, Mr. Paxton?" Rianne asked with a laugh.

"No! I . . . that is, I . . ."

Her rich, contralto voice carried a strong flavor of Scottish brogue. "Not my everyday wig, I assure you. Rather, my impression of Cleopatra's," she explained, turning about so he could see it in its full glory. "Given, that is, that she lived in modern times. It isn't finished, of course, until Mrs. Choate approves. I predict she'll ask for many changes—worth a respectable number of pounds, by the by, before the ball. Come see, children."

She walked to a work table that was covered with great bolts of fabric, pieces of ribbon, spools of thread, and assorted pairs of scissors and other sewing tools. The rest of the shop was in an equally unorganized but fascinating state of disarray: fine pieces of English and French furniture—chairs, divans, and sideboards—sat next to roughly hewn crates full of supplies. Along the length of one wall, shelves were crammed with colorful materials. On another were pinned sketches of gowns, wigs, parasols, gloves, hats, and shawls. From a gilded box, Rianne produced a tiny golden pin-backed thimble. "Each of my major customers receives one of these," she explained, "to be worn as a symbol of my art. An ingenious touch, wouldn't you say?"

"Indeed," asserted Jason, who couldn't help but admire the pleated frills of her intricately embroidered silver-and-purple gown, the way in which it puffed out dramatically to either side of her ample hips, and the fashionably tight sleeves that stopped at the elbow, leaving several inches of fine lace ruffles to encircle her lower arms.

"Doesn't he look good, Aunt Rianne?" Colleen asked. "Aren't you at all surprised to see him?"

"The gentle slope of his eyes tells me he's even more the dreamer than when I observed him last. He seems a man whose soul partakes of an ephemeral music we mortals shall never hear. Surprised to see him? No. Little surprises me. I knew he'd return someday." Her eyes twinkled merrily as she winked at Jason. "And I suspected, I'm bound to say, that my niece would be there to fetch you and whisk you away before another female had time to claim the prize herself. A job well done, I'd say."

"Aunt Rianne!" Colleen protested. "Please . . ."

"There shall be no hypocrisy in this shop. There's enough hypocrisy in this once-free city already. I speak to the point— be it kind or cruel. And the point here is surely romance. I see it in the eyes of both of you. And I say to you, my good niece, that yours is a choice well made. My advice is not to tarry, for men are not unlike the noble steed that brought you here. They need to be captured, tamed, and bridled. As one who has never quite achieved that goal, I speak from experience. But I shall neither reveal to nor bore you with details of my past. Instead, I'll treat you to a pot of genuine Scottish tea, a luxury that has perhaps of late eluded our distinguished composer. To be in possession of such tea leaves in days such as these is not, you understand, a slight achievement. It's already steeped. I shan't be a moment."

"I know she seems a little grumpy," Colleen explained as Rianne swept out of the room, "but she does have a smiling heart. You'll see."

"I think she's wonderful," Jason said.

Colleen replied by kissing him on his mouth at the very moment Rianne reentered and cleared her throat. Blushing, Colleen quickly moved away from Jason.

Rianne placed the tray and tea set on a small mahogany Pembroke table and began to pour. "'Tis nothing to be ashamed of, child. Passion is the lifeblood of what would otherwise be a paltry existence. What is art without passion? Would the composer not agree with such a statement?" she asked, handing him a dainty porcelain cup.

"The composer," Jason replied, "has been taught in the great capitals of European culture that art is the product of reason."

"But are they reasonable men who take such a position?" Rianne asked. "Or are they, creatures of a dying civilization, simply unaware of their own deaths?"

"Call them what you will. There are, nonetheless— Mmm, this tea's delicious. Yes, there is a number of geniuses among them."

"Ah," Rianne replied. "But what of the undiscoverd geniuses of this vast land? Why, in this city alone I myself am familiar with dozens of artists intent on developing styles of their own, quite independent from, and indifferent to, I might add, what may be considered artful in Europe. Many of my own designs, you will note, vary widely from the European norm, even though I must, I admit, be practical in offering the women of Charleston gowns that they consider fashionable."

"Then you aren't adverse to selling your wares to the wives of those sympathetic to the Crown?" Jason asked, curious to test the extent of Rianne's patriotism.

"On Tory Row, a street less than a quarter-mile from where we sit, my reputation for needlework is as formidable as among those who share my own adversion for our English lords and masters. I'm a practical woman, Mr. Paxton, dependent on my own wit and talent. I place survival above all else."

Jason wasn't surprised when Colleen protested. "But only a few months ago you said that certain causes are worth dying for!"

"Indeed I did, though 'tis not inconsistent with my belief that we better serve our cause alive than dead. Do I make myself clear, Mr. Paxton?"

"Clear as a bell, madam."

"But enough talk of war! I suppose you've come to Charleston to see Mr. Courtenay and Mr. Ponti."

"You know them?" Jason asked. "I mean, other than by notoriety?"

"Extremely well. They are kind and noble gentlemen, if somewhat bizarre, and I know of their great affection for you. They speak of you often, and I take it as a great compliment to my niece's charms that you chose to visit me before them."

Jason appreciated Rianne's courtesy and the fact that, unlike practically everyone else, she had not pressed him on political matters, as though she had detected his sensitivity to such issues. "And visit them I must," he said, noting the time. "It's getting late in the day to arrive unannounced, so if I might excuse myself," he said, rising from the table, "I'd best leave now."

The word *leave* alarmed Colleen. "Would you mind terribly, Jason, if I went with you?" she asked as she remembered her aunt's words—"my advice is not to tarry." The thought of being separated from Jason, even for a few hours, disturbed her. Besides, she wanted to know all the people important to his life, and that included his patrons.

The corners of Rianne's mouth turned in an approximation of a smile. "I think that's a splendid idea," she said, pleased with Colleen's forwardness. "It would be most illuminating for Colleen to make their acquaintance—that is, if you have no objection."

Jason preferred a private reunion with his benefactors, but his hand was forced. "None at all," he said, hiding his irritation.

Rianne shook a finger at him. "I trust you'll have my niece safely escorted home at an hour that will raise none of the eyebrows of my prying neighbors."

"My word is as good my deed, madam," he said before kissing her outstretched hand and noticing that her skin, although wrinkled, was extremely soft and pleasing to the lips.

❦ *Chapter 10* ❧

"We must hear about everything, from your first day to your last," insisted Piero Sebastiano Ponti.

"Give Jason time," replied his friend and constant companion, Robin Courtenay. "The lad's just arrived."

The two gentlemen, each in his late fifties, sat in magnificent matching Hepplewhite armchairs whose seats and back cushions had been designed and embroidered by Robin himself, a distinguished craftsman who, despite his soft-spoken manner, was given to unbridled extravagance. He wore a small turban awash with bright colors, an item, Jason reported, that was all the rage in London among writers and painters.

"I knew that . . . when I gave it to him . . . last Christmas," Piero sniffed. His high tenor voice, in contrast to Robin's deep-bottomed baritone, was strained, and he spoke in nervous spurts, with only a slight trace of an Italian accent. Piero was a short, compact man whose small frame and tight britches, complete with shiny plated buckles at the knees, gave him a much younger look. Both he and the portly, slower-speaking Courtenay sported identical shoes, pumps fashioned from green-dyed Moroccan leather.

Across from them, Colleen and Jason sat squeezed together on a petite divan. The extravagance of the room—the frescoes on the ceiling, the gold-gilded frames on the portraits on the walls, the tucked-and-pleated blue satin drapes—had rendered

Colleen speechless, at least for the moment. Only a short while before, she had seen the two men greet Jason as if he were a long-lost son—with loving embraces, and, in Piero's case, tears of joy.

"'Tis a marvelous home you have here," she complimented them. "Have you lived here long?"

"Just a century or so," Robin joked. "It was my father's and his father's before him."

"The decor is magnificent," Colleen said.

"Aside from ancestral inheritances—a painting here and there," Piero noted, "the arrangement of the furniture, flowers, and such is of my design. Robin will be the last to say so, but many of our best pieces are of his own making. His artistry extends beyond the making of mere instruments. He crafts furniture, he sews, he even weaves tapestries!"

"My friend," Robin was quick to say, "would have you believe my talents exceed my girth. 'Tis not true. I'm a mere dabbler. You, Jason, are the true artist among us, and I yearn to hear more about your musical adventures abroad."

"As do I," echoed Piero. "Were it not for my duties in the kitchen, I'd gladly stay to listen. But I'm off to put the final touches on a dinner that you, Jason, and Miss McClagan simply must share with us."

"Only if I can be of assistance," Collen chimed in, accepting the invitation for both of them as she followed Piero from the parlor.

In the kitchen, Colleen decided that there was something warm and almost maternal about the Italian. When she and Jason had first arrived, his immediate concern had been for Jason's health, insisting, all evidence to the contrary, that the musician was far too thin.

"This is the first of only a long series of feasts that will serve to fatten up our mutual friend," Piero gushed as he busily tended his goose, sauces, and boiling squash.

"Might I help in some way?" Colleen asked.

"There's not a thing for you to do, *angelo mio*," he assured her. "'Tis enough for me to be able to feast my eyes upon you as I work. Spontaneity is the key to my culinary methods, and I'm afraid my infamous lack of discipline makes assistance nearly impossible." The smells were divine, and Piero's eyes twinkled as he frequently sampled the food. "I consider cooking a noble pursuit. Within my repertory are dishes from no less than a dozen civilized lands—and some decidedly uncivilized. Would you mind passing my snuffbox? One small inhalation and I'll have my wits about me again."

The tiny box sat on the window sill overlooking a gracious courtyard where a ring of white and pink azaleas encircled a gushing stone fountain. Colleen peered out the window and saw, extending from the second story of the stately Georgian edifice, a wrought-iron balcony twisted in the shape of twin peacocks, an appropriate symbol, she realized, for the home's inhabitants. The same peacocks had been painted in miniature on the lid of the snuffbox. Handing the container to Piero, Colleen asked him whether he and Robin were akin to the macaronis, a group of affluent young Englishmen who, some years back, formed the famed macaroni club in London and became known as the epitome of flamboyant dressers. She remembered the line from "Yankee Doodle": "He put a feather in his cap and called it macaroni."

"Oh, no, dear child," Piero replied as he quickly and expertly tapped a goodly amount of the powdered tobacco on the palm of his right hand and sniffed it into each nostril. "We are part of no group or movement. We follow our own instincts and live according to our own rules." As the snuff took its effect, he rolled his jet-black eyes toward the wood-beamed ceiling, which, even in the kitchen, had been decorated with the bodies of dancing angels and nimble cherubs.

"If you weren't so young and unspoiled, my dear Colleen, I'd offer you a pinch. It's nothing your aunt would admit to, but I can assure that she can testify to the strength of this mixture, though I'll grant that she's far more discreet in its usage than I. I'm afraid I find the mixture—a rich Carolina tobacco blended with special herbal plants grown in our garden—yes, I find it quite irresistible . . . The bird! *Dio mio!* . . . I'm about to overcook the blessed bird!"

He ran to the massive hearth that dominated an entire kitchen wall where he opened a cast-iron door in the stone wall next to the open fire and slid out a metal box that served as an oven. Colleen watched him as he juggled his herbs and spices like a chemist. Wigless for the moment, his bald head with its semicircular ring of silver-gray hair glowed with a deep olive complexion. His dark eyes darted and his small hands were in constant motion. His movement was graceful, if somewhat exhausting to observe. He set the steaming fowl in a warming pan, checked a black pot full of sliced squash swimming in a pungent sauce, nodded, then replaced the lid. As he cooked, he prattled on about his proud Italian heritage, his two great-uncles who had been cardinals, his great-great grandfather who had been a duke, and his own father, a successful Venetian merchant who, while Piero was in his teens, had disappeared during a winter storm on the Adriatic. Shortly afterward, his mother had died in a fierce outbreak of the Black Plague. The inheritance had been substantial and, by nature a cultural explorer, Piero found himself drifting from country to country until the lure of America drew him to the colonies, where he finally lost his wanderlust and found a home. The story was told with a good deal of pathos, a degree of self-pity, and a large dose of histrionic humor. Piero spoke whimsically and rapidly as, with flourishingly elaborate strokes, he painted a rich, white sauce over the thin-skinned goose.

Thirty minutes later, Ned, a handsome young male servant with ebony-colored skin, poured wine in silver goblets as dinner was served in the formal dining room, which combined the ambience of a museum and concert hall. There was a still-life painting of grapes ripe with an eerie reality, a tapestry depicting an Arthurian legend, and an impassioned interpretation of the crucifixion in which one could practically hear the cry of agony falling from Jesus' half-opened mouth. In each of the four corners of the room sat musical instruments, themselves notable and moving works of art. A virginal, a small oblong keyboard instrument, had been crafted and painted by Robin as though it were a canvas. A landscape complete with shepherds, maidens, and grazing sheep was depicted with great sensitivity and care for detail on the raised section above the keyboard. A spinet, pianoforte, and harpsichord had been decorated in much the same way, showing scenes of ladies at court and noblemen at play. As dinner began, Colleen, who, seated next to Jason, faced Piero and Robin, decided they were among the most fascinating men she had ever encountered.

She was touched by Robin's gentle manner, and she could see why he had exerted such a strong paternal influence on Jason. His speaking voice was melodious and comforting as he expressed himself precisely and without pretense. Full-faced with expressive green eyes, bushy brows, and plump cheeks, Robin looked decidedly older than his companion. He also exhibited the strange characteristic of blinking very slowly. In fact, the rhythm of his blinking seemed to set the carefully measured pace of his speech. She watched him as he patiently sipped his white, bitter wine while Piero drained a second glass and started on his third.

"The goose is succulent, and the sauce most subtle," Robin praised his friend's efforts.

"Hear, hear!" agreed a smiling Jason, happy to be back in what he considered his second home.

As the meal was consumed, the two men returned to questioning Jason with the concern and curiosity of caring parents about every aspect of his long sojourn. They both listened with obvious pride, though they expressed their feelings much differently. Upon hearing of Mozart's words of praise for a composition of Jason's, Piero exclaimed, "One genius smiling upon another!" Robin simply nodded with quiet satisfaction. For her part, Colleen felt a trifle neglected.

"You've accomplished a great deal," Robin told Jason. "I feel well rewarded that whatever faith Piero and I have invested in you has been returned tenfold by virtue of your continued devotion to your art. Naturally, you'll stay with us as long as you like"—Jason had explained the tense situation with his father—"as there could be no place more suitable for your work than the apartment upstairs. I worry only that these troubled times might be an annoying distraction from your true artistry."

"True artistry," Colleen spoke up unexpectedly, "must help shape these troubled times."

"In these troubled times, dear lady," Robin replied, "I've learned to avoid discourse concerning politics among friends."

"And yet such discourses are unavoidable," Colleen rebutted. "Might I be bold enough to ask the nature of your political sentiments?"

"My, my, Jason," said Piero. "Your lady friend is a fiery Patriot, there can be no doubt."

"And you, sir?" she asked the Italian.

"Foreign born and a guest on these shores, I find myself confused by the turn of events," Piero confessed.

"Neither of us," Robin spoke deliberately, "is terribly fond of the king's forces breathing down the necks of the fair citizenry of Charleston. Yet what can one person do? I'm afraid we're essentially quite powerless. As you can see, we lead a somewhat insular and quiet, domestic life."

"But everyone must do whatever he can . . ." Colleen began her usual impassioned argument, only to be interrupted by Jason.

"Now that we've had dinner, shall we return to the parlor?" he suggested.

"Splendid idea," Robin agreed.

Piero led the way to the parlor, where Ned set out tea and tiny, delicate chocolate cakes. Seated in the same positions they'd occupied before, their talk lingered on for another half hour as Jason mentioned some of his observations of European banks and businesses.

"Still toying, then," Robin asked, "with working with your family business?"

"That depends on Father," Jason said with a shrug. "I hope so."

"I don't see why you shouldn't," Robin agreed with a nod of his head. "You're a man with a variety of talents and interests. It's a great blessing to be able to move freely from art to commerce, and back again."

"As long as we can do so as free citizens." Colleen returned to her former argument.

No one responded. Piero was tired, and the twinkle in his eyes seemed to be fading fast. Robin, his palms resting on his generous girth snugly covered by a white-and-black-striped vest, was also fatigued.

Surreptitiously, Colleen allowed the toe of her right shoe to glide up and down Jason's calf.

"I dare say," Robin finally announced, "that the elderly contingency had best be excused for the night. Ned has already prepared your room, Jason, though I suspect that you may want to show Miss McClagan the music library before escorting her home."

Colleen suddenly felt a surge of gratitude for Robin that overcame her contempt for his indifferent politics. He understood! He was allowing them to be alone! He and Piero kissed her and Jason on both cheeks before leaving the room. "Your return," Robin said, addressing his protégé, "has already enriched our lives. I can only pray that your artistry grows in whatever direction the gods decree. Good night."

Piero and Robin retired to their rooms, which, along with the parlor, kitchen, and dining room, were on the first floor. Jason led Colleen to the second story, where, past several spare bedrooms, an elaborately carved double door opened to a large music library. Colleen gasped. The astounding beauty that faced her was almost too rich and varied to be digested. Paintings in gilded frames hung everywhere. The ceiling was frescoed with mermaids, satyrs, and pink-faced cupids. Books and folios— as large a library as Colleen had ever seen—filled a half dozen shelves. Dozens of instruments, strings, lyres, flutes, and brasses lay on tables.

Jason sat at a harpsichord and let his fingers wander over the keys. "I was thirteen when my father decided I should move to Charleston in order to further my education. I studied the usual courses: Latin, Greek, mathematics, philosophy. . . . and music, which happened to be taught by Piero. I'd never played an instrument, but the school owned a harpsichord, and perceiving how quickly I learned and that I had, as he put it, a natural talent, Piero invited me here." Remembering, he turned slowly to take in the whole room. "Can anyone imagine how I was affected by the experience? I'd entered a new world, one I never so much as suspected existed. It was as if all the world's artistic riches had been placed in front of me, and I was allowed to pick and choose what I wanted. In the weeks that followed, I spent hour after hour on these instruments, to the neglect of most of the rest of my studies, as my father learned all too soon."

"And he? . . . " Colleen prompted.

"He came looking for me. In a rage, he was. The very idea of his son, a Paxton, being interested in music to the exclusion of everything else almost gave him apoplexy. And of course," he added with a chuckle, "the appearance of Robin and Piero on the scene didn't help. I tried to explain to him that they were perfectly benign, but I might as well have been talking to the Atlantic. He pulled me out of here by my ear, which was red for days afterward. How long ago was that? Ten, eleven years? I remember it as if it were yesterday."

"But you returned," Colleen said softly, moved by his story and the fact that he'd confided such intimate details of his youth to her.

"Yes. Against his wishes, I came back." Abruptly, he rose, led her to a far corner of the room, and invited her to sit next to him on the bench facing an exquisite virginal. "I gave my first recital three months later on this instrument," he said, chording absentmindedly.

Colleen sat silently and studied the mural painted on the raised board above the strings. A golden-headed Apollo, his long, thick hair knotted at the nape of his neck, held a milk-white lyre on his lap. His fingers stroked the strings, his small mouth was open, his head lifted in song. His eyes were enraptured as he sat beneath the giant palm tree of Delos, surrounded by his faithful muses, nymphs posed in pirouettes, their arms raised above their Titian curls as they danced in nearly transparent yellow frocks. The beardless, soft-skinned god himself was naked.

The chords took on shape and definition. A melody, soft, sinuous, and haunting, crept in. Looking at the painting of blue-eyed Apollo, listening to the surging melody, a warmth passed from Colleen's neck to her breasts, from her breasts to her thighs, until at last she was filled with the rhythm of the sweetly measured music.

"You were irritated," Jason finally said as he continued to play, "because we didn't discuss your poetry."

Colleen was surprised at how well he read her mind. "How did you know that?"

"The look on your face. The way your lips pursed. The tension in your arms and hands. But there's really no need to worry, you know. Robin and Piero are sincere souls who recognized your intelligence and wit."

"I so much wanted to tell them," Colleen confessed. "I wanted to feel part of this world . . . of your world."

"I understand," he whispered, and then he let the flowing notes speak for him. His fingers flying over the keyboard, he looked into her eyes and felt the words returning to his lips. "I love you," he wanted to say, just as he had said in the ravine. He held his tongue, though, reminding himself that the time spent with Colleen, and the powerful infatuation, must soon come to an end.

With the sound of music ringing through the room, Colleen found herself first humming, then finding words that fit the newborn melody with a natural grace:

> Like gentle Apollo whose selfsame song
> Lingers on my lips so soft. How long
> The strains of your love play upon my heart
> Pierced by cupid's quivering dart . . .

At that point, words and music ceased, and despite Jason's reservations, he turned to Colleen and took her hands in his. "Your words, my music," he whispered.

Slowly, Colleen moved his hands to cup her breasts and gently leaned forward to bring her lips to his. And in the kiss that followed, there were words and music enough to send their souls soaring beyond words and music, to a place where ecstasy reigned, and love was the lord of all.

～ *Chapter 11* ～

Sleep was impossible. Stimulated yet frustrated by the evening's events, Colleen tossed and turned. The May night was uncomfortably hot and humid, especially in the small, dainty bedroom of her aunt's home from which she watched row after row of restless clouds race across a full yellow moon. Clad only in a thin cotton chemise, she was covered with perspiration. She wiped her forehead, cheeks, arms, and neck with a damp towel, but nothing relieved the sticky persistence of the cloying night.

She could still taste the sweetness of Jason's moist lips against hers, still feel the agony of being left by him at her aunt's door, the memory of the secret ravine, and dawn in his arms in her very own bed. She wanted him again, and the separation from him was difficult and painful. Why was he at Piero and Robin's and she at Rianne's? What would he say if she threw on a cloak, raced over to his patrons' home, rapped on the door, and insisted that they sleep together that night and every night thereafter for the rest of their lives?

No, such foolishness must be avoided. Proper ladies were forbidden to comport themselves thus. Proper ladies were to sit daintily at elegant dinner parties, listen attentively, and register wonder as worldly gentlemen impressed them with their erudition and influence. Despite what Jason had said to her in the library, was he really any different? He and his friends were the most fascinating, most cultured creatures Colleen had ever met, yet they looked upon her as though she were a precious porcelain doll, incapable of speech, not to mention thought. And what of their politics? They spoke as if the war were but a trifle compared to their protégé's musical career. And what stance had Jason himself taken in that particular discussion? The one he usually took—perching somewhere on a fence, nodding agreeably, arguing with no one, hiding behind a façade of affability and diplomatic restraint. When, oh, when—Colleen asked herself as a ragged line of lightning cut the sky and, seconds later, distant thunder boomed—would he declare his true sentiments? How could he possibly restrain his feelings so long? How could he not defend his homeland? How could she love a man who didn't love freedom as deeply as she?

For the better part of an hour, she stared out the window and wished for the relief of rain. Too soon, though, the thunder and lightning moved off to the west, leaving in its wake a still-stifling humidity that served only to increase her frustration. "Damn him!" she whispered, pulling on a light wrap. Silently, she crept downstairs to light her candle; stealthily, she slipped back up to her room. She was her aunt's niece, was she not? And damned if she'd be intimidated by a pair of macaroni peacocks or, for that matter, Jason. Quivering with rage, she extracted paper, ink, and quill from the small portable secretary Rianne had left in her room, propped herself up in bed, and set to work. She'd show them, she mumbled as the first words spilled out and onto the paper. She'd show them all what one person could do in the name of the cause that tugged so insistently at her heart: the cause of independence and liberty.

Jason saw the same lightning, heard the same distant thunder, but felt a much different sort of confusion. Like Colleen, he was unable to sleep as he sat on the side of the bed in the room he had always considered his hideaway. He'd taken off his nightgown, and his nude, lean frame was bathed in sweat. He breathed the heavy night air with difficulty. How long had it been since he'd had a decent night's sleep? Time blurred as a myriad of thoughts and feelings competed for his troubled attention. He was happy to be back in the house which, in the past, had provided him with so much comfort. In certain ways, Piero and Robin understood him better than anyone else, even his sister Joy. In other ways, though, they understood him not at all, and it was difficult to speak to them of the mental turmoil that had brought him back to America.

Colleen. His mind filled with thoughts and images of Colleen. Her words and spirit ran through his memory—that and her soft, gentle skin, the silky ease with which they had negotiated the dance of love. Never before had he felt such intensity. He thought of her, alone in bed, and the gnawing hunger returned, the excitement arose. "Damn it!" he cursed aloud, angry at the recurrence of such confusing and private thoughts. Still, the confusion would not quickly be laid to rest.

After all, her reflected, staring out the window at the pale yellow moon, Colleen was right. They lived in troubled times when art must follow action. It was not a time for composing music or falling head over heels in love. It was a time for planning—and acting. His position was unique. The high esteem in which the British held him was an invaluable weapon not to be wasted. That very image of himself as a political naïf content to mingle with representatives of the Crown allowed him vital access to the headquarters and homes of Loyalists and English officers. He had to take advantage of that image, he decided, and quickly. He sighed when he thought of the word and considered the dangers. Yet the word was inescapable—spy. He was going to spy. He was going to live two separate lives, have dual identities. More and more, his plans jelled and the inevitability of his mission became clear. He needed time to think and plot and work out the details by himself. He needed the seclusion that Piero and Robin could supply. And mostly, for all her good intentions, he needed to stay away from Colleen, before their wreckless, passionate affair brought calamity to them both. Yes, he vowed to himself as he reclined on the bed, as his ardor faded and a worrisome sleep finally triumphed over his anxious thoughts—he had to force himself to stay away from the beguiling, altogether too lovely and alluring Colleen Cassandra McClagan.

"Miss McClagan is at the door," Ned announced as Piero, Robin, and Jason enjoyed a late breakfast at the dining room table.

"A most persistent young lady, is she not, Maestro?" Piero asked Jason.

"Most persistent," Jason agreed, not certain whether he was sad or glad.

"Please see her in, Ned," Robin instructed without a moment's hesitation as he fluffed his loosely tied white embroidered neckerchief.

Moments later Colleen swept into the room with the energy and grace of a bright-eyed deer. She wore a forest-green gown and snow-white bonnet, and was smiling as though the war were already won.

"Methinks I see a vision of eternal youth," offered Piero. "You must sit down and share our food. We've a rare syrup and . . ."

"No, thank you," she said. "I've come to read you something I wrote last night. Would I be troubling you if I recited these few lines?" She glanced up, fearing rebuff.

"Not at all, my dear," Robin was quick to say.

Jason feared the words to which she referred was the love poem she had sung the night before, but he was wrong. Without further ado, Colleen cleared her throat and made the announcement. "I've written this conceit to a melody that is on everyone's lips—'Yankee Doodle.' I shall half sing, half recite, so that none of the meaning will be lost:"

> Major Embleton came to town, he hoped to be a hero
> But stormed upon a picnic fare where ruffians
>   numbered zero.
> Randy Embleton, keep it up, Randy, you're a dandy,
> Beat the rebels at their game, and with the food be
>   handy.
>
> He made an arrest with regal pomp, most certain of
>   his peg-o,
> In reaching for his pistol true, he drew a turkey leg-o,
> Randy Embleton, keep it up, Randy, you're a dandy,
> Beat the rebels at their game, and with the food be
>   handy!

Piero laughed uproariously, and Robin managed a tight smile as Colleen read and sang three more stanzas, each more biting than the last.

Jason was impressed, but also alarmed. "What do you intend to do with this?" he asked.

"Print it as a broadside and post it on the streets of Charleston. Let the people know what a pompous fool this Embleton really is."

"I think it's something we should discuss," Jason suggested, paling.

"We?" asked Colleen with indignance and surprise. "Why, the deed's practically done."

Seeing that it was neither the time nor place to engage himself in an argument, Jason asked Piero and Robin to excuse him and Colleen. Learning that she had walked to the Georgian town house, he offered to accompany her home.

Annoyed at being rushed out of the house, Colleen was also pleased at the prospect of spending more time alone with Jason.

Ned brought the buggy from the carriage house, and once behind the reins of Cinder, Jason felt a bit more in control of the day's events. He decided to ride around the city for a while and take the occasion to, as gently as possible, break off his relationship with this baffling woman.

Happy to learn Jason wouldn't be taking her directly home, Colleen returned to the discussion of her broadside. "I've decided to call it 'The Battle of Brandborough,'" she said. "I think that's a wonderful title, don't you?"

"No." Jason was frankly annoyed.

"You're cross."

"Quite."

"Why?"

"Satire doesn't suit you," he said as the buggy made its way toward Market Street, which was filled with the cries of vendors hawking vegetables and flowers. Black women carried baskets of ferns atop their heads as clean-shaven English soldiers bartered with big-bellied merchants. The air was scented with the aroma of roasted chestnuts, the sky a miracle of contrasting light—powder blue mixed with menacing clouds of sinister gray, the sun dancing in and out, the ocean breeze now tame, now frisky.

"Satire," Colleen contended hotly, "is a most potent tool for political retaliation. Are you forgetting Mr. Dryden and Mr. Pope? Surely they..."

"...were men of the world," Jason finished, interrupting Colleen.

"That's unjust!" Colleen complained with mounting anger. "Criticize my verse if you will, but not my gender. Would not these words have the same effect on their readers as those composed by a man? Would, in fact, the gentle reader know, from the language itself, that it was penned by a woman? I think not. Nor would the reader care."

"'Tis not the point," Jason said as they rode by the Dock Street Theater, which, in spite of the British occupation, was advertising the celebration of its forty-fourth anniversary with a gala production of, ironically, Shakespeare's *All's Well That Ends Well*.

"Then sir, what *is* the point?" Colleen asked.

"That you can be indiscreet, Colleen, and, if you'll permit me to say, foolhardy."

"I've told no one of this broadside."

"Save Piero, Robin, and myself."

"And neither you nor your dearest friends are to be trusted?"

"I trust them with my life," Jason said with frustration. "But I'm not so sure about the servant who was listening outside the door. Not to speak of your judgment, which I'm sorry to say I'm beginning to suspect."

The remark struck home. Jason saw that he'd wounded her far more than he'd intended and, as they passed by the porticoes, belfry, and towering spire of St. Philip's Church, by the tiny shops of silversmiths and cabinetmakers who displayed their smaller pieces on the street, he tried to explain himself. "I fear for you," he admitted. "I understand the English. I lived with them for three years. I know how they approach war. 'Tis no game, Colleen."

"And neither is my verse!" Colleen snapped, her rage flaring anew. "I can't speak for you, Jason Paxton, but I fear neither the British nor any other tyrant who would take from me what's rightfully mine. And this," she said, pulling out the paper on which her broadside was written, "is mine, my free expression, my heartfelt conviction that . . ."

Suddenly Jason grabbed the paper and quickly crumpled it in his fist. Colleen watched in disbelief and was on the verge of registering violent protest when she saw, facing them in front of the Old Customs Exchange, Major Randall Embleton. Having just dismounted from his horse, he had noticed Jason and was approaching the buggy. Four of his red-coated aides, men whom Jason and Colleen recognized from the picnic, accompanied him.

"How nice to see you in Charles Town, Mr. Paxton," the major said, greeting him with a salute.

"Good morning, Major," offered Jason, inconspicuously dropping the crumpled parchment at his own feet. "You remember Miss McClagan, I trust."

"'Tis my honor once again." He bowed, but not before lustily eyeing her.

Colleen stared coldly into space. The sight of Embleton, with his oversized features and ostentatious medals—the very man she had spent a part of the night parodying—filled her with contempt.

"I was actually on my way to see you, Major," Jason said, alighting from the buggy. "I was wondering if you'd object to my visiting my brother-in-law. I presume you're caring for him in there," Jason said, pointing to the fading brick and peeling wood of the Old Customs Exchange building, currently being used as British headquarters and a high-security prison.

"Object? Why, sir, I'd be pleased," Embleton replied slyly. "For anyone gracious enough to provide us Europeans with a taste of the culture we so sorely miss, why, it's a small enough request. Besides, who better than you might be able to enlighten the poor bloke with some sane Tory reasoning. Yes, certainly, go in and see the lad. In exchange for the favor, I know you'll be pleased to grant me a request of my own. I've spoken to Tarleton about you, and he'd be pleased to know a date when you'd be free to give a recital at his home. There are many more English gentlemen here who appreciate fine music than you might imagine. As you may have heard, he's taken over the Sitwell mansion, on Logan Street. Seems like the old man keeled over and died last week. Accommodating of him, wasn't it?" Embleton chuckled.

Colleen was appalled by the officer's attitude—Alexander Sitwell had been one of Charleston's bravest Patriots—and equally appalled that Jason would permit himself to prostitute himself before the warlords who held the city captive. "He called you a Tory," she whispered to Jason as Embleton marched off toward the building. "Are you going to allow that? Aren't you going to . . ."

"Shh!" Jason put his finger to his lips.

Colleen's face had turned scarlet. She was furious; she could no longer tolerate what she considered Jason's sickeningly obsequious behavior. How else could she look at him but as an effete musician whose only interest in life was pleasing the powerful and rich? "I'll say and do as I please," she snapped, "and leave you to your friends!" She reached down, snatched up the crumpled parchment, took the reins, and rode off indignantly.

Jason started to call her back, but Embleton's remark stopped him.

"What troubles Miss McClagan?" asked the bulbous-nosed major. "She seems frightfully upset."

"I don't have to tell you, Major, of the wiles of women," Jason answered coolly.

"Indeed you don't." Embleton smiled. "I've been known to have something of an accurate eye for various female dispositions, and I'd therefore place Miss McClagan in an especially hot-blooded category. What say you, Paxton?"

"I'd say that the major knows his ladies."

The men went through the huge paneled doors engraved with figures of cotton, tobacco, and other symbols of commerce. Inside, the Old Customs Exchange building was a combination of decrepitude and charm. Dozens of regular English soldiers in their scarlet uniforms and Embleton's own elite green-coated colonial guard monitored the hallways and worked at scattered desks. A large portrait of a drowsy King George III had been placed on a wall in the high-windowed central room from which Embleton, eliciting smart salutes from everyone he encountered, veered to the left and, with Jason close behind, threaded a winding path, a virtual maze.

The section reserved for prisoners had been used as a carriage house attached to the main building. It smelled of stale food and fresh urine. The air was damp; the light was dusty and grim. Rodents scurried up walls and along filthy ledges. Jason noted each turn, then fixed the location of the many windows and doorways in his mind. He continued following Embleton, past cramped cells with men collapsed on the floor, men groaning in pain, men who appeared to have been abused or beaten. In the corner in a tiny cell, Allan Coleridge slept on hard dirt.

"You've a guest, Coleridge," Embleton barked.

Allan opened his luminous gray eyes, and at the sight of Jason, he spang to his feet and spat at him. Jason turned away barely in time. The spittle clung to his sleeve like a milky, oozing badge of shame.

"Get the bastard traitor out of my sight," Allan said with contempt, "before I break through these bars and strangle him with my bare hands. I'd rather be visited by Satan himself than by a man who'd betray his own family. The sight of him makes me sick."

"I hoped I might be of some help, old boy," Jason said, playing a role for Embleton even as Allan's curses drowned him out.

"'Tis no use," Embleton sighed with some amusement. "At least you tried, my good man."

Jason endured his brother-in-law's abuse for a few more minutes, all the time memorizing as much of the prison's layout as he could.

"You see," Embleton remarked, leading Jason out, "reasoning with these heathens is quite impossible. I learned long ago that the lash, not the tongue, is all they understand. It's become a policy for which I've gained a deserved measure of fame here in the colonies." With that, he called his aide, "Benson, you're to administer a strong two dozen lashes to the first man who gives the guards the slightest bit of trouble today. Bring all the prisoners into the courtyard so that they witness the punishment and see for themselves what insubordination will bring them."

"Don't you think that's a bit excessive, Major?" Jason asked, fighting the urge to tell Embleton exactly what he thought of him.

"To the contrary, Mr. Paxton. I appreciate your artistic sensitivity, but these are stubborn people. Word will go out as to what awaits the rebels in the Old Customs Exchange. One way or another, their spirits will be broken."

The major escorted Jason to his office, where, he suggested, they have a spot of sherry. Jason accepted. The room was large, and Jason was surprised to see that Embleton worked in an atmosphere of no small disorganization. A slew of dirty cups and mugs, half-emptied teapots, and wine bottles was scattered on the tops of tables and desks. Maps were strewn everywhere. Battle plans hung from the walls by small nails. Bits of food—bread, slices of pork, and a variety of fruits—sat in baskets and upon platters. While the English officer sipped sherry and waxed eloquent on his favorite European music of the day, Jason cast furtive glances at the strategic maps and plans. The musician encouraged Embleton to expand upon his views and talked at length in order to buy himself time, all the while casually moving about the office, reading upside down when necessary, organizing the great bulk of information in his mind, much as he organized the notes of a symphony on the piano-forte. Before Jason left, Embleton had made him commit to a definite date—ten days hence—for a recital.

Outside, his head dizzy with a strange swirl of confidence and despair, Jason looked around, hoping that Colleen might have returned with the buggy, but saw instead another familiar carriage pull up in front of the Old Customs Exchange.

When Hope emerged, her eyes met her brother's. She looked stunning but distant in an outfit of deep purple as she heard Jason explain how he had come to see Allan.

"Did they allow that?" she asked coldly.

"Yes, but he wasn't overjoyed at seeing me."

"Will they let me see him?"

"I can speak with Embleton and—"

"Never mind," Hope cut him off. "I can do that myself."

"I might have more sway and . . ."

Hope began walking toward the entrance to the old building. "Please," Jason continued, "if you're staying at Father's apartment here I'd like to visit with you and explain . . ."

Hope never turned around, never bothered to acknowledge her brother's pleas. She proceeded straight ahead through the open doors, into the building.

Jason could do nothing more than walk away through the narrow cobblestoned streets of the city. The morning had turned even more humid. The sun was hidden behind a bank of dark gray rain clouds. He felt a few drops on his head and hands as he walked not by design, but by instinct, watching the flower sellers running for cover as the wind and the rain came down. It didn't matter if he got wet. He welcomed the relief from above. Let it rain! Let it pour! The row of small, French-looking buildings on stately Queen Street seemed like a painting to him. In his mind, he heard a symphony—the angry roar of firing cannons, the plaintive song of soaring birds, the formal meter of measured minuets. He struggled to put them all together, and yet he couldn't. He realized that he would have to live with the disonance until a structure of sense, a manageable motif, prevailed. Meanwhile, he walked in the rain and thought, walked through lovely, troubled Charleston, walked and told himself that, yes, it was a cruel way to break off the relationship, but at least the deed had been done. And if, an hour later, soaked to the bone, he turned a corner and found himself on Meeting Street, quickly approaching the home and shop of Rianne Mary McClagan, it was only because the house was directly on the path back to Robin and Piero's. He had no intention of stopping, no intention of offering any further explanations. Neither, though, had he expected to be greeted by the sight of a resplendent carriage that stopped him dead in his tracks. With a shock of recognition, he knew that the carriage sitting directly in front of Rianne's belonged to Buckley Somerset. He didn't even consider going inside. He couldn't face another confrontation, not at that moment. Instead, his heart filled with jealousy, he turned on his heels and walked way, taking a longer path back to the home of his patrons.

Chapter 12

Buckley had arrived at a most inopportune time. Colleen was in a rage—angry at herself for having left Jason, angry at Jason for having courted Embleton, angry at the world for being so unjust.

"I must tell him something, dear," Rianne insisted from the hallway outside Colleen's bedroom.

"Tell him I died of consumption during the night."

"Really, Colleen!"

"Tell him I can't see him today."

"I've already done so and he insists on waiting. He says you promised to see him here, and while I sympathize with your plight, I must say that a brief appearance shouldn't be all that painful. I hold no affection for the young man myself. Still, it doesn't hurt to be civil. May I tell him that you'll be down?"

"You may say whatever you please, Aunt Rianne," Colleen replied stiffly.

"Good. Then we shall see you in the parlor in a very few minutes."

Silence. Blessed silence. Colleen thought about her situation, about Jason and Major Embleton, about Buckley Somerset and his family fortune, about her new lyrics, which she had recopied and presently held in her hand. She read the piece again. The more she read, the more she considered her state, the less she wanted a scene with Buckley. Too much had happened. Too much, especially with Jason. Her words to Rianne forgotten along with her polite intentions, she threw on a hooded cloak, stole down the back stairs, and quietly slipped out the rear door. She was off to see Ephraim Kramer, and the fact that it was pouring rain did not deter her one bit. She placed the parchment inside her blouse, next to her breast, protecting it from the wet with the warmth of her body. She walked quickly down the darkening streets as the frightened whinny of horses responded to the sudden crack of thunder. The farther she went, the braver she grew, the more exhilarated she felt. The air was alive with the excitement of electrical change. Several times she looked over her shoulder, half wishing that she were being followed. Nothing could stop her! Just let them try! She turned up one alleyway and hurried down another until, on a tiny side street, close enough to the harbor to hear the sound of waves crashing against the battery walls, she reached her destination. The overhead sign read: EPHRAIM KRAMER: PRINTER. Out of breath, seeing that his door had been padlocked, she felt her heart beat even faster. When there was no response to her insistent bangs, she cupped her mouth with her hands and screamed, "Mr. Kramer! It's Colleen! Please, open your door!"

From the second story, a small head, wrinkled as a raisin, raised a window. A raspy voice chided Colleen. "Get out of the rain, child, before you catch your death of cold! Go back home! Get!"

"I must speak with you!" she pleaded.

"There's nothing to speak about," he said, nervously looking up and down the street. "Now go home."

"If you don't let me in, I'll continue to scream until King George himself hears my cry."

"Be still, be still. Come 'round back and I'll let you in," Ephraim Kramer conceded, mumbling something about the madness of women.

Once inside, Colleen began to take off her drenched cloak. "Not so fast," said the elderly man in a quivering voice. "I've let you in, not invited you to stay."

In Kramer's cramped kitchen, Ephraim was dressed in rough work trousers covered by a large ink-smeared smock. He was a diminutive man, much shorter than Colleen. His hairless hands were small, and his tiny ears looked as if they had been pressed against the sides of his head. In his beady brown eyes, despite what seemed an apparent hardness, Colleen saw a special kindness and courage.

"You've been nothing but a pain to me, young lady," he said to her, "and I'll have no more of it. I've decided to stop all this secretive printing. I've toyed with my luck long enough."

"What are you saying?" asked Colleen, not quite prepared for still another disillusionment.

"That the Sandpiper has chirped her last. 'Twill chirp no more. Listen to me, Colleen. I'm an old, feeble widower who has but a few years to live. And, with your permission, I'd like to live them in peace, or, for that matter, live them out of prison. Things have changed since the British seizure. Things have worsened. I've been visited twice in the past week by Embleton's men. They searched this place high and low for signs of seditious material. I told them that for the past thirty years I've printed nothing more substantial than the notices of local merchants and a modest letter of inconsequential activities among the citizenry. They didn't believe me, though. They compared all my type to that used to print the Sandpiper's pages, and they made a mess of the place in the process."

"They didn't find the spare set of type, then?" Colleen asked, relieved.

Ephraim's face broke into a toothless smile. "Not so much as an ampersand." He tapped the grain bin, in whose fake bottom the incriminating type was hidden. "Not a single *e* or *m*. Or period, for that matter."

"Then what's stopping us?"

"My good sense. I'm closed for the summer and will stay closed until the climate changes for the better. Heat's an affliction for an old man like me. Along with floggings and hangings. And mind you, they're afflictions that can strike the young as well."

"You aren't old, Mr. Kramer. You're young as spring itself, and I love you," Colleen said, kissing him on the cheek.

Ephraim backed into a chair and grumpily brushed off the kiss. "We'll have none of that," he warned. "I'm no longer tempted by women, not even one as pretty as you."

"But I'm sure you'll be tempted by this," she said, pulling out her satire and presenting it to him.

Ephraim fished out a pair of rimless spectacles from his vest pocket, put them on, and read, and in spite of his best efforts, he couldn't fight back a wide grin and several rich chuckles.

"Damnation! But you're a mischievous female!"

"It's for the love of freedom, Mr. Ephraim. The love that beats in all our hearts."

"Oh, but I'd love to see Embleton's bloated face when he lays eyes on this."

"Then you'll print it?"

"Not on your life. This one could cost us our necks."

"You *must* print it. I'll help you, no matter how long it takes. I'll follow all your instructions, just as I did last time. We'll work through the night if we have to."

"We'll do nothing of the kind, Miss McClagan. For all your wit and winning ways, I'll not risk my life and my livelihood."

"You've already risked it. We risk it every day that we continue allowing them to imprison us in our own homes. Dear Mr. Kramer, can't you see that?"

"I can see only that I won't be persuaded this time. I dislike the Crown's impudence as much as anyone, but I've worked all my life to build this small enterprise, and I'll not see it destroyed. No, Miss McClagan, the answer is a definite and unalterable no!"

Colleen nodded as if in complete accord with the elderly printer. Without further ado, she pulled the grain bin away from the wall and stooped to remove the backing strip, in front of which lay the tray that held the Sandpiper's type. There wasn't, she explained, a moment to lose.

Sometime during the evening, Jason remembered Piero knocking at his bedroom door and announcing that Cinder had been brought to the carriage house by one of Rianne's servants. The Italian had also asked whether the young maestro cared for dinner. Not presently, Jason had replied, and he retreated once again into himself.

It was close to midnight. The sudden squall that had sprung up an hour earlier had subsided and, from his window, he could see a few stars twinkling through a sky of broken clouds. Cinder's return without a note or message was discouraging. It was evident that Colleen was convinced, as was seemingly everyone dear to him, that he was conspiring with the enemy. She no longer trusted him and, by her silence, was obviously ending their friendship. The brief union was broken. Well enough, Jason thought. That was what he'd wanted. Finally, his mind was clear to concentrate on action. It was time to formulate a precise plan, find someone he could trust to pass information to the rebels—a difficult task, as scattered and disorganized as they were—and then get to work.

Restless and troubled with an excess of pent-up energy, he donned breeches, blouse, boots, and the great woolen peasant's cape from Parma, then crept silently out of the house without waking Piero and Robin. In the carriage house, he saddled Cinder and rode out into the darkened streets, past the many churches, past the silent marketplaces and the multitude of shops, past the wharves and fishing boats. A circuitous route of back alleys and hidden paths led him past the sentries guarding the roads leading out of the city, and within an hour, he urged Cinder into a gallop as he left Charleston behind and rode deep into the night, into the countryside where, he knew, he would find the solitude he needed.

On he rode into the marshlands and along the dense coastal swamps that he'd explored and loved so well during his school years in Charleston. With the storm far behind, the sky was brilliant with radiant, silver-white stars. The smell of rain-saturated earth, wet moss, and the nearby salt marshes mingled and became a single perfume that cleared his head. Moonlight lit his path as he ventured farther and deeper into the wilderness with only the heavy breath and drum of the dun stallion's hooves on the damp ground breaking the wondrous silence.

How long did he ride? How many times did his thoughts turn to Colleen, to his father, his sisters, to Peter Tregoning, and to the filty cell that Allan Coleridge was forced to inhabit? Nothing made sense, and yet he kept riding, riding through the night, riding until the first hint of dawn faded the smaller stars and brushed a thin coat of gray over the eastern horizon. And then, suddenly, he saw it—the eerie phosphorescent glow of swamp gases, a magical lumination that had been as much a part of his childhood as the morning sun. What was it that they called the ghostly, flickering light?

Will-o'-the-wisp! His heart pounded as he repeated the words aloud. "Will-o'-the-wisp. Will-o'-the-wisp!" He drew rein. Whinnying in protest, Cinder came to a sudden halt. The night silence closed around as Jason watched, waited, and found his answer.

The harmless, illusive will-o'-the-wisp—always to be chased, never to be caught. That was the game that boys loved to play, chasing thin air, chasing the mysterious, magical light.

Well, it was a game, he realized, that deserved playing again, only this time with deadly serious intent, and not nearly so harmlessly.

"Yes!" he shouted, his voice ringing out, shattering the silence before being swallowed by the swamp. He clutched the gold Paxton amulet that hung on the chain around his neck, and he knew, knew, knew that it would work. "Yes!"

Suddenly, filled with the thrill of purpose, he whipped Cinder toward the already vanishing glow. He'd wanted to become a part of the struggle for freedom, had wanted to dare and die, if need be, but on his own terms, as his own man. He had searched and, chasing the intangible, had at last found . . .

The will-o'-the-wisp, will-o'-the-wisp, no one can catch, the will-o'-the-wisp! . . .

Dawn was breaking over Charleston's bay just as an officer of the British Army, flushed from a bawdy night in a house of ill repute, happened by the Fierce Lion Inn, whose doors and shutters were closed tight. On the door, however, he caught sight of a newly printed broadside, and despite his great fatigue, he stopped to read. A minute later he ripped the paper from the door with great fury and berated a private patrolling the streets.

"Why hasn't this slanderous piece of sedition been long removed?" demanded the officer.

"Begging your pardon, sir, but I'm not much of a reader, so I wouldn't know what's on the paper. If it helps, though, sir, I can tell you that I've seen a good half dozen of the same posted 'round about. I can't tell you who's done it, but there's more than a few of 'em, you can be sure."

"Well, damn it, man," barked the officer, ripping the broadside in half, "I want you and everyone else on patrol to tear every last one down—I don't care how long it takes."

"Yes, sir," said the private, saluting.

But by then, most of Charleston was slowly awakening, and from East Bay Street to Logan and Murray Boulevards, from one end of the city to the other, among the fishermen along the Ashley and Cooper rivers to the clergymen opening their rectory doors to the newborn sun, dozens of copies of "The Battle of Brandborough" were being passed from hand to hand. If one listened hard, one could hear muffled giggles and chuckles. Some folks tried to control themselves, others couldn't, until, like a soft white cloud above the city, a low roar of laughter seemed to arise everywhere from large clusters of citizens gathered on street corners, in front of candlemakers' shops and bakeries, even on Meeting Street, where, from her second-story window, her face, hands, and arms smudged with fresh, black ink, and her mouth broadened in a wide, triumphant smile, Colleen Cassandra McClagan had the supreme satisfaction of watching her readers react with alacrity to her labor of love.

PART II

PART II

⤜ *Chapter 1* ⤛

It was the second week of June as two Tory soldiers rode swiftly along a trail ten miles outside Charleston. The night air was sticky and hot, their horses tired and thirsty, but the greencoats pushed on. They had been instructed by Major Embleton to arrive at Fort Santee by daybreak with a vital communiqué for the commanding officer. The road was bordered on the west by the dark, putrid-smelling swamp. Thick clouds danced across the moon, blocking the silver light and turning the mood of the dark night somber and stark. The men knew the countryside well and weren't disturbed by the strange sounds coming from the wilderness—the buzzing insects, croaking frogs, screeching birds. Nothing, though, could have prepared them for the sudden swoop of what seemed a flying figure leaping from the swamp.

A few feet in front of them, the mysterious will-o'-the-wisp blocked their way, moving quickly, knocking the first Tory from his horse and skewering his chest with a quick rapier's thrust. The man fell helplessly to the ground, crying in pain. By then the second soldier had unsheathed his own sword and moved to challenge the masked Wisp. Both horses neighed and reared as the men slashed at one another, the sound of steel striking steel ringing out in the night. Jason fought furiously, surprised at his opponent's strength. He took a blow powerful enough to throw him from his horse, spilling him in the gooey, soft edge of the swamp. He scurried to retrieve his rapier, lay low, and emerge at the very moment the Tory was approaching. Jason was able to return the favor, spilling the soldier from his horse. The man recovered his sword in time to accept the Wisp's challenge. On foot, a brutal battle ensued. The Tory was larger and stronger than the reed-thin musician, and with the tremendous force of two thunderous blows, he knocked Jason back to the ground. The musician realized he was foolishly unprepared and clearly outmatched. He saw his patriotic mission coming to a quick and lethal end. Natural agility, however, enabled him to regain his footing. Toe to toe against the Tory, he breathlessly held off the strikes as best he could, but it was useless; he knew he couldn't last long. In that very instant, Jason heard the voice of his father reminding him that any two brutes could bang blades together. Panting, he dropped the tip of his rapier, and the Tory went for the bait, lunging and throwing himself off balance. In a moment of composure, the Wisp took his advantage, plunging his sword through his adversary's heart. Both relieved and sickened by another man's death, Jason turned to the first Tory, whose life had also drained from his body. With no time to waste, no time to think, Will-o'-the-Wisp searched the pouches of the Tories' horses and found the secret message he had overhead Embleton discuss. Within hours, the parchment, containing specific battle plans against rebel forces, was anonymously placed under the door of the home of one of Charleston's most reliable and effective military strategists, a Patriot of singular dedication.

Shirtless and soaked in sweat, Jason raised the ax and lowered it on the massive log with all the strength at his command. Chips flew. The blazing summer sun beat down mercilessly as the musician feverishly labored in the enclosed backyard of his patrons' town house. Again and again, he attacked the wood with impassioned tenacity. The sinewy muscles in his back and arms ached with exruciating pain, but Jason pressed on, not allowing himself a minute of rest. He worked the tough wood for a good half hour. When he was through, he chinned himself on a long, solid branch of a giant oak tree, raising and lowering his torso again and again until he was ready to fall with fatigue. Yet he wouldn't fall, he wouldn't stop until he was satisfied that his morning routine had sufficiently taxed his hardening body. In the afternoon, he'd repeat the process, adding a number of strenuous exercises—climbing, running, diligently practicing his swordplay for hours on end. When he grew tired or bored, he redoubled his efforts, pledging never again to ride as Will-o'-the-Wisp in anything but a state of absolute preparedness. As he pushed himself on, grunting as he lifted weights of greater and greater bulk, he moved to a stirring, marching melody inside his head, an obsessively rhythmic cadence that had him pulling and straining until he felt his stomach tighten into a slab of iron, his legs and arms turning to cords of steel.

The city of Charleston was clutched in a paralysis of political tension. Its narrow streets seethed with intrigue, its citizens weary of a scrutinous and heavy-handed military presence. Unrest could be felt, liking a rising fever, in taverns, public parks, and private homes. In one such home, deep in the damp recesses of his candelit basement, Ephraim Kramer spoke in whispers to Colleen Cassandra McClagan.

"Have you heard what he's done now?" he asked.

"No," she answered. "Tell me."

"He's a madman, he is, but he's got courage—I'll say that. Single-handedly, in the dead of night, he raided the English arsenal at Mason's Swamp. They chased him till dawn, but not a trace. They say he vanished into the swamp like thin air. Will-o'-the-Wisp—that's what he calls himself. And this time he got away with a bushel of pistols and a barrel of muskets that he delivered the next morning to the Continental Army at Colonel Buford's doorstep without even bothering to introduce himself. Snuck into camp, left the guns on the ground, and rode off before anyone knew he'd been there."

Colleen's amber eyes were all afire. "If the Sandpiper devises something about him, Mr. Kramer, can we print it and put it out?"

"If I say I'll deny you, I'd only be fooling myself again, eh?"

She kissed his cheek and left quickly, hurrying back to her aunt's house, where quill and parchment awaited her.

That night Captain Peter Tregoning and Joy Exceeding Paxton strolled along East Battery under the silver light of a pale half moon. English warships, like floating forts, guarded the harbor. The June night was humid and still.

Joy took Peter's hand, felt the perspiration, and saw in his eyes the unmistakable look of anguish.

"You didn't want to see me, did you?" she suggested.

"Of course I did. I was truly pleased to see that you went to the trouble to learn that I'd been reassigned here. But for you to come to Charleston might have been a mistake. Your father must..."

"I told him I wanted to be with Hope. She won't leave Charleston until Allan is freed. Father hasn't seen your letters, nor does he know you're here."

"Joy..." Peter began, but interrupted himself with a deep-throated sigh belying the stiffness of his military posture.

"What is it? Please tell me, Peter. It's as if you're a thousand miles away tonight."

"I just returned from Waxhaws." His voice was whisper-quiet. He could barely speak. "I went with Tarleton and Embleton. Buford led a band of four hundred Continentals against our two hundred fifty. The Patriots fought poorly, though. They were inexperienced and inept on the battlefield. We trounced them thoroughly, but then..." He hesitated, forcing back what actually looked like tears. "Then..."—he swallowed hard—"...Tarleton and Embleton went mad. We'd captured more than two hundred men and they ordered us to..." Again he stopped, closed his eyes, and finally said the words, "They ordered us to run the prisoners through with swords and bayonets."

"Peter!" Joy threw her hand over her mouth and gasped. "Could you...did you..."

"I was one of the commanders," he said. "I relayed the orders. I watched it happen."

Now his eyes flooded with tears as Joy took him to her breast. Silently, the proper English soldier wept in her arms.

"I must say—he was quite fabulous," Rianne reported, all aflutter in a silver-threaded burgundy gown and a sky-high powdered wig decorated with clusters of tiny white pearls.

"How could you have possibly gone?" Colleen was outraged as she confronted Rianne in her own workshop.

"How could I have possibly missed it?"

"For all practical purposes, you were consorting with the enemy."

"Nonsense. Many a music-loving Patriot was there, though Colonel Tarleton and Major Embleton were too glassy-eyed from their English sherry to take note. What pompous fools they are! But, oh, the music was divine!"

"He played?"

"I thought you weren't curious," Rianne teased.

"I'm not," Colleen insisted.

For the next few seconds Rianne slowly removed her white silk gloves and let silence prevail. Finally, her niece surrendered.

"Well, did he or did he not play?" Colleen asked.

"Like an angel, my dear. An absolute angel."

"I really don't want to hear about it, Aunt Rianne, but if you must tell me, I'll force myself to listen."

Rianne removed remnants of fabric from a wicker chair and sat majestically, folding her hands on her lap, making herself comfortable before she cleared her throat and spoke in carefully measured phrases. "To begin with, poor Alex Sitwell's manor will never be the same. The major stripped it of its furniture and replaced the fine pieces crafted here in Charleston with extraordinarily vulgar new rubbish from England. But no matter, the parlor's still a lovely room, with its bay windows and the light from the south garden falling so gently on the assembled guests. In the first row, naturally, were Tarleton and Embleton themselves, as well as a whole assembly of decorated British officers. Before the recital began, I saw Jason speaking with a red-haired officer. From what you've told me, I gather that was Captain Tregoning. A handsome lad, I must say. I also saw that Joy Exceeding was in attendance, and I was most pleased that she wore a floral-designed gown of my own making. A dear child, that Joy. Robin Courtenay and Piero Sebastiano Ponti were very much in evidence. Robin wore a remarkable yellow-and-black turban as tall as my wig, while Piero donned a red vest and a waistcoat as white as freshly fallen snow.

"As to your Mr. Paxton . . . well"—she shook her head as if all description were futile—"he appeared wigless and terribly somber. His gray greatcoat and white blouse were as undistinguished as they were proper, more befitting of a schoolmaster than a musician. Not in the least dashing. Naturally, the unusual curliness of his hair lends great dramatic effect to his person, particularly when he sits down to play. And, oh, my child, play he did! Before the music began, the man looked . . . I would say . . . troubled. Of course, he was charming to all in attendance, but he seemed, beneath the surface, out of sorts. When his fingers danced o'er the ivory, though, it was as if the room had been raised upon a soft cloud and lifted toward blissful heaven. His instrument was a chamber organ newly arrived from London, an enormous piece, which at first glance I took for a sideboard. Even Robin seemed impressed. The elongated silver pipes were encased above the keyboard in a chamber of bejeweled cut glass. And when Mr. Paxton played, the sound seemed to emanate from the very soul of the composers—a sonata by Muzio Clementi, brief pieces by Martini and Giacomo Puccini, a delicious opus by Johann Christian Bach."

"And nothing by Jason himself?"

"No, which was strange, I thought. And it did appear, on reflection, that he was holding part of himself in careful reserve. His execution was divine, and yet, oddly enough, one waited for something more."

"His conscience—that's what it was. The guilt of betrayal! He's a monster, Aunt Rianne, he's a scoundrel and a..."

"Well, then you'll not care to learn that the monster and scoundrel asked to be remembered to you."

"What did he say?" Colleen had to know.

"Only that he very much regretted not having seen you this past month. He wondered whether you were still in Charleston."

"And what did you say?"

"What any respectable aunt would say under the circumstance. I spoke the truth. I said you were here."

"And then what did he say?"

"My dear, 'twas a brief encounter indeed. Many others were waiting to congratulate him on his performance. He kissed my hand and bade me a good afternoon. I curtsied and wished him well."

"He's a scoundrel!" Colleen cried, running from the room, "a monster!"

> While Tarleton murders our innocent lambs
> And Randy hosts recitals sublime
> The Will o' the Wisp continues to prey
> Upon those who would foster these crimes

In pursuing his capture, the English fox
Gets lost in the woods and the swamps
The more futile his attempts to find his own tail
The more our Wisp laughs and romps

      —the Sandpiper

With one violent stroke, Major Randall Embleton ripped the broadside in half. "Has Tarleton seen this slander, Benson?"

"I'm not certain, sir."

"Well, I want it stopped, and I want it stopped now!"

"Referring to the broadsides, sir," Benson asked cautiously, "or Will-o'-the-Wisp?"

"Both, you bloody fool!" the major exploded. "With no mercy shown to printer, poet, or bandit. I'll make examples of them, I will. I'll break the neck of this pesky Sandpiper and cut the throat of this wispy pest. Their blood will flow in the streets so that all can see what awaits those who mock and defy the king's authority in this godforsaken colony."

Chapter 2

Colleen awoke at dawn. Rays of sunlight peeked through her window and, even at the early hour, the heat of summer had begun to build. It was the first day of July. The air was humid, and the sky, while not threatening, was filled with fabulous formations of billowing white clouds. It took her a second to remember where she was—not at home at her father's farm, but in Charleston, at her aunt's house. Where had she been in her dream? Angrily, she remembered Paris, and that Jason had been there, and he had taken her to the opera, and afterward, in his secluded studio he had . . . She blocked the rest of the dream from her mind. Such dreams were frivolous, and though they haunted her night after night, she was determined to erase them from her mind.

Getting out of bed, stretching and yawning away the fatigue that clung to her eyes like morning dew, she remembered the powerful thoughts with which she had fallen asleep the night before. Late that afternoon, Jeth Darney had paid her a visit and reported that, in spite of rebel losses at Mock's Corner, Lenud's Ferry, and the already infamous battle of Waxhaws, British brutality had inspired an unprecedented number of new recruits to join the Continental Army. "Never seen anything like it before," Jeth had said while downing a glass of Rianne's sherry. "The revolution's turned into a bloody civil war, least-ways in this colony. Friend agin' friend, family agin' family."

The news of the growing bands of volunteers had been encouraging, and with morning light, she dressed quickly in an orange frock of patterned gauze that lent her hair a misty, golden glow. Downstairs she left a brief note explaining that she'd be home no later than noon. It was not yet seven A.M. Once outside, a sense of optimism, even gaiety, sang through her heart. Hidden within the multilayered petticoats of her skirt was her newest lyric, which, she was certain, would do even more to encourage men to join the fight for freedom—men unlike Jason Paxton who could be made to see that nothing, not even their own private gain, was more important than the struggle against the Crown. The shopkeepers mopping the sidewalks in front of their stores suggested a fresh metaphor to Colleen. The English would be washed away, she told herself. Hope burned within her, and, even more, a certain faith that, if it were a game the occupiers were playing, she would win. In the past month since being in Charleston, the Sandpiper had written and, with the help of the children of jailed patriots, distributed no less than a half dozen biting broadsides. At night, in taverns and homes wherever Patriots assembled, the words, sung to familiar melodies, soared defiantly from one side of the city to the other. *A game indeed!* She smiled to herself as she picked up the pace of her walk, threading her way through the narrow streets and tiny alleyways, not bothering to see whether she was being followed, not caring, knowing that, no matter what, her mission would be accomplished because, in spite of their warnings and ridiculous posters threatening the arrest of those involved in seditious activity, people like herself or Ephraim Kramer or the wondrous Will-o'-the-Wisp would be neither frightened nor silenced.

She thought of a story she had heard of the campaign in New York at the outbreak of war in 1776 when a Patriot, surveying British troop movements for General Washington, had been captured and ordered hanged. He had been denied a trial, a clergyman, and even a Bible. Yet with the noose around his neck, his eyes were clear and calm, and his brave words were never to be forgotten. "I only regret," said the young Nathan Hale, "that I have but one life to lose for my country."

The memory of that story set Colleen walking even faster. Now she couldn't wait to reach Ephraim and show him her newest call to arms. Oh, how he'd love it! For all his initial hesitation, he, too, had proven a brave and hearty soul, a splendid man who . . .

Something was wrong. Terribly wrong. When she turned the corner on Legare Street and began to walk the few paces down to Kramer's shop, she saw four Redcoats posted at his door. What were they doing there at that hour of the morning? Her heartbeat quickened and her throat turned dry. Quickly, instinctively, she ducked into one of his neighbor's gardens. There, among beds of flowering pansies and petunias, she found herself waiting, listening, staying flat against the side of the brick wall, out of sight. Minutes later she heard a struggle, then the sound of her friend's voice, the old man's voice, crying, "It's a mistake, you're making a mistake, it's not my press, it's not my doing!" Never before had she heard such utter terror trapped inside a human voice. She wanted to break out of her hiding place, step forward and fight for her friend—how, she wasn't certain—but instead remained frozen, unable to budge for fear of recognition. Fear had her paralyzed.

Seconds later, when she heard the soldiers take him away, she slowly, cautiously emerged from the alleyway to see that a large crowd had formed and was following the arresting party. She slipped in among the several dozen people, feeling protected in their numbers. As they trailed behind Ephraim and the soldiers, their ranks grew. Soon a hundred or more citizens had formed something of a parade. Colleen hoped they'd understand the injustice of the arrest and demand Kramer's release. Instead, they merely gossiped among themselves, curious to see where the soldiers were taking him. Colleen grew even more frightened as she realized they were heading toward the Old Customs Exchange. Once they were there and she saw that a gallows had been constructed in front of the main doors, she desperately tried to awaken herself from this nightmare: *This wasn't happening! This couldn't be true!* She was nearly sick to her stomach, her mouth parched with panic.

She edged her way toward the front of the now enormous crowd. Hundreds watched. The event had been timed to coincide with the hour when Charlestonians were up and about, engaged in early morning activities. Colleen thought of making her way to the first row, but stopped at the second, partially hidden by a tall gentleman in a fancy wig who stood in front of her. She looked around the man and saw that Embleton was on the platform, and that Ephraim's eyes mirrored the specter of sheer terror.

"So that the more critical among you," declared the major, his saucer eyes bulging with purpose, "be satisfied that there's English justice even during the bloodiest of wars, this man, this rebel printer, will not be hanged. He has only to reveal the name of his accomplice, the would-be poet whose insidious and silly rhymes have done so much to rile the more rebellious factions among this otherwise civilized community. The gallows will be dismounted, the affair brought to a quick end. The printer will be imprisoned, but his life spared. What say you, then, Ephraim Kramer? Will you name this Sandpiper?"

For a second, Colleen considered running, screaming, racing to the gallows and strangling the major herself. But instead she did nothing except hold her breath and fight for control. Her hands shook and her heart beat madly against her chest. *How had they found out? An accident. A horribly cruel twist of fate. A surprise visit by English troops. Perhaps he had been working in the basement.* She hid behind the tall man, her eyes closed tightly, her hands clenched in fists. Silence, long seconds of silence. *Who knew why? Only that it had happened.* She dared to peek around the man to see Ephraim and—dear God!— she was certain he had spotted her. She shut her eyes again, as if that would make her disappear, only to hear a cry from the gallows: "I'm an old man! Spare me! Spare my life!"

"You know the condition," Embleton pronounced loudly.

"I don't want to die . . . please, please . . . I'm . . . I'm afraid to die . . ."

"Then speak," ordered the major.

Suddenly Ephraim was silent, defiantly silent. Not a word, not a sound from him or the throng of people assembled. Colleen's eyes were still closed—*this isn't happening, this can't be happening*—and when she opened them against her will, she saw only a flash of images: soldiers struggling with the frail printer, the noose around his wrinkled neck, Ephraim's sweet, harmless neck. His eyes, widened with terror, more alive than any eyes she had ever seen. His voice, now pleading for mercy. Then a sound she'd never forget—a release, a thump, the hideous crack of bone, an anguished groan. His neck broken, his head slumped to one side. She opened her eyes to see that his were also still open. His pupils were frozen in a silent scream. Would that death erase that gaze! Would that death shut his eyes, eyes that still stared into hers! And then, all control vanishing, she suddenly felt herself falling, falling into a deep, dark abyss of quiet and solitude. . . .

She opened her eyes to the sound of chirping birds and the sight of spreading vines. She was in a secluded section of King's Park, seated on the ground beneath a great oak tree, nestled in his arms. The face of Jason Paxton had never seemed more compassionate or loving.

"What . . . where . . ." she began to ask.

He calmed her with a gentle kiss. "You fainted," he explained. "I caught you, and brought you here. 'Tis nothing more than that. I was standing near you all the while."

She looked around and saw a white gazebo beyond which a pair of swans swam upon a still, small pond. In the distance, church spires extended into a sky still crowded with clouds.

"Ephraim!" she suddenly remembered. "He was so afraid."

"He was a man of singular courage. His silence was courageous."

"And I . . ."—her breath quickened—". . . I'm nothing but a loathsome coward."

"There was no way to help, Colleen."

"But I . . . I . . ." And the tears streamed from her eyes. Finally, she exploded with a series of body-wrenching sobs, weeping uncontrollably, as a child, a small infant, lost, afraid and filled with unspoken pain. All the time, Jason held her, kissing her forehead and assuring her that she'd be all right, that life would go on, that her friend hadn't died in vain.

For a great while, she let his words of kindness soothe her wounded heart like a salve. She felt protected, loved, and understood. He never reminded her of his earlier warnings, never chided or rebuked her for foolish behavior. He was merely there for her to lean upon. She allowed herself to be comforted for a few additional moments before standing up suddenly, wiping the tears from her eyes, and walking quickly to the latticed gazebo. Jason came to join her.

"No!" She stopped him before he entered the gazebo. Her mood had changed drastically. "Don't come any closer."

"I don't understand."

"Who informed on Ephraim? How do I know it wasn't you? Or Robin? Or Piero? How do I . . ."

"Oh, my sweet angel," he declared, meeting her accusation

with even deeper understanding. "My heart cries for you."

"I don't need your pity. Just let me be."

"Please, Colleen, surely you see..."

"I see nothing and trust no one, least of all you."

"Then I'll see you home."

"You needn't bother. I know the way."

"Let me just..."

"It's useless, Jason. You can't begin to fathom what I feel. If only I had helped Ephraim. No one can understand my remorse. Please, just let me be."

Jason turned and walked away, his head down, his pace agonizingly slow. It was what he wanted. He had no room for love. His steps might also lead to the gallows. Why drag her with him? Better to let Colleen live with the cruel lesson of that heartless morning. Still, he worried about her more than ever. There was no use in denying it. He cared, cared deeply about this fascinating and fragile woman.

It was only after he was gone that Colleen suddenly remembered the lyrics that she had hidden between her petticoats early that morning. She searched for the paper, but to no avail; the broadside was no longer there. Panic and fear welled in her breast. Had someone noticed her drop it? And if it was gone, she had no copy.

An image of Ephraim. She wavered, fought back the tide of revulsion and sorrow that threatened to engulf her, crushing the last vestige of her spirit.

She could have saved him.

Her fault, not Jason's or anyone else's.

Oh, God in heaven, her fault...

∾ *Chapter 3* ∾

Jason was drained of emotion as he rode back toward his patrons' home. He went over the scene in his mind—how he had spotted Colleen in the crowd, stood behind her and held his breath as he waited for Ephraim to speak her name. He, too, had considered charging the gallows, protesting with words or action, doing anything to stop the hanging and Colleen's incrimination. At a certain point, though, he sensed that Kramer would neither betray her nor could Embleton retreat from this public threat. All he could do was catch Colleen when she swooned and, in the confused and shocked aftermath of the execution, carry her to the carriage loaned to him by Robin and Piero.

Now he brought the carriage back to Easy Bay Street. Robin was in his shop at the back of his house; Piero had gone to market seeking the ideal eggplant for the evening's dinner. Jason went to the music library, shut the door, and for the next several hours emptied his heart onto the virginal in what became an improvised requiem for Ephraim Kramer. The motif was mournful and slow, the tear-stained notes filled with pain, as if nothing but this dirge could express the sorrow in Jason's soul. He made no attempt to notate the composition, but merely allowed himself to cry through his music as he bent and swayed with the heavy, minor chords.

At sunset he found himself walking from the house, through

153

the garden, across the street to stare at Charleston Bay. The sight never ceased to fascinate him—ships of commerce, ships of war, the islands and vast ocean beyond. With Ephraim's death, the miracle of the changing light seemed especially poignant. Why had he died? Was there really a point to it all? Jason thought of the two Tories he had killed—his countrymen—and wondered whether his own exploits were worth the bloodshed. Or was it all, as the bard had said through the lips of a bereaved Macbeth, "a tale told by an idiot, full of sound and fury signifying nothing"?

The beauty of light, the way in which the majestic clouds caught the gold and pink of the setting sun over the untamed lands to the west, filled Jason with inspiration and troubled awe. How was one to respond to a world in which a decent man was dragged to a twisted, tormented death under a sky that hours later sang a symphony of breathtaking colors? What was one to say? What to think? And what of Colleen? Jason wanted to see her and hold her for as long as it took to convince her—and himself—that, yes, there was some sense to it all, that beauty would prevail in the end. But would it? And would the view of stark brutality, the awakening to a new reality, break her spirit and render her forever fearful of a world too cruel to abide? Still, as much as he wanted to speak with her, he knew he couldn't. Responsibility demanded that he leave her alone, forget her. There was nothing to do but walk.

Walk along the long battery wall of this war-weary city, walk away the doubts and insecurities, walk until he came upon the darkening docks and glanced out toward sea to watch the arrival of a ship. At first he thought it might be one of the two vessels owned by the proud Paxton consortium. But instead he made out the Somerset coat of arms. It was the *Bountiful,* whose longboats, Jason could now see, were delivering a shipment of black human flesh. In from Africa by way of New Orleans, the huddled men and women, for all the wonder in their eyes, seemed of great nobility to Jason. As the first of many boats neared shore, he couldn't help but speculate whether one man in particular, of wide nose and high cheekbones, was not a prince among his people. Yet his hands and legs were chained, his chest and back scarred with the marks of a brutal whip. Who knew of the culture of these people, their religion or language? Who cared? The absurdity, the inhumanity, the horror of it all! And that woman—climbing from the boat, in chains like the others, yet unlike them, for her flesh was shiny and scrubbed, not encrusted with filth like her fellow prisoners; her long neck so thin and supple, her hands so delicate—who was to say that she was not a queen? And why, on a slave ship, had she been kept in such a delicate condition? And what was this? The captain of the ship was approaching the woman, setting her free from her chains and bringing her over to an admiring Buckley Somerset.

Jason strained to hear the conversation, but he was too far from the two men.

"Here she is, Mr. Somerset," said the amicable, hook-nosed captain. "Just as I promised you, sir. Pick of the lot. She was one of the tribal chieftain's wives, and the prettiest of them all. I'd say even prettier than that beauty I brought you last summer. You can see that we've fed and bathed her. Even splashed on a bit of perfume. I know you like them to smell sweet. Can't say that I blame you."

Buckley, regally attired in dark velvet, looked her over lasciviously as if she were a side of beef. The captain did indeed know his taste. Her long limbs and thrusting breasts were much to his liking. It was delightful, he thought to himself, how he could have any woman of his choosing. Women were brought to him from around the world, and yet he couldn't forget that damned doctor's daughter. Why couldn't he lose this obsession for Colleen? Why couldn't he strike her from his mind? Was it because she had refused his every advance. No matter, he decided, he'd lose the image of that cold-hearted damsel by treating himself to this luscious, dark-skinned beauty.

Generously tipping the captain and thanking him for his courtesy, Somerset led the young woman, shoeless and frightened, to his carriage, parked inconspicuously inside a narrow alley, shoving her inside and then following, pushing closed the curtains.

Seeing all this, Jason was incensed at more than the fact that Somerset was indulging his lust at the expense of a human being who had been torn from her home, thrown in the bowels of a boat, and shipped halfway around the world in order to pick cotton and so enrich an already rich man. He felt sickened by the very greed and cruelty of mankind. Without thinking, he ran to the carriage, responding to the cries of the African woman, and, with full force, slapped the rears of Somerset's team of steeds. The horses bolted, charging off wildly, blindly,

with a dazed Buckley cursing and flinging open the door to
see what had happened. Jason had ducked out of sight, though
he could see that Somerset's fancy breeches were at his ankles,
his swollen member shrinking fast.

Three weeks after Kramer's hanging, Rianne sat in the privacy of her bedroom as night fell upon the troubled city. De-
signing a flamboyant costume on a pad placed upon a small,
delicate table facing a window overlooking the courtyard, she
found concentration impossible. Her mind went back over the
past twenty-one days. For all her worldliness and bold demeanor, she was deeply disturbed and concerned for her niece's
welfare.

She remembered the awful morning. Having heard from a
neighbor of Kramer's hanging, she assumed immediately that
her niece, too, had been imprisoned, and until Colleen arrived
home that afternoon in a state of emotional collapse, she was
closer to panic than at any point in her life. She considered
going to the Old Customs Exchange, yet that very act could
be seen as incriminating. She saw no choice but to stay home
and wait. And, oh, the relief she felt as Colleen finally walked
through the door! Her peace of mind, though, was frightfully
short-lived; the fact remained that the officials were searching
for Kramer's collaborators. Were they on Colleen's trail? Had
someone spotted her at Kramer's house? And which neighbors
could and could not be trusted? Rianne felt responsible. She
knew that it was largely her influence that had pushed Colleen
into action. Never had she guessed that events could take such
a wicked turn. Just as painful was the emotional condition of
her ailing niece.

Colleen's eyes revealed the fact that she had looked death
in the face, and not recovered from the sight. She was sick.
She slept for hours on end, late into the morning and often into
early afternoon. She couldn't face the day with its bright summer sunshine and blue sky, the same conditions under which
Kramer had been hanged. She blamed herself for his murder.
She couldn't forget that it was she who had convinced him to
print her propaganda. His face, his open eyes, his lifeless head
fallen upon his right shoulder—the image haunted her awake
and asleep. Where once she felt the energy of hope, she now
felt only despair.

There were moments when she conjured forth the old images

of bravery. She tried to read Thomas Paine and think of Nathan Hale, but they seemed heroic figures from another lifetime. She had lost touch with the woman who had responded so passionately to those men's courage. Oh, to regain that faith! But faith, like her love for Jason Paxton, had come to seem almost childish to her. She had seen what the world was really like. Poor Ephraim, kind Ephraim, gentle Ephraim, publicly humiliated, brought to his knees, made to suffer and die on her account.

The thrice-daily rap on her door never failed to startle Colleen. Her first thought was that the soldiers had come to arrest her. Someone, a neighbor of Kramer's, had turned her in. Her breath shortened, her heartbeat quickened, only to have her aunt's firm voice assure her that she'd brought a tray of nourishing food. Colleen ate very little, and her loss of weight was apparent. She hadn't been out of the house since the morning of the hanging. Her coloring had transformed from vibrant tan to pale white. Every day Rianne considered removing her niece forceably from the bed, sending her home, or making her work. She understood, though, that Colleen's anguish was deep, and it would take time for the wounds to heal. Not indulgent by nature, the aunt nonetheless found herself mothering this motherless, guilt-ridden child—at least for the time being.

Leaving her thoughts behind, Rianne put down her design— it was useless trying to work—and walked slowly to Colleen's room. She rapped gently on the door. "May I come in?"

"Please," replied a frail and faraway voice.

Colleen was still in her nightgown. Rianne began to protest, but reminded herself to be patient before she spoke. "I hope you remember that by this time tomorrow, your father will be here. We've exchanged any number of letters. I've tried to put him off, but he'll wait no longer. He's coming to bring you home, Colleen."

"No, no . . . I can't go back . . . I can't leave!" Colleen cried.

"I myself prefer that you stay. But it's conceivable that you'll be better off in Brandborough."

"I can't be with my father. He can't—he won't—understand. No one understands except you. Don't you see? If I leave this house, I'll be followed. They probably already know, and they're just waiting."

"No one knows anything. If they did, they'd be here already."

"No matter what, I have to stay with you. I must! I'm . . . I'm . . ."

"I'll do what I can, child, but you, too, must find the fortitude to speak to my brother rationally and with composure. If he sees you in this condition, he'll take you home, no matter how forceful my pleas. I'll say that you've suffered from a slight flux. That will explain your loss of coloring. Beyond that, though, you must present yourself as normally as possible."

Some twenty-four hours later, Dr. Roy McClagan stood at Rianne's door wearing a thin, battered cloak and tired expression. His salt-and-pepper whiskers were unkempt, and he appeared even more stooped than usual. His straight-backed sister, taller than he, bent down to kiss him on both cheeks.

"Where's my Colleen?" he asked.

"Where she usually is, dear brother. In her room reading. You've raised quite a scholar. Night and day she pores over the classics."

"The classics, or the seditious tripe of which you're so fond."

"Perish the thought! It's Ovid and Virgil, Dante and the mighty Milton. I tell you, I can't get her out of the house. She's devoted herself to the study of fine literature and lofty poesy. I know you're proud of her, Roy."

"She's a smart lass, she is."

"And she's missed you."

"And I her," he said, sinking into a wing-backed armchair in Rianne's parlor. " 'Tis lonely without her. I've come to bring her home."

Rianne didn't protest—at least not for the time being. All things considered, she felt that going home would only exacerbate her niece's ailment. Eventually—and soon—Colleen needed to be brought back out into the light of reality. The isolated farm would only deepen her retreat. And with every passing day, Rianne was convinced that Colleen's involvement had not, and would not, be disclosed.

That evening Colleen appeared for dinner, and Rianne was relieved to see how hard her niece worked to create a semblance of normality. She nearly succeeded. She treated her father affectionately and tried her best to satisfy his inquiries. Yes, she had been reading a great deal, studying her Latin and Greek;

yes, she had learned to appreciate the ancient poets as never before; and no, she wasn't getting out much. She was over her mild flux and felt fine. She was simply enjoying a period of quiet reflection.

Her father knew that something was wrong, but couldn't quite identify the ailment. Her speech was lifeless and her dimpled cheeks drained of their glow. She smiled hardly at all. Where was her old energy and spark?

"Well, then," he finally said to her while sipping on his after-dinner port, "you'll be packed and ready to leave on the morrow."

Colleen's eyes darted toward Rianne, looking for hope. "'Tis something your father and I will discuss tonight," Rianne assured her. "You look tired. I think a wee bit extra sleep might do you good."

When she was gone, Roy lit his pipe and turned to his sister. "What's wrong with my child?" he asked with genuine concern. "She acts as if there's been a death in the family."

"She's matured. Charleston has matured her. That's why she must stay."

"Out of the question."

"'Tis her preference."

"No doubt to see young Paxton."

"On the contrary. I'm the only one who sees him. Weeks ago he gave a recital for Major Embleton."

"Glad to hear it. But she leaves with me in the morning nonetheless."

"The riders who ruthlessly raid the countryside do not give you pause for thought?"

"We've not been bothered by them in Brandborough."

"Which doesn't mean the danger's any less."

"I'll run the risk. Has she packed her trunk?"

"Then I'll simply have to tell Buckley Somerset to change the arrangements," Rianne announced, ignoring her brother's question and feeling pleased with herself for having improvised this fabrication. While it was true that Somerset had sent messages and had come to the house at least a half dozen times, Colleen had consistently refused to see him.

"What arrangements?" asked the doctor.

"To escort her to the costume ball at Somerset Hall here in Charleston at the end of August. He so had his heart set upon taking Colleen that I naturally insisted that she accept."

"Has she?"

"She most certainly will."

"And so Buckley can fetch her at Brandborough."

"'Tis an impossibly long way to travel for a ball, and I doubt if he'll agree. The lad's here for the remainder of the summer, tending to family business. He was most pleased to learn that Colleen will be staying. He seems to enjoy visiting her often."

"If my daughter isn't pulling me in one direction, you're pushing me in another. Something's amiss, Rianne, and methinks you're to blame."

"Physicians, gentle brother, can be such fools. You look for maladies where none exists. For the next five weeks I shall be preoccupied with the design and creation of dozens of costumes. 'Tis a nearly impossible task, and in addition to enjoying my dear niece's company, I dare say I could also use her invaluable assistance."

"You've taught her to sew?" Roy was surprised.

"There's nothing, absolutely nothing," Rianne assured him as she straightened her wig, "that a McClagan woman cannot do."

～ *Chapter 4* ～

Taking a break from his afternoon work at the pianoforte, Jason entered the Roaring Lion, a popular coffeehouse filled with men engrossed in intense conversation. He knew that the patrons were rebels—this was a well-known gathering place—and as much as he wanted to share his thoughts with them, enjoy their camaraderie and shed his mask as a loner, he said nothing. He sat by himself and looked around the room, thick with smoke. The walls consisted of bare, worn bricks, and the floor was covered with sawdust. At the table next to his, Jason overheard the whispers of two men deep in a dialogue they both seemed to relish.

"I'm willing to wage that he'll strike again by week's end," said the first man, whose broad, bald head seemed connected to his shoulders by a series of ever-widening chins. "He'll go after that supply post outside Bentfork; I'd bet my mother's soul on it."

"Would be far too rash an act," disagreed his companion, who spoke through a rugged toothless grin. "The Wisp's too smart for that. He knows they'll be waiting for him at Bentfork. No, I think he's gone back to the swamps. Biding his time, he is, waiting for the moment when the moon's high and the guards are down."

Jason was amused and pleased that his actions had stirred such passionate interest. For a moment, he was able to take

his mind off his new composition, which, in spite of his best
efforts, was going slowly. There were certain sounds he was
trying to incorporate into formal musical structures, as unorthodox as they might have seemed—the sound of hoofbeats,
a horse galloping across the marshes, the incessant buzz of the
Carolina cicada—sounds he associated with his midnight rides,
the most recent of which saw him intercepting a secret transport
of military weapons from Brandborough to Charleston after
seeing a letter regarding the shipment on Embleton's desk during one of his visits to the major.

Dividing his life in half was not conducive to productive
creative work. Composing by day and raiding by night was a
bit of madness he found hard to accept. Yet he couldn't stop.
For a week after the execution of Ephraim Kramer, he had
eased off and even considered retiring his disguise, the costume
of Hamlet's ghost that he had borrowed from Piero—the deep
gray breeches and blousy shirt, the gray cloak and mask that
covered his head. He had almost been swayed by the pleadings
of his patrons—the only people aware of his dual identity. For
them, it wasn't a matter of politics. They argued solely out of
concern for their friend's welfare. They feared his capture and
execution, and yet when he rode off at dark, they said not a
word. Instead, they stayed up all night, unable to sleep until
they heard the sound of Cinder returning to the carriage house.

Seated in the Roaring Lion, Jason also thought of Colleen.
She had never left his consciousness, day or night, whether he
sat at the harpsichord or rode through the swamps. Once he
had stopped by Rianne's to ask after her well-being, and to see
whether she was still in Charleston. The seamstress had said
yes, she was there, but he could tell by the look in Rianne's
eyes that all was not well. Assuming that Colleen's frightened
guilt had deepened, he didn't bother to ask to see her. He knew
she'd refuse, and, besides, he was determined to keep his vow
to romantically disentangle himself from her. None of that,
though, could speak for the longing in his heart. Only music
could convey such feelings, and yet reaching her with music
was impossible. He thought of her fiery spirit, and then the
fearful look in her eyes in King's Park. Would that he could
cross the barrier and carry her back, back to his secret ravine,
away from Charleston, even America, back with him to faraway
Parma or the palazzi of ancient Venice.

Daydreams! Fantasies! He ordered coffee and sighed. His

eyes burned from the smoke. He felt isolated and alone. Oh, how he longed to share his thoughts with an understanding soul! He glanced out the front window and studied the people passing by: a beggar; another group of chained slaves; fishermen; farmers; merchants; a steady stream of humanity passing through this crowded city . . . and then Peter Tregoning.

"Peter!" Jason ran from his table out to the street, where he hugged the soldier, in full view of the Roaring Lion's curious patrons. A great outpouring of emotion on the part of both men was instantaneous, and yet when the embrace ended, the musician and captain were left with an extraordinarily strained feeling. Their lives were bound up in secrets far too intimate and dangerous to exchange.

Could Jason dare mention that which troubled him most—Kramer's hanging, Colleen's disturbance, his veiled double identity? It was unthinkable. And as much as Peter had come to appreciate Jason's sympathetic ear, as often as he had confided in the American while the two lived in London, he, too, couldn't possibly divulge matters of his secret heart. The massacre at Waxhaws and his growing love for Joy Exceeding were not issues that he felt free even to mention. The conflicts and contradictions in both men's characters made them painfully wary of each other. They had never known a time in their lives when they needed a friend more, and yet that friendship, a source of such satisfaction for the past four years, choked on the words that neither of them could utter.

"Will you be in Charleston long, Peter?" Jason asked.

"I'm not prepared to disclose the secret plans of my superiors," he replied, using jest to cover his discomfort. "You jolly well know that the military mind is as fickle as a woman's, and there's no telling where they'll push me next. 'Tis rather like a chess game, isn't it? We're no more than mere pawns."

"I'm very glad you're well, Peter," Jason said, sensing the pain beneath his friend's inscrutable demeanor. "You're looking fit."

"And you seem to have developed bags under your eyes, old boy. If I didn't know you so well, I'd assume that the local ladies have been tiring you out."

"It's my music."

"Please, spare me that same lame excuse. I heard enough of it in London. Isn't your Miss McClagan about? I didn't see her when you played for Major Embleton."

"I haven't seen her myself. I've been concentrating on composing."

"To the exclusion of all else?"

"I'm afraid so."

"And what, may I ask, are you working on?"

"A suite in a somewhat experimental vein."

"I presume this is going to be the startlingly original American music of which you often spoke."

"It will certainly be startling."

"And when can I look forward to hearing you perform this masterpiece?"

"Upon completion, I assure you."

"That is, if the rival factions in this bedeviled colony don't decide to use your harpsichord for firewood."

"Things surely aren't that bad, are they?" Jason tried to sound nonchalant.

"I'm afraid it's getting a bit uncivilized around here."

The chitchat continued for several minutes more, with both men realizing the ways in which they were skirting the real issues between them. In spite of this, they couldn't help but feel the genuine and strong affection they held for one another. They promised to meet again soon, though neither specified how that would be accomplished.

"It was good seeing you, chap," said Peter.

"Take care, my friend," Jason replied.

Feeling profoundly frustrated and unsatisfied by the encounter, Jason watched Peter walk stiffly out of view. Sighing, the musician turned back and reentered the Roaring Lion, only to be pelted in the face by a raw egg. The impact stung him, and as the dripping yolk stuck to his eyes and eyelids, he couldn't possibly see who had thrown it. He heard only a roar of laughter followed by a rousing chorus of the "Liberty Song." The sound of Colleen's own lyrics ringing in his ears along with the profanities of the rebel patrons who had witnessed his friendly meeting with an English officer filled him with deep despondency. He was enraged and humiliated. Yet whom could he charge? Whom could he fight? He swallowed his fury and left, walking a short block to the river, where he soaked his face clean. He knew he needed to get out of the city.

Without explaining to Robin or Piero what had happened, he changed clothes quickly and saddled up Cinder. He had no plans, wore no disguise, and rode off into the late-afternoon light without a thought of where he might be going or why. He carried papers given to him by Embleton himself—identifying him as an artist with privileges to move freely around the colony—and thus the sentries guarding the roads leading outside Charleston let him pass. The countryside seemed to call to him, as it did so often, as a friend who asked no questions and made no demands.

Enchanting stretches of wilderness awaited him. Aging willow trees shaded his face from the sun, and wept for him. Faster and faster he rode his steady steed, wishing that the wind in his face and the fragrance of the land could clear his throbbing head. For all the blinding speed with which he raced across the landscape, there was no escaping the terrible ache in his heart. He was tired of being despised, despised by his father and his sister, despised by the woman he loved, despised by the very compatriots he strove to aid. Yet there was no way out. His plan had been perfect, had indeed worked wonders, with even greater potential ahead. To continue, though, meant further misunderstanding and required a depth of unrewarded courage that Jason wasn't sure he possessed. He wanted to quit, resign from the whole bloody business of living. Never before had he felt so depressed, and the very fact that he fell into such reveries filled him with remorse. What was happening to him? What was this God-awful war doing to him and everyone he loved so dearly?

Riding through groves of trees and patches of swamp, Jason passed through a section of one of the Somerset plantations. The sight of slaves bent over in the vast fields of cotton did little to lift his sagging spirit, though the song they sang stopped him in his tracks. He climbed off Cinder and, standing under a solitary cypress at the edge of the field, listened. One worker in particular caught his eye and ear.

A man well into his seventies picked but a few yards from Jason. His hair was dove white, puffy bags sagged beneath his eyes, and his large hands were callused and swollen. His spirit, however, was undeniably happy. His hypnotic baritone voice was soothing, rich, and honey-soaked. He sang of despair, but also of joy. There was no doubting the message of his song: his troubles would be transcended, there'd come a better, brighter day, a more loving way, a time when man and his God would be joined as one, forever, glory hallelujah! And despite the tedium of his work and the abjectness of his condition, his golden voice was filled with hope, so much so that Jason felt his eyes swell with tears. His heart was touched, his soul stirred. This, he understood, was the miracle of music, the strength of the human spirit: despite everything, beauty would survive—if man sought it, if man sang it.

"I see my message reached you, Paxton," Major Randall Embleton announced the next morning in his office. "Decent of you to drop by. Care for a spot of tea? I'll have my aide fetch you a cup."

"Thank you kindly, Major," Jason said, curious to learn why he had been summoned to Embleton's massive, messy office in the Old Customs Exchange. He wasn't really concerned that the English official might suspect him, though naturally he was on guard. He welcomed this new opportunity to look over the papers, maps, and plans that were invariably scattered about.

"Care to drop in on your brother-in-law, Paxton?"

"I think not. I'm afraid a visit from me is of little comfort to him."

"So I assumed, but I was hoping nonetheless that you'd encourage him to behave. Because he's a relation of yours, I've gone out of my way to tolerate the bloke. But he's becoming more and more difficult. My men say he's a swift pain, practically daring us to flog him. Well, we'll flog him all right. We'll do a lot worse than that if he doesn't behave. Why can't he and the other obstinate rebels understand that the more they curse, the more I'll see them bleed? I'd have thought that the elimination of the old printer would have demonstrated something. Well, at least we haven't heard a chirp from the Sandpiper since Kramer was hanged. I'm pleased to say that I've put those half-literate broadsides to a stop."

Jason suppressed an angry response and welcomed the arrival of Embleton's aide with a tray of tea as an opportunity to change the subject. He understood that his brother-in-law's life was threatened, and yet the one way to save him—to free him from prison—was something he hadn't yet devised.

Benson left quickly, and the major, his large stomach protruding in rolls from the tight waistband of his uniform, dropped the subject of Allan Coleridge with a final comment. "It's clear," he said to Jason, "that you've as little interest in that ruffian's welfare as I."

Content to allow the matter to rest there, Jason veered the

conversation toward military history. Playing to the major's vanity, Jason encouraged Embleton to demonstrate his familiarity with the great battles of the Middle Ages. His long, self-satisfied monologue, accompanied by his usual practice of pontificating while parading back and forth, gave his guest ample opportunity to scan the office. Ten minutes later, it took a loud rap at the door to interrupt him.

"Enter," he ordered.

Buckley Somerset, a scarlet-plumed hat upon his periwigged head, his hand on his hip, stood in the doorway with a sly smile on his face. Oddly enough, his waistcoat, vest, and trousers were covered with a fine film of dust, and even more peculiar, he smelled of smoke.

He was surprised to see Paxton, yet ignored him. Nothing could spoil the good news he had come to report to Embleton. "You'll be pleased to learn, Major, that the Bronson farm has been burned to the ground."

"Splendid!" exclaimed the Englishman. "You saved us the trouble."

"A group of my own men, organized and led by me, attacked only a few hours ago. We found that the damned rebel farmer had been hiding grain and livestock marked for requisiton. We took possession of the cattle and grain and transported it to one of our plantations just north of the city. We await your further orders, Major."

"A job well done, Somerset. You local gents have a feeling for who's hiding what around here. You're to be commended. Of course you know young Paxton."

"The tunesmith?" He laughed, instinctively touching the bridge of his nose. "Yes, I've known him since he was a young schoolboy tripping over his own gawky legs."

"Well, I'm glad you're both here," said Embleton, "because you're precisely the two men I've been considering for a critical post I've decided to create. Commander of the Continental Tory Militia—that's what I shall call it. A brigade of rough-and-ready men to supplement our efforts in the Brandborough and Charleston areas, and beyond. What do you say to the idea?"

"Bloody good," Buckley blurted out, "but why you'd consider the harpsichordist here is beyond me. I'm not certain he knows the difference between a musket and a baton."

"Indeed he does." Embleton rose to Jason's defense. "We've had long discussions on military matters, and the gentleman is as well versed as anyone I've encountered in the colonies. He knows his weapons as well as his symphonies, and, what's more, he has the respect of the region's most prominent Tories."

"Begging to differ with you, Major," argued Somerset, "but those very people, my dear colleagues, barely know who he is."

Alarmed by the conversation, Jason felt obliged to speak, addressing his remarks to Embleton. "I'm flattered by the consideration, but honesty requires that I represent myself as a musician, not a soldier."

"Nonsense, Paxton," Embleton retorted. "There's no sweeter music you could make than the patter of patriotic rabble being put to flight. You're very much in the running, lad. I shall take but a few weeks to make my decision," he said, looking back and forth between the two men and obviously savoring the competition he was provoking between them. "I'll announce the appointment at the costume ball, which your grandparents, Somerset, are so graciously hosting."

"I'm afraid," Jason was quick to add, his mind plotting schemes, "that I've not been invited to the gala."

"Oh, nonsense," Embleton insisted. "An obvious oversight on Somerset's part. Am I right?"

Buckley hesitated for a second, saw there was nothing he could do, and said, "Why, certainly he's welcome to attend. If one of the flautists falls ill, Paxton could be especially valuable."

"Yes, yes," said the major, dabbing at his lips with a silk kerchief. "Now you two run off. I've a full day ahead. Our prisons are overflowing with rebel scum who grow more unruly each day. They and the beastly heat make the colonies intolerable this time of year. Oh, to be back in London and the seat of civilization! Good day, good day."

Outside, in front of the gates of Old Customs Exchange, Jason and Buckley stood together for a brief moment.

"I warn you," Somerset said, jabbing his finger into Paxton's chest, "stay away from her at the ball."

"Stay away from whom?"

"Colleen McClagan. She'll be attending with me—at her own request, I might add, and she'd not appreciate any distractions from the likes of you."

"I wouldn't think of it. I respect your privacy far too much to interfere with any private matters you might be negotiating.

Though the other day you seemed to be having a bit of trouble with your newest paramour—what with your carriage running wild. I'd have sworn you'd lost your breeches, just as you lost your purse at the picnic. Do take better care of yourself, Buckley," Jason said before bidding good-bye to a flabbergasted and infuriated Somerset.

Chapter 5

"You'll not tarry in this room another moment," Rianne insisted
as Colleen turned from her reverie at the window, her movements slow and weighted with self-pity. "Now mark me well,
Colleen McClagan," said Rianne. "I've coddled and cradled
you long enough. It's been a month since you've closed yourself
up in my house, pouting about and feeling sorry for yourself.
I'll have no more of it. I thought I was helping by letting you
be, but now I see that my lenient attitude has allowed you to
fall into a dangerous state of melancholy. Melancholy is understandable. 'Tis part of the lives we must lead, but you've
gone too far. You're indulging yourself in melancholy much
as the obese man indulges himself in sweetbread. Such indul-
gences lead to sloth, surrender, and, even worse, early death.
If you prefer not to live, have the courtesy to extinguish yourself
quickly. But please do not drag out the ordeal in this perfectly
lovely bedroom. Do you hear me? Is my meaning clear?"

"I know you mean well, dear Auntie, but . . ."

"Save your drooling affection for another day. I'm not interested in sentiment now, Colleen, I'm interested in work.
There's but one decent remedy for melancholy, and that's forth-
right, diligent, God-fearing work. Will you work now, woman,
or not?"

"I . . . I . . ."

"Good. You've made the right choice. You'll select your

outfit for the day, and then you'll walk downstairs, where you'll assist me, beginning now. There are costumes to make, dozens of costumes, and none more important than the one that you'll be wearing. I have every clever seamstress in Charleston due here within the hour, and I'll not have them find you in this state."

"Costumes? For what purpose?"

"For the purpose of not attending the Somerset costume ball in a state of undress."

"Oh, that. I completely put it out of my mind."

"Well, put it back in, because you're going," Rianne said as she helped her niece out of her nightgown and into her undergarments. "And Buckley Somerset is to be your escort."

"You're jesting."

"Not in the least."

"I refuse."

"You can't. You're the one who requested that he be your gentleman for the evening."

"How is it possible?"

"Through Rianne McClagan, all things are possible. I made the request in your name."

"You're no better than my father."

"You'll find that I'm a good deal worse. I consider myself far more ingenious."

"And if I refuse to go?" Colleen asked with a sign of the old defiant spirit in her voice.

"Then you'll be sent home."

"Why? Why are you doing this to me?"

"Somerset was a convenient ploy to convince my brother to leave you here, a ploy, I'd dare say, with which you yourself are most familiar."

"It'll be horrid."

"It'll be a splendid evening. The Somerset Ball is the event of the season."

"They're the most sinister Tories in South Carolina, and you know it."

"Indeed I do. But what you don't know is for that one evening identities will be so confused as to render the line between Loyalist and Patriot most insignificant. You'll be surprised just who will attend. Even I will be going. Some of my wealthier patrons have secured an invitation for me. They want me there in the event that their costumes require repair during the evening. But come, finish dressing. There's work to be done. I'm satisfied to see you agitated. By week's end, I intend to agitate you a great deal more."

Week's end came quickly for Colleen. The shop was bustling as her aunt overwhelmed her and the other six seamstresses with work. Rianne eliminated all discussions of worldly and metaphysical matters. Customers, among those the city's most prominent citizens, came in to check on the progress of their costumes, and, for each, Rianne had a kind and comforting word. At the same time, she let the client know firmly that she'd appreciate not being bothered again, and that, without further interference, the deadline would be met.

"Aside from the Christmas season, the Somerset Ball provides me with the year's largest income," she told her niece one night after the other ladies had left. Aunt and niece sat at a large worktable, Rianne sewing furiously, while Colleen, like the assistant to a surgeon, passed her needles and threads, buttons and bows. Rianne was careful to involve Colleen in certain aesthetic decisions involving color, fabric, and design, but when her niece complained that she was tired and wanted to rest in her room, the older woman flatly refused. "You're to stay here and work," she insisted.

Rianne knew what she was doing. While Colleen's melancholy did not fade immediately, her energy began to surge slowly. She responded to the challenge—the dozens of small tasks, the fact that she was accomplishing something, albeit stitching a collar to a dress. The nightmare was not yet over. Her mind was still plagued by her responsibility for Ephraim Kramer's death, but her aunt's demands dominated her days. She had no choice but to chase after a bolt of blue cotton or a piece of lace. The bustle of the busy shop had a not unpleasant rhythm. "Hurry!" Rianne demanded, working with the speed of a rabbit and the tenacity of a beaver. "And when you've found the fabric, you'd do well to make us all a bit of lunch. We'll eat right here at the table. No time for dallying, not now."

Thus went the daily routine. They awoke at daybreak, worked with the hired helpers all morning, all afternoon, and, when alone for the night, by lantern and candlelight, they labored on. Rianne made a list of the various costumes and posted it on the wall so everyone could see what progress had been made, and the amount of work still to be done. No doubt, there was drudgery to the tasks, especially since Colleen's contributions were essentially secondary. There was also a distinctly creative side to the activity that awakened her dormant imagination. The costumes themselves were marvels of invention as they hung around the shop in various stages of completion—the shepherdess outfit, the Renaissance courtier, Neptune and Nero, mermaids and barmaids, and soldiers of fortune. No matter how great her desire to retreat to the bedroom, Colleen couldn't help but imagine the effect the outlandish costumes would have on the partygoers. Little by little, in spite of Buckley Somerset, she found herself anticipating the evening with a degree of pleasure. For the first time in over a month, she was actually looking forward to something, and that, Rianne noted with satisfaction, was progress.

Considering everything, all work was going well until late one Friday afternoon when Colleen happened to glance out the window and caught a glimpse of Jason driving by inside a carriage with Piero and Robin. She thought of waving, of running from the house to stop the carriage so that she might speak with him. Instead, she did nothing. She'd sworn not to see him, not even to think of him. But think of him she did. For the remainder of the afternoon and late into the night, she dreamed of his gentle fingers and sleepy eyes and the fugue they had played together, she and he, outside of time, deep in the recesses of a green ravine known only to them.

Ethan Edward Paxton blew out the candle and closed his eyes. He had broken a promise made to himself years ago. He had just reread the letters written to him by his deceased wife when they were still courting. So many decades ago. Why, of all times, had he chosen now to relive those memories? What a foolish act! What sentimentality!

As he struggled toward sleep, he wondered why he had changed his mind. Why hadn't he visited the widow Jarvis? God bless that woman, always so willing and anxious to take him in. Her generous bosom and warm, wide thighs had satisfied him on many a cold and lonely night. Her carnal appetite was nearly as large as Ethan's, just as her demands were small—a bit of affection and a few words of appreciation for the hot apple pie she never failed to bake him. Why, then, hadn't he seen her in so long? Why hadn't he ridden to her place that very evening and comforted himself with simple physical pleasure? Perhaps it was because she was too simple, or because having once known the meaning of love, it was difficult for Ethan to settle for less. His wife had the soul of a poet, the sensibility of a true artist. In that way, Ethan had to admit, she was very much her son's mother. Her son, he thought, her lost son, giving recitals for the conquering generals, aiding and abetting his fiercest foes.

Ethan turned on his side, and still sleep wouldn't come. Where was Joy? Why hadn't she returned from Charleston? When would Allan be released? And would the Paxton business ever recover from the grueling hardships imposed by this war? Production was down by a third, and another quarter of their agricultural output had been requisitioned by the greedy British. The Paxton ships had been out of service for months. Rather than acquiesce to the Crown's choking taxes and and trade restrictions, Ethan had decided to dock his vessels and wait until he could operate when and how he damned well pleased— which wouldn't be until the scoundrels were sent a-swimming back to London. Soon, Ethan decided, no matter how great the odds, no matter how strong their hold on the South, it would happen soon. And as far as sentiment went—his wife's old love letters and his son's sweet sonatas—the hell with it all! There was work to do and a war to be won. The dead and deserters were to be forgotten. Half enraged, half heartbroken, Ethan Paxton finally fell into a shallow, uneasy sleep.

Downstairs and out back, on a ridge overlooking the moonlit grounds behind the Paxton home, Joy Exceeding and Captain Peter Tregoning shared a hammock that rocked silently between two sturdy trees of aging oak. The summer night smelled of flowers as they lay side by side, whispering so that the sound of their voices blended with the croaking cicadas. From time to time, their mouths would meet. Their flesh perspired as desire inflamed their bodies and quickened their breath.

"We mustn't," Joy insisted.

"He doesn't know you're home yet," replied the red-haired soldier.

"I must tell him."

"He's already asleep. Wait till morning," he urged, watching the moonbeams play with the wondrous curls of Joy's long chestnut-colored hair.

"And where will you stay?"

"With you, my love . . . here in the hammock, there on the ground . . . please . . ." he entreated as he looked into her softly sloped green eyes.

"'Tis all in vain, Peter. You promised if you saw me home, you'd turn right around. You're needed back in Charleston."

"I created an excuse, a job to be done in Brandborough."

"Please, Father can't know. Jason's been enough for him to contend with."

"And yet," Peter reflected, "there seems more to your brother than meets the eye."

"What do you mean by that?"

"Only that his heart belies his actions."

"He's not a Tory, is he?"

"Oh, God, no. We practically lived together in London, and if it's one thing I'm able to judge keenly, it's a man's political character. No, your brother's no follower of the Crown."

"I've always known that. I could read his heart when I was with him yesterday. I've tried to convince Father and Hope of his patriotism, but to no avail."

"Perhaps Jason wants it that way."

"But why?" asked Joy.

"I'm not certain. With Jason Paxton, one can't be certain of anything."

"All this confusion, Peter. Are you really certain that you want to keep seeing me?"

"Certain beyond reason, sweet Joy," he whispered as he kissed her ear, her mouth, and her throat, pulling her blouse below her shoulders, and lower yet, bathing her hardening nipples with kisses, pulling her to him, easing her from the hammock to the damp earth. There, hidden behind a grove of high, dense bushes, she surrendered to his ardent yearning, his probing fingers, his swollen passion. Slowly but surely, he drew moisture from the heart of her desire as he tasted the soft, smooth skin of her thighs with the tip of his tongue, his open palms caressing the small of her back and the curve of her buttocks, as he pressed his hard need against her undulating loins, as he kissed the side of her neck, kissed her half-closed eyelids, as he followed the shape of her delicate breasts with his lips, whispering warm words of love in her ear while gently, sweetly, inch by precious inch, entering the deep ecstasy of Joy's most private and sensual chamber.

* * *

Ethan Paxton, dressed in coarse work pants, the muscles in his arms bulging against his snug, half-sleeved cotton shirt, his eyes bloodshot from a night of restless, troubled sleep, listened to his daughter with suspicion as they sat at the breakfast table. Sometime during the night she had arrived, escorted by an unknown and elderly merchant traveling all the way from Boston. A likely story.

"And the English soldier?" asked Ethan as he sipped his freshly brewed coffee, trying to contain his anger.

"What soldier is that, Father?" she asked, sensing the controlled rage in her father's voice, which alarmed and frightened her.

"Please, don't play games with me. You know precisely which soldier I mean—the one you took a fancy to at the picnic."

"Oh, *that* soldier. I think he's in Charleston."

"Think? Are you saying that you haven't seen him?"

"I'm saying that I think I need to bring you more coffee, Father—that and a sweet roll." Joy got up from the table and started for the kitchen.

"Stay where you are, young lady. I asked you a question, and I want an answer."

She froze in place. "I . . . I . . ."

"You've been seeing him. Isn't that the truth?"

"The truth . . ." She couldn't complete the sentence.

"The truth is that I must have done something gravely wrong in bringing up you and your brother," said Ethan, feeling as if the world were crumbling around him. "Neither of you have a modicum of pride for our family or our family's independence. First Jase went over to the other side, now you. Deserters both."

"You're wrong," Joy answered, her voice trembling with emotion. "We have pride, great pride. You've taught us that, Father, and we love and respect you with all our heart. It's only that . . ."

"You don't understand the meaning of respect." Ethan cut her off, his anger building. "If you did, you'd tell that English dog to go back where he came from."

"Dog? Why, he's the most perfect gentleman . . ."

"Then you do admit to seeing him."

"Am I not free to see whomever I please?"

"Not when your friend is pointing a musket to our heads. God gave you more sense than that."

"God gave me the sense to know a true friend when I see one."

"Damned impertinent daughter!" Ethan exploded, shouting and rising as he swept his coffee cup from the table. It smashed and splashed against the wall, and yet the noise of its break paled in comparison to Ethan's shattering voice. "If you're to whore for the British, at least get them to pay you well!" His eyes flashed with fury as he pointed his finger directly at his daughter's quivering lower lip. "Go back to Charleston. I'm in no need of you here. Hurry and perhaps you can catch your soldier boy. I saw him riding away at daybreak. He'll not have gone far. He looked tired. The poor swine had obviously been laboring all night."

Sobbing, Joy ran from the room.

Chapter 6

There were three great Somerset plantations in South Carolina—the one run by Buckley himself in Brandborough; the one overseen by his father and mother, Marble Manor, halfway between Brandborough and Charleston; and the grandest of all, the most splendid in the colony, or, as some claimed, the entire South: Somerset Hall. Just a few miles away on the outskirts of the city, it was the immense estate on which Jason had paused to hear the song of an elderly slave. The slave population of Somerset Hall was, in fact, larger than in most Carolina villages.

At eighty-five years of age, Hugo still lived there with his wife, Paulina. Both invalids, they nonetheless made certain that their yearly masked costume ball, an event that had assumed legendary proportions among the region's aristocracy, was carried out with the same extravagance for which it had been known since its inception some five decades earlier.

That was the year, 1730, when Colonel Hugo had sworn that his new home would be the city's undisputable showplace and a monument to the glory of his name. A half century later, that distinction remained unchallenged. It wasn't merely the grandeur and serene beauty of the main house that so dazzled the eye; it was also the gardens, themselves a wondrous testimony to the human cultivation of nature.

The colonel had employed no less a figure than Michel Henri LeBlanc, Europe's leading landscape artist, to design the grounds. LeBlanc had accepted the commission only on the provision that he have fifty slaves at his disposal for three years, and Somerset had agreed. The result was breathtaking: a dozen terraces rose in subtle gradations before reaching a high plateau upon which a gushing fountain, an exact duplicate of the masterpiece sculpted by Giovanni Bernini in the Piazza Navonna in Rome, was serviced by two separate spring-water wells. From the third floor of the great house one could gaze down upon a system of butterfly lakes that appeared just as lovely and graceful as the winged creatures upon which they had been modeled. The three acres of formal gardens had the frozen elegance of Versailles. The lush grounds were bejeweled with a potpourri of exotic bushes—lime, strawberry, ginger blossom, and pomegranate—lining the walkways with thousands of exotic flowers that changed monthly. Every day for the past fifty years, a dozen slaves roamed this botanical marvel, removing fallen leaves and petals from the paths, maintaining the grounds in a meticulous and perpetual state of beauty.

The house itself had taken six years to build. More than six thousand tons of brick had been brought over from England. The work of the president of the Royal Academy of Architects, Sir Hanford Alexander, Somerset's was the first and only commission he had accepted in the colonies. For three years, at Hugo's expense, Alexander and his assistant lived at the Prince of Wales, Charleston's foremost inn. There he ate, drank, and drew renderings—all to great excess. Like a master chef scrutinizing the ingredients of a subtle soufflé, he personally selected each piece of hand-sawn lumber. While Alexander labored away at the inn, Colonel Somerset grew nervous. Whenever he'd visit the famed architect, the great-girthed gentleman would inevitably be at his desk in his room, red-nosed and slightly tipsy, a frothy mug of ale in hand and a buxom wench by his side. Somerset had been told that Sir Hanford was married to a distant niece of the king, a Teutonic iceberg of a woman not known for her great beauty. He understood that the architect was inclined to abuse his liberty in this far-off colony, but couldn't help worry that his house, like Sir Hanford's gait after a half dozen ales, might be lopsided.

The colonel's worries were unfounded. The house did not

tilt; it was a sturdy and magnificent structure. The main portico was supported by four Ionic columns of Tuscan stone. A juxtaposition of rose-shaped windows lent a delicate, dignified aura to the edifice, the pure white color of which was preserved by a yearly coat of fresh paint. The massive front door, sculpted of polished mahogany, opened to a wide oaken parquet hallway that ran three hundred fifty feet to the rear of the house. Everywhere one looked, one was dazzled by opulence—inlaid tables of black marble and gold, long silk drapes of burgundy red, sapphire blue and emerald green, huge English landscape paintings by William Hogarth and Joseph Highmore, and portraits of the Somerset family painted in the somber Dutch and Flemish schools of Jan Vermeer and Han van Meegeren.

To the east of the downstairs hallway was a drawing room, to the west a library and map room. Toward the rear, the dining room was large enough to accommodate a state dinner, and the furnishings, many carved by Thomas Chippendale and George Hepplewhite themselves, stood like stately pieces of sculpture. A mahogany-and-pine stairway led to the second floor, which contained, in addition to a half dozen drawing rooms, a grand ballroom in which the famous Waterford chandelier hung.

The enormous chandelier was created in two tiers, from each of which extended twelve solid cut-crystal arms. On each arm was a series of blown-glass figurines—fawns, foxes, blue jays, flamingoes—developed by Venetian craftsmen on the Adriatic island of Murano and shipped to Charleston over a period of two years. At the rear of the ballroom, a white-stoned balcony, as wide as the room itself, looked out on the vast gardens and hundreds of acres of Somerset land beyond.

For the past two weeks, the estate had been a whirlwind of activity as preparations for the masked ball gradually intensified. At last, with the Saturday sun setting and the musicians arriving, everyone, from old Colonel Hugo to the woman cleaning crystal in the kitchen, felt the tingling drama of this fabulous evening beginning to unfold.

"Would you please make certain my tail is in order?" Piero requested with something close to hysteria in his voice. "If it falls off, I'll be mortified."

"'Tis firmly in place," Robin replied as he gently pulled on the fabric to make certain it was secure.

"Where's Jason?"

"I expect him to be down directly. Be patient, Piero. The night promises to be long and trying. We must pace ourselves accordingly."

"I worry so much about the maestro, I can hardly sleep."

"Calm yourself. Jase can take care of himself. You remember, years ago, the way he beat back Buckley Somerset, right in front of our house. Jason plays sonatas with rare tenderness, there's no doubt, but our musician is also something of a tiger."

"He may be, but I'm not. I'm not at all certain I can go through with this scheme. I said I would, but now I'm not certain."

"If I was agreeable, I don't see how you can object."

"Because I'm the one directly involved, not you, *caro mio.*"

At that moment Jason Behan Paxton, dressed as a harlequin, complete with floppy, pointed hat, multicolored baggy pants, and painted face, bounded down the stairs. One look at his friends and he howled. Piero was dressed as a peacock, plumes and all, and Robin was outfitted as a portly yellow-flecked butterfly. The three costumes themselves, conceived and sewn by Robin, were ingeniously crafted, and yet the musician couldn't help but laugh.

"Begging your pardon, maestro," said Piero, "but I do think that for orginality and boldness of design, Robin will not be outdone."

"You're forgetting the handiwork of Rianne McClagan," replied Robin as the three men prepared to leave the house for the carriage. "There's no more compelling reason to attend the ball than to see what stimulating fantasies Rianne has conjured up this year."

Rianne lowered the black lace fan to reveal her face. She was dressed as a Spanish contessa in a flame-red gown, stiff lace collar, beaded stomacher, high mantilla, and matching red comb stuck in a wig two feet high, black and shiny as panther skin.

"Good evening, Mr. Somerset," Rianne said by way of greeting Buckley at her front door as she quickly inspected his buccaneer outfit—tight black breeches, full white shirt, silver-brocaded vest, black pumps with gold buckles, white bandanna around his forehead, cummerband-held rapier around his waist, and black velvet patch over his right eye.

"Good evening, Miss McClagan. You look enchanting. Is your niece about?" Buckley asked with his usual impatience.

"She's about to fall from exhaustion. I'm afraid I've over-worked her. Preparing costumes can be such a chore. Thank goodness that job is behind us." Rianne sighed, casting a glance toward the empty, silent workroom, which only a few hours before had been a hub of frantic activity in which eight women labored to meet the deadline. After weeks of strips and streams of colorful fabrics covering every inch of the place, the room had been transformed to its former condition, neat as a pin.

"I presume Colleen is dressed and prepared to leave with me straightaway," Buckley said, not in the least interested in hearing about the seamstress's work. "As a host, I'm expected to be there early."

"I'll fetch her myself," Rianne said, deciding that she shared her niece's low opinion of Buckley.

Somerset took a few steps from the doorway into the hall, and went no farther. He was too excited about seeing Colleen to sit down. Finally, he was to be with her. All these months, she had tried to resist him, but it was no use. Her resistance had only added to his determination and longing. Clearly, she was prepared to surrender. After all, she had asked him to take her to the ball. Where was she? He had to see her, had to have her. . . .

From the other end of the hallway a vision in green and glittering gold floated toward him. He was viewing the goddess Diana, and for a second, his heartbeat stopped. Never before had he seen a feminine figure of such grace and beauty. Her gown of moss green was decorated with full and quarter moons. Her long blond hair was adorned with acorns. She carried a bow, and a small sack of arrows was slung across her lovely back. On either side of her, she was accompanied by two thin grey-hounds, growling softly as they approached Somerset, who took a few discreet steps back. Her amber eyes shone like jewels through a mask of white silk satin brocade.

Seeing Buckley dressed as a pirate, she felt her heart sink. Still, she was determined to make the best of the evening. The five long weeks of feverish sewing had done something to her—what, she wasn't sure. She was neither melancholy nor joyous. Yet her costume gave her a small sense of courage, just as

Rianne had hoped, a daring that she had lacked for so long. It was as if she had left her former self somewhere in the aftermath of Ephraim's execution and was reappearing as a mythical huntress. Her dogs and arrows, special gifts from Rianne, provided her with a measure of protection. She felt heady and strange, for this last Saturday night in August was her first time out in nearly two months, and something told her that anything might happen.

The Roman centurion wore a heavy metal helmet with a dark brush running over the top. His armor clanked as he walked to the back of the alleyway, behind the Paxtons' Charleston town house. There, under moonlight, he spotted an angel whose sheath of sheer ivory silk was framed by two light, wire-framed wings. Thousands of white goose feathers had been painstakingly pasted over the garment by Rianne and Colleen, and upon her head sat a garland of silk peonies, violet and pink.

When the soldier took off his helmet, his disheveled red hair gave him a funny look. Joy didn't care. They embraced, and kissed, and kissed again.

"Did you tell Hope?" Peter asked.

"I told her that you'd arranged for her to visit Allan. At first she said that under those conditions she preferred not to see him at all, but finally she changed her mind. She's going to see him later tonight."

"Does she know that you're going to the ball with me?"

"She didn't ask about my escort, and I didn't mention you. There are certain things Hope and I can't discuss. You and my brother head that list."

"Have you heard from your father?" Peter asked with concern.

"Not since I came back to Charleston. Father's not quick to forget."

"When he understands how I arranged for Hope to see her husband, perhaps he won't be as angry with you and..."

"Please, Peter, let's forget all that tonight. Tonight I have this mask. No one will know me, and we can dance, Peter, we can hold each other and..."

He interrupted her sentence with a kiss. For many minutes

they stood there, wrapped in one another's arms, until they were finally able to break away. Together, the centurion and the angel walked to his coach, where they left the Paxton town house behind and followed a long trail of elegant carriages, each carrying excited passengers dressed in fantastic attire moving slowly and steadily toward Somerset Hall.

~ *Chapter 7* ~

Something in the air was different—an especially strong summer breeze, a luminous moon that looked full to the point of bursting, twin shooting stars falling in opposite directions. Colleen felt uneasy, intrigued, alive. As she and Buckley made their way toward the main house, he made a point of calling many of the male servants, lined up in blue cutaway coats and white knee breeches, by their first names. Despite his costume, his voice tipped them off, and they greeted him with solicitous bows. "Good evenin', Master Somerset, good evenin'." At first Colleen was reluctant to part with her greyhounds. She still felt shaky and insecure, but she finally allowed Buckley to entrust them to an attendant.

For all its splendor, the house seemed slightly ridiculous to Colleen—pompous and pretentious, like Buckley himself. The evening's bizarre atomsphere, however, lulled her into suspending judgments. The great gala had more the feeling of a dream than reality. As she and Somerset climbed the main staircase, heading for the second-story ballroom, he didn't cease pointing out the treasures—the furnishings, paintings, and enormous tapestries—that his family had accumulated, treasures all to be bequeathed to him. Colleen couldn't concentrate on his comments, for ahead of them was a Renaissance courtier with lavender codpiece and silver slippers, a knight in shining armor, a barmaid with a flimsy low-cut off-the-shoulder blouse, and Cleopatra herself.

Inside the ballroom, the madness was even more delicious. A twelve-piece ensemble played a selection of popular minuets and quadrilles. A brown bear danced with an elf. On one side of the room a huge feast had been set upon a round rosewood table as large as a small lake. An enormous Wedgwood soup tureen held a pinkish-white shrimp bisque. Platters of roasted squab and cornish hens were piled two feet high, and a wigged servant carved slices of pork roast onto the plates of the hungry revelers. A steaming rice pilaf, a Charleston specialty, with colorful bits of tomato, okra, and cloves, was being spooned from large crystal bowls. Piping-hot trays of porgies and hen crabs were emptied almost as soon as they arrived at the table. The aroma of *gâteau-patate* filled the room—a sumptuous mixture of boiled sweet potatoes, cream, eggs, butter, sugar, and cinnamon. Great piles of persimmons stood in a pyramid at one end of the table, and, in addition to dozens of freshly baked cream pies—peach, strawberry, and chocolate—a huge English trifle, soaked in wine and sprinkled with macaroons, sat in a compote dish of pink-colored porcelain.

Servants circulated around the ballroom with trays of fine wines and aperitifs, and clearly the partygoers were thirsty. Though the costumes themselves had the effect of intoxication, the revelers were anxious to push themselves even further as they readily down glass after glass of sparkling liquors. It was as if an inebriated state of mind made them less self-conscious about their ludicrous disguises.

Dressed as Indians or monks, men felt free to ask women whom they'd never dare ask before to dance. When their wives objected, they pleaded innocence. "I was certain that she was your Aunt Helen," protested a gentleman in wolf's clothing.

Unable to refuse Buckley's invitations to dance, Colleen nonetheless found herself looking around with growing amusement. The enormous ballroom had filled to capacity. Dancers were bumping into dancers, and more than once did Colleen feel a wandering hand on her thigh and buttocks. Their identities hidden, men were taking liberties. It was with great relief that she spotted the entrance of Rianne, who was instantly surrounded by admirers, customers who wished to show the seamstress how glorious they looked in her costumes.

By Rianne's side was a man, taller than she, who had taken on the appearance of a Chinese warlord, an outfit that Colleen herself had helped construct. Several weeks back, the niece had asked her aunt whom the outfit was for, and most mysteriously Rianne had refused to say. Now Colleen understood. The warlord was her escort. A man of broad shoulders, he appeared in black quilted evening pajamas. On the back of his overblouse a ferocious, fire-breathing dragon was stitched in loud reds and purples. A large obi sash, holding an ivory-handled sword close to his abdomen, encircled his waist. His wig was as black as Rianne's, with a long ponytail protruding from beneath a small red silk skullcap. Layers of black mascara and eye pencil, along with small dabs of wig cement, had turned his eyes an astounding almond shape. Long false nails painted bright lacquer-red were held in place with a special adhesive. But underneath it all, who was he?

Colleen went over, expecting to be introduced. Much to her amazement, she wasn't. Rianne used the evening's whimsical mood to avoid formalities, and when the niece, filled with curiosity, pressed the issue, her aunt merely presented the gentleman as "my Oriental friend." The man spoke in a mock Chinese accent, making it impossible to identify his voice. Rianne seemed most pleased at the attention her escort was attracting and did nothing to mitigate the mystery. After all, she reasoned, she was entitled to a bit of private romance.

Buckley was anxious to get Colleen back on the dance floor and into his arms. He knew that by the end of the evening she'd be his. That, coupled with his anticipation of Major Embleton's long-awaited announcement, heightened his already ebullient mood.

Their eyes met, their hearts knew, and she suddenly stopped dancing with a surprised Buckley and simply stood there, facing the harlequin. Those sleepy, sloped eyes could belong to no one else. He was flanked by his peacock and butterfly friends, whose effusive praise of Colleen's outfit went on for several minutes. All the while, Buckley, quick to recognize Paxton, tapped his foot impatiently, taking a menacing stance he thought suitable for a buccaneer.

Jason resented Somerset's attitude. A sense of competitive anger rose through the musician, who, in Buckley's costume, saw the reflection of his own childhood fantasy. He, too, had thought of attending the garish affair as a pirate, but had rejected the notion, wanting to wear something less threatening. Suddenly he felt foolish in his clown's costume.

"You cut quite a figure as a jester," Somerset sneered sarcastically. "It suits you well, though I'm surprised that you're not here with the orchestra. Earlier I saw a lanky boy carrying their fiddle cases and naturally assumed 'twas you."

"I'd like to cut his throat," Piero whispered to Robin as he went to his snuffbox for a quick snort.

"The figure of you as a pirate, Buckley," Jason shot back, "is hardly one I would have anticipated. I was certain you'd be far more specific in your choice, a unique character from history, perhaps."

"Whom did you have in mind for Mr. Somerset, maestro?" Piero was pleased to provide his protégé with the setup.

"Figures more suited to his own refined personality—say, Attila the Hun, or Caligula, perhaps."

Colleen felt herself stirred by the nasty exchange, silently pleased to see Jason so untypically aggressive. For a moment, all her anger and doubts about the musician vanished, and she was disappointed when, with the formal introduction and entrance of Colonel Hugo Somerset and his wife, Paulina, all conversation ceased.

It was an extraordinary moment, and Colleen was grateful to be standing next to Jason, Robin, and Piero, whose sensibilities, in this instance, matched her own. Like her, they couldn't help but see the strange humor of the situation: carried in atop a table whose legs were lifted by four large slaves was the colonel himself—thin-faced, half blind, his palsied hands waving to an ocean of guests he could only barely see. A round of hearty cheers greeted the old man, dressed as a Crusader, who appeared more than a little baffled and senile. Behind him, his Paulina was dressed as Little Bo Peep, a diminutive elderly lady in a baby-pink shepherdess dress. she wore a large pink bonnet and carried a staff adorned with pink satin bows. Her face seemed frozen in a painted smile as she led an actual sheep on a leash. Trailing the sheep, a slave carried a small shovel to tidy up after the woolly creature.

In a tentative, high-pitched voice, Colonel Hugo welcomed his guests and introduced Major Embleton, whose last name he failed to remember. The major, dressed in full battle regalia, stood in front of the orchestra and asked them to play "God

Save the King." They did so as many of the guests sang along, while others, such as Colleen, flatly refused. When the song had been sung, the major cleared his throat and began to speak as Jason prayed that he not be chosen for the Tory post.

"I understand that on a night such as this no one is enamored of speeches"—a lusty cheer went up—"so I shall be brief and, even more, do what I can to keep your spirits light. That shouldn't difficult with the news I bring, for there's victory to report. In the north-central sector of this colony, General Cornwallis has turned back a large-scale attempt on our supply base at Camden. Indications are that the rebel forces led by Gates and deKalb have been severely trounced in what purports to be an even larger triumph than the one so satisfactorily effected here in Charles Town. With this great victory, there can be no doubt that the South is secure for those loyal to King George the Third." Embleton paused for the inevitable cheers, mixed with more than a few faint derisive cries.

"The second happy note of the evening concerns an appointment I wish to make—the Commander of the Continental Tory Militia. Believing that it's vital that the post be filled by a Loyalist who hails from this great region, I've decided upon a gentleman whose gallantry, honor, and skill are beyond question or reproach. I am speaking of"—the major let the guests wait a few seconds as he cleared his throat again—"the grandson of our most gracious host, Colonel Hugo . . . Buckley Somerset."

Deeply disturbed by the news of the defeat at Camden, Jason nonetheless breathed a sigh of relief as Buckley grinned from ear to ear, grabbed Colleen's hand, and tried to lead her toward the orchestra and Major Embleton. She refused to budge. Showing something of her old self, she was furious and ashamed of her escort, wanting nothing more to do with him. Why had she allowed Rianne to involve her in this? Where was her sense of integrity? She moved instinctively to Jason's side and let Buckley make his tedious acceptance speech by himself. When he was through and the music began again, Jason danced her into the far reaches of the ballroom, away from Buckley, who was busy accepting congratulations from his many Tory friends.

Colleen and Jason responded to the minuet with identical rhythms. They floated together, easily, naturally, hands and legs moving with the same syncopation. At least for a while, this goddess and clown returned to the state of grace that had greeted them his first day back in America, at the picnic and in the woods. The slightest touch, the mere brush of their skin, renewed the excitement and sent them dancing farther and farther away from the crowd, until they found themselves in a distant corner of the balcony, overlooking the gardens. Dressed as they were, given their moods and desires and the glow of silver moonlight, it was all Jason could do to keep from embracing Colleen. Suddenly she reached out to him, placing her head upon his chest.

"This isn't right," Jason whispered, angry at himself for abandoning his vow to leave this woman alone. "Not here, not now."

"Then when?" Colleen asked. "When can we be together again? When can we run away? It matters not where."

"Everything matters—that's the problem."

"Must we think about everything? Can't we just be ourselves and be happy? Ever since . . ."—she hesitated before saying it—". . . since Ephraim, I've done nothing but think. Oh, Jase, I'm so tired of thinking. Please just hold me and say that this bloody business will soon be over and there'll be nothing to worry about, no bad dreams, no fearful nights, just you and me and moments like this, peaceful and . . ."

"But there is no peace, Colleen. We can pretend, but to what avail? You heard Embleton's news."

"Embleton and Buckley Somerset are simple, vain men who . . ."

". . . wield enormous power of which we must be cautious."

"Please, Jase, don't you understand that I've been cautious for weeks, so cautious that I've been afraid to live? But now you and I must start to live. Somehow and somewhere, we must be together, Jase. We must."

Confused by Colleen's new attitude—the last time they were together she had accused him of betraying Ephraim—Jason reminded himself that he hadn't time to contend with this perplexing female. His critically calculated plans for the evening would go awry if he didn't act soon, and so he tried to extricate himself from the situation as best he could. Unfortunately, there was no easy way.

"Let me take you back to Buckley," he urged Colleen.

"What? Is that some sort of cruel jest?"

"Not at all. After all, he is your escort."

"If you love me, Jase, if everything you have ever said to

me is true, then you and I will walk out of here this very instant and never look back."

"That's impossible." He shook his head, unable to look her in the eye, but determined to keep to his own way.

"Then your hypocrisy is exactly as I thought." Her voice started to freeze. She felt herself grow tense as she longed for the two greyhounds that Rianne had given her, the only companions she could trust.

"I ask only for time and understanding." Jason took her hand, but she withdrew it quickly.

"How can I understand what you refuse to let me see? Who are you, Jason Paxton? Are you a musician or a clown, a Tory or a rebel? What am I to believe when you tell me nothing?"

"What am I to believe when you tell me everything? Who are you? A rebel, a would-be artist, or a love-struck girl?" Jason retorted. "You tell me, Colleen, just who is the hypocrite?" He turned on his heels and walked away, unable to witness how his words had stung her, how the tears came to her eyes, the eyes of his beloved. He tried to tell himself there had been no other way. Time was of the essence this night. Someday he would make her understand. Someday . . .

In the gardens below, near the outer rim of the magnificent *fontana del moro,* where Bernini had depicted a Moor attempting to tame a dolphin, the gentle spray of spring water touched lightly upon the faces of the centurion and angel who, far from the crowded ballroom, spoke to one another in the language of love. Colleen watched them—now touching, now separating, now touching again—as a stream of warm tears ran down her cheeks. The keen edge of his reproach had cut her to the quick. "Jason, I hope never to see you again," she whispered as strains of elegant Mozartian music wafted through the night air, somehow adding to her sorrow and pain.

"'Tis not a foregone conclusion that the scheme will work, maestro," said Piero as he slipped nervously into Jason's harlequin outfit while the musician donned the gray cloak of Will-o'-the-Wisp. They were inside Piero and Robin's carriage, which they'd left at a remote section of the vast Somerset grounds.

"I've no doubt it will work," Jason replied. "Just do as we planned. Act as if you're drunk. Don't speak directly to anyone, yet be certain your presence is in evidence."

"Your shoulders are broader than mine," Piero complained, reaching for his snuff.

"There's not a soul who'll notice," Robin assured him, "and with these heightened shoes, the ruse will be complete."

The clown and the butterfly left the carriage and headed back to the ballroom. Jason waited, made certain he wasn't being watched, and then walked a quarter of a mile to a tree where, earlier, he had tied Cinder. Minutes later, he rode off swiftly, deep into the moonlit night.

Chapter 8

Hope left the Old Customs Exchange in silent despair. Her meeting with Allan had lasted barely a half hour. She was shocked by his weak condition and pathetic appearance. His once muscular, stocky body had thinned markedly. Fifty pounds lighter, head lowered, eyes sunken, he whispered to his Hope words she shuddered to hear. "They're flogging us," he told her, "the bastards are flogging us every day." He began to show the scars on his back, but the sentinel stopped him. When Hope started feeding him food she had prepared—plump breasts of chicken and pieces of cake—the guard interfered again. She began to argue and verbally abuse the English soldier, but Allan put his frail finger to her lips. "Don't," he told his wife, "they'll boot you out. I've seen 'em."

"He wouldn't dare touch me," Hope snapped, showing her husband a defiant strength he had never before seen in her.

"You don't understand their brutality," he said.

"I understand," she whispered intensely, squeezing her husband's hand and looking squarely in his eyes, "that one way or another, we're getting you out of here."

"'Tis hopeless."

"'Tis only a matter of time. Believe me. Meanwhile, you must never give up. That's what they want. They want your spirit, Allan, but they won't have it, will they?"

Allan saw the expression of courage in his wife's burning eyes. She had her father's pluck. For the first time since he was jailed, over three months ago, he managed a small smile.

"I know what you've been through," she said, placing her hand behind his neck. "Most men would have crumbled by now. But not my Allan. It's going to take more than a handful of bloody Redcoat jailers to keep you down. Now here's something to help your spirits," she said, quickly glancing around to make certain that the guard wasn't looking, then slipping pieces of chicken along with a slim bottle of whiskey into Allan's shirt.

"Be strong," Hope whispered in Allan's ear before leaving him. "I know better than anyone that you possess a passionate endurance that can outlast a whole army of these English fools."

"I love you," the farmer said to her, amazed by the force of her optimistic conviction.

"I love you, Allan," she replied, fighting back tears, as she let go of his hand and walked away.

In spite of her brave façade, it was clear to Hope that, slowly but systematically, her husband was being beaten to death. Nothing had prepared her for this realization. Choked with fury and agonized frustration, she hurried through the streets of Charleston, back toward the Paxton town house, unaware of the cloaked figure who, from a distance, had been following her path, making certain that she was undisturbed by the rowdy soldiers who stumbled from the pubs and inns.

The pirate had found his prize, a veritable goddess, and, for what seemed the hundredth time, led her around the dance floor. He was ecstatic. This was the greatest evening of his life. He had been chosen, above all his colleagues, to lead his people in battle. He had humiliated his arch rival. He only wished his parents could have been there to hear the news, but illness had kept them from attending. What a pity, for his victory had been proclaimed in the most public manner possible, and he was convinced that there was nothing in the world that could not be his—including the amber-eyed beauty with whom he danced.

"'Twas between me and the clown," he told Colleen with smug satisfaction. "Embleton himself said so. The two of us were called to his office. 'But Major,' said I, 'the man may be suited to strike a clavichord, but certainly not a rebel. Let the women and musicians be, and the men shall win this war for you.' He laughed heartily and, as you can see, he agreed. Paxton! The mere thought of him in battle is enough to make me howl."

At which point Somerset did howl—from pain. Colleen had stepped on his foot with great force, but professed innocence. "So sorry," she offered immediately, not certain whether she was angrier at Buckley or the man he was ridiculing.

From across the ballroom, she caught sight of the floppy harlequin hat and, in spite of herself, stretched to see whether he might be coming her way. He wasn't. She watched as her aunt and her Chinese warlord passed by, and she noticed that Rianne's frivolous mood had heightened. She simply smiled at her niece, saying, "You look too serious, my dear. Remember—revelry has its place."

Even during a revolution? Colleen wanted to reply, but there was no time. Rianne and her Chinese-styled companion had disappeared into the crowd, and Colleen, still forced to listen as Buckley received compliment after compliment on his new post, felt herself more torn and baffled than ever. Wherever she looked, she seemed to see the floppy harlequin's hat, and whenever she started to follow it, she stopped herself. He had clearly rejected her, so why pursue him? Why, indeed! Why not drink instead? Drink—that seemed such an easy solution to her sour state of mind. Why hadn't she begun earlier? Wasn't her aunt right, after all? Revelry! She took a glass of brandy from a tray carried by a servant and quickly drained it. The results came suddenly. A light-headedness, almost a giddy release. She gasped, each breath soothing her throat. Another servant, another tray, another glass, this time port. What was real and what was make-believe? Was there actually a war outside this gilded palace, and, if so, what were these dancers— these bears and butterflies, courtiers and fops—what were they doing whirling around the room? And, oh, how the room whirled! Who was tending to life's somber responsibilities?

It didn't matter, nothing mattered, because Colleen was goddess of the hunt, and hunt she would. There! There was the clown, the man who, despite all his mysteries, dominated her dreams, awake and asleep. As Colleen walked up to him, determined to give him another piece of her mind, he saw her coming and cruelly turned away. Still she pursued him, feeling more like Diana the huntress than Colleen, until she finally caught the sleeve of his comical blouse, only to have him withdraw his arm, as though her touch had repulsed him. The words he spoke, in a strangely contorted voice, cut through her heart like a sharpened surgical tool used by her father to slice human flesh: "Away, woman!" he barked. "Away!"

Allan Coleridge had fallen asleep. Hope's whiskey had put him under, and he was certain that the whisper in his ear was part of a dream. When he opened his eyes and saw a man wearing a gray mask with only small slits cut out for his eyes, mouth, and nose, he felt even more alarmed.

"Can you walk?" asked the man in a disguised voice. "If not, I'll carry you."

"Where are we going?" Allan wanted to know.

"We're getting out of here."

Outside his cell, Allan saw another three dozen prisoners assembled. What were they doing there? A half dozen guards had been knocked out or tied up. Windows and doors were wide open. Still groggy and slightly hung over, Allan joined the others in following the masked man in the gray cloak outside. Outside! Oh, the sweet smell of freedom! The deliciously cool night air! But no time to stop. The men climbed in the back of a large covered cart used for transporting farm animals, and suddenly they were off, their liberator driving a team of horses through the back alleys of Charleston.

"Did you see him, Allan?" asked Jack Spike, one of Coleridge's fellow prisoners, as they bounced up and down while the cart headed toward the countryside.

"I was sleeping," Allan confessed.

"My God, man," said Spike, one of the fiercest rebels in the colony, "I never seen nothin' like it before. He was lightnin', he was. The way he broke away the bars and snuck in through the side window just above my cell. I saw it all, I did. Like lookin' at one of those drama plays the fancy people pay to see. He comes in and takes two guards at once, bangin' their heads together so mightily that they're both out in a flash. Little noise, and then he's on the third guard, knockin' him out with a blow from his right fist, the likes of which would down a bear, I swear. Now he charges the fourth guard, with no time for the bloke to see what's a-comin'. Smack! He slams into his belly and knocks the breath from him, ties him up—the man's no killer, Coleridge, that's the strange part—but he's lightnin' on his feet, and when the last two limeys hear the clamor and come a-lookin', why, he's ready with rope. He catches them 'round the neck and has 'em gagged and helpless in less time than it takes a hound to mount a bitch and there we are, our bloody cages open, and the rest of the ignorant English blokes too far away in the Old Customs Exchange to hear a peep. Can you imagine it? One on six and the day is his. He's the one they call Will-o'-the-Wisp. I'd bet my dear dead mother's arse on it. It's him, all right, and he's sprung us free. My God, what a night!" Spike slapped Coleridge on the back as they continued bouncing through the countryside.

Behind the reins, the Wisp was all concentration, obsessed, transformed as he always was on his missions—no thoughts of goddesses or music—riding, riding, riding, running the team of strong horses through the woods and swamps, riding no less than eight miles north of the city until he reached a secret encampment of rebel forces.

"'Tis no friend of the Crown here!" he shouted, keeping the sentinels from shooting. "I'm carrying Patriot prisoners in need of medical aid and decent food. Will you help them now?"

A lusty cheer went up from among the rebel forces who had come out to inspect the cart. But by the time the men climbed down and embraced their comrades-in-arms, Will-o'-the-Wisp had mounted the great dun stallion he'd brought with him and ridden off like the night wind.

"Are you ready to leave now?" Buckley asked Colleen as at least half the guests had already gone.

"Yes, immediately," she replied, deciding that she could no longer stay in the same room with Jason Paxton. The drink had brought her mood first up, then down, and, with a dozen different thoughts whirling in her head, all she really knew was that she wanted to escape this madcap party, and right away. The farther away from him, the better. She bothered to say good-night to no one, not even her aunt.

Her greyhounds were pleased to see her. Their ready affection was something she welcomed, while Buckley paid them not the slightest attention.

Somerset's head was high in the starry sky. Never in his life had he felt more confident. He knew that nothing could deter his plans as he, Colleen, and the twin beasts stood inside the portico, waiting for his carriage to be brought around.

The fresh night air, in combination with the goodly quantity of alcohol she had consumed, startled and refreshed Colleen. Ten minutes later, riding in the carriage, she saw that they'd passed by her aunt's street without stopping. "Where are we going?" she asked Buckley in an alarmed voice.

"Trust me, my dear," Somerset said, offering a sly smile.

"I want to know where we're going. I *demand* to know."

"I'm taking you home with me."

"Have your man turn the carriage around and take me back to my aunt's."

"I'm afraid I can't. You see, your aunt's not expecting you."

"Of course she's expecting me! What are you talking about?"

"I spoke with her at the ball and explained that you'll be spending the weekend with me."

"That's out of the question. Aunt Rianne would never allow such a thing."

"On the contrary, she seemed pleased at the prospect. I had the feeling she welcomed the opportunity of being alone with her Oriental friend."

"This is impossible," Colleen said.

"Perhaps you don't know your aunt as well as you think. No matter, we'll have a splendid time. You've not seen Marble Manor before, and you'll love the place."

"I'm not the least interested in seeing Marble Manor."

"It's but mid-road between here and Brandborough. Mother and Father are expecting us. I've some business to tend to there, but I assure you that nothing will interfere with our pleasure. We'll be there well before daybreak."

"This is insane. I've no provisions, no clothes other than this foolish costume."

"Your costume's delightful, and Mother has nothing but clothes. Your head will swim with choices."

Colleen considered protesting further, considered striking Buckley or leaping from the carriage. If she gave the command, would her greyhounds attack him? Probably not. Nothing had gone right, and for all the heartache she'd suffered at the hands of a silly clown, Colleen was tired. Why had Jason deserted her? Why had her aunt allowed her to be whisked away? Too many unanswered questions, too little energy left to fight. She leaned back in the carriage and tried to convince herself that this was her fate, that fighting wouldn't help, that she had no choice but to remain in the company of this bold buccaneer.

Chapter 9

It was nearly two A.M. when Rianne told Billy Hollcork that enough was enough. Hollcork was an old friend of hers, a hulky, big-boned tanner who had been in love with the seamstress for years. Once in a great while she allowed herself the pleasure of his tireless passion. Tonight had been one such memorable occasion. She had dressed him in a Chinese warlord's outfit, taught him to mumble a couple of Oriental-sounding phrases, and taken him to the most aristocratic ball on the Charleston social calendar. The fact that her escort had been a tanner was a private joke of no small delight to Rianne as she introduced him to the refined ladies and gentlemen whose costumes she had created. Afterward, in the intimacy of his small living quarters behind his shop, she let the middle-aged Hollcork show his appreciation for having gained entrance to the splendid mansion. Unlettered but bright, Billy was a splendid physical creature—dark-haired, full-faced, barrel-chested, and long-legged—with a keen understanding and appreciation of the female anatomy. The fact that he and his surroundings carried the masculine fragrance of sharp-smelling leather did nothing to detract from his strapping appeal.

"You're a prince, Billy," said Rianne after straightening her wig and gown. "There's not another man in these parts to match you."

"Then when can I see you again, Rianne?"

"Whenever the fancy strikes you."

"Then I'll be knocking at your door tomorrow." He smiled with his almond-colored eyes.

"That'll be a tad too soon."

"See there? It's going to be another six months before you grant me your favors. You're a cruel woman, Rianne McClagan, you are."

She kissed him on his broad nose. "Take me home like the gentleman you are, Billy. We should both count ourselves lucky for this night. It's one I won't soon forget."

Fifteen minutes later she found a note slipped under the front door of her house.

My dear Miss McClagan,

At your niece's request, she and I will be spending a few days at Marble Manor in the company of my mother and father. You can be assured that Miss Colleen will be treated with the utmost respect and propriety.

Most cordially yours,
Buckley Somerset

Rianne silently questioned the correspondence. Would Colleen have indeed asked to go home with Somerset? She seriously doubted it. Yet it was also true that her niece had acted quite peculiarly at the ball. Rianne had seen her quarreling with Jason Paxton. She knew her niece well enough to realize that she wasn't above using one man to spite another. In days past, Rianne herself had employed such tactics. Surely, though, the fact of Buckley's military appointment had infuriated Colleen. Rianne thought about the matter for a few minutes, the note still in hand. Between politics and romance, which was the stronger passion for a young woman in love? The answer was obvious. Politics had given Colleen the fright of her life, and, yes, it was possible, Rianne concluded, that her niece had decided to torment the musician by making it known that she was not only Buckley's companion for the evening, but for the next several days as well.

The following Monday, in a sun-soaked open fruit market still buzzing with talk of the Wisp's spectacular Saturday night break-in at the Old Customs Exchange, Rianne spotted Piero

Sebastiano Ponti squeezing plums and pears. He was dressed in a breezy, blousy outfit of yellow and orange silk.

"Delicious evening, was it not, Rianne?" Piero asked.

"Absolutely scrumptious. The costumes fashioned by Robin had a wonderfully feminine touch."

"What is your meaning?" Piero asked defensively.

"Only that your companion is a man of delicate talent."

"Delicate would not be a word I'd apply to your mysterious companion last night. Might I be bold enough to ask his identity?"

"And ruin the mystery? Heaven forbid! You may guess, but I'm sworn to secrecy."

"I'd swear that I detected the distinct odor of leather. The outline of the gentleman's massive physique brought to mind a certain tanner."

Rianne suppressed a smile and said wryly, "You're a far greater connoisseur of the male physique than I."

Piero didn't suppress his smile. "If we weren't friends, Rianne, I'd be a trifle concerned that we know one another far too well. We're two creatures with a decided predilection for pleasure," he said, reaching into his snuff pouch for a quick pinch for each nostril.

"Private pleasures," Rianne added, "are often the most attractive."

"Speaking of attractiveness, where is your fair niece this fine afternoon?"

"She's spending a few days at Marble Manor," Rianne was quick to say, knowing that the loquacious Piero would immediately report the news to Jason—which would be exactly what her niece would want. "Buckley Somerset and his parents were kind enough to invite her."

"Oh, I see," Piero said nonchalantly, hiding his excitement at learning so juicy a tidbit and already calculating the earliest possible moment to convey the information to his protégé.

Having arrived at Marble Manor close to dawn, Colleen spent nearly all day Sunday asleep. When she awoke, she barely remembered who and where she was. The bedroom, with its frescoed ceilings and pink-painted walls, was magnificent. A half dozen gowns her exact size hung in the splendid armoire. Undergarments in a variety of styles were neatly folded and placed in a drawer of a tall, baroquely sculpted bureau. Colleen chose a modest mauve gown and, at six o'clock, walked down the wide staircase, into the oblong dining room, where she saw that places had been set for two. She assumed that she and Buckley were to eat alone, and that, after dinner, she'd be faced with fighting off his advances. Sighing, she took a seat and resigned herself to her fate. She noted that the dining room, like the hallways, had Italian marble floors—gleaming, beautiful, and cold. In fact, the marble motif, giving the house an especially severe character, was visible everywhere—marble columns by the front door, marble fireplaces, carved marble mantelpieces. what else was one to expect at Marble Manor?

Several minutes later, she looked up to see Miranda Somerset walk through the door. Her jutting chin and fierce slate-gray eyes told Colleen that she had to be Buckley's mother. A diminutive woman with small hands, a thin neck, narrow mouth, petite nose, and excessively wrinkled skin, she wore a great deal of jewelry and makeup. Her wig was decorated with long light blue ribbons that unfortunately kept falling in her face. She walked with a black cane bejeweled with rows of large, fabulous turquoise stones. The cane seemed to be for effect, for she carried herself erectly, with no trace of a limp or any other physical impairment.

"My dear," she said, extending her hand, which Colleen took quickly as she rose from her chair. The two women sat on opposite sides of the table. "I believe I saw you once as a girl. Your father came here for a medical emergency, undoubtedly related to my husband. My husband's been sick since I've known him. You couldn't have been older than ten. I was struck by your beauty then, and am even more so now. I understand my son's burning obsession with you, though I warned him earlier today, as I will warn him throughout your visit, that he's behaving quite foolishly. You're undoubtedly a rebel at heart. If not, you would have married him months ago and had all this." With dramatic flourish, she waved her hand around the extravagantly appointed dining room, pointing to the great tapestries, the gleaming silver urns. "My silly son laughs at the notion of women having political convictions and calls me half crazed. That's how he speaks to his mother. Well, he's not too old to be slapped across the face, which I was forced to do earlier today. His father exerted absolutely no discipline upon the lad, and the job was left to me. No son of mine will address me in that tone of voice. Half crazed? Perhaps I'm

fully crazed, but I do understand the mind of women. I've
heard stories of your mother and your aunt, and I expect you've
inherited much of their wildness. Am I wrong?" Miranda didn't
stop for a reply. "I am not wrong. I see it in your eyes. A wild
woman, much like his mother, would naturally attract my son.
We won't be eating meat tonight. To pick on the carcasses of
dead animals is an unholy and barbarian act. Jesus himself fed
fish to his followers, and so who am I to object to fish? I am
sixty-three years old and have never been sick a day in my
life. Fish, vegetables, and fruits are the keys to longevity. Do
you consider that a half-crazed notion? My husband eats flesh
every day and has been debilitated by one form of sickness or
another for the past two decades—now he can barley lift his
little finger, not to speak of other parts of his failing anatomy—
yet they call him reasonable and sane. Is it insane to speak to
the birds in the morning and the owls at night? Did Saint Francis
of Assisi do any less? Are you familiar with your saints, Miss
McClagan? Do you understand that snakes and turtles have
much to teach us human beings? If I tell you that among my
closest friends are two bumblebees named Cleopatra and Cae-
sar, would you understand? They speak to me in a language
far more succinct than our own. *Serve the flounder!*" she suddenly shouted to the servants in the kitchen. "And where in
the name of our merciful Lord is my wine? I want my wine!"

During dinner, Miranda drank excessively. She didn't stop
talking for a minute. Her voice was high-pitched and squeaky
as she bounced from subject to subject with only the slightest
thread of logical connection. In the midst of one of her discourses on her husband's poor eating habits, she called in a
slave to cut from her wig the long ribbons that kept falling in
her face. The slave did so only with great difficulty, since
Miranda kept drinking, talking, and eating all the while.

"I suspect that if women ran things in this colony, we could
have avoided the chaos that presently surrounds us. Don't you
agree, my dear?" she asked Colleen without giving her time
to answer. "Our greatest monarchs have been women. Is there
an epoch any more splendid than the Elizabethan? Here the
primitives are incapable of appreciating feminine genius. They
are barbarians in this colony, and nothing more. My father, as
you probably know, was an English lord, my mother of royal
blood. He came here to satisfy a foolish wager. Had he listened
to mother, I'd still be living in London. The notion of smart

society in South Carolina is symbolized by my father-in-law's yearly costume ball, an event that reeks of vulgarity. For years, I've refused to attend. True nobility would never, under any circumstances, agree to mix with the sort of riffraff that worms its way into Somerset Hall. Do you observe nature, Miss McClagan? If so, you will see that cardinals are cardinals precisely because they will fly with no other birds. Their blood is pure, their red coloring as brilliant as the blazing afternoon sun. Now that August is nearly behind us, one hopes that the heat is passing. Will you join me in prayer? Dear Lord," Miranda said, closing her eyes and folding her hands, "we pray for a cool September. And a quick end to the rebellious rascals who run amok." She opened her eyes and stared into Colleen's. "Am I offending you, Miss McClagan? How is it that you're a rebel?"

"I'm merely your guest," Colleen said tactfully, more astounded by this woman than angered by her politics. Who could take her seriously? Colleen rightly guessed that Mrs. Somerset's credibility was notoriously low. Never had she met a person of such volatile emotions and moods.

"Your eyes are full of rebellion," Miranda went on. "I warned Buckley, but he thinks I'm mad. He's mad for you because you won't have him. I've spoiled the lad. He's inherited my breeding and my temperament. By nature, he grows bored with what he has and infatuated with what escapes him. Beauty is destructive. It feeds upon itself. If you were a man, Miss McClagan, you might be leading an army. I know, for I would be charging you with a force of my own. I would plot my own strategy and select my own generals, all of whom would be women. Think of Joan of Arc. We have much to learn from the bees, highly intelligent and organized insects. There is but one queen. Are you at all interested in bees, Miss McClagan?"

"I would rather doubt it," Buckley answered for Colleen. He appeared in the doorway wearing a silver-colored cape and shiny black boots.

"The ladies are dining alone tonight," Miranda informed him.

"You'll forgive my mother," Buckley explained to Colleen, "but she has a tendency to rattle on a bit."

"I resent that."

"She's really quite a remarkable woman," Buckley continued.

"You speak of me as if I were dead."

"If you're through with your dinner, Mother, I'd like to . . ."

"I am *not* through. The flounder is far too salty and I'm demanding that fresh pieces be cooked. Miss McClagan has not eaten a bite, and rightly so."

"Miss McClagan and I will be having coffee and cakes on the terrace. If you'll excuse us, Mother . . ."

"I demand that this woman be sent back to her aunt's sewing shop. She will lead to your ruination just as surely as hell burns beneath this earth."

"That will be quite enough, Mother!" Buckley demanded sharply.

With that, Miranda arose from the table, took several steps toward her son, and held him with her commanding gray eyes. For the first time since she had known him, Colleen saw fear on Buckley's face. Clearly, he was afraid that the woman would strike him, and so he sheepishly backed away. "Please," he begged with the uncertainty of a small boy, "let there be no further embarrassments. We have a guest."

"A traitor whose beauty belies her treachery!"

"Hold your tongue!" Buckley found the courage to exclaim.

Swinging with furious velocity, the flat palm of Miranda's right hand caught Buckley on his prominent chin. The slap came too quickly to duck, and snapped back his head. His skin flushed red. For a second, Colleen thought that Buckley's eyes would fill with tears, but somehow—she had the feeling only because of her presence—he was able to maintain himself. He took Colleen's hand and quickly escorted her from the table to the terrace, while his mother, having made her point, stormed from the room, ranting about the weakness of the male species.

The terrace overlooked what must have been a huge expanse of land, but the warm, moonless night revealed little. A slight breeze blew from the west. Creaking crickets and croaking frogs blended with the harmonious strains of singing slaves heard faintly in the distance. Trying to pretend nothing had happened, Buckley promised Colleen that he would take her on a tour of the property in the morning. As a black woman served after-dinner refreshments, Colleen noticed him taking several deep breaths in an attempt to regain his composure.

Buckley couldn't deny it: Colleen had seen a side of him no female had witnessed before. At once, the thought repulsed and excited him. He had brought the bewitching doctor's daugh-

ter into the very bosom of his family. This was the intimacy
he had sought for so long. It mattered not that she knew his
mother was eccentric or that his father was an impotent invalid.
What mattered was that she was here, and that she was his.
He had her now, and he would never let her leave—ever.

"I want you to have anything you desire," he said before
escorting her back into the house. His plan was to demonstrate
restraint by gently kissing her cheek before leaving her at her
bedroom door. There would be time for longer, more ardent
kisses tomorrow. It was enough for tonight to put her at ease
and assuage her fears. And yet even a fleeting, innocent peck
left Buckley hard with driving desire as he turned toward his
mother's sitting room, where for the next thirty minutes he and
Miranda debated and abused one another as they had done ever
since he was a boy. Fascinated by it all, Colleen pushed her
door slightly ajar so she could hear the vituperative argument.
It was only with the sound of another violent slap that the
crescendoing cries ceased. As he had done so many times
before, Buckley raced from his mother's room, down the stairway, out into the open fields toward the slave quarters, where,
unknown to Colleen, he demanded the submission of a robust
female slave, pre-selected by Jack Windrow and Sam Simkins,
the overseers who ran Marble Manor with iron fists.

The next morning, taking a carriage tour of the plantation,
not nearly as large or extravagant as Somerset Hall, Colleen
learned from Buckley that Windrow and Simkins had once
worked for Ethan Paxton in Brandborough. "The fool fired
them," Somerset explained, "and I gave them work immediately."

"Why were they fired?" Colleen asked.

"Their view of managing men differed from Paxton's. They
understand the way to deal with darkies is through force and
fear. The Africans are strong but lazy children and must be
treated as such. Ethan Paxton looks down upon this slavery
business, and consequently is on the verge of bankruptcy. He
mistook these men's efficiency for cruelty," Buckley said,
pointing to his overseers, who, with whips in hand, were leading two black boys from a vast field of cotton.

Jack Windrow was in his forties, a wall-eyed albino of
medium height who wore a large-brimmed hat to protect his
pink-white skin. Because of the strange movement of his eyes,

it was impossible to tell at whom or what he was looking. Sam Simkins was slightly older and shorter, with broad shoulders and thick forearms. He had enormous hands and a tiny forehead. His black bushy hair, dark complexion, and thick, angular eyebrows gave him a menacingly bearish appearance.

"Bastards were gossipin' out there 'stead of pickin'," Windrow reported in a surprisingly high-pitched voice. "They didn't see us comin' up behind 'em, so they kept chatterin' away. Got some news out of 'em that's pretty interestin'. Think you oughta hear it for yourself, Mr. Somerset."

The black boys couldn't have been older than sixteen, Colleen observed as she and Buckley stepped out of the carriage. Their doe eyes conveyed a mixed sense of defiance and fear. Tall and wiry, they looked like brothers.

"We ain't done nuthin', suh," said the older of the two, stepping forward and addressing Somerset.

"Speak when you're spoken to, boy," Simkins barked while snapping his whip on the ground. The teen-ager jumped back.

"What is this news?" Buckley asked impatiently.

"They said they heard it last night," Windrow said. "They were laughin' about Will-o'-the-Wisp and how he sprung the rebel prisoners from the Old Customs Exchange Saturday night."

"What! Why, I haven't heard a thing about it," Somerset said, upset not only by the information, but by the fact that he was learning it from his slaves.

"News spreads among the niggers like swampfire," Sam Simkins drawled. "I think they sing messages across the fields like they must have done back in the jungle."

Colleen's heart fluttered with joy. Again the Wisp had struck, only this time at the heart of the English command, liberating prisoners from under Embleton's very nose. Allan Coleridge was free! For the first time since Ephraim had been killed, she felt inspired to write a new broadside. Lyrics danced through her head. The Sandpiper lived again.

"Damnation!" Buckley shouted. "As Commander of the Continental Tory Militia, I should have been informed of this outrage by a personal envoy of the English command at Charles Town!"

Feeling happier by the minute, Colleen wanted to tell Buckley that in spite of his new post and pretentious title, he'd obviously been forgotten by Embleton. Wisely, though, she said nothing.

"What should we do with the niggers?" asked the albino, who seemed to be looking at Somerset and Colleen at the same time.

"Whip the bastards!" Buckley commanded angrily.

"That'll teach 'em to pick instead of talk," Windrow concurred.

"No!" Colleen shouted suddenly, taking a few steps toward the overseers and the two boys.

"We'll take 'em to the barn," Windrow suggested, "so's not to upset the little lady."

"You'll whip them right here and now!" Somerset ordered with a gleam in his eye as he grabbed Colleen by the arm and brought her back to his side. "Ten strong lashes each."

"They've done nothing," Colleen protested. "They only spoke of what they heard, not what they did."

"Quiet, woman! You'll quickly learn why the Somerset plantations are famous for maintaining absolute order and discipline."

Held fast by Buckley, feeling as hopeless as the day Ephraim Kramer had been hanged, Colleen turned her back as the air whistled with the sound of the hissing whip. The first boy's agonized groan was met by Colleen's own cry for mercy. Still the lashes continued, as did the bloodcurdling screams, again and again and again. When it was finally over, out of the corner of her eye Colleen saw both boys flat on the ground, shivering, their backs marked by a pattern of jagged red lines. Windrow and Simkins, breathing heavily, stood over them, their leather whips dripping blood as Buckley, smiling with sinister satisfaction, led a weeping Colleen back to the carriage.

Later that afternoon, back in her guest bedroom, Colleen regained her composure. She had been weeping uncontrollably for Ephraim Kramer and the two black boys. At some point, though, her sobbing had ceased. What good were spilled tears? Enough of the Tory politics of Buckley Somerset and the hopeless equivocations of Jason Paxton! it was time to get to work. Slowly but deliberately, she began composing a verse about the Wisp's daring escapade. The first draft was rough, and so she wrote a second, and a third, and a fourth, until she felt satisfied enough to start considering ways to have the broadside printed. She'd have to make inquiries about other printers, make other contacts. The thought frightened but thrilled her at the same time. Finally, her courage was back. How good it felt! There was something worth fighting for, something worth dying for, and she could no longer hide in her aunt's sewing shop until the war had ended. Aunt Rianne was right. Work was the best antidote to melancholy, but meaningful work, patriotic work, work for the revolution. Reading over her lyrics, she grew more excited. The people needed to read this. She needed to get back to Charleston immediately.

It was sunset when she came downstairs and asked one of the slaves to locate Buckley. Impatiently, she paced up and down the central hallway as she waited. At one point she glanced into the mammoth library and caught a glimpse of a pathetically palsied man peering at a book with the aid of an enormous magnifying glass. Through the lense, his left green-gray eye appeared larger than his head. This, Colleen assumed, was Miranda's husband. The sound of approaching footsteps drew her attention back toward the entrance of the house, where Buckley bounded through the front door.

"An envoy of the major's just left," he said to Colleen, his voice filled with excitement. "Embleton was certain that the Wisp was hiding north of Charles Town, and consequently had concentrated his efforts to capture the swine in that territory. That's why we received no notification of the escape. But now they've picked up a trail heading south, in this very direction. I've alerted my full work staff, and at sunrise tomorrow I'll be going out with a dozen of my best men, Windrow and Simkins among them, to search these swamps for the slippery rebel. I intend to find him myself. I want to be among those cheering when he's strung up like a common criminal."

"He'll be impossible to catch," Colleen couldn't help but blurt out.

"You delude yourself, my pet. If he's within twenty square miles of Marble Manor, he's as good as dead."

"I want to go back to Charleston tonight."

"That's impossible. I can spare no men to accompany you home. Besides, you've just arrived."

"I'm being held against my will."

"Come, come, let's not exaggerate," Buckley said, changing his tone to one of salacious delight. Slowly, he looked over Colleen and spoke in a low, sultry voice. "After all, it was you who asked me to the ball. Finally, I'm beginning to understand you, Colleen McClagan. There are women who give in easily, those who give in not at all, and finally those who derive a degree of pleasure by merely postponing the act. I've come to see that you, my dear, fit into the third category. Yes, you'd have me wait, and wait, and wait again. You've sensed that I delight in a certain measure of subtle teasing. But of such games we've had enough. Tonight," he announced decisively, a sneer dancing across his lips, "there'll be no more waiting. You and I alone will dine at eight. Then, after our long night together is finally consummated, if you aren't too exhausted to travel tomorrow, I'll see that you're safely escorted to Charles Town— but not, mind you, before we take the pleasure that we've denied ourselves for far too long."

The strangely intense manner with which he spoke these final words alarmed Colleen. She realized that no matter what she did and said, there was no getting out of Marble Manor till the morrow.

Back in the bedroom, she put on a nightgown and tried to nap, but sleep wouldn't come. *I must escape. I must find a horse and hurry back to Charleston. Somehow, I have to flee this dreadful place.* But common sense told her it was impossible. Where were the stables? Who would help her locate a horse and saddle? She didn't know the territory well enough to find her way back to Charleston, and, even worse, traveling alone in the dead of night was treacherous and foolish. She was trapped. A loud rap at the door snapped her away from her reverie.

"Master Somerset says I needs to give you this dress, ma'am."

Colleen opened the door to a short, bright-eyed young black girl who spoke with a lisp. "He says you gotta wear this here dress, an' I needs to take all the other clothes away to make sure you wears it. He says I gotta do it, so please let me do it, 'cause if I's don't, Master Buckley, he gets mean, an' when he gets mean he likes to take out that whip o' his. Lord, have mercy, when he takes out his whip!"

"Come in," Colleen instructed the slave, "and do as you were told to do."

Appreciative of Colleen's cooperation, the girl placed the black dress carefully on the bed and busily gathered up the contents of the armoire and bureau, putting the clothing into a large box just outside the door.

"But the undergarments, you're leaving me with no undergarments."

"Sorry, ma'am, but Master Buckley hisself says there can't be nuthin' in here 'cept that there gown and some petticoats I's leavin' you an' a pair o' shoes. You gotta wear jus' what I's leavin' you, an' I can't say nuthin' more 'bout it 'cept that when it comes to things like this with ladies an' clothin', Master Buckley is mighty funny, an' ev'ryone 'round here knows 'bout it, so we listen an' don't say a word."

Colleen thanked the girl and closed the door behind her. What choice had she? She couldn't wear a nightgown. Yet, how could she submit to the humiliation of dining without undergarments? *What if I refuse to go downstairs at all? What if I simply remain in this room?* Colleen answered her own question: Buckley would refuse to allow her to return to Charleston. He'd keep postponing the day of her return until she finally subjected herself to this foolishness. More and more, she was seeing a clear-cut pattern to his perversions. The picture of dining with him under such conditions made her flesh crawl, and yet, greater than that repulsion was her desire to leave Marble Manor.

At seven-forty-five she put on the petticoats and pulled the gown over her head. The luxuriant black velvet garment was exquisite, but the daringly low-cut bodice was far too tight. It forced her small breasts up and out, exposing at least half of Colleen's hard, round nipples. She had to admit that the feeling of the fabric against her skin was provocative. The gown fell to the floor and trailed a few feet behind her. The absence of undergarments, the feel of air against her legs, thighs, buttocks, and pubis also aroused her, in spite of Colleen's best efforts to resist. *For the revolution,* she told herself. *My job is to get back to Charleston and fight for freedom. If even this must be endured in order to realize that goal, so be it.*

Buckley was already at the table, and as soon as she entered the dining room, he stood and, with lascivious relish, inspected her from head to toe. He, too, was dressed in a black velvet suit—did he wish to match hers?—tight at the waist, with rows of tiny cultured pearls stitched around the floppy lapels. His gray perfumed wig was coiffed in pageboy style, and his tall black boots shined to a mirror finish. Momentarily forgetting her state of partial undress, even Colleen had to admit that he struck a dashing pose.

"You look divine," he told her in a sensual whisper, "or should I say devilish? Mother herself never looked more ravishing in that gown."

"This gown belonged to your mother?"

"Indeed it did," Buckley reflected as he seated Colleen at the table and sat beside her. "I still remember seeing her wearing this very garment. I was a young lad no older than twelve or thirteen, and she seemed . . ." Realizing he was revealing a bit too much, he cut himself off.

"Won't your mother be dining with us?" Colleen asked.

"I'm afraid not. She's in a separate house on the plantation we call Miranda's Retreat. For her own good, we have to keep her there for a few days until she's rested enough to return to the normal world. Mother has a tendency to fly off the handle. As a young woman, though, I can assure you that there was no more seductive female in all the Carolinas."

Colleen saw that there was something different about Buckley. It was as if he had drunk a strange potion. His eyes were glazed. He twitched slightly. His usual habit of touching the bridge of his broken nose was intensified. Her stroked his wig as he delighted in the daring position of Colleen's breasts. For a moment, she was fascinated by this mysterious change in his mannerisms, but the draft beneath her dress brought her back to herself, remembering that she was furious with him.

"Never have I been put in such an insulting and demeaning position," she said angrily as she noticed the perfect elegance of the table—the white linen tablecloth bordered with Irish lace, the delicate bone china and exquisite silverware reflecting the eerie, flickering light of long tapered black candles.

"And never will you regret a moment of this marvelous evening. Tonight, my sweet pet," he continued speaking in a throaty whisper, "you will learn the difference between shallow pleasure and deep ecstasy."

"If you have the slightest intention of . . ." she began warning him.

"My intention is to bring you joy—penetrating and fulfilling joy, joy such as you've never tasted before."

"And if that sort of joy holds no interest for me?"

"You've only to let me know."

"Then be so advised. First thing in the morning, I want to . . ."

"You speak of tomorrow," he said with a growing sense of

confidence, "before you've allowed yourself tonight's delectable delights. At least enjoy your meal. We're dining on a plump goose prepared in a sauce certain to sweeten your sour disposition."

A liveried slave carried in a carafe of wine. Were it not for the dim candlelight, Colleen might have seen that the liquid was slightly strange in color, more orange than red. The taste, too, was a little foreign to her palate. It was pleasing, however, and to get through this dreadful evening, she told herself, a glass of spirits might be just the thing she needed.

The meal commenced, and as soon as she had drained the first goblet of wine, she noticed a subtle alteration in her perception. The change was not unpleasant, nor was it the usual light-headedness that came as a result of drinking. Her thoughts fogged as her senses sharpened. The food tasted noticeably succulent. She was especially aware of her tongue, and the feeling of naked skin beneath her gown. After a few sips from her second goblet of wine, a warm flush of eroticism spread as she watched Buckley watching her. He smiled slyly and brought his own goblet to his lips.

"You're enchanting," he continued speaking in whispers, "and worth these many months of waiting."

Suddenly the fog within her mind thickened as her skin seemed to sizzle with heat. She knew it had to be the wine. She had been drugged.

"What is it you've . . ." she began asking, but then lost her train of thought as she felt the toe of his leather boot lift her velvet gown and caress the back of her left calf. Feeling a thrilling chill pass over her body, she shivered as the boot slowly moved up to the softness of her thigh. The chill turned to a wave of warmth washing over her limbs. Involuntarily, moisture flowed from her pubic flower. Again, she struggled for reason. "No . . ." she started saying. "I've read of these aphrodisiacs, and no one will . . ." But by then Buckley was standing behind her, blowing on the back of her neck, kissing the lobes of her ears, allowing his perfumed fingers to tingle the tops of her breasts. She found herself breathing harder, felt herself slipping further away, falling from the even plane of reason into an abyss of forbidden bliss. *No,* said her former self, *this is horrid, this is wrong, this horrible man is using me. Stop! Stop!* But the sensation of his lips on her now exposed areolae, the way in which his flicking tongue traced the outline of her stiff, pointed nipples had her faint with desire. He had only to take her hand and lead her from the table. Then, with one swift movement, he lifted her in his arms and carried her up the great staircase toward his bedroom, one hand cradling her back, the other working busily beneath the petticoats of his mother's gown.

He kicked the door open, and through semi-conscious eyes Colleen saw a room darkened by black velvet drapes. The thick smell of burning incense hung heavy in the air. A variety of swords was nailed to the wall, and strewn across the bed were two large black leather whips. The sight of such instruments of pain was nearly enough to awaken Colleen from her sensuous stupor, when suddenly he pressed his mouth upon hers, his tongue probing, pushing, pleading. "Say no," he begged her. "Deny me as you've always denied me. Make me wait, my pet. Please, prolong my agony, prolong my pleasure. Not yet, not yet."

Confused by his sexual histrionics, she wasn't prepared to act out a drama. Seeing that, he grew angry, throwing her on the bed, lifting her gown and petticoat to her waist and placing a whip in her hand. "Let me just look at the beauty of this sight," he said, his voice shaking like a little boy's. "Now!" he shouted. "This is how I've always wanted you! This is how I shall take you!"

And take her he would have, were it not for a gun blast from downstairs as loud as the boom of thunder. Leaving Colleen on the bed, he charged from the room and ran down the hallway to the top of the staircase. There below him were Jack Windrow and Sam Simkins walking through the main doorway of the house, their hands tied behind them. Following the overseers was a line of a half dozen other white men who worked as plantation supervisors and guards. They, too, had their hands tied. Finally, pushing them all on with a rifle-barrel Kentucky pistol, was a masked man in a flowing gray cloak who, to disguise his voice, spoke through a short tube. Spotting Buckley at the top of the stairs, he aimed his gun at Somerset's head.

"The damned Wisp!" a half-drugged Somerset whispered to himself as the house slaves hid in the kitchen or ran out the back door.

"Get down here and open your safe!" demanded the strange-voiced rebel. "The money will go to Bronson so he can rebuild his farm you so cruelly burned. Hurry, man, before I blast you into the fires of hell!"

Enraged but afraid for his life, Buckley did as he was told. Joining the party of prisoners, he led them into the library, where he emptied one of the family safes, filled with gold coins, into a sack provided by the Wisp. There was something familiar about the outlaw's mannerisms, though Somerset's mind was too foggy to see through the disguise. In turn, the masked man tied Buckley's hands, but not before demanding and receiving a key to the library. He gagged each of the eight men and locked them in the room. In the hallway, carrying the sack of gold, he looked toward the staircase. There, staring down at him, was Colleen.

Reeling in a semi-stupor, not quite sure whether she was asleep or awake, she spoke his name: "Will-o'-the-Wisp."

He hesitated before going to her. Still wanting to protect her from the knowledge of his identify, he had nonetheless come here, in large measure, to carry her away. Having learned her whereabouts from Piero, he had been drawn inevitably to the plantation. Could he do any less than free her from this marbled prison?

Slowly she walked down the stairs, afraid of losing her balance, afraid that it all might be a dream. Slowly he walked up to meet her.

"Is it you? Is it really the Wisp?"

"Yes," he said, speaking through the tube.

"Then take me with you. I'm . . . I'm the Sandpiper."

"There's no time to waste. We must flee . . . now!"

At that moment—whether through the last, lingering effects of the drug or her own natural instinct—she pulled him toward her, stripped off his mask, and gasped. Before she could say his name, he covered her mouth with his and kissed her for what seemed an eternity.

"Jase!" she whispered when he let her go. *"Oh, dear God! It was always you! Jase!"*

Still clinging to Buckley's sack of gold, he seized her hand and, seeing that her legs were barely steady enough to support her, lifted her in his arms and carried her outside, where Cinder was waiting. The fresh night air brought her back to reality. As they galloped off, the startling texture of the stallion's back-side against her bare bottom threw Colleen into a drugless but heightened state of erotic arousal. Jason offered her his cloak, but she refused, for as they flew through the night, thundering through the plantation into the wild countryside, she wanted to feel the full force of the warm wind against her face and chest and half-exposed breasts. She wanted to experience this, the most thrilling moment of her life, in all its unleashed glory. Were they being chased? Would they be caught? She felt no fear. Let them try! Her arms wrapped around Jason's waist, the horse bouncing steadily and rhythmically beneath her, she felt the power of the great beast, the power of Jason Paxton, her own power and determination that linked her to this mighty, mysterious man who was everything she had ever dreamed— and more, so much more!

Miles beyond the plantation he led the horse into a dense wood, wonderfully fragrant and fresh. He veered from a beaten path and wound his way through a maze of trees and thick bush before stopping at a small, hidden grove. Quickly, without a word, Jason carried Colleen from the horse, spread his cloak upon the ground, and gently set her there. *Yes! Yes!* she thought. *My Wisp! My Jase! My fondest fantasy is real! My most cherished wish is coming true!*

"The English will be looking for us around here," she said.

"Let them look. No one—not even Somerset—could find this grove. It's another of my secret childhood hideaways, still unknown by other men."

"Then we're truly safe?" she asked, looking into his eyes with tender admiration.

"For now," he answered, his hunger for her love hardening by the minute.

Despite all their denials and vows, their misunderstandings and mistakes, they had never stopped wanting one another, not for a second, and finally, in the wild forest where they had first tasted the joy of their impassioned desire, they reached for each other with a feverish urgency no mortal could resist. *Three months without him,* thought Colleen, *three long months!* She opened her arms to him and together they rolled around in a sensuous, impatient embrace. She led her lover's hand beneath the velvet gown so he might discover the extent of her excitement. Curious about her extraordinary state of undress, he assumed it was the result of having to flee from Marble Manor in so a great hurry. Too aroused and thrilled to ask questions, he freed himself of his straining breeches and, within the time a bolt of lightning could pierce the midnight sky, he filled her with the burning, bulging expression of his love. She received him with ecstatic joy, wrapping her legs around his, urging him on, her nails dug deeply in his back, his tightened muscular buttocks rising and falling furiously, faster and faster, as she gave herself over to the frenzied convulsions. She was a rushing river whose banks overflowed, he a mighty, massive ship roaring through her savage currents. Her gasps, her moans, her cries, and her final scream of sweet release shot through the trees, straight to the heavens, where she envisioned a thousand cupids singing and dancing with unabashed delight.

Afterward, wrapped in his cloak, wrapped in one another's arms, there was music on their lips. Together they sang the same melody heard the day he had come home from England.

"I always knew," she whispered to him as she placed her hand upon his cheek and gently stroked his moonlit skin. "In the deepest part of my soul, I knew this song was ours. I felt your music, and your bravery . . . oh, Jase, I love you, I love you more than life itself."

Enjoying a relaxing, deep satiation he hadn't known since he last loved Colleen the day of the picnic, he felt blessed to have this precious woman cradled in his arms.

"I love you with all my heart," he whispered in her ear, kissing her lightly on her nose, on her still-warm lips. Her naked skin burned with slowly cooling passion. For a long while they lay there, she singing their song, he humming along. Yet in spite of this moment of quiet contentment, he couldn't help thinking that eventually night would give way to day and, in spite of his best intentions, the complexities of their lives were hopelessly intertwined, the dangers they faced suddenly more imminent and lethal than ever before.

PART III

~ *Chapter 1* ~

Commander Somerset of the Tory Militia
Searched for the Wisp long and hard.
Thus it was a shock when he was spotted
In Buckley's own backyard.

The rebel was there, without a doubt,
Somerset had only to bring him down.
But Will-o'-the-Wisp took the upper hand,
Turning Buckley into a clown.

"No, I don't think it's funny, not at all," Jason remarked
with decided anger as the rest of the company in Robin's ornate
parlor—Piero, Robin, and Colleen—laughed heartily. It was
the first week in September.

"Oh, come, come. You must admit that it's somewhat amusing," suggested Piero, nervously rubbing his thumb beneath
his nose as he felt the tender hairs of a new moustache growth.
"What's more, Miss McClagan reads her work with great verve."

"I think it's foolhardy," Jason snapped. "And it would be
even more foolish for the lyric to be circulated."

"I quite agree with Jason," commented a pensive Robin as
he rested his folded hands upon his considerable girth. "In spite
of its wit, it would be prudent to put the poem aside for the
time being."

"It's too late," said a confident Colleen. "I've given it to Frederic Pall, who's printing it even as we speak. Sometime during the night, the broadside will be nailed to the doors of pubs and shops throughout the city, where . . ."

"Colleen," Jason broke in sharply, "I warned you about this. We were lucky enough that your story about escaping the Wisp was believed by Somerset. What's the point in pushing our luck? And, besides, who is this Frederic Pall?"

"A most marvelous printer I met yesterday."

"And immediately decided he could be trusted?"

"I knew within minutes. He has a heart of gold and is willing to risk his life for the revolution. Isn't that enough proof? He was forced to flee from Augusta, where he printed books of patriotic poems. He's also an actor. He's just taken a role in the Shakespeare play at the Dock Street Theater. He knows absolutely everyone. His credentials are impeccable. He carries personal letters of recommendation from Benjamin Franklin and Sam Adams. He knew Ephraim well. Sometime back, he even served as Ephraim's apprentice."

"So it was Ephraim who first introduced you to him?"

"No. I met him for the first time yesterday morning. He was with Benjamin Long, the bookbinder, who's the most respected Patriot in the city. They both came to call on Aunt Rianne in search of a hiding place for a large quantity of forbidden books—one of which is a new number by Thomas Paine. Knowing my aunt's political persuasions, Long reasoned that she'd be helpful. Of course, she was. We had tea together, and during the course of the conversation Mr. Pall said that he knew of an abandoned press in working order here in the city, but he had no place to keep it. It occurred to me that if my aunt's basement could hold the books, it could hold a press as well. Rianne was a bit reluctant, but we finally convinced her."

"So they carried in the press in the bold light of day?"

"Hidden in a carton with dozens of fabric bolts and dresses spilling out of the top so as to give the appearance of perfectly normal activity."

"And you saw fit to give him your broadside and reveal your identity—just like that?" Jason asked skeptically.

"It was a matter of blessed fate. I was looking for a printer, and one was delivered to my very door. Wouldn't you call it providence? And is it not a great deal safer to have this material printed in my aunt's home rather than have me walking the streets, as I did with Ephraim, hoping not to be followed?"

"Who's to say that this Frederic Pall is not being followed?"

"Who's to say any of us is not being followed? But there's a limit to the precautions we must take. Being prudent is one thing; being inert is quite another."

"I don't like it, Colleen," Jason scolded. "This is no time for you to return to your old tricks. The loss at Camden and Fishing Creek only strengthened the Crown's stranglehold on the colony. You need only to step outside and look around. Tory and English soldiers are everywhere. They've increased the manpower here by nearly twenty percent. Moving in and out of the city without being stopped and searched is nearly impossible. What's the point of riling them up with another barb? Why must you persist in these games?"

"They're *not* games, Jason," Colleen said with dire seriousness. "I thought by now you understood that."

"Come, Piero," Robin said discreetly. "I've designed you a new robe, just as you requested, and I'd like your approval on the fabric. Will you join me in my studio?"

"Well..." Piero hesitated, hating to miss the rest of this fascinating exchange between lovers. "I suppose so. *Scusate, per favore.*" Bowing, he and Robin left the room.

Alone, Jason and Colleen rose from their chairs and met in the center of the room, where they grasped hands.

"I asked you not to come here," he reminded her. "'Twas a rash and reckless act."

She stood on tiptoes to kiss his mouth. He didn't resist. "I couldn't stay away. It's been three long nights since we escaped together, three nights of not being able to sleep. Haven't you missed me? Haven't you yearned to..."

"Yes, yes. I've wanted you more than I care to mention. In spite of all my noble intentions to stay aloof, my heart has claimed victory over my head. But, damn it, our heads will soon be severed if you don't realize the deadly situation we face. This is not the time to taunt Buckley and Embleton."

"No one suspects you. No one suspects me."

"Are you certain? Walking these streets, I've the feeling that everyone and everything are suspect. You're moving far too quickly, Colleen."

"But how will the people know of your exploits at Marble Manor if we don't tell them?"

"Eventually word will be spread."

"But in this besieged city, our people are crying out for hope—now, not eventually. How else can they endure the chains that bind them to their homes and shops? How else can they live with their fears? Hope. The Wisp brings them hope. And so does the Sandpiper. For in your actions and my words live the dreams and faith of thousands of men, women, and children, all praying for freedom. Can't you see that, Jase? You're not the Wisp any more than I'm the Sandpiper. The people are. We're merely their instruments, the symbols of their courage and determination. That's why they must know of your triumphs. You must understand that it's worth every risk."

Jason sighed and shook his head, obviously moved by what had just been said, but frustrated at his inability to convince her to curb her activities. "You're a remarkable woman, Colleen McClagan. A month ago you were hiding behind sewing tables, and today you're back risking your neck for the revolution."

"While I was at Aunt Rianne's and so full of fright, I read something in a book she gave me. It was a Greek philosopher— I forget whom—who said that courage is not simple fearlessness. The truly courageous individual is one who, having harbored fears, finds the strength to overcome them. That thought gave me hope. And so do the selfless acts of the Wisp."

"I appreciate that, Colleen. I appreciate you. I love you for your stamina and your courage. But I also want to impress you with the cold, hard facts of reality. In your verse, for instance, you speak of Buckley as a clown. Did it not occur to you that someone might make a connection between that reference and my costume at the ball?"

"No, I didn't think of that. But surely no one will..."

"Why take such a risk? Why make such an association?"

"You're far too sensitive, Jase. I don't think..."

"And this Frederic Pall. Have you discussed him among your rebel friends? Are you certain that he isn't..."

"If you'd read his letters of recommendation, you'd understand why I resent your inference," Colleen blurted out, cutting him off, her voice growing angry. "Sam Adams refers to him as one of the most dedicated Patriots in all the colonies. You still don't give me credit for having any sense. By now you should realize that we're truly partners in this..."

"For all the love I feel for you, Colleen, I must say that I don't need a partner. I don't want a partner. My plan was that no one except my patrons would know of these midnight rides. I've wanted to protect my family and you from..."

"Spare me from your protection! Won't you understand once and for all that I don't need protection? I have a mission in this war as great as any man's, and with the help of God I'll fulfill that mission or die trying."

For several seconds, they looked into one another's steadfast and stubborn eyes. Then, at the exact same moment, the discord quickly fading, they found each other's arms, lips, mouths, and tongues.

"Will you play for me?" she whispered in his ear.

"Whatever you like." He felt himself melting.

In the library, he wooed her with Mozart, his military posture turning into sweet, subtle melody. Later, with an almond-colored sun sinking into the garden beyond his bedroom window, their bodies danced to a long, sensuous symphony of love.

"It'll never cease, this love of ours," she said afterward as he cooled her neck with kisses.

"Promise me you'll be prudent," he urged. "For the sake of our love, promise me that, at least for the moment, the Sandpiper will retire."

"If you insist..."

"I do."

"Then I promise," she said, kissing his nose while she crossed her fingers tightly behind his back.

Frederic Pall held Major Randall Embleton and Buckley Somerset with his slanty, icy blue eyes. Wigless with wispy blond hair falling below his shoulders, his concave chest gave a decidedly passive appearance. The clothes he wore—a dark brown waistcoat, a jet-black blouse—were in noticeable contrast to his pale, rubbery skin. His elongated face was strangely mercurial. At times his visage exuded the tenderness of a kitten; other times he projected the aura of a sly fox. To a slow, steady rhythm, he continually tapped his long, graceful fingers upon his knees. He spoke with a fluent theatrical accent that could be bent to fit a wide variety of characters.

"Let me be plain about the matter," he said in a tone that was all business. "'Tis solely a question of money. I'm asking for nothing less than a hundred pounds sterling."

"Why, that's outrageous!" Embleton slammed his fist on his monumentally messy desk, causing papers to scatter in every direction. He was on the verge of ejecting the man from his office.

"With your permission, Major," Buckley interceded, "let's hear the man out. He's said, after all, that his information is nothing short of spectacular."

"That it is," said Pall, "if you still harbor an interest in the positive identification of the rebels known pseudonymously as the Sandpiper and Will-o'-the-Wisp."

Embleton and Somerset both rose at the same instant. Their jaws dropped; their eyes widened with impassioned interest.

"Of course! Of course!" the major declared.

"Money is no object," Buckley announced, deciding that if he himself had to pay the price, he would—which was one of the reasons Pall had requested that the plantation owner be at this secret meeting. "Just give us the names—now."

"It's not quite that simple. The arrangement will be effected in two stages. Today I'm prepared to deal only with step one— the first revelation. Within a week, I shall return to deliver the second name."

"With whom do you begin?" asked Somerset.

"And how do we know your information is correct?" inquired Embleton.

"My proof is incontrovertible. So confident am I that I'll defer full payment until a week from today, when I'll disclose the name of the Wisp."

"So you still don't know who he is," Buckley deduced.

"He's as good as named," said Frederic Pall, pulling a rolled piece of parchment from his coat. "Read this."

Embleton grabbed the document and Buckley read over his shoulder. It was the verse concerning Colleen's escape.

"This must never see the light of day!" Buckley demanded. "Name this Sandpiper so we can string him up this very day!"

"I'm afraid, kind sir," Pall replied, "that if we are to catch your elusive Wisp, this broadside must be distributed. If not, its author, whom I know to be in direct contact with the bandit, will be lost to me forever. As things stand now, she is as innocent of me as a lamb."

"*She!*" shouted Embleton. "You don't mean that the Sandpiper is a female!"

"One Colleen Cassandra McClagan by name."

"My God!" Somerset gasped as he fell into a chair, mumbling with a dazed glaze over his eyes. "Mother was right . . . Mother is always right. . . ."

"The McClagan woman!" the major shouted. "How extraordinary! She's a beauty, if I remember correctly, with those strangely yellowish eyes. In fact, was she not the woman whom you brought to the ball?" Embleton asked Buckley.

"Yes," answered the printer, "and the one whom the Wisp captured from Marble Manor."

"You didn't mention anything about a woman being captured," the major said to Buckley.

"I was about to tell you," Somerset lied, "but then Mr. Pall arrived early and . . ."

"Ye gods!" Embleton bellowed. "This woman has been extracting information from you for months. You've been taken in by the oldest trick of them all, a seemingly innocent female who . . ."

"I can assure you, Major, that she's learned nothing from me, absolutely nothing."

"It doesn't matter," Embleton said excitedly. "All that matters is that we've got her now."

"*I've* got her," Pall reminded the men. "She placed this document in my hands, just as I placed a printing press in the basement of her aunt's sewing shop. I have her absolute trust."

"Then why didn't you ask her to name the Wisp?" Buckley wanted to know.

"Timing, gentlemen," Pall said coolly, squinting his eyes. "'Tis all a matter of timing. In one meeting, I did quite enough. To rush matters would lead to suspicion. She's a trusting and extremely bright woman. Her impetuousness, though, led her to indiscretion, in spite of the shock of having seen her former ally, Ephraim Kramer, hanged in public."

"So that's why the swine wouldn't name his accomplice. A woman!" Embleton observed. "How novel, how clever . . ."

"I still insist that this broadside be stopped," demanded Buckley. "What purpose does it . . ."

"Let not pride interfere with progress," Embleton interrupted. "Our Mr. Pall is right. The McClagan woman must be led to believe that nothing is awry. We'll have that shop watched every minute. We'll follow her everywhere she goes. There's no doubt she'll lead us to our man."

"You could follow her all you like, but one false move on

your part, Major," said Pall, "and the game will be up. I suggest my approach is far more subtle. Leave this flighty Sandpiper to me and by this time next week the true name of your troublesome Wisp will fall from my tongue like gentle rain from the summer sky."

Something suddenly flashed through Somerset's mind—the image of a clown at his grandfather's ball. But, no, that was absurd, absolutely impossible. He dismissed the thought quickly.

"Yes, you have a point," declared the major. "If you can prove the Wisp's true identity, you'll get your hundred pounds next week, Frederic Pall, whomever you may be."

"I'm a mercenary, an occasional printer, but principally an actor by trade. In fact, I've been asked to take over for the chap who's been playing Parolles in the local production of *All's Well That Ends Well*. Seems as though the poor fellow, discovered to be a rebel by his crazed father-in-law, a rabid Tory, was shot in the back. I do hope you gentlemen can find the time to see me perform, though I must admit that this extraordinary state of war is a drama greater than any conceived by even the mighty bard. It has created a number of fascinating parts for those whose training has equipped them for the roles. This isn't my first performance in the service of public good and private gain, and I assure you it shan't be my last."

"Yes," said Embleton, "my reports from Georgia indicate you were a most effective spy."

"An actor," Pall corrected him, "who takes great professional pride in his performances."

Buckley had heard little of this, his mind still preoccupied with Colleen. Once he had gotten over the initial shock, a slow fuse had begun to burn through his body, finally reaching his brain, where the explosion was evident by the fire in his eyes and the rage of his shouting voice. He screamed without restraint. *"I want that wench's neck! I won't rest till the bloody bitch is dead!"*

~ *Chapter 2* ~

On a muggy mid-September afternoon, Jason took a brisk afternoon walk to his family's town house in Charleston. He knew
that Joy had been spending time there with Hope, but now that
Allan was free, he wondered whether his unmarried sister was
in Charleston or Brandborough.

Strangely enough, the front door was open, allowing the
musician to go inside without knocking. There, in the empty
parlor, seated on a wooden crate, her head in her hands, Joy
was sobbing her heart out. The place had been stripped of all
its furniture. The rugs had been picked up from the floors; the
walls were bare. When Joy saw her brother, she arose to embrace him. Shaking, she held him for a very long time before
the two of them sat down on the crate.

Jason looked at his sister, her eyes puffy with tears, her
body weak from sobbing. He tried to comfort her by putting
his arm around her shoulders. "Just take a deep breath," he
said, trying to console her, "and tell me what happened."

"The English military command has appropriated the house,"
Joy said, sniffling. "They say it's because of Allan being at
large, but I know they've been looking for any excuse to punish
the Paxtons. They've ransacked the house, they've taken everything. Soon they'll be back to padlock the door."

"We'll find a way to get it all back."

"It's not that, Jase. It's Father. When I was told that the

233

English would be closing up the house, I had no choice but to go home to Brandborough. I never thought he'd do it, but he blocked the front door. He stood on the porch and shouted at me. He called me a traitor and said never to come back to Brandborough because now that Allan had escaped he was afraid I'd find out where he and Hope were hiding and tell Peter. I reminded him that it was Peter who arranged for Hope to see Allan, but Father would have none of it. So I came back to Charleston only to find that the servants have been dismissed and that by day's end I'll be barred not only from our childhood home, but from our house here as well."

"Why didn't you come to see me?"

"I was about to, but you found me first. What's going to happen, Jase? Where am I going to go? What am I supposed to do?"

A rap was heard at the front door, followed by the firm footsteps of a soldier. Instinctively, Jason stood, his body tensed before he saw Captain Peter Tregoning appear in the archway of the parlor. Joy looked at Jason for an instant before she ran to the Englishman and embraced him. As he was being held by Joy, Peter's embarrassed eyes met Jason's.

A few seconds later, Joy asked her brother, "Do you think it's terrible? Do you think I'm a traitor?"

Jason regarded his sister and his friend. "No," he answered, "I don't think you're a traitor. I know your heart, and it's pure as gold. You're caught, we're all caught," he said, his eyes turning to Peter, "in the web of war."

"I just found out about the appropriation," Peter said with sincere concern. "I've tried to intercede, but it's impossible. Frankly, I was surprised, given Major Embleton's regard for you, Jase, that this action wasn't averted."

"In his mind," Jason answered, "he separates me from the rest of my family."

"Just like Father," Joy added.

"Did you see your father yesterday?" Peter asked her.

She told him the story. When she was through, she once again raised the question of her future.

"You'll come with me to Robin and Piero's," Jason told her. "They have the room and . . ."

"I couldn't, Jase. I barely know them. I'd feel like an intruder."

"What about Colleen McClagan?" Peter asked, addressing both Jason and Joy.

"Her Aunt Rianne has often told me that if I needed anything in these troubled times, I was merely to ask," Joy said. "I think I'd feel far more comfortable there than with your patrons, Jase."

Jason tried to hide his concern while searching for a good excuse as to why Rianne McClagan's was not a suitable place for Joy. The intrigue surrounding that house alarmed him. Anything he said, though, would reveal more than he wished to disclose.

"Will you take me there, Jase? They're so fond of you. Will you ask them with me?" Joy knew of the romantic involvement between Colleen and Jason. Jason had also told her of Dr. McClagan's disapproval. In her brother's affectionate alliance with Colleen, Joy felt a comforting parallel to her own relationship with Peter, something that the English soldier had himself sensed when he made the suggestion. She was also genuinely fond of the flamboyant Rianne and quick-witted Colleen. She looked forward to greater intimacy with them both.

"I'm not sure they have the room," Jason said.

"Rianne's house isn't small," Joy observed.

"Whatever you do, hurry," Peter urged. "Embleton's assigned a rough lot of Torries to close down this house. According to the schedule I saw, they're due within the hour. You don't want to be here when they arrive."

"They're not going to damage the property, are they?" Jason asked.

"Since the house can be put to good use, I doubt it. These are men, though, who aren't given to restraint. Some of them have had their own houses destroyed. In every part of this colony, emotions are out of control. I've just returned from Fairview, where we fought in conjunction with a brigade of Greencoats. We stormed the village, which, as you know, had been a rebel stronghold. My orders were to capture and hold the town, but the Tories couldn't be controlled." Peter paused to sigh. It was obvious that he was trying to maintain his composure, though the fresh memories still racked him with pain. "The Tories went wild, burning down every home and village in sight. Our soldiers followed suit. I tried to stop them, but it was impossible. The order from Embleton was to drive out the rebels at any price, but, believe me, Jase, when you see a forty-five-year-old man shoot a twelve-year-old boy in the back, you start wondering why and what in the name of a merciful God . . ." Realizing he had gone too far in confessing his equivocation about his service of duty, Peter stopped himself.

Jason sensed that his friend wanted to go on and relieve himself of the torturous guilt. "I understand," the musician said, moving toward the archway where Joy and Peter were standing. He put a consoling arm upon the soldier's shoulder before going on. "In war there are atrocities on both sides."

"I realize that," Peter replied. "I've seen the horrors of battle before, but there's something about this conflict that chills the civilized soul. Perhaps because I'm so far from my own soil, in a land that seems remote . . ." He lowered his voice and, finally uttering a thought that had been locked in his mind for months, said in a choked cadence, ". . . a land that seems so clearly fated to cast its own destiny."

"You've recognized that?" Jason asked, marveling at his friend's changing spirit.

"It would be hard for a sensitive soul not to, Jase. Never before have I encountered a people whose sense of individuality is so powerful. I fear . . . I know in my heart that our mission here is doomed."

"In spite of the strength of your position in the South?"

"I can't help but see beyond the temporary positions of the opposing forces. Something large, extraordinarily large, is happening in these colonies. I feel as though I'm witnessing a great birth. The horrible part is that I've been ordered to murder the child."

"Oh, Peter . . ." Joy gasped as she felt the excruciating dilemma in which her lover found himself.

Jason's eyes filled with tears as his friend's words touched his heart. "And yet . . ." he began to say, but found himself unable to speak.

"Yet I'm duty-bound," Peter completed the thought. "I'm an Englishman with sworn royalty to the Crown."

"Even if . . ." Joy started to speak.

"There are no conditions to a soldier's loyalty," Peter said firmly, trying to bring himself back to his former bearing.

"You've come here to alert us to leave our home," Jason

spoke up. "I'm touched by your devotion to my sister and myself, Peter. But isn't that, in and of itself, an act of questionable loyalty?"

"'Tis a question I prefer not to ask myself," he answered. "I know I care for your safety. I cherish your lives."

"And we cherish yours, Peter," Jason added, realizing that the discussion should go no further. "You'd best leave before us. Now, more than ever, it's important that we not be seen together. I'm afraid that's especially true for you and Joy."

"One way or another," Joy whispered as she hugged her man, covering his face with tear-stained kisses, "we must see each other, we must talk."

"I'll do whatever I can," he promised. Looking directly into Jason's eyes, the young Englishman extended his hand. The musician grasped it in his, but the emotion of the moment brought the men into one another's arms. They embraced for a few intense seconds before, without another word, the soldier left the siblings to their wistful thoughts.

"I don't like this, I don't like it at all, Ethan Paxton," Dr. Roy McClagan said as they sat side by side in the buggy, Paxton's strong hands on the reins. Slowly they rode through fields, forests, and swamps going west from Brandborough. They had been traveling through the starless night a full hour, their silhouettes in stark contrast—the erect, athletic farmer and the stooped, wizened physician. They had another hour to ride before reaching their secret destination.

"I promised you'd be well paid, Doctor," Ethan assured him.

"'Tis not the money, but the danger."

"The message I received today was unmistakably urgent. These men are sick. They've no hope for help save you, so put your doubts and fears in your back pocket, and be comforted that you're a vital part of a noble cause."

"Some comfort! Some cause!" Roy scoffed. "I'm making this trip, Ethan Paxton, only because you've assured me these men are patients of mine from Brandborough. I want no part of your rebel uprisings, but I can't allow a patient to die for lack of care, no matter how foolish his political persuasions."

"While your head is hard, your heart is wise. Eventually, you'll cheer as we throw these tax-mad British off our land."

"Save me the pain of your convictions, Ethan Paxton, and

quickly lead me to the wounded. I want this night's work concluded as quickly as possible."

For the rest of the arduous ride, barely a word was spoken between the two men. They were both preoccupied with thoughts of their daughters. Again and again, Ethan reviewed the painful scene between himself and Joy. He had all but disowned her, yet what else could he do with a woman who'd slept with the enemy?

In his coat pocket, Roy carried a letter from Colleen. He had to admit that she sounded more like her own self. In these violent times, though, he wanted her home. In his last letter, he had again raised the question. She replied by mentioning her pleasant weekend at Marble Manor, failing to add a word about her capture and "escape" from Will-o'-the-Wisp. Fortunately, news of the escapade had not reached Roy. "I shall be coming home soon, dear Father," she had written, "but for the present time, I'm content helping Rianne in the shop and continuing my study of classic literature. To be a scholar or a seamstress—that is the question." Roy smiled when he read that, knowing full well his daughter felt no such conflict. Still, Colleen's words had successfully charmed her father into not pressing the issue of her immediate return, for even if he had, he realized, there was no guarantee that she or her stubborn aunt would pay him the least mind. Most of all, he wanted Colleen to be happy. If staying in Charleston for a while longer gave her pleasure, then so be it. At least Rianne would see to it that his daughter stayed out of mischief.

Worriedly, Roy watched as Ethan slowly guided the horse and buggy though a shallow swamp. But for the steady slush of dark water, the buzz of mosquitoes, and the occasional sound of a slithering, hissing snake, the night was silent. The doctor began wishing that he'd never been persuaded to make this journey.

"I presume that, were we lost," said the doctor, "you'd so inform me."

Ethan laughed. "I could no more be lost in these swamps than in my own bedroom. Be assured, Dr. McClagan, that we'll be arriving soon. Solitary lies just behind the other side of that cypress grove where the swamp ends."

"Solitary?" Roy asked.

"It's land, wonderfully rich and perfectly hidden." As Ethan spoke of Solitary, his voice filled with enthusiasm. "Nearly

four square miles of flat, fertile meadow, a virtual island surrounded on all sides by swampland and acre upon acre of tall,
sturdy cypress. I discovered this place when my children were
infants, and we've been going there ever since. They love it
as well as I—at least they *did*. 'Tis where we Paxtons will
finally root ourselves in the earth. The moment we've won this
war and chased the British home, I intend to build a commodious house there and cultivate substantial fields of cotton and
corn."

"A dream, Ethan Paxton. You're a man given to dreams."

"It's as real as the medicines in your case, Doctor. The
swamp ends here, and in a few minutes we'll be through these
trees."

Even in the dark night, Roy could make out the beauty of
the land. Slightly elevated, it arose from the swamp and trees
like a hidden paradise. Here and there stood groves of tall oaks,
but, for the most part, Solitary seemed a natural lawn of mammoth proportions. The doctor could well appreciate Ethan's
affection for the land. "Where are the wounded?" he asked the
farmer.

"In a moment, you'll see for yourself."

In the dense center of one of the larger groves of oaks, Roy
spotted a group of tents. By prearranged signal—a cry simu-
lating the hoot of an owl—Ethan announced their arrival. Within
seconds six men and one woman emerged from the tents. Roy
recognized Hope Paxton, her husband, Allan Coleridge, and
the other five men, each of whom he knew well. He had treated
all of them at various periods of their lives, some since they
were children. Hope, in a coarse gray robe, greeted the doctor
with gratitude and warmth. The others, ranging in age from
twenty to fifty, followed suit. Among them were Ned Flats,
the paunchy bread maker, and Tom Jobete, the silversmith
whose wife's first baby Roy had delivered only a month before.

"You must do something, Doctor," Hope urged, her brow
wrinkled with worry and fatigue. "I've tried to bring down their
fevers, but to no avail." She pointed to the men most in need
of medical attention—Jimmy Morris and her husband, Allan.

A fire was made as Roy went about his examination. One
man displayed all the signs of dysentery; he complained of
painful cramps and bloody stools. But Coleridge and Morris
had symptoms far more severe. They shook with a feverish
chill, their tongues were covered with a yellow-green crust,

and their hands trembled. The doctor detected purplish spots spread over their peeling skins.

"What is it, Doc?" Jimmy Morris asked. He was a slight, gawky lad in his late teens. Roy had brought him into the world and remembered every detail of the stormy night when the miracle had taken place. The doctor never forgot a birth, carrying the joy of a healthy baby in his heart forever after.

"Is it bad?" asked a frightened Jimmy.

Roy knew it could well be typhus, but didn't say so, wanting to avoid panlic. "Courage, my boy," he responded. "We'll see what we can do to relieve your discomfort."

"I chill easily," Allan said in a voice straining for strength, "but I expect it's nothing more than fever blisters and a nasty cold. Am I right, Doctor?"

"Your attitude is the correct one, Mr. Coleridge. Determined mental defenses have been known to beat these maladies back. Be of good cheer."

After the examinations, Roy took Ethan aside and spoke directly. "Three of these men, including your son-in-law, must return with us. They require beds and continual supervision."

"Impossible," Ethan answered. "It was hard enough to make our way at night. During the day we'll be unable to move about without being observed. Three times last week my property was searched for escaped prisoners. Because of Allan, I'm highly suspect."

Roy brought his voice to a whisper. "It could be typhus."

"The devil be damned!" Ethan said disgustedly. "Will it spread. Has it already?"

"I think not. I'll examine the rest of the party, but these are the early stages when, with conscientious and continual treatment, the men could be saved and the malady checked. This surrounding doesn't help a bit. They must be brought to Brandborough—immediately."

"You know as well as I that it's swarming with Tories and Redcoats. We might as well bring them to the hangman himself."

"Mr. Paxton, I warned you before I came that the patriotic cause is one that fills me with dread. We are subjects of the Crown. Theirs is the brute force that rules this region. But I came here out of humanitarian concern, and now that I've made my diagnosis I can only tell you what is absolutely necessary.

Ignore me and these men, along with your daughter, may not survive another two weeks."

"Then we'll take them back tonight."

"I'm glad you understand."

"We must take them to your house. You must care for them there."

"What! I've risked my neck just by being here now, but under no circumstances will I . . ."

"You speak of risk, Dr. McClagan, but these men have risked their very lives so that you and others like you might keep what's rightfully yours. You're a fortunate man. Your services are always in need and the English haven't yet decided to tax your practice. But your farm has been taxed, and your crops are selling at a third of the price they're worth. Whenever they like, they'll appropriate your land, and then it's only a matter of time before . . ."

"I will not involve myself in your scheme, Ethan Paxton."

"Scheme! Is saving the lives of honest men a scheme? Are you a physician, Dr. McClagan, or a cynic? You call yourself a humanitarian, but no true humanitarian would leave these men alone to die in the wild."

Ethan stopped talking as he saw Hope approaching.

"Please be candid with me, Doctor," she said. "I must know the truth."

"The situation's grave," her father whispered.

"But not without hope," McClagan added, glancing over at young Jimmy Morris, who, sitting upon the ground, shivered beneath a thin blanket.

"Then you'll care for these people?" Ethan asked.

"They're my patients," Roy heard himself saying, "and I'll do what I can."

Shortly before dawn, a caravan of two buggies and two stallions arrived unnoticed at the McClagan farm. By nine that morning, in the back rooms of his house, with the help of Hope, Portia, and several other servants, Roy had set up temporary beds for all six rebels.

Part of McClagan's mind was in a panic. Wondering how in the name of God he could be taking such a foolhardy risk, he was glad that Colleen had decided to stay in Charleston. At least he hadn't involved her in this great danger. In the pit of his stomach, he felt the awful, gnawing fear of being discovered. Stronger than that fear, though, was his sense of obligation to his patients, whom he treated with ointments, salves, and herbs, gently wiping their perspiring brows and cooling their feverish skin with fresh spring water while reassuring the men he would heal them; to the best of his ability.

Chapter 3

On the way to Rianne's shop, on the street Jason saw a discarded copy of the Sandpiper's broadside concerning Buckley. He picked it up, read it quickly, and threw it back down as four Redcoat soldiers hurried by on horseback.

"What is it?" Joy asked.

"Propaganda," Jason answered, reflecting on Colleen's persistence in publishing the tracts. He frowned and felt his old anger and fears for her safety return. Another group of British military men, these on foot, marched by, their muskets resting against their shoulders. It seemed as if there were more soldiers than civilians in Charleston. The city, once open and inviting, had turned inward and anxious. The streets had been given over to the army, to the greencoats as well as the red, and on this humid September afternoon, normally a time when the citizenry found any and every excuse to congregate in the city's many markets and parks, those public gathering places were half deserted, creating a forlorn and forbidden atmosphere.

Joy slipped her arm into the crook of her brother's elbow and gave him a soft, loving squeeze. "Thank you for seeing me through this, Jase," she said. "You're the one person who doesn't demand explanations or apologies from me about Peter. I don't have to say a word, and yet I know you understand. I don't know what I'd do without you."

"You've done as much for me," he answered, knowing that

in his family, Joy alone accepted and supported his affection for Colleen without question or judgment. "If families can't help one another, Joy..."

"If only Father felt that way," she interrupted.

Jason reflected upon the twisted misunderstandings that so cruelly divided his family. "Perhaps one day he, too, will understand," he said, searching his own soul for optimism. "I just hope that day comes soon," he added wistfully.

At the seamstress's shop, a servant led the Paxton siblings into the parlor, where they seated themselves in stiff, wingbacked chairs and awaited Rianne's arrival. A few minutes later, she appeared with a buoyantly curious Colleen at her side. Seeing Colleen's sparkling eyes and ready smile, Jason's anger about the broadside quickly fell away. He arose courteously and kissed the hand of the aunt as well as the niece, noticing that Colleen's fingers were smudged with printer's ink.

"To what do I owe the honor of this visit?" the seamstress asked.

"I'm afraid," Joy answered before her brother had time to speak, "that we've come here under rather embarrassing circumstances."

Joy and Jason related the story together, careful not to interrupt one another or put their father in too unfavorable a light, demonstrating both discretion and compassion in telling their tale of family distress. Captain Peter Tregoning was never mentioned.

"Why, naturally you may stay here, my dear," Rianne offered the minute their case had been stated. She'd always been extremely fond of Joy and—like her brother, Roy—had a soft spot in her heart for souls in distress. "Your faith and trust in me," she told Jason and Joy, "is highly flattering. I'm sorry for the unfortunate conflict with your father. Alas, I've a similar situation, somewhat in reverse, with my own brother."

"You presume we're Loyalists, Miss McClagan," Jason said, "but I want you to understand that, apart from appearances..."

"Fret not, Jason Paxton," she broke in. "It matters not to me how you view this bloody conflict. I know you and your sister to be people of good conscience. We'll care for one another as human beings, not political entities. Now, if I can persuade my niece to share her bedroom with Joy..."

"Most gladly!" Colleen exclaimed, delighted to have an

opportunity to get to know Joy better, a person she, too, had always liked and admired.

"Then the matter is settled. you'll move your garments in . . ."

"I'm afraid," Joy said with fresh embarrassment, "that most of my clothing is back in Brandborough. What remained in Charleston was taken from our house by the greencoats. I have a few things, but lack even essential . . ."

"You'll lack nothing here," Rianne stated. "Of all the places in this colony to arrive *sans* wardrobe, you've chosen the ideal establishment. Why, we have garments of every stripe, for every size, figure, and taste."

"I hope you'll allow me to help you with the household duties as well as the sewing," Joy offered. "I'm quite handy with needle and thread."

"You're a dandy, I'm sure. I'll put you to work within the hour if you're not careful," Rianne responded, realizing that allowing Joy to work would make her feel useful and wanted.

A servant entered the room and whispered something into Colleen's ear. Colleen thought for a few seconds—Jason could hear her thinking—before she said, "Aunt Rianne, could you show Joy around the house? She hasn't seen the living quarters before. There's an old musical score in the basement that I wish to show Jason. it won't take but a minute."

"Of course, my dear," Rianne said, eyeing her niece with suspicion but content to go along with what seemed a harmless plan.

Jason followed Colleen through the shop to a door that led downstairs. "Where are you taking me?" he asked.

"Shh!" she said, putting a finger to her lips. "You'll see in a second."

She led the way down the staircase into the dark, damp basement. Jason tripped over a bolt of fabric, but Colleen was there to catch his fall. He felt embarrassed, allowing her to lead the way as she held his hand. "I was told he's at the trapdoor," she said, lighting a candle.

"Who?"

"Frederic Pall."

"Wait, Colleen," Jason said with some alarm in his voice. "I don't think it's a good idea . . ."

"Nonsense. You were suspicious of him. Well, now you'll see for yourself the sort of rebel he is."

Several mice scurried over Colleen and Jason's feet. She shuddered, squeezed the musician's hand, regained her composure, and walked to the back of the basement, where she found a small stepladder that she ascended and expertly opened a trap door leading up to the backyard. Daylight flooded the basement. The startling light caused Jason to take a step back. Seconds later, though, the same light was blocked by an intense face peering into the opening.

"Colleen?"

"Yes, Frederic. There's a ladder beneath you. Lower yourself carefully."

He did so, as Jason noted the snakelike dexterity with which the slim, slithery figure negotiated the steps of the ladder. Before Colleen replaced the trapdoor, Jason had a few seconds to examine Pall. His shoulder-length blond hair, his piercing blue eyes, and his sunken chest all gave the printer a singular, almost bizarre, appearance. Jason's suspicions grew. Perhaps it was jealousy, Jason thought; perhaps it was the fact that Colleen had called Pall by his first name. No matter, with the door back in place and another candle lit so that the basement flickered with long yellow shadows, Colleen introduced the men to one another.

"'Tis a rare pleasure indeed," Pall said, turning on all his theatrical charm. "I've heard much about you from my friends in Europe."

"Oh?" Jason asked with studied wariness.

"Indeed. You're a musician and composer, if I'm not mistaken, and the son of Ethan Paxton."

How does Pall know so much? Jason wondered.

"Here's the printing press that I told you Frederic brought last week," Colleen said as she drew back several enormous pieces of fabric that had been thrown over a worn but operative press. "Isn't it marvelous?"

"Where did you get it?" Jason asked, aware of the fact that by merely being introduced to Pall, Colleen had let this stranger know that he—a musician and friend of Major Embleton— knew the Sandpiper's true identity. What else had Colleen told Pall? Jason wondered.

"The press is a loan from a rebel friend who shall remain nameless," Frederic said cautiously. "But if I may say so, Mr. Paxton, I sense that you don't trust me."

"I don't, Mr. Pall."

"Then perhaps my letters of recommendation would put your mind at ease."

Frederic produced the documents, which Jason read carefully by candlelight before saying, "I have no way to authenticate the handwriting."

"If my sources are correct, Mr. Paxton," Pall retorted haughtily, "I might remind you that for the last several years you've been off in Europe pursuing a musical career while many of us have stayed home to fight a war. My efforts on behalf of this revolution are a matter of record. Nonetheless, I'm pleased to learn that you're a supporter of our cause, if indeed that's the case."

"I'm a friend of Colleen's."

"A very close friend, I see," Pall commented as he saw Colleen take the musician's hand. Even at this early moment, there was no doubt in the actor's mind that he had his man. He'd been certain that Colleen would introduce him to the Wisp, though he hadn't thought she would do so this soon. How simple the task! How sweet the reward! Still, he was able to suppress any flush of victory from appearing on his face. He knew he had to be careful not to tip his hand.

"And from where do you hail?" Jason asked, still digging for information.

"From wherever our great revolution has last led me," Pall replied, ready to meet the challenge of Paxton's questions. "I've no home, save where duty calls. I've been in Philadelphia, I've been in Atlanta, and now I'm needed here, where the Crown's vicious stronghold tightens about our necks with each passing day."

"'Tis strange," Jason added, "that you knew of my reputation as a musician."

"Not in the least," Pall said casually, twisting his face into an expression of thoughtful sincerity, speaking as if the words had been written out beforehand. "I'm a printer, but also something of a thespian. I've friends throughout England and the Continent who keep me abreast of the latest artistic developments. You've been mentioned many a time. I'm also aware that you performed at Major Embleton's home here in Charleston. I'm sorry to have missed the recital."

"Purely an artistic event," Jason said defensively.

"A convenient camouflage," Colleen added.

Jason shot Colleen an angry look that Frederic did not fail to see.

"Might I ask about your European friends who mentioned me?" Jason turned the questioning back on Pall.

"Why, of course." Frederic paused, placing his right leg upon the first step of the ladder, his chin resting upon his hand. "Let me see . . . could it have been my good friend Luigi Boccherini?"

"The musician?" Jason asked in amazement.

"The same. When last in Tuscany—several years back— we struck up a rare friendship and have corresponded ever since. I'm a great admirer of his string quartets."

"Then you know music."

"I love music. And musicians fascinate me. I can't pass through Paris, for instance, without seeing my good friend François Barthelemon."

"The violinist?"

"And composer. His *Pelopida* is among the loveliest operas in the French language."

"But what brings you to Charleston, Mr. Pall?" Jason asked, still not satisfied by any of Frederic's answers.

"My work in Atlanta was discovered by the British. They didn't look favorably upon the patriotic pamphlets I was printing. Consequently, I was forced to leave Georgia in something of a hurry. Fortunately, my network of friends led me to this press and, I might add, to a part in a Shakespearean comedy as well."

"But won't the English officials from Atlanta have an easy time tracing you to Charleston, especially as an actor?"

"Oh, but there's little chance. You see, I'm quite an expert at changes in identity. The true rebel must go by many names, and under many disguises. In Atlanta, with the aid of a multiplicity of wigs and a great deal of greasepaint and rouge, you would not have recognized me as the man who stands before you."

The more they spoke, the more suspicious Jason became, in spite of—or because of—Frederic's glib responses. For all his surface charm, Pall had too many ready answers for Jason. He seemed to know every well-known revolutionary in the colonies. "He knows Thomas Paine himself," Colleen said, giving Pall an excuse to relay stories of his friendship with the famed writer. He spoke of the revolution with singular zeal, and Jason could see how Colleen's openheartedness and patriotic fervor led her to believe this man's many tales. Jason did not believe him. He found the man unctuous and cunning. Yet the musician knew himself to be in a most precarious position. Pall now knew he was a confidant of Colleen's. Jason had no choice but to go along—and find out what he could later.

"You've arrived just in time, Frederic," Colleen said. "I wrote a new broadside early this morning. If you could print it now, I could have the boys put it out tonight. Our people will be heartened, I know. 'Tis a verse of hope and needs to be read by all in despair."

"You're an angel of good faith, Colleen McClagan," Pall declared. "Souls such as yours will keep the fire of revolution burning bright. Am I right, Mr. Paxton, or am I not?"

Jason remembered his many meetings with Embleton and the goodly amount of acting that had been required of him. He recognized in Pall an actor of far greater ability, but someone whose facial expressions, poses, and smiles appeared shallow and forced. "Miss McClagan has only the best intentions," Jason replied finally.

"We'll leave you alone to your work, Frederic," Colleen said, "and wish you well. My aunt will be looking for me."

The two men shook hands before taking their leave. Pall held Jason with his eyes for several awkward seconds. "It was a privilege to met you, Jason Paxton, and a comfort to realize that you are so close a friend of so great a patriot. I trust you'll come to see me as Parolles in *All's Well That Ends Well,* just as I hope the next time you perform your music, I'll be among those privileged to attend."

Jason nodded without replying. He felt a growing alarm spread through his heart and mind as he followed his lover from the basement, up the stairs, and back through the shop, where Joy was already working, under Rianne's watchful supervision, on an elaborate gown.

"The girl's an absolute gem," Rianne announced. "With two nimble helpers, both of whom refuse to accept even the most modest wages, I'm sure to have a markedly profitable year—despite the ravages of this endless war."

Jason wished his sister good-bye. "You're upset about something." Joy sensed the concern in her brother's eyes.

"Only your well-being."

"'Tis my concern now," Rianne informed them. "So you go back to your friends and your music. This home is secure."

After wishing the women a good day, Jason walked with Colleen to the front door. She stepped outside with him and asked, "Well, wasn't I right? Isn't it marvelous the way Frederic came into my life, just as I needed a printer? Don't you see how he and people like him are guaranteeing our victory? I didn't even know that he had lived abroad and knew so much about music and . . ."

"I wish to God, Colleen," Jason said with pointed irritation in his voice, "that you hadn't said that about my camouflage. You might as well have called me Will-o'-the-Wisp right then and there."

"And if I had, there'd be no harm done. Frederic Pall's someone we can trust."

"I don't like the man," Jason said flatly.

"What?"

"I said I don't like him. And I don't trust him—not one bit."

"What about his letters?"

"Who's to say they're not forgeries?"

"Jason Paxton," Colleen drawled as she looked at his troubled eyes. "If I didn't know you better, I'd say you were jealous."

"I'm not in the least jealous. But I do worry about someone who just happens to appear from nowhere, with so many names on the tip of his tongue. I suspect he's both a brilliant actor and a brilliant fraud."

"For God's sake, Jase, help arrives and you're too suspicious to believe it's really help. Or is it because Will-o'-the-Wisp wishes no competition, no other man who has the courage to . . ."

"Please, Colleen, you're making me angry. I welcome all help. But there's something about that man that . . ."

"That what? If anything, he reminds me of your trusted patrons, Piero and Robin, only with real revolutionary conviction. He's erudite, but he's also brave."

"And Piero and Robin aren't?"

"This man is printing my broadsides. That's the simple fact of the matter. He's printing them when no one else has been willing. I'd say that's proof."

"Proof of the fact that he's learned the Sandpiper's identity and now may have some fairly accurate notions about the Wisp."

"You're imagining this. In truth, I didn't say a word about the Wisp."

"There was no need to. Introducing me was enough."

"That's enough, Jason! Were he a spy, I'd have been arrested days ago."

"If he were a spy he'd string you along, hoping you'd lead him to the Wisp."

"All this to tell me to stop writing my verses! Well, I won't stop. You needn't invent any more stories about secret spies in my basement, Jason, because you won't convince me. My work is vital, and my work goes forward, with or without your support."

And with that, she stormed into the house, slamming the door behind her.

~ *Chapter 4* ~

Jimmy Morris stared at Roy McClagan, his eyes filled with terror. The teen-ager knew he was dying.

Since returning from Solitary two days ago, the doctor had turned Colleen's room and his back study into a temporary hospital where all six men were confined to cots. Jimmy was in the most critical condition of all. The physician had isolated him from the others and had brought him into his own bedroom. He had stayed by his side all night, giving him a series of emetics that had induced vomiting, but there had been no sign of progress. The fever raged unchecked, Jimmy's pulse was feeble, and the awful yellow-green crust coating his tongue had hardened. Still, Roy mixed his herbs and ointments, steadily toiling for six straight hours, pushing himself beyond endurance. Black night had turned to charcoal gray, and as the gray turned light, as the tip of morning sun met the horizon, the frail lad began speaking in a barely audible voice.

"I'm . . . I'm afraid . . . I don't want to die . . ."

The physician, kneeling at Jimmy's side, put his arm around the feverish boy and spoke gently to him. "I've not met a man—no matter how brave—who wasn't afraid, lad. But you, you're braver than most. I see it in your eyes. You've done what you've thought was right, haven't you?"

"Dear God, please don't let me die, not now, not this soon.

I've still never known a lady. I want to live . . . I want . . ." But he was too weak to speak the words.

"You're strong and you're young and your spirit won't be broken, Jimmy, not for an instant." Roy took the boy's hand in his.

"Stay with me . . . I'm afraid . . . please stay . . ." the teenager whispered.

"I'm with you, laddy. I'm not going anywhere."

Filled with frustration and anger that there was nothing left to do—his mind exhausted, his own body at the point of collapse—McClagan felt the teen-ager's hand go limp as his life expired with the first rays of a new day. The doctor's eyes filled with tears as he stood up, looking at his patient for a few silent seconds, only to have his mournful concentration broken by the frantic cry of a woman's voice.

"Hurry!" Hope screamed. "Allan's having convulsions! Run!"

The stooped-shouldered doctor ran to Colleen's room, where Hope, Allan, and two of ther other rebels were staying. Coleridge was twitching and shaking like a pathetically wounded bird. He flayed his arms and kicked his feet in writhing paroxysms of pain. "Do something, Doctor, for God's sake!" Hope urged, dressed in a cloth robe, her long hair streaming wildly down her back.

For an hour, Roy struggled and labored over the once powerful and fearless rebel. It was no use. By the time the radiant sun had burned off the scattered morning clouds and the sky appeared as clear and blue as the ocean, Allan Coleridge was gone, and his wife, Hope Ellen, was beside herself with grief. She sobbed, she threw herself upon her husband's lifeless body, she screamed at the heavens for the injustice of it all.

Roy swallowed hard, fighting to maintain his composure, feeling his heart thumping wildly against his chest. His house stank of medicines and death. Portia and the other slaves were petrified. One grave was being dug, and now another. Ethan would have to be notified. These other men would have to be watched even more carefully. There was no time to fall apart; ther was work to be done. Roy put his arms around the grieving Hope, whispering in her ear that God worked in mysterious ways. Trying to comfort the widow, though, his heart beat even faster; for, on Hope's hands, he saw the faint markings of purple spots, a telltale sign that the typhus's lethal spread had yet to be stopped.

* * *

Frederic Pall had awakened at noon in the small room he occupied in a boardinghouse on the northern edge of the city. The day before, he'd completed the printing of Colleen McClagan's latest broadside and spent much of the night supervising its distribution by the children of rebel prisoners. He sat on his bed, amid his rumpled sheets, and read over his part in *All's Well That Ends Well* for a solid hour. Nothing pleased him more than to lose himself in one of Shakespeare's psychologically complex roles.

The lines still ringing in his ears, he selected his outfit for his afternoon outing—a green waistcoat, black trousers, black boots, a high white powdered wig, and a feathered orange tricorn. He expertly painted his pale complexion a deep olive, adding several beauty marks around his mouth. Pleased with himself at having done such a superb job in uncovering the identity of the Wisp, he walked briskly to King's Park. Jason Paxton indeed! It was all so clear to Pall. The musician cleverly camouflaged (wasn't that the Sandpiper's very word?) his rebel sentiments by hiding behind his musical notes. Who would suspect a composer who had lived abroad for most of the war? Frederic knew, though, that Ethan Paxton had a reputation as a hotheaded rebel. Like father, like son. *Ah, yes, Jason Paxton, your days are numbered, your game is up.*

Secluded in a corner of the park, Pall spent another hour rehearsing his lines—this time aloud—his heart thrilling to Shakespeare's relentless iambic pentameter. At three o'clock, pleased with his practice for the day, he left the park and headed for the Old Customs Exchange. He planned to surprise Embleton with an early visit. It was a pleasant afternoon indeed to collect his hundred pounds.

He was just about to walk through the front gates of the Exchange when he nerly bumped into Jason Paxton. Deftly, Pall turned his head and walked away. The actor was certain that Jason hadn't seen him, and even if he had, the wig and heavy makeup would have hidden Pall's identity. Grateful for avoiding what might have been a most unfortunate confrontation, Frederic made his way to the Dock Street Theater. Why was Paxton going to the Old Customs Exchange? To steal more information? It mattered not. By tomorrow morning, the major would be informed. For the time being, Pall decided to concentrate on tonight's performance. He would rehearse his lines for a third time. He knew he would be brilliant—brilliant in depicting this character, brilliant in earning his bounty. As he walked along Charleston's narrow alleyways and cobblestoned streets, in the silence of his mind he recited that single sliver of Shakespearean wisdom he cherished most: "All the world's a stage,And all the men and women merely players.They have their exits and their entrances;And one man in his time plays many parts. . . ."

At the moment that Jason walked through the gates of the Old Customs Exchange, his mind was on Frederic Pall and, more pointedly, the play, *All's Well That Ends Well*. After spending three hours at the pianoforte that morning—three frustrating hours when, in the light of political events, his music continued to seem less and less relevant—he took down a folio from Robin's vast library shelf and reread the play. The part of Parolles was nothing short of extraordinary, especially in light of yesterday's meeting with Pall. The character, a worthless companion to Bertram, the play's hero, was variously described as "a snipt-taffeta fellow," "a red tail'd bumblebee," and "a damnable both-sides rogue." The more Jason read, the more concerned he became. He knew his negative reaction to the actor was more than mere jealousy. No, this man, like the character he portrayed, was rife with duplicity.

So great was Jason's concern that by mid-afternoon he was unable to sit still any longer. He would have to take action. He decided to visit Embleton to see for himself whether the major harbored suspicions about him. He understood the Englishman well enough to know that, whatever his military talents, the man was incapable of hiding his doubts. Jason would be able to tell in very short order whether the British command was aware of his secret rides.

He had no trouble gaining entrance. Embleton was in a jovial, expansive mood. He'd just received a report that the opposition had been relatively quiet in and around the city of Charleston. His campaign was working. With the certain capture of the Sandpiper, along with the impending arrest of the elusive Wisp, the two great romantic figures of the local rebel movement would be hanged publicly, thus crushing the very symbols of the Patriots' hope. No more broadsides, no more midnight raids.

"Paxton!" he said. "Why, you're just in time for a spot of afternoon tea. Or if you'd prefer sherry, I'll drink along with you, my good man."

Prepared for a greeting of considerably less warmth, Jason accepted the offer of sherry and took a seat across from the major's wildly disorganized desk. He was careful not to snoop, as was his usual practice, and instead kept his eye on the bug-eyed officer himself for any signs of mistrust. Embleton poured them each a full glass of sherry, after which they lifted their glasses and toasted one another's good health.

"I've pleasant tidings," Embleton said, placing his feet upon his desk and stuffing several small macaroons into his mouth. "I've been looking at maps, plans, and casualty counts all bloody day and can happily report that we're slaughtering these rebel beasts like pigs. 'Tis only a matter of time before resistance completely collapses. But enough thoughts of battle. It will do my heart good to speak to a true artist whose spirit soars above such worldly matters."

Jason searched the Englishman's shining black eyes and friendly tone for a hint of sarcasm, but found none. "'Tis always a pleasure to converse with you, Major, though today I've come with an inquiry I hope you won't find troublesome."

"You've captured your brother-in-law and wonder whether to shoot the bastard yourself or turn him over to us?" Embleton laughed heartily at his own joke, his oversized ears twitching with merriment.

"No, not quite."

"Go on, go on."

"My father's home here has been appropriated and I was wondering..."

"Oh, yes, I saw something about that pass over my desk. At first I thought it might inconvenience you, and then I... was reminded that your father has given us nothing but trouble from Brandborough. He openly defies the military command in the region and refused to pay a farthing of taxes. Were it not for you, Jason, he'd have been behind bars long ago. However, we've decided to let him be. I know that you and he have been on the outs ever since your return, and I concluded that the house would serve you no purpose. Was I wrong?"

"Not really." Jason decided to back off, increasingly convinced that he was really in no danger of being discovered. Embleton still believed firmly in his Tory sentiments.

"I would have thought that by now you'd have your family convinced of the inevitability of British rule," the officer continued, pleased with the sound of his own voice. "Having lived in our fair land, you were privileged to see with your own eyes the invincibility of our mighty empire. But, alas, these rebels are stubborn by nature, and I can no more blame you for your father's misplaced patriotism than for your colony's pathetic absence of refined culture. Which brings me, dear Jason, to a musical note. When can we expect another recital? Ah, but I've missed the sound of music ringing through the rooms of my Charles Town home!"

"Whenever it pleases you, Major," Jason offered, deciding to drop the subject of his father's town home and placate Embleton any way he could.

"A week from tonight would be most pleasant. It would give me time to issue invitations. When would that make it? The third Wednesday in September. I'd like to plan something special, particularly in view of the fact that our military fortunes are so secure. It will be an important sign to the citizenry that cultural life, in spite of our presence—indeed, because of our presence—is flourishing. Tonight, for instance, I plan to attend a performance of *All's Well That Ends Well,* another example that this city is functioning quite well on every significant level."

Jason was alarmed to hear the play mentioned. He wondered immediately whether there was a connection between Embleton and Pall, but knew he couldn't possibly ask the question.

"So will you agree to this concert, Jason?"

"Most definitely."

"And what will you play?"

"A composition of my own making, something I've been working on ever since I returned from London."

"Most commendable. An original composition. I applaud your ambition. It will be an honor to host a recital in which a new musical creation will be debuted. Might I suggest that you dedicate your work to King George the Third himself and his enlightened sovereignty over this land?"

Jason took a deep swallow of his sherry, covertly bit his lip, and looked Embleton in the eye. "A suggestion well made, Major. It will be my honor to do so."

*   *   *

Robin and Piero left their home before Jason returned from his meeting with Embleton. They had been invited to dine at the home of a friend and then planned to attend the evening's performance at the Dock Street Theater. It was Jason's suggestion that they see the play, and they agreed most readily. The musician wanted a firsthand report on Pall's theatrical abilities without showing up himself.

Dinner was quite pleasant, and at seven-thirty their servant, Ned, drove them to the theater in their elaborate coach. Dressed in contrasting outfits—Robin's coat, blouse, trousers, and wig were snow white; the wiry Piero was decked out in solid black, from head to foot—they made a noteworthy entrance into the theater, with their canes, their capes, and their extravagantly bejeweled slippers. Piero was especially proud of his new moustache.

The intimate auditorium, which seated no more than two hundred fifty spectators, was divided into boxes, pit and gallery. The proscenium arch framed a scenic area twenty-five feet deep, with only five feet of off-stage space on either side. The stage was tilted toward the audience. The raked pit consisted of eight wooden benches painted bright red. Raised above the pit level and surrounding it in a semi-ellipse was a single row of boxes where individual chairs accommodated the theatergoers. The highest-priced tickets were for this section. The gallery, where the cheapest seats in the house could be had, was located above the boxes.

Naturally, Robin and Piero were seated in one of the choice boxes, close to the stage, decorated with thin gilt railings. The half-filled theater was dimly lit by small six-branched chandeliers hung on the back of each box, while the stage was illuminated by oil lamps that would be raised and lowered, depending upon whether the scenes depicted night or day.

Just as Piero inconspicuously took a snort of snuff and was enjoying the pleasant effects, he felt a gentle nudge from Robin's elbow against his waist. There, being seated in the box next to them, was Major Randall Embleton and two of his aides. Piero began to whisper something to Robin, who, the more discreet of the two, put his finger to his lips, quieting his Italian friend as the players took their places upon the stage.

Throughout the comedy, both men couldn't help but feel anxious by their proximity to the British commanding officer, remembering how earlier Jason had confided his fears to them.

He'd expressed his concern that Pall was a spy and was perhaps connected to the British high command. In light of that statement, Embleton's bulky presence kept both men in a state of extreme tension.

Yet, in spite of their nervousness, Robin and Piero were vaguely bored by the production. It was not their favorite Shakespeare play. Lacking the festive aspect of the bard's other comedies, it neither sang nor soared with the sort of wit that was Robin's particular delight. Piero recognized the plot from an old tale of Boccaccio and preferred the original Italian narrative to this watered-down adaptation. There was, however, no denying the extraordinary talent of Frederic Pall, who enacted the role of Parolles with singular concentration and conviction, easily overshadowing the other characters. Robin also saw exactly why Jason had been concerned: the man played the part of an imposter and poseur with uncanny verisimilitude. Could this be mere acting? He thought not. It took a rogue to play a rogue this convincingly.

At intermission, as was the custom in the colonial theaters of Philadelphia, Boston, New York and Charleston, the players entertained the audience with entr'acte diversions. It was at this point that Pall stepped forward and, much to the spectators' delight, juggled various colored objects in the air and recited love poems in German and French. What's more, he sang a few English ditties and did something of a dance, moving from the ridiculous to the sublime back to the ridiculous in the wink of an eye. Robin and Piero were impressed and did not fail to see the utter enthusiasm with which the pudgy major applauded the man's efforts.

After the play itself was over, the musician's mentors applauded lightly and then left quickly before Embleton turned around. He hadn't noticed Robin and Piero. They'd met the major at Jason's last recital and had no desire to renew the acquaintance. Instead, they went directly home to report to Jason that Embleton had attended the play and to relay their concern about the thespian's alarmingly true-to-life portrayal.

"I, too, am concerned," Jason said as his fingers danced over the pianoforte in the cavernous music library, "but after seeing Embleton, I'm certain there's no present danger. I'm not under suspicion—I know that for a fact—and next week's recital will give me another several weeks of unhampered freedom."

Chapter 5

"Yes, yes, quite satisfactory, dear boy," Randall Embleton said, seated behind his office desk, as a white-wigged Buckley Somerset sat in the major's office in the Old Customs Exchange and described the work of his Continental Tory Militia. In a series of lightning-fast raids, he and his men had burned a half dozen rebel farms in the area. There was great excitement and pride in his voice as he described the bloody work of his two aides, Jack Windrow and Sam Simkins. "My men," he informed the major, "instinctively go for the jugular. They understand that it requires nothing less than a quick knife in the abdomen or a cold bullet to the brain to convince these Patriots that theirs is a lost cause."

"Precisely. I'm pleased to see that the noose around the rebels' necks is tightening."

"We're choking them to death," Buckley added with a smug smile of satisfaction on his lips.

An aide entered to announce the arrival of a certain Mr. Parolles in the outer office.

"Ah, it's Pall playing theatrical games again. Yes, yes, send him in at once. Perhaps he has news for us."

Frederic Pall entered in the guise of an agricultural worker. Wigless, his mouse-brown dyed hair was in wild disarray, and his rubbery elongated face, covered with splotches of mud, resembled a horse. He wore garments of coarse fabric and covered two of his front teeth with a black gummy substance in order to appear partially toothless.

"Brilliant!" Embleton said, slapping the thespian on his back. "You were brilliant last night. And this morning I'd not recognize you for all the tea in Boston Harbor. Surely you remember Buckley Somerset."

"Indeed," the thespian said through a toothy grin.

"Have you the name of the Wisp?" Somerset arose from his chair and approached Pall. Embleton leaned forward and sat up alertly.

"Have you my hundred pounds?"

The major opened a side drawer and pulled out a bulky pouch. "In silver, Mr. Pall, if it so suits you."

Frederic's eyes lit up. "It suits me just fine."

"But first the name, and the proof," the Englishman insisted.

"'Tis so obvious, I must admit to feeling somewhat guilt-ridden in relieving you of so substantial a sum for so simple a deduction."

"Guilt-ridden or not," Somerset said, "tell us the name, man, before we change the conditions."

"Calm yourself, Buckley," Embleton advised. "Mr. Pall is an actor, and actors are inclined to present information in dramatic form. A good actor—and our friend here is indeed good—understands the subtle element of suspense. Let us just enjoy his performance. There's no doubt the Wisp will be named, for it's certain that Mr. Parolles will not leave without his remuneration."

"A keen mind have you, Major. You understand me well. Would, though, that you understood all artists as well."

"I pride myself in thinking that I have a rare and, might I say, refined affinity for the arts."

"But the arts and artists are two different things," Pall added.

"For God's sake!" Buckley shouted as he impatiently paced the room, nervously playing with the bridge of his broken nose. "Get to the point, Pall. Name the Wisp once and for all."

"We were talking of art," Frederic continued, speaking slowly, enjoying tormenting Somerset a little longer, "and art, you will see, is most relevant to this morning's revelation."

"Your train of thought eludes me," Embleton confessed.

"'Tis precisely your affinity with artists that has blinded you to what otherwise would be an inescapable conclusion."

"What are you saying?" the major asked.

"That you've been fooled."

"By whom?"

"An artist, a sensitive soul who's been in your very home and . . ."

"Jason Paxton!" Buckley's voice rose as his heart sank. "You're saying that the Wisp is Jason Paxton!"

Pall's mouth widened into a devilishly sly smile.

"Impossible!" Embleton insisted, bolting from his chair, storming around his desk and standing nose to nose with Pall. "You're saying this to embarrass me. Why, I know Jason Paxton as well as my own blood brother. The man's a Loyalist through and through. He harbors nothing but contempt for his mindless rebel family. They don't even speak to one another. He's a cultivated and brilliant composer who . . ."

". . . happens to be a brilliant spy," Pall finished the major's sentence.

Buckley sank into a chair, his eyes glazed, his mind crazed with thoughts of violent revenge. He was speechless in the face of what he understood to be the absolute truth.

"But Paxton was in this very office yesterday," Embleton continued in dismay.

"As he's been here time and time again," Frederic reminded the officer, "learning what he can about the British military effort."

"Damn it, man!" Embleton slammed his fist on his desk. "What proof have you?"

"He was introduced to me by the Sandpiper herself, in the basement of her aunt, the seamstress Rianne McClagan. To be with Paxton and the young poetess is to understand in a minute's time that they are not only conspirators, but lovers as well. I've not the slightest doubt that he kidnapped her from Mr. Somerset's farm, that he was responsible for the raid on this prison that freed his brother-in-law, that he . . ."

"Enough!" the major said, looking slightly sick as he returned to the chair behind his desk. "What say you to this, Buckley?"

Somerset found speaking difficult. His stomach was in knots, his brain on fire. Finally, in a pained voice, he spoke barely above a whisper: "I never thought he was man enough. I never thought he had it in him. But, yes, this actor is right. It all makes sense. He knows these swamps, he's had access to information, he's used the camouflage of his music. Deep down he's no different—no better—than his outlaw rebel father. Both bastards, both scum. He and the whorish McClagan woman, hanged together, side by side...." Buckley's breath quickened, his eyes widened. "I'll be there, by God! When their necks snap I'll be the last thing they'll see on this earth, and I'll be laughing, oh, I'll be smiling at them both...."

"Jason Paxton." Embleton reflected as he slowly saw the inescapable truth of it all. In the silence of his shocked mind, he reviewed the events of the past summer. "Jason Paxton. Yes. Of course. It was him. It was him all along. It seems as if the musician has made something of a fool of me."

"I'd have to agree with that," Buckley said.

"Quiet, you love-sick schoolboy!" the major exploded. "Were it not for the come-hither smile of the rebel girl and your own petty jealousy, you'd have had your wits about you and been able to identify and capture Paxton months ago. He's made you look far more ridiculous than me."

"I beg to differ with...".

"Say nothing more, Buckley, or in the blink of an eye I'll strip you of your command. Now is the moment for sagacious reflection."

"It's obvious," Somerset said, "that we must..."

"Nothing is obvious!" the major snapped, cutting him off. "The fact of the matter is that I've invited Paxton to perform at my house a week from yesterday. He told me that he's written a suite which, at my suggestion, he agreed to dedicate to the honor of our sovereign. I've already issued invitations to many of the leading citizens of Charles Town."

"I see." Buckley smirked.

"You see nothing!" Embleton shouted as Pall picked up the pouch of silver upon the desk, agreeably testing its considerable weight. "You'd expect me to cancel the event. You're thinking it would be an occasion on which my misplaced confidence would render me even more naïve. Well, you're wrong. I plan to carry on exactly as planned."

"You can't," Buckley complained. "Paxton and his harlot must be arrested immediately, within the hour, before they grow suspicious and flee the colony. My men and I will apprehend them ourselves."

"You and your men," the major retorted, "will tend to your own business for the next six days. No one—absolutely no one besides the three of us in this room—must know of the

Wisp's or the Sandpiper's identity. I have every intention of going forward with the recital. In fact, I will expand the festivities and invite twice as many guests as I had intended. Yes, it couldn't be more perfect if I had planned it. Right now, neither the girl nor the musician is the least bit suspicious. We'll keep them in their state of blissful ignorance and shepherd them safely and securely to my home, like obedient sheep to slaughter. I'll make certain that they're all there—Jason Paxton, Colleen McClagan, her aunt, those two foppish fools whom Paxton calls his patrons—the whole bloody lot of them. We'll let the man play, we'll listen to his dedication, we'll applaud his artistic efforts. And when it's all over, I'll have my say. Oh, indeed I will! Never before will an arrest be made with more finery and flourish. I'll have an extra two dozen men stationed in positions that will have them wondering—and worrying themselves sick with fear—from the moment they step into my house. We'll give them ample time to consider their fate. Then I shall humiliate this man and woman as no human beings have ever been humiliated before. Trick me, will they? Why, they'll be writing about the arrest of the infamous Will-o'-the-Wisp and his Sandpiper in history books for centuries to come. Through his duplicity, he has afforded me a moment of sublime glory. And then, Mr. Buckley Somerset, you may have your fun. As a symbol of the local Tory cause, you will join me in personally leading the procession back to this building, where the gallows will be waiting. I'll have my men arouse the citizenry from their beds. I'll make certain that the crowd numbers in the thousands. There, under the brilliant light of a hundred blazing torches, this city will witness an execution the likes of which it has never known before, nor will ever know again. For not only will we break the necks of our two artistic lovers, but we will break their conspirators' necks as well—every single last one of them."

"What of their fathers—Ethan Paxton and Roy McClagan? Surely they're in on this," Buckley observed. He had found himself somewhat sexually aroused during Embleton's detailed description of what was to come.

"Deal with them however you like. It's their children who most concern me."

"You'll be interested to learn that Paxton's sister Joy is also staying at the McClagan house," Pall informed the men without interrupting his second count of the money.

"We'll not exclude her from the hanging party," Embleton said.

"Oh, to see Paxton's blood flowing like rich red wine," Buckley whispered, his throat parched from heated excitement.

"Yes, my friend," Embleton declared as he walked back behind his desk and plopped into his chair, folding his hands in front of him. "It seems that in the end we all shall have exactly what we want."

"Not quite, Major," Pall spoke up. "You're a pound short. I count only ninety-nine."

"Allow me," Buckley offered, fishing a sterling coin from his vest pocket and flipping it in the actor's direction. Frederic caught the silver handily and threw it atop the pile as Embleton and Somerset remained silent, privately entertaining fantasies of sweet, vicious revenge.

～ *Chapter 6* ～

Jason swept Colleen up in his arms and kissed her long and passionately, forgetting his music and the formal setting of Robin's fabulous music library. He could concentrate on his composition no longer, not with her sitting beside him on the pianoforte bench, not with her thigh touching his, the fragrance of her skin strong in his nostrils. He had held himself back long enough. His resistance had shattered.

Opening her mouth with his insistent tongue, he felt that her excitement was as great as his. There was not a moment's hesitation on her part as he led her to his bedroom. Piero was in the kitchen and Robin in his workshop. Besides, who cared? Certainly not they. All the unbearable distresses of war, of this precarious life of dual identities, had built up inside him. His body was rigid with tension, hungry with desire. In these five months since he had been back in America, his only real emotional and physical release from his heavy political burdens had been with Colleen. Before his meeting with Embleton, he'd been convinced that her trusting nature had compromised their secrets. At this moment, though, he was reassured. The major had seemed as enamored of Jason as ever—perhaps more so—and what anger the musician had felt toward his lover dissipated as they embraced, easily falling upon his bed, his hands caressing her neck and breasts, much as he had caressed the ivory keys of the pianoforte—with delicate patience and extreme loving kindness.

She lowered the bodice of her dress and moaned softly as she felt his tongue tracing her already-erect nipples. She felt him probing beneath her slips and petticoats, his long fingers gently stroking her soft thighs and barely touching—as if to tease—her pubis, overflowing with love's natural liquids. With her own hands, she thrillingly touched his thick, stiff staff of ardor, encircling it with her fist and squeezing him ever so fleetingly. He responded with immediate appreciation, helping her out of her clothes, throwing off his own, kissing her stomach, her waist, her moist fluff, her hidden lips until she asked him—until she begged him—to commence the frenzied dance. He gave little of himself at first, knowing the effect it would have on Colleen. She demanded more, and more he gave, a little at a time, until finally his thrusts were long and deep and felt on the sides, at the very back, in the very center of her being. She moved up to meet him, positioning her legs against her chest, seeking his mouth with her own, kissing him, thanking him, urging him on and on and on, flying with the feeling of this free and frantic union, her fingers digging into his spine, into the twitching muscles of his buttocks, as finally, with one last thrust, they met upon a thundercloud hung high over a meadow and, in a single explosion, spinning, tumbled and fell to soft earth below.

"Oh, I love you so much, Jason Paxton." With her muscles she kept him inside, wanting all of him, all of him forever.

"My little Sandpiper, my sweet little Sandpiper," he said, wiping the tears of joy from her eyes.

They held each other for a long while before letting go. Lovingly, he dislodged himself and rolled over onto his back, remaining next to Colleen. She turned on her side so she could run her fingers through his dark curly hair as she peered into his sloped eyes, losing herself in his dreamy, faraway expression.

"Sometimes it seems like a fairy tale," she said to him.

He smiled and answered, "For a moment, perhaps, but no more."

"And yet I believe that a happy ending will be ours. Don't you, my darling? Don't you believe that?"

He lifted his head from the pillow and sighed. "I believe

that you're a remarkable woman, Colleen McClagan—bright and beautiful, but sometimes silly and stubborn."

"You blamed me for Frederic Pall. Is that why you call me silly? But you've seen that nothing has changed. We've an ally—that's all."

"And a long way to go before this war is over."

"But being assured of Embleton's continuing trust, you'll be able to learn whatever you need about their maneuvers. You can ride again, my gallant Will-o'-the-Wisp, just as the Sandpiper will record and report your efforts. We'll undermine them at every turn," Colleen said, now sitting up in bed. "They'll never stop us, Jase. Never."

"For a while, I want us to stop."

"Why?" she asked with alarm in her voice.

"I told you only part of what transpired between the major and myself. I didn't tell you that he asked me to give another recital."

"And you agreed?"

"I felt as if I had little choice—either that, or raise new suspicions. In any event, I'll not be riding—nor will you be writing—until after that event."

"I wish you wouldn't express your feelings as absolute demands."

"I'm sorry, but I need to keep my concentration on purely artistic matters."

"For how long?"

"A few days. The recital's next week, and this suite is not entirely complete. I've been working on it since I returned from England. At first, the inspiration came fast and furiously, but recently the music's faded from my mind. Before, when I rode through the swamps and woods, I heard in Cinder's breath a certain syncopation. The sound of leaves crushing beneath his hooves suggested musical flourishes. the birds had me thinking of piccolos; the frogs were bassoons. Now, though, the forest is no longer an orchestra. the forest is merely the forest. I hear the sounds of the animals, the babbling brooks, and whistling breezes as nothing more or less than what they are—the spontaneous and glorious sounds of nature. I love them for their own sake. I no longer feel the need to translate them into a frozen and artificial form. The essential work of this war—to free ourselves of our captors and regain the integrity of our lives and land—is what compels me, Colleen; that's what keeps me awake at night. I suppose this is what you said to me months ago. I argued with you then, with only half a heart. Tonight we're in unison, with all our hearts."

"But you'll always love music, Jase. You're far too blessed with musical talent ever to ignore it."

"Once this war is won, I'm not certain what any of us will do. I know now, though, that my commitment is to freedom first. The extreme irony of all this is that, in order to protect both my identities, I must make a respectable showing at this recital. I must force myself to complete this work. It will be a fitting close to a strange chapter in my life, an original composition dedicated to the very enemy we work daily to defeat."

"The king? You're dedicating this to the king?"

"Embleton's idea. What would be gained by refusing? He sees me as the model Tory. So why give him any reason, especially now, to doubt that image? Satisfying him will only further serve our purposes."

"To that end—and the strengthening of our love—I commit my very heart and soul."

"Dear Colleen," Jason said and exhaled softly. He put his arm around her slender shoulder and brought her closer to his side. "Sometimes the fabric of our very survival seems so threadbare."

"Yet it's stronger than it appears, Jase. It will hold together," she said with her customary optimism. "I know it will."

"Once this recital is behind us," Jason said, "the road ahead is sure to seem that much clearer."

"Will I be able to be in attendance when you play?"

"I'm not certain. You may have lost your best entrée in Buckley Somerset."

"Would that it were so. In fact, he sent a message to my aunt's this very morning, asking after my well-being and wondering whether I'd recovered from the ordeal at Marble Mansion. He indicated that he'd like to see me at my earliest convenience."

"Then that's your ticket to the recital, my dear."

"If that's the only way to hear your music, I'll endure even Somerset," she said, bringing her mouth to his chest.

It had been four days since Ethan Paxton had left Hope, Allan, and the rebel band in the care of Dr. McClagan. Four days without a scrap of news. One would think the doctor would send word of the progress being made, thought Ethan, as he decided to see for himself. His patience had worn thin. After notifying his servants that he'd be back by nightfall, he mounted his steed and headed up the coast toward the McClagan farm.

The third week of September, and still no relief from the muggy heat. The vast ocean was flat and lifeless, tiny wavelets weakly lapping the sun-parched shore. Ethan was in an especially foul mood. The night before he'd received a report from a former employee in Charleston stating that not only was the Paxton town home physically occupied by the Tories, but that Joy was living with the seamstress Rianne McClagan and Jason was to give another of his musical recitals for the English high command. He ached with the reminder that his own son was a traitor. What greater infliction could fall upon the Paxton family honor? What greater pain could shatter a father's soul?

The faster Ethan rode, the greater his concern grew. Why hadn't McClagan sent him a message? He had great confidence in McClagan's competence as a doctor. He knew the gravity of Allan's condition, but hadn't Roy been optimistic that constant medical attention would bring him back? Ethan knew that the doctor's apolitical outlook was based upon a certain cowardice, but he also knew that when it came to the care of his patients, McClagan exhibited rare devotion and skill. Then why hadn't he received a progress report? Ethan would have made this trip earlier if he hadn't been concerned with rumors that the Tories were planning raids throughout the countryside. It made him uncomfortable to leave his home, uncomfortable to ride in the open. To be safe, he followed a hidden path a quarter-mile inside the swampy woods that ran roughly parallel to the coastal path. Perspiring and feeling out of sorts in both body and mind, Ethan nonetheless rode full force. He was a rugged man, powerfully built and not easily deterred, no matter what his mission. Life hadn't been easy in the colonies. Nothing was easy, Ethan reflected—nothing, perhaps, save surrender.

As he rode up the hill leading to the McClagan farmhouse, he immediately smelled the stench. Was it the awful flesh of dead animals? No, it couldn't be. . . .

Having heard the approach of Ethan's horse, Roy McClagan hurried to his front porch. Tied around his head was a makeshift mask, a piece of white cloth with sections cut out for his nose and mouth, giving him an eerie ghostly appearance. Thin, wild strands of long white hair fell over his near-bald scalp. His eyes were horribly bloodshot, more red than white. His mouth was tight-lipped and drawn, his arms limp. Bent over, he seemed even more stooped than usual. He removed the mask to reveal a four-day growth of sparse, uneven beard.

"Where are they? What's this awful smell?" Ethan asked even before he dismounted.

"Turn around and come no farther."

"Where are they, McClagan? Where's my daughter?" Ethan dismounted and started toward the farmhouse.

"In the name of God," Roy urged, holding up his hand, "stay away!"

"Tell me."

"They're gone." The physician sighed, looking down at the wooden slats of his porch.

"Gone? . . . Who? . . ." Ethan forced the questions from his lips.

"All."

"Impossible."

"Unspeakable horror. The worst I've seen."

"And Hope? My Hope?"

Roy raised his tear-stained eyes to meet Ethan's. "I lost her last night. I tried . . . dear God, I tried. . . ."

Out of control, Ethan ran to the porch and grabbed Roy by his bloodstained blouse. "You said you could save them. My daughter, my Hope, you said . . . you promised. . . ."

"A deadly typhus took them all," Roy whispered. "The fever came over them all like a hurricane. There was no hope . . . none. . . ."

"Fool! Incompetent idiot!" Still grabbing him by the blouse, Ethan lifted Roy's frail body as if it were a sack of potatoes. He began to strike the man with his free hand before his senses returned. Seeing the pain in the doctor's weary eyes, Ethan could no longer hold back his own tears. He released Roy.

"Allan, Hope . . . all of them?" Ethan asked again, still trying to fathom the enormity of the loss.

"She was the last to go. She was so brave, by my side, helping me with them all. With no strength of her own, she created strength from sheer will. Her last words before she passed . . ."—Roy stopped, choking—". . . were to thank me."

"My Hope," Ethan muttered, his face moist with flowing tears.

"You must go," Roy said. "I sent my few servants and slaves away two days ago to their friends and relatives, paying them wages for the month to come."

"What about you? Were you affected?"

"It seems that the infection's spread was limited to those who had banded together in Solitary. There were no signs that either I or my servants have been touched by the typhus. I've disinfected the house as best as I can. The only safe course, though, is to evacuate and stay away for a day or two."

"Then you'll come to Brandborough with me."

"My presence would be a burden."

"Where will you go? You can't stay here."

"I haven't even thought of where I'd . . ."

"The matter is settled. You'll return with me."

"That's very kind of you."

"Where's my Hope now?" Ethan asked, his voice cracking. "Can I bring her home and place her beside her mother?"

"I'm afraid not. I buried her myself in the middle of the night. To expose us would only . . ."

"I understand," Ethan said, recognizing the extent of Roy McClagan's enormous courage. "Can you show me to the graves? I need to be with my Hope this one last time."

Roy nodded, then led Ethan behind the house, in back of the great oak tree where seven graves had been dug. The doctor stood in front of the grave on the extreme right where the dirt was still fresh. Not a word was spoken. Roy left the father alone to kneel in front of his daughter's remains, his face in his hands. The physician, who had reached his back porch, stopped and turned around, looking at the bereaved father. He thought of his own precious Colleen and prayed for her safety. He nearly walked back to the grave to comfort Ethan, but he stopped himself, realizing that this was a moment when Ethan Paxton needed to be alone.

Fifteen minutes later Roy emerged from the house. He had packed two bags—the larger one with medicines and instruments, the other with a few clothes. Ethan hadn't moved, still kneeling before Hope's grave, still burying his face in his hands.

Roy walked toward him. "We'd best be leaving," he whispered.

Ethan didn't answer.

A few minutes later, they rode silently down the hill, Roy on his steed, his head bent toward the ground, Ethan atop an old beat-up buggy. To the east, the blue-green ocean spread to infinity, though each man, consumed with the pointed images and heart-rending emotions of death, failed to notice.

⇜ *Chapter 7* ⇝

Buckley Somerset's attitude bothered Colleen a great deal. On Jason's suggestion, she agreed to see him, but as they sipped tea in her Aunt Rianne's parlor, she grew increasingly uncomfortable, and not for any of the old reasons. Sitting there in his white wig and red velvet waistcoat, he wasn't in the least forward. His demeanor had changed. He expressed gratitude that Will-o'-the-Wisp hadn't harmed her, but asked no questions about the abduction. Before, he had always seemed so sexually hungry in her presence, about to pounce at any moment. On this late morning, though, he appeared especially self-satisfied. Why? Colleen couldn't help but wonder.

"I was wondering if next Wednesday evening you might enjoy accompanying me to a recital that Major Embleton is hosting in his home," Buckley said, his voice untypically calm.

Colleen was hoping that he'd ask, yet she was still put off by his casual tone. "Yes," she answered after a brief pause. "I'd like that very much."

"Without even knowing the nature of the recital?" Somerset inquired, pleased to have caught Colleen off guard. He knew that she knew Jason was to perform.

"I'm sure the program will be delightful, whatever it is."

"Indeed." Buckley smiled smugly. "In fact, our old friend Jason Paxton is to perform a new composition. I understand he's dedicating it to the king."

How did he know that? Colleen wondered. Embleton, of course. Buckley and the major were friends. What was so strange about that? Nothing, and yet . . . "It should be fascinating," Colleen commented.

"Most fascinating, in fact so fascinating that I was hoping your aunt could attend as well. I know she's a lover of the arts and would certainly enjoy it. Might I invite her myself?"

Another strange turn of events, Colleen thought. Why would Buckley bother to invite Rianne, a seamstress? And how was he authorized to do so? Was he speaking for Embleton? Or, after the grief he had given Colleen at Marble Manor, was he simply trying to make amends and act the part of a considerate gentleman?

"I might add that it's been reported to me," Buckley continued, "that Joy Exceeding Paxton is staying here. It appears as if both she and her brother cannot abide by their father's rebel sentiments. In any event, please tell her that she will not be excluded from the recital. I know how she adores her brother, and an invitation will be sent to her as well."

"She'll be well pleased," Colleen answered, amazed that news of Joy had spread so quickly.

"Until Tuesday, then," Somerset said, standing at attention. "I'll be honored to take all three of the ladies of this household in my carriage—that is, if you don't object, Colleen."

"Why . . . not at all," she said, still perplexed by his curiously solicitous manner.

Outside, with the door closed behind him, Somerset couldn't help but smirk. *Oh, the beauty of it all! The absolute glorious beauty! Trapped. The rats were trapped.*

The next day Hanford S. Windsor, a colleague of Peter Tregoning's in the British Army, sat atop a military carriage and directed two proud steeds on a circular tour of the city. He had nowhere in particular to go, but as an English officer, he would not be questioned. In the carriage below, the curtains drawn, sat his friend Peter, for whom he was doing this favor, and Peter's paramour, whose name Hanford had sworn not to reveal.

"Must we ride about in circumstances this mysterious, Peter?" Joy asked. "It seems silly."

"It would be silly to do otherwise," Peter said nervously,

opening the curtain a few inches in order to peek outside. "This city is seething with intrigue. 'Tis unwise to trust a soul."

"Why this sudden suspicion?" she asked as she moved her body next to his, taking his hand in hers, looking into his freckled boyish face with eyes filled with sympathy and love.

"A change of climate," he reported, "at the Old Customs Exchange. There's great movement about, high-level meetings which, for the first time, I've not been privileged to attend. Embleton had fallen into the habit of seeking out my opinions on certain key maneuvers, but no more."

"Do you know why?"

"I have not the slightest clue. Suddenly I've been excluded from everything. I have no present assignment. And there's absolutely no explanation."

"Do you think it has to do with me? My father's reputation as a rebel, and the business with Allan . . ."

"Yes, for all our discretion, we may have been seen. We can't chance it again."

"And what of your friendship with Jason?"

"'Twas widely known. In fact, Embleton once complimented me on my choice of companions. He has the highest respect for your brother. In fact, I've always presumed that it was my relationship with Jason that first put me in Embleton's good graces."

"These webs are far too intricate to be fathomed."

"Yet fathom them we must if we're to survive."

Joy sighed before asking, "Can't we ask your friend to keep riding until we reach some land, some place, some paradise where men have learned to treat one another with love and respect?"

"Oh, dear Joy." He responded by putting his arm around her shoulder and bringing him closer to her side. "Your heart is so pure. When I think of what lies ahead, I wonder whether my own heart can endure."

"Why do you speak so sullenly?"

"A week ago, before I was shut out from the strategy sessions, I learned some of the impending plans. It seems that after his victory in Camden, Cornwallis is convinced that South Carolina is permanently secure. He's moving into North Carolina, having instructed Major Patrick Ferguson to protect his left inland flank. Ferguson may need help."

"Is that the same Ferguson whom my father so constantly cursed?" Joy asked. "The man who invented some weapon or other?"

"The same. His breech-loading rifle can be fired five or six times a minute. Like Tarleton and Embleton, he's something of a mad butcher. He and his men have set on a course of ruthless pillaging—burning homes, killing whole families."

"They must be stopped!"

"The Scot-Irish frontiersmen who man the mountains west of the Carolinas are said to be fierce fighters. They're basically apolitical by nature, but Ferguson is doing his best to alienate them, thus turning them into rebels. There have been reports of massacres, and now there are fears that the frontiersmen will soon retaliate. Embleton's been told—at least as recently as a week ago—to be prepared to reinforce Ferguson if necessary. Cornwallis wants his flank protected—at whatever cost."

"So you'll be leaving?" she asked fearfully.

"I've no idea. That's exactly why I'm so out of sorts. For what purpose are they keeping me in the dark? And even were I asked to join Ferguson and the pillaging, I'm no longer sure I could stomach the task."

"Perhaps your superiors have sensed that, Peter."

"I doubt it. I've voiced these views to no one except you and Jason. These are attitudes I've kept locked in my heart. This arbitrary maiming and slaughtering of innocent people, perpetuated by the greencoats as well as the Redcoats . . . why, it's nothing I could have ever imagined possible."

"You accuse me of idealism, my dear Peter, but you're as pure-hearted as any creature on God's green earth."

As the carriage ride continued, so did their conversation, with Joy expressing fear for her father, for Allan, and for Hope. She told Peter about the invitation from Somerset through Embleton, and that, too, alarmed the soldier. Why was Joy being given a special invitation? And why hadn't he been asked, as was the case for the first recital, by Embleton himself? He'd been told nothing of the concert. Questions, questions, his head was full of uncertainties. In spite of his doubts, though, he was unable to think further as Joy brought her face to meet his. There, as they rode through the captive city, their mouths and hands sought one another's soft comfort. They escaped from the fearful puzzles of the outside world into the heat of a warm embrace. Unable to do what they would have done on the dewy grass or upon a great feather bed, there in the darkness of the carriage—the wheels steadily turning, the vehicle bouncing to what seemed a sensual rhythm—they satisfied each other with their tongues and fingers, probing deeply, stroking sweetly, allowing their passions, at least for the moment, to chase away their fears.

Later that afternoon when Joy returned to Rianne Mc-Clagan's home, she found the seamstress and her niece in the workshop, busy with their needlepoint while listening to a man who, for all practical purposes, had the appearance of a pirate. His left eye was covered with a patch, his lined face was marred by a series of deep scars, and a majority of his teeth were missing. Even worse, he smelled as if he was in immediate need of a soapy bath.

"This is my friend Jeth Darney," Colleen said, introducing the bizarre-looking old man to a curious Joy. "He's just come in from New York with news of the war."

"Aye, and 'tis a treacherous time," Jeth said excitedly as he sipped a tall glass of sherry provided by Rianne. "Traitors and turncoats—that's what they're discovering. Before I snuck onto the good ship *Suffolk*—the one that's sitting right there in Charleston Harbor—by bribing the bleeding British cook, I heard me enough to fill a book, I did. The worst is about Major General Benedict Arnold. You've heard of him, ladies, haven't you?"

"Yes, of course," Rianne replied, looking up from her needlepoint.

"He's the commanding officer of the Continental forces that reoccupied Philadelphia earlier this year," Colleen stated.

"*Was.* And is no longer. Right now he's fighting for the British."

"What?" Colleen exclaimed.

"So help me God, ma'am. He sold the Hudson River to the Crown, he did. Some months ago, I was told, General Washington, who's no one's fool, caught Arnold with his hand in the sweets' jar. He was misusing public funds. Seems as if Arnold had found himself a young bride—Peggy Shippen by name—twenty years his junior, with an eye for fancy clothes—no reflection on you, Miss Rianne—and glittering jewels. Peggy, they say, is something of a Tory. Anyways, as we all know, a woman can do strange things to the mind of men, especially between the marriage sheets. Not that it was completely Peggy's fault. Not at all. The two of them were connivers and somehow figured out how to win back Washington's trust. Arnold convinced the general to give him command of West Point. Meanwhile—and methinks it was because the bills were piling up from pretty Peggy's purchases—Arnold was strapped for coin and began, if you can believe it, a correspondence with a certain British major, John André, head of all the Crown's spies here in the colonies."

"Mr. Darney, how do you know all this? How can you be certain what you say is true?" Joy asked skeptically.

"Certain as I'm sitting here looking at you, missy. You see, this here André fellow was captured not long ago in Tarrytown, New York, and inside his stockings they found these letters from Arnold. It was all there, in cold black and white. Arnold, that worthless scum, was planning to turn over the whole bloody fort at West Point to the British in return for a commission from the Crown to fight on its side."

"Has Arnold been apprehended?" Colleen asked.

"I'm afraid not. Word of André's arrest got to him in time and the traitor escaped. He's fighting for King George now, he is."

"That's horrible," Joy said, thinking of everything that Peter had told her about the English army.

"What of André?" asked Rianne.

"Oh, he'll swing from a tree. Clinton will try to convince Washington otherwise, but old George won't forget our Nathan Hale—did they give him a chance, and did they even grant him a trial?—and there'll be no pity wasted on André."

"My God," Colleen said softly, remembering her disquieting encounter with Buckley earlier in the day, "our own officers are deserting the cause."

"Arnold's an ugly exception," Jeth said spiritedly. "I've heard of no others, and besides, with five thousand Frenchmen to boost the Continental Army, all's far from lost. The rebels are hungry for a big victory, and speaking of food, Miss Rianne"—he paused, draining his glass of sherry and casting his one good eye around for the bottle—"might I prepare a feast for you lovely ladies tonight? Miss Colleen and her good father used to claim I was the best cook in all the colonies. If you've a little lamb or mutton, I've just the recipe to set your hearts a-dancing. What say ye?"

"I say you're looking for a free meal, Jeth Darney, and, under those terms, I'm pleased to give you one—that is, if you'll go out and bathe before you begin cooking."

"Wouldn't do it any other way." He smiled while scratching his head. "And if it wouldn't make any difference to you, ma'am, I might just sleep down in your basement tonight, as I've done before, making no disturbance or . . ."

"How long do you plan to be in Charleston?" Rianne asked.

"Oh, I won't be bothering you for more than a few nights. I'll slip back down around the harbor tomorrow and see which way the winds are blowing. I was able to sell a few items to a rebel acquaintance earlier this morning, so I'm fixed for a while. Some dandy muskets and knives I liberated from the *Suffolk*. Didn't get nearly the price I deserved, but that's the cost of patriotism. The problem is, what with this Benedict Arnold business, it's getting harder to tell friend from foe, if you catch my drift."

"I do," Colleen said, feeling increasingly anxious about the state of affairs.

Chapter 8

The Monday before Jason's recital, Ethan Paxton arrived back in Brandborough, where a number of people stopped him on the street to warn him of English and Tory troops in the area conducting house-to-house searches. Paxton took the news in stride, too preoccupied with the death of his daughter to grow alarmed. Roy McClagan, who rode next to him, reacted with more apparent apprehension. His deep-seated fear of the English returned in the form of a nervous stomach. Yet, what could be worse than his experience of the past days and nights? His most pressing concern was for Colleen.

"I must ride to Charleston," he said to Ethan as the two men entered the Paxton home. They stood facing one another in the foyer.

"We'll make the trip together," Ethan promised. "No matter how despicable their political persuasions, I must tell Joy and Jason about their sister. But not today. You and I both need at least a night's rest. I can see in your face that you haven't slept in days. Let me show you to a bedroom."

"I prefer to leave immediately," Roy said. "I fear for my daughter's safety."

"She's a rebel, isn't she?" Ethan asked, shocking McClagan with the directness of the question.

"I fear she is," the doctor answered, too weary to be anything but honest. "And, strangely enough, she is enamored of your son."

Paxton, still weak with grief himself, shook his head. The world was so strange, so unfathomable. His Tory son, McClagan's rebel daughter. In spite of everything, though, he felt a deep bond with the doctor—for his dedication and courage in trying to save those lives; for the fact that, like himself, he was a father who loved his daughter; for the notion that their children might well be in love with one another. "All our differences," Ethan said, "seem so insignificant."

"In the face of death," the stoop-shouldered physician added, "all things appear insignificant."

A half hour later, in the privacy of their separate bedrooms, the gentle doctor cried himself to sleep while the rugged farmer stared into space.

Piero Sebastiano Ponti, dashing about the kitchen, preparing the evening meal, took an especially hefty snort of his special-blend snuff. He looked at the engraved invitation that he had just received by messenger and called Robin.

"Trouble with the stew?" asked the potbellied instrument maker who arrived from his workshop holding a metal file.

"Read this, if you will."

Robin looked over the engraved invitation and raised an eyebrow. "Strange that we should receive this after a personal aide to Major Embleton came by yesterday to request our presence."

"Last time we received no invitation whatsoever," Piero remembered. "Jason simply brought us along."

"It's as if they're almost *too* anxious to have us attend," Robin observed. "Do you smell something wrong, my friend?"

Piero sniffed, feeling the effects of his snuff. "In truth, I don't know what to think. Perhaps we should mention this to Jason."

"I'm reluctant to disturb him. He's been practicing for two straight days now, though I can tell by the sounds that he's still struggling. A distraction would not be beneficial."

"As long as you're convinced that nothing's wrong," Piero said.

"Who can be convinced of anything these days? Suspicion is more rampant than the swarms of our famous Carolina swamp mosquitoes. We've all been bitten by the bug. Perhaps, though, it's merely a matter of Embleton's being better organized this time around, what with the city so neatly under his thumb. You weren't considering not attending, were you?"

"Perish the thought! Wherever Jason goes, go I. I was only fearful that . . ."

"Yes, I understand, but we'll simply have to live with our fears, and carry on as best we can."

"Begging your pardon, sir, but I understand that tomorrow evening Jason Paxton is giving a recital," Captain Peter Tregoning said as he stopped Major Randall Embleton in the halls of the Old Customs Exchange.

"Yes, yes," the flatfooted superior said in a huff, avoiding Peter's eyes.

"Not wanting to appear out of place, Major, but I was just wondering, since I consider Paxton to be not only my friend, but a dear friend of my family in England, whether I might be expecting an invitation?"

Embleton thought quickly. He had intentionally struck Tregoning's name from the list, knowing full well that he and the musician were chums. Having learned that the captain had been seen with Paxton's sister, he'd also excluded him from all sensitive planning sessions. These associations with the rebel family meant that the captain could no longer be trusted. Stories of Benedict Arnold had reached the major. Allegiances were short-lived. On the other hand, Embleton certainly didn't want to cause Peter any alarm. If he were in cahoots with Paxton, he might well tip him off. No, that wouldn't do at all.

"You received no invitation? A silly oversight. I'll reprimand my secretary at once. I look forward to seeing you there. Good day, Captain."

"Thank you, Major," Peter said, saluting sharply.

After dinner, Colleen went to see Jason. Robin was reluctant to disturb him, but the concern on her face caused him to change his mind. He called the musician down from the music library to the parlor.

When Jason entered the room, looking thinner and more withdrawn than usual, Colleen dashed to his side, as if he were in grave danger. They embraced and, as he held her body, he could feel her shaking. Filled with their own fears, Piero and Robin remained for the discussion that followed.

Colleen told of her visit from Buckley Somerset and Jeth Darney, reporting each incident in ample and careful detail. When she was through, Robin relayed the story of their double invitations. Jason listened to them all intensely.

"Colleen, Rianne McClagan, my sister Joy, Robin, and Piero . . ." Jason reflected— ". . . it seems rather obvious that he wants everyone there."

"Why?" Piero asked nervously. "That's the question."

"My mind has been so concentrated on my music," Jason confessed, "I've had to brush all other concerns aside."

"Yet the concerns are here, Jason," Colleen said.

For a long while, Jason thought. Was it *really* that unusual? Or was Embleton not merely being polite, wanting to show one and all that an original work by a distinguished composer had been written and would be debuted while the city was under his enlightened command? He knew that Piero was certainly an alarmist, and could have easily set off Robin. Colleen might well be suffering a relapse of her fears from the hanging of Ephraim Kramer. Besides, it was too late. What could he do at this point?

"Cancel the recital," Colleen said. "I beg you."

"And give Embleton a real reason to suspect me?" he asked.

"I'm afraid," she said, moving from her chair to his, falling at his knees and grasping his hand. "I'm afraid something dreadful will happen. I feel it in my bones."

Jason looked into her bright amber eyes and saw the fear. He brought her hand to his lips, kissing her gently and then speaking confidently in a reassuring voice. "Last week 'twas I who expressed such doubts. Now that my outlook has brightened, yours has dimmed. It seems as if this business of fear changes hands as quickly as a thief's ill-begotten lolly. But all of us must remember"—he raised his voice, casting an eye at Piero and Robin—"that we aren't thieves. We have stolen nothing. Our cause is just. Our aim is true. Our challenge is formidable. To meet that challenge is to conquer the fear that lurks within. Anything else is defeat."

Stirred by his noble sentiments and sweet, sloped eyes, Colleen was persuaded by Jason's words.

Later, in the home of her aunt, alone in bed, she heard the sound of scattered musket fire breaking through the thick silence of night and slept not a wink, thinking how much this man meant to her, how futile life would seem without him,

how she loved him with all her heart and soul, how she longed
for him—now and evermore.

"Master Buckley," announced one of the house slaves who
had known him ever since he was born, "your mother is here."

Somerset, who had been taking an afternoon nap in his
bedroom at Somerset Hall, leaped to his feet. "What!"

"Yessuh, with Mr. Windrow an' Mr. Simkins, suh. They
jus' come in."

Buckley threw off his sleeping gown, threw on some clothes,
and raced down the great staircase. Waiting for him at the
bottom, her bejeweled black cane by her side, her arms opened,
ready to embrace her son, was Miranda Somerset, looking
remarkably vibrant and young.

Buckley stopped at the fifth step. He didn't want to be
hugged by his mother. He didn't want to see his mother. Tonight
was the recital, perhaps the greatest evening of his life, and
the last human being in the world with whom he wanted to
contend was Miranda.

"How did you get out?" he asked her bluntly.

"Am I a prisoner?" she asked him, her eyes flashing, a
series of pink ribbons cascading from her wig. "Am I not a
free woman?"

Standing a few feet behind her, the albino Jack Windrow
and the muscular Sam Simkins shrugged their shoulders. "We
tried to tell her," Simkins explained. "But she insisted."

"My instructions," said Buckley, who had wanted his two
toughest aides at the recital that evening, "concerned only you
and Jack, not Mother."

"Mother was bored with Marble Manor," Miranda piped in
with her operatically high-pitched voice as she dropped her
arms to her sides. "Mother was bored with caring for Father,
who cares for nothing except his old maps. Your father's a
fossil and I care not a whit who knows it. I've just spent the
last week riding over the plantation, charging into the woods
by myself, chasing off rebels. I've cleared the countryside of
the dreaded Patriots. At first your men were reluctant to follow
me, so I rode out with my band of women. But now the men
recognize my leadership and jump at my commands. I left
Marble Manor with the satisfying assurance that I've made the
grounds secure. Therefore, it's with blissful serenity that I've
come to Charles Town to speak to the crocuses. I dreamed of

them last night. They begged for my attention, these lovely flowers that grow in Charles Town, so different from my irises, so much more expressive and in need of social intercourse. You need me, my son, to make certain that you eat not a bite more of contaminated meat before your body goes bad like your father's. My in-laws are too sick and senile to care for you, and who, may I ask, is in charge of the kitchen at this ridiculous estate? The estate should be sold at once. 'Tis far too large to be maintained, the expense is too great a burden, and the slaves are undisciplined. I shall oversee its sale."

"You shall do nothing of the kind. I'll have you escorted back home," Buckley said, trying to maintain his composure as he bravely came another step closer to his mother.

"You'll have your mouth washed out with lye if you're not careful," she said as her son wisely backed away. "Now, where's this Colleen McClagan? Bring her down here at once."

"Mother," he spoke softly, trying to calm her, "Miss McClagan is not here."

"You've lied before and you'll lie again. She's upstairs, even as we speak, lying in wait, in your very bed. I've come to warn you again, Buckley. Give her up or face your ruin."

He took the remaining steps to the bottom of the grand staircase and waved Jack and Sam from the house. "We'll speak later," he told them. "Now, Mother," he said, finding the courage to take her hand and lead her along the hallway toward the kitchen, "it may be a good idea for you to see to my meals. You're right—my stomach is lined with God knows how many unclean beasts."

"I'll be neither humored nor distracted." She looked at him with penetrating gray eyes. "You're under that woman's pernicious influence."

"You're imagining things, Mother."

"And you lack the imagination to understand the ways of women. Who was it who said, 'Beware of women who deceive with the eye and soothe with the body'?"

"I've no idea."

"Why, it was I, you fool! I've been telling you that ever since you were old enough to fall prey to the temptations," Miranda continued harping as they entered Somerset Hall's massive kitchen. "And fall you have. Time and again. With tavern girls and slave girls—and now an unruly rebel. When will your appetite be satiated?"

"Will you supervise a feast of fish for me tonight? I'm in need of nourishment."

"Why?-Will you be going out? Will you be leaving me here alone?"

"We'll eat early. I have an engagement later."

"With McClagan, no doubt?"

"Mother . . ."

"I knew it! Bacchus himself, god of wine and frivolity, never drank himself into a stupor as dense as yours, my son. If you're to see that woman tonight, I'll be by your side, I swear it. Only I can protect you from a destiny of certain doom."

Buckley began to complain. But, as he pondered the point again, he thought: Why not? Why not allow his mother to see his role in the arrest, the humiliation, and the hanging? Why not finally please the old lady? Why not show her that, when it came to Colleen McClagan, he hadn't been so stupid after all? Together, mother and son would share a satisfying last laugh.

Chapter 9

"It'd be best not to see them before the performance begins," said Frederick Pall, disguised in the soot-laden clothes of a chimney sweep, to Randall Embleton at four o'clock on the afternoon of the recital.

"You told me that she'd written a new broadside," the major said, sitting behind his desk, tapping his fingers together, "and promised you'd deliver it. I want it."

"I mentioned it, but she was reluctant to have it printed now. I sensed a growing suspicion on her part, so I simply left in a hurry. She didn't ask me to print a thing, and I didn't feel it prudent to press the issue. Methinks it's best to leave things as they stand."

"I want this broadside delivered to me. You have access to the seamstress's house, do you not?"

"Through the cellar, yes."

"And you know where she keeps her work?"

"By the press."

"Then you'll retrieve it. Simply wait until they leave for the recital. Buckley's escorting the lot of them. Once they're gone, get me the poem and bring it to my home. Even if Paxton's begun to play, it will make no difference."

"It's not worth my trouble."

"You're a mercenary bastard."

291

"Mercenary perhaps, but my parents, Loyalists both, were married in the Church of England."

"How much will it take?"

"Twenty-five pounds sterling."

"An outrage!"

"Find someone else who has entrée to the McClagan house."

Embleton knew he had no choice. "Twenty pounds and not a shilling more."

"I'll accept your offer, but only with the understanding that I won't be able to give you the document in front of the audience at the recital. When word gets out, my life won't be worth a pittance. The murdering rebels will see to that."

"I'll have a man waiting by the door. Give it to him and he'll get it to me. No one will be any the wiser."

"He'll get the broadside as soon as he hands me the silver."

"You'll get your lucre, Pall, but I want that verse. When Paxton is through at the pianoforte, I intend to include this little Sandpiper in our cultural soirée, and I want her complete *oeuvre*, from the earliest lyrics to her most recent. I want this whole bloody city to see that there's absolutely nothing they can hide. I want the devastation to be total."

Seeing there was no dissuading his benefactor, Pall, still in disguise, left the Old Customs Exchange and wound his way through the streets of Charleston. The evening's performance of *All's Well That Ends Well* had been canceled by Embleton himself, who wanted nothing to compete with the recital. Feeling a bit uneasy that he had to return to the McClagans', the actor spent a few hours reading *Othello*—oh, how he longed to play Iago!—before setting out on his official mission. Packing a small bag with a change of clothes, he wore his chimney sweep disguise as he walked across town to the seamstress's home. A gentle twilight was falling over the captive city as Frederic stopped some fifty yards away from his destination. There he lurked at the corner, where, after a few moments, he witnessed the arrival of Buckley Somerset's splendid carriage. In a few more minutes, they'd all be off and Pall could make his move.

"I think it's ridiculous," Colleen said to her aunt, "and quite surprising as well."

"You, of all people," Rianne retorted. "You're as bad as your own father. What right have you to question *my* escort?

What's more, lower your voice before he hears your rude remarks. He's downstairs waiting."

The women stood in Rianne's bedroom as the seamstress put the final touches on her extravagant wig. It was a masterwork, built upon tiers ascending to the sky. The wig was more resemblant of a tower than a hairpiece. Her gown was fashioned from startling orange velvet. Her wrists, neck, and fingers were covered with jangling jewelry. Colleen, in contrast, seemed almost retiring in pale blue. She wore no wig at all, her lustrous hair twisted in a bun atop her head.

"You're nervous," Rianne told her niece as she applied a final touch of makeup, "and understandably so."

"I am," Colleen had to admit. "I couldn't sleep last night, couldn't eat all day, and..."

"Which is precisely why I've asked Billy Hollcork to attend this recital with us. A measure of security will surely..."

"But he hasn't been invited, Aunt Rianne."

"*I've* been invited, and no doubt would not be expected to attend without benefit of escort."

"Buckley was to take us all."

"Mr. Somerset can accompany you and Joy. I prefer to go in Billy's wagon, which, he told me, has been freshly painted and tonight, just for the occasion, will be pulled by both his horses. He's a kind and considerate man, he is, and has been patiently courting me for years. I fear that I've treated him with something less than proper respect, inviting him through the back door, as it were. Well, I've had enough of my own hypocrisy. You're right to think that these are fearful days. We must surround ourselves with friends—people we can truly trust—no matter what the social costs. As far as my fine lady clients are concerned, if they think less of me for befriending a tanner, they can take their business elsewhere. Let them find a seamstress in this war-torn city whose wares compare to mine!"

Colleen listened carefully to her aunt and admired her even more for her strength of character. "Would that I could forgo Buckley and ride to Embleton's with you, Aunt Rianne."

"You needn't fear. Jason's music will surely calm the boiling blood of these English beasts, at least for this one evening. Let us descend. I think your Mr. Somerset has arrived."

* * *

Hardly able to contain his impatience for the events of this delicious evening to unfold, Buckley had successfully convinced himself that his mother's presence would not be a hindrance. In fact, he thought it a brilliant touch: by bringing Miranda into Rianne's home, the unsuspecting rebels would be thrown off track even more.

If Rianne's wig was a tower, Miranda's resembled a baroque church, a sculpted mass of fabulous curls and dips, a dazzling work of flamboyant art. She walked with Buckley into the seamstress's home, her queenly purple gown trailing behind her. Still not apprised of the true situation by her son—he could never trust her with such delicate information—Miranda saw her role strictly as his protector.

A servant of Rianne's escorted them into the parlor, where Billy Hollcork, whose formidable physical presence came as a shock to Buckley, stood waiting for Rianne in an ill-fitting dark waistcoat.

"Hollcork?" Somerset asked the man who for years had done tanning work for Buckley's grandfather.

"Pleased to see you, Mr. Somerset," Billy said, taking Buckley's relatively small hand and shaking it with such force that the aristocrat winced in pain.

"What are you doing here?" Somerset asked, not bothering to introduce his mother, who was too preoccupied inspecting what she considered the tawdry furnishings to be offended.

"I'm taking Miss McClagan to the recital."

"You are, are you?" Buckley commented as he looked over the tall, powerfully built tanner. Somerset's mind raced with questions. Why was Rianne taking this man, this peasant, to the recital with her? It made no sense. But alas, thought Buckley, dressed in an impeccable ensemble of green scarlet-edged wool and sleek red-brown boots, it also made no difference. No doubt Hollcork was part of the rebel clan. Somerset regarded Billy's thick neck and envisioned his massive body swinging from the gallows. The more the merrier.

Minutes later, Rianne, Colleen, and Joy entered the parlor. Surprise registered on the three ladies' faces as they encountered Miranda Somerset, standing erectly, a turquoise-jeweled cane by her side.

"It's been years, Miss McClagan," Miranda said to Rianne. "When was the last time? Oh, yes. When I commissioned you to make a gown that came out ridiculously wrong."

"It came out splendidly right, Mrs. Somerset," the seamstress shot back, "if perhaps a shade too sophisticated for your taste."

"My son tells me your sophistication has led you to request this gentleman to, shall we say, attend to your needs tonight." Miranda nodded toward Hollcork, indicating she had heard every word exchanged between Buckley and the tanner.

"Would that your beloved husband could tend to your needs," Rianne retorted, well familiar with the gossip concerning Buckley's father.

"Husbandless spinsters," Miranda said, addressing her son, "are notoriously jealous women, prone to acts of moral repugnancy."

"Frustrated matrons," Rianne replied, addressing her niece, "are given to foolish redundancies, malicious behavior, and mindless accusations."

"Seamstress or not,' Miranda quipped, pointing accusingly to the bottom of Rianne's gown, "your petticoats are showing."

"I'm afraid," Rianne retorted, "that it's your senility that is showing. Those are not petticoats, but part of the outer garment."

Joy and Colleen stood watching, spellbound by the confrontation between the two women: Miranda short and tense as a nervous bird; Rianne taller and every bit as feisty. So intense was the animosity that Rianne had forgotten to introduce Joy and Colleen to Billy, which she finally did with apologies to all.

Buckley moved quickly to Colleen's side, wanting to glean as much pleasure from the evening as possible. "You look divine tonight," he said. "You've the beguiling look of a poetess. If I didn't know you better, I'd swear you were an enchanting weaver of lyrical verses."

The remark struck Colleen's heart, and Rianne's as well, just as Buckley knew it would. Slowly, he wanted to give her time to consider her fate. Subtly, he would let her know that she was doomed.

"Your niece is a damned rebel," Miranda blurted out, "and my Buckley's a fool for not seeing it."

The statement startled everyone. For several seconds, the silence was deafening.

"Oh, no, Mother," Somerset finally piped up, continuing his charade, "you're far too harsh in judgment. Miss McClagan, like her aunt, cares absolutely nothing for politics. They, like their friend Jason Paxton, are merely lovers of art. Am I right, Miss Paxton?" Buckley turned to Joy, dressed in a delicate gown of muted pink bordered by flowery lace. "I presume that you, too, are part of this cozy little band of purely artistic souls."

Joy, who was still not aware of either Colleen's or her brother's secret identities, was nonetheless frightened by Somerset's dripping sarcasm. In his voice, she recognized the tone of murderous intent.

"I have not the talent of my brother," she answered discreetly, wishing the evening to be quickly over.

"Well, then, shall we make our way to see just how talented your brother is?" Buckley suggested.

"Meat," Miranda said, sniffing tenaciously. "I smell the distinct odor of dead carcasses. Has meat been consumed in this house tonight?"

"Mother, we've no time to discuss culinary matters now."

"Rianne McClagan, I see you for what you are." Miranda pointed to the seamstress. "You kill defenseless animals. You train your niece to plot against the Crown."

"My dear Mrs. Somerset," Rianne replied coolly, her nose tilted slightly toward the ceiling, "I'm afraid it's not our evening meal you're smelling, but your son's rather peculiar perfume."

Having seen Buckley's carriage and Hollcork's wagon pull away from Rianne McClagan's house, Frederic Pall made his move. Leaving his bag in a bush, he managed to remove the board covering the trapdoor leading to the basement. Then, after looking around to make certain he wasn't being watched, he carefully jumped into the cellar. He landed feet first and, pleased with his athletic agility, expected to quickly retrieve Colleen's latest broadside and be back out in a few seconds. What he hadn't expected was a callused hand around his neck and the point of a long knife poised a fraction of an inch from his left eye.

The knife blocked his view, but it looked as if the man holding it had only one eye.

"Tell me your true purpose, or you're as good as dead," said a scowling Jeth Darney.

"I'm here as a friend of Colleen McClagan's," Pall replied in a strange accent that disguised his theatrical training.

"Then why not use the front door like her other friends?"

"This is our usual way."

"To be stealing in like a thief in the night?" asked the suspicious sea cook.

"If you'll stop choking me and take that knife away, I'll explain."

Jeth let go of Frederic's neck, but he kept the knife in place. By Pall's very smell, he didn't trust the man. "Explain yourself—now," Darney demanded.

"It isn't easy with that blade about to dig into my eye."

Jeth lowered the knife, holding it close to Pall's stomach. "Who are you?"

"I might ask the same of you," Frederic said, repulsed by the strong smell of tobacco on Darney's breath.

Jeth let Frederic feel the point of the knife against his navel. "I'm asking the questions."

Was this one-eyed man himself a thief? Pall thought. Was he in the process of robbing the McClagan home? Frederic had no way of knowing. Still, he had to take a chance and say something. If he were a thief, politics wouldn't matter to him; if he weren't, the chances were he was a rebel associate of Colleen's.

"I'm here in the name of freedom."

"Whose freedom?" Jeth asked, still skeptical.

"The people of this colony. Colleen and I have been working together, and I presume, if you're a good man, you honor the cause that should bind us all."

There was something about Pall's glibness that Darney didn't like.

"You still haven't said who you are," the actor commented.

"A guest of the family," Darney replied, pointing to the blankets on the floor that served as his bed.

"Then surely you know of our work together." One way or another, Pall was determined to get to the printing press and find that broadside. He wanted his extra twenty pounds.

Colleen had told Darney about her surreptitious lyrics. She'd also expressed her fears about this evening's recital—another reason Jeth was doubly suspicious of Pall.

"I'm the printer," the actor finally said.

"I see," Darney said.

"If you allow me," Frederic went on, "I'll prove it to you."

Jeth, his knife pointed at Pall's back, allowed the actor to lead him to the darkest corner of the dank, musty cellar, where Frederic removed a large cloth revealing the hidden press. Pall's eyes looked around quickly and spotted a sheet of parchment on a stool next to the press. He knew it was Colleen's latest lyric. "I was to run off a broadside tonight."

"Colleen and her aunt said nothing about your coming."

"Maybe they forgot."

"Maybe they didn't know."

"They knew, all right," Pall said, thinking quickly. "But on the other hand, I'll not stay if my presence makes you uneasy. I can come back. Wait. . . ." Frederic suddenly tensed his body and pointed toward the open hole through which he had descended. "Do I hear someone coming?"

At that moment—when Jeth turned to look—Pall slipped the parchment under his soot-soiled blouse.

"I don't hear a blasted thing," Darney said.

"Probably just a dog. No matter, I'll be leaving. When Colleen returns, please be good enough to say I was by."

How did this printer know Colleen was gone? Had he been watching the house? Did he know about the recital? Jeth silently debated whether to keep him at bay in the shadows of the cellar or let him go. Strange, how anxious he seemed to leave.

"No harm, then," Darney said, deciding he'd learn nothing by detaining him. "I'll tell the lady you were here. On your way, then."

"We're all in this fight together, aren't we?" Pall asked rhetorically.

"I suppose," Darney answered.

"If you'll give me a hand, I'll be out of here in a jiffy."

Jeth helped him up through the hole, and as he did, he noticed something under Frederic's blouse. What was that parchment he was carrying next to his heart?

"Better stay where you are for just a minute," Darney warned, quickly deciding on a course of action. "The greencoats have been swarming around this place. Let me just go 'round the house to make sure the coast is clear."

"You're kind to do so," Pall replied, secretly gloating that another one of his performances had been so well received.

Jeth quickly gathered up an assortment of weapons, hid them on his body, and then ran up the stairs, through the shop, out onto the street, and met the actor in the backyard. "All clear," he said.

Frederic was off into the night. He could almost hear the jingle of those silver pounds in his pocket. What he didn't know, though, was that, from a few dozen yards back, armed with pistols and knives, Jeth Darney was following his every move.

⤳ *Chapter 10* ⤳

"No, you fool!" Randall Embleton barked at his aide, who carried a dark uniform ito the major's dressing room. "I want my whites for tonight along with the fringed red epaulets, the full assortment of medals, and my white braided campaign wig. Hurry! I hear some of the guests arriving already."

The aide saluted and left promptly as Embleton turned back to the mirror, where he continued curling his eyelashes with a special scissors, a chore he had always carried out in strictest privacy. He was as happy as a man who had certain knowledge that a voluptuous and eager lady awaited his attention. Perhaps happier. Never had he anticipated an evening with greater pleasure.

His aide returned, leaving the white uniform behind. Slowly, relishing all that was to come, Embleton stepped out of his dressing robe and donned his formal attire, silently rehearsing his speech. Once dressed, he regarded himself in the mirror with enormous satisfaction. The trousers were a bit snug—the major had grown fond of the Carolinian fried foods—but his girdle lent him a smooth, altogether presentable appearance. Dressed all in white—even his special officer's tricorn was white—he appeared absolutely dazzling to himself. Peering out his bedroom window overlooking the street, he smiled smugly at the sight of the arriving carriages and the presence

of a dozen red-coated soldiers standing smartly at attention by
his front door. It would all happen too quickly—that was Embleton's only concern. He wanted to—nay, he *intended* to—
savor every second of this delectable soirée, where each detail
had received his undivided attention. Spraying himself with a
variety of substances—powder for his wig, perfume for his
neck—he caught one last glimpse of himself in the mirror and
wholeheartedly approved of what he saw.

"Please be good enough to follow me," said the Redcoat
standing directly at the front door to Buckley Somerset, Miranda, Joy, and Colleen, who was already alarmed by the number of British soldiers. Was this a military or cultural affair?
Inside, they were escorted through the house to the rear parlor,
a large room where some fifty chairs had been neatly set up.
Half the seats were already occupied, and against two walls
another dozen Redcoats stood, muskets in hand. Why so many
soldiers, and why were they so blatantly positioned? Buckley's
party was taken to the very front row, where seven chairs sat
directly before the pianoforte. Two of those chairs were occupied by Robin Courtenay and Piero Sebastiano Ponti, who
had arrived only minutes before. The gentlemen arose and,
with formal graciousness, greeted Colleen, Joy and Somerset,
and Miranda.

"It's been several years, madam," Robin said respectfully
to the great-wigged woman.

"It was several lifetimes ago that we knew each other,"
Miranda replied. "I presume that you do believe in reincar-
nation, an ancient belief held sacred in certain corners of the
world. I, for instance, am certain that, religious differences
aside, I embody the spirit of Joan of Arc, who . . ."

"Mother," Buckley interrupted, afraid that this would happen. "I'd like you to sit next to me."

For the moment, Miranda was silent, seated at her son's
left. Colleen sat between Somerset and Piero. She resisted
asking the Italian about Jason's whereabouts. Reading her mind,
though, Piero whispered, "The maestro is in the garden relaxing
before his performance." Colleen looked beyond the glass doors,
where she saw her lover seated on a bench in a corner of the
garden, a short brick wall to his back, his eyes calmly closed,
the very portrait of the artist in gentle meditation. He was

wigless, dressed in a simple gray waistcoat as the light from the parlor's torches and candles lent his lanky figure a shadowy glow. Oh, how she longed to go to him, to sit beside him, to wish him well and tell him how much she loved him! She admired him even more for enduring this charade so that his fearless work might continue.

A few seconds later, almost sensing the warmth of Colleen's loving stare, Jason opened his eyes and smiled into hers. His smile spoke volumes. Colleen could see the love and concern in his eyes. In fact, the musician had been preoccupied with the same thoughts as hers.

At the last recital, not a single guard was in evidence. This time he counted at least two dozen. Why? What was the purpose, especially inside the parlor itself? Was Embleton worried about a rebel attack? It seemed hardly likely. No matter; Jason struggled back toward relaxation. In a few moments he would begin to play, and this composition, which had been boiling within him ever since he had returned to America, would finally find formal expression. It was enough to look up and see Colleen's lovely golden eyes. In returning her glance, he offered her a deep measure of sympathy, an unmistakable look of love.

Buckley intercepted the silent exchange. He was barely able to contain his fury. How these lovers pined for one another! Oh, to see them strung up, side by side! He knew he had no more than two hours to wait for his sweet reward, and yet seated there, his index finger playing compulsively with the break in his nose, Somerset counted the seconds ticking away as he turned to greet the arrival of a group of wealthy Tory friends and wondered when in hell Embleton would appear so that the festivities might begin.

"Lovely setting for a recital," he said to Colleen, forcing her to divert her eyes from Jason. "If you were only a poet, you could compose a sonnet about an evening such as this."

Colleen didn't reply as waves of terror chilled her bones.

Dressed in full dress uniform, Peter Tregoning left the officers' quarters of the Old Customs Exchange and walked to the stables, where he saddled and mounted his steed. He had supervised a meaningless practice maneuver all afternoon— another frivolous assignment he'd been given—and was tired, thus the decision to ride rather than walk to Major Embleton's.

The sky was already dark, and leading his horse around the front of the massive building, he saw a number of flaming torches. When he paused to inspect the nature of this unusual activity, he felt his throat turn dry and his heart beat madly against his chest. Dozens of workmen were hurriedly putting up gallows. There could be no doubt about it. He tied his horse and walked toward the front of the building, his mind racing with questions: Why? Why this time of evening? Why so many workers? And why the frantic pace? This was evidenced by the shouts of the greencoat in charge: "Hurry! We've got only an hour to get this thing up! You lugs over there—move those beams!"

"Will there be a hanging tonight?" Peter asked the Tory in charge as he rode his horse.

"Can't say a word about it, Captain. Just following orders."

"I see," Peter said, convinced that the secrecy, the decision to wait till the last minute, the fact that the construction was to be done within an hour all had some connection with the event to which he had managed to invite himself. Taking one last glance at the bustling crew, he walked slowly back toward his mount. A humid, misty film had fallen over the city, lending a swampy feel to the moonless night. Riding through Charleston, Peter saw danger in every alleyway, danger behind every door. His mind filled with images of the massacres he had witnessed, he felt strangely disconnected from his past as, with greater speed, he rode on, as if on a mission of desperate urgency.

As soon as Billy Hollcork's two-horse wagon pulled up to the front door of the Embleton town house, the same red-coated guard who had escorted the Somerset party smartly stepped forward and helped Rianne step down. Billy rode on farther down the street to tie his horses to a post.

"I'll take you inside, Miss McClagan," the soldier said.

Shocked that she had been identified by name, she nonetheless replied coolly. "Thank you, but we had best wait for my escort."

"Escort?" the Redcoat asked. "I wasn't told you'd be attending with anyone besides your niece. She's already inside."

"Well," she said snappishly, wondering why this party was so carefully planned, "I happen to be attending with Mr. Hollcork, who will be here presently."

"I'm afraid, madam, that I won't be able to admit him."

"What! Why, that's outrageous!"

"I have my orders."

"You have your nerve. If you don't want me standing out here shouting to the heavens and disrupting this affair, I suggest you admit my friend at once."

"What's wrong, Rianne?" Billy asked as he joined her at the front door.

"They say you can't come in."

"If you'll excuse me for a moment, madam," said the soldier, "I'll see what can be arranged."

Tapping her foot as she watched the guests arriving—several of whom had been customers—Rianne grew testier by the minute. It didn't matter to her that many of the other attendees smirked at the sight of Billy Hollcork and presumed that the seamstress and tanner, try as they might, couldn't gain admittance to the exclusive recital. She was furious that her choice of an escort was being questioned.

At that moment, Captain Peter Tregoning arrived. Having met Rianne at the costume ball, he greeted her warmly and shook hands with the broad-shouldered Hollcork. "Shall we all go in together?" asked the Englishman.

"We're waiting for orders," Rianne said wryly.

"I don't understand."

The guard reappeared. "Seat her in front and keep him in back," the Redcoat announced, relating Embleton's orders. "We don't want to cause any commotion."

"If you'll follow me, madam," the Redcoat said, "I'll be honored to seat you."

"And my gentleman friend?"

"He's welcome to view the recital from the foyer."

"Listen here, lad," Peter interjected as the soldier sharply saluted.

"Good evening, Captain."

"I'll be taking Miss McClagan and Mr. Hollcork inside as my guests."

"Begging your pardon, sir, but I've instructions that you, too, are to view the recital from the foyer."

"What!"

"We'd better stop arguing," Rianne said with relief that Billy was being allowed inside. "The recital is about to start. At least you and Billy can keep each other company, Captain."

Astounded and alarmed, Peter knew that further arguments wouldn't help.

Rianne was escorted to the front row of the parlor, where all the straight-backed chairs were now occupied. The room buzzed with excited conversation as Rianne accepted her greetings and sat next to Miranda.

"Where's your mountainman friend?" Mrs. Somerset asked.

"Apparently there's a shortage of seats."

"I'm not surprised they didn't let him in. At least some standards still remain intact."

"In fact, he's here," Rianne replied while an interested Colleen leaned over to listen to her aunt's conversation. "He's in the back."

At that point, the entire front row—Joy, Rianne, Miranda, Buckley, Colleen, Piero, and Robin—turned around. At the very rear of the long room was a small foyer in which stood a dozen or so spectators—people of obvious lower class. Peter and Billy towered over the others.

Buckley laughed to himself; that Jason's dear friend was relegated to the back was a source of great amusement. He was even more pleased when he saw that his men had finally arrived. The wall-eyed albino, Jack Windrow, and his stocky sidekick, Sam Simkins, joined Hollcork and Tregoning in the foyer.

Joy had to fight herself from going to Peter. They looked at each other with a mixture of pained concern and deep desire. Since the afternoon in the military carriage, they hadn't seen one another. Joy felt a series of frightening questions running through her mind. Why wasn't he allowed in the parlor? And why were those sinister former employees of her father standing next to him?

"The house looks stunning," Miranda said to Rianne. "A fine example of how good breeding can restore even the most banal decor."

"When this manor belonged to its rightful owner, Alex Sitwell," Rianne said loud enough for the five British officers seated directly behind them to hear, "I considered it a model of distinguished taste. This English-made furniture has the look of another time and a different place—a foreign place. I greatly preferred the pieces that were crafted here in Charleston."

"Charles Town," Miranda corrected, "has its would-be artists and artisans. They're little more than pretenders. To the eye of a European, this land is still barbaric, as are its artifacts."

The banter between the women would have continued if Major Randall Embleton had not entered the parlor through a side door. He had waited until the last minute, hoping that Pall would deliver the broadside he so badly wanted. Thus far, there was no sign of the actor. Smiling nonetheless, walking erectly, the major looked around for Jason. For a moment, he panicked. Had the bastard escaped? Quickly, though, he spotted him in the garden and, with great relief, motioned him inside. Jason came in and sat himself at the pianoforte bench, only a few feet from Colleen and the others who sat in the first row. He looked out into the audience, at the officers and the mannered ladies and gentlemen, and then, unexpectedly, in the back, he saw Peter, Hollcork, Windrow, and Simkins. Why wasn't his friend seated in the parlor? What was going on?

"I'm glad that each of you is here tonight," Embleton said, appearing resplendent in his dress-white uniform as he stood directly in front of Jason and faced his audience. "You will be witness to not only a cultural event of no small significance, but a number of astonishing revelations that go beyond the realm of music. In fact, this evening's activities will be divided into two discrete sections, only the first of which will be conducted in my home. Alas, I hope my remarks are not confusing. The suspense will be lifted to everyone's—well, *almost* everyone's—satisfaction. First, we shall be treated to an original composition by Mr. Jason Paxton, and then I shall have more to say about the second half of tonight's entertainment. Before Mr. Paxton plays, however, I'd like to acknowledge the presence of another artist in our midst, Miss Colleen McClagan. Miss McClagan"—Embleton paused, gallantly gesturing toward the lady—"we are honored to have you here, as well as Mr. Paxton's sister, Joy Exceeding, Miss Rianne McClagan, aunt to the artist, and Mr. Paxton's distinguished patrons, Mr. Piero Sebastiano Ponti and Mr. Robin Courtenay."

The major stepped aside and sat in a chair that faced the audience a few feet from Jason. Now that he had let this rebel gang know that the game was up, he wanted to enjoy looking at them, one by one, as the anxious musician exercised his fingers briefly before placing them on the ivory keys.

Already Embleton saw terror in the Sandpiper's eyes. He smiled at her sweetly. Her aunt seemed no less anxious. Randall nodded at the extravagant lady. Joy Paxton looked confused. Not for long, Embleton thought. And Paxton's absurd champions, those effeminate fops, oh, how they began to perspire! Give them time to think about it! Let them enjoy their maestro's recital! Let the music play!

∽ *Chapter 11* ∽

The smell of kerosene, then a series of sudden explosions. Heat everywhere. Fire! The house was on fire! Roy McClagan leaped from the bed and looked out the window of the Paxton home in Brandborough. He saw two of Ethan's farmworkers strewn across the grass, their faces up, their backs stained with blood. The house was surrounded by greencoats, excitedly setting torches to the kerosene-drenched porch, flames licking a dark, misty sky. In a volley of gunfire, three of Paxton's house servants running from the house were shot—one in the stomach, another in the neck, a third in the head. They fell to the ground, bleeding, screaming.

Run! Roy thought to himself. *I've got to run!*

Ethan Paxton ran into the room, his eyes blazing with fury. "Follow me! Hurry! We've got only seconds!"

How long have I been sleeping? Roy thought to himself as they scurried down the smoke-filled staircase through the house to the kitchen. He vaguely remembered that he and Ethan had tried to leave for Charleston earlier that day, but fatigue had overcome the physician, and Ethan, fearing Roy was growing ill, considerately suggested that he rest a few more hours before they made the trip. Now this.

As they ran into the kitchen they heard a violent pounding at the front door—the butt of muskets against wood—and then gunfire, windows smashed, the shouts of angry men. With the greencoats in the house, greencoats running down the hallway,

Ethan watched Roy push a small section of the kitchen wall that magically gave way, leading to a secret passageway. Immediately, Paxton pushed the wall back in place and led McClagan to a narrow wooden staircase. "Take my hand," Roy whispered as he reached out behind him and made contact with Roy. They were in total darkness. "One step at a time. Slowly."

The men descended into a space that was more the size of a large tomb than a basement. Surrounded on four sides by hardened dirt, Roy felt a rodent nipping at his naked toes. He kicked the animal, and the rat scurried off. The hole in the ground stank of feces and mildew, and breathing was difficult. The men stood next to each other, smelling the burning wood from above, hearing the wild hoots of the raiding party.

A lifetime, thought Ethan Paxton, a lifetime up in flames. He had been in the fields when the Tories came, and by the time he arrived at the house, his half dozen employees had all been killed. Realizing there was nothing to do but save the doctor and himself, he forced himself to maintain this defensive posture, although inside he was half mad with the urge to go up and fight, to shoot, to kill the bastards who had murdered his people and burned his home.

Death and destruction, thought Roy McClagan. When would the murdering stop? And what of Colleen? *Dear God,* he prayed, *nothing else matters, if only my Colleen is safe.*

Colleen saw her life ending. Hers and Jason's. She understood that they were trapped. Embleton's words; the soldiers; the invitation to Rianne and Joy; being seated in the front row— the signs were everywhere. Would they be shot? Or hanged like Ephraim Kramer? Either way, there was absolutely no escape. She tried to think of Nathan Hale. If she were to die, she would try to do so bravely. But the knowledge that her exploits might also lead to her lover's demise filled her with shame and horror. How had they found out? Where was the leak? Squirming in her chair, she had her answer immediately as she glanced toward the back of the room where, in the corner of the foyer, she saw a figure who resembled Frederic Pall handing something to one of the soldiers who, in turn, slipped him what looked like a money pouch. *Pall has betrayed us! Jason has been right all along! How could I have been so stupid, so naïve? I've killed him! The one man I loved! The one love of my life!*

Meanwhile, Jason silently prayed for a moment of bravery as he prepared to play, for he knew he had to play. There were no other options, at least not now. Playing for the next forty minutes would at least give him time to think, and to postpone the inevitable. Meanwhile, before touching the ivories with the tips of his fingers, he looked at Colleen one last time. If his eyes could speak, they'd have said, "I love you, no matter what. I love you with all my heart."

Mere seconds before Jason began to play, Embleton suddenly arose and lifted his hand. Jason, Rianne, Colleen, Robin, and Piero all knew that the end had come even earlier than expected. Given the screaming panic reverberating inside their heads, they each remained remarkably composed, even though Piero, with the palm of his hand covering his nose, sniffed an especially large quantity of his special-blend snuff.

"You'll excuse me, dear maestro," the major said, "but I was led to understand that this piece was to be dedicated beforehand. You'll not disappoint me, I know."

Jason sighed, his heart heavy with fear, yet pounding with a strange sort of unvanquished pride. He looked the officer in the eyes with fierce determination, said nothing, defiantly lifted his fingers, and began playing a music that was, at once, so startling, so amazingly original that even Embleton—who, after all, was still a music lover—allowed his request to go unanswered. Let the musician play, he reasoned. The bloody encore would come soon enough.

The composition was in three sections. Colleen understood that Jason had written this opening movement out of the fabric of his childhood. She could picture the swamps and woods—oh, his secret ravine!—where he had romped and played as a child. She felt all the innocence of youth in the whimsical motifs, the cascades of notes, the playful arpeggios. There was a suggestion of Irish, German, and French folk melodies and a strong flavor of the haunting songs sung by the Africans who had been brought to these shores in bondage. It was sympathetic music, open to an astounding variety of sounds, and quite unlike anything the audience had heard before. Watching Jason rock his upper torso back and forth to the lilting rhythms, Colleen was almost able to forget about the doom that awaited them. Never had she felt closer to this extraordinary man.

Jason paused at the end of the fifteen-minute opening section, breathed deeply—staring at the keyboard, maintaining

his concentration against the invasion of a thousand thoughts—
then began the next movement just as one of the Redcoats
handed Embleton a rolled piece of parchment. Colleen under-
went the terrifying experience of watching the major read her
latest broadside—she recognized the paper—and enduring his
gleam of satisfaction as he looked up at her, a sinister smile
playing upon his lips.

"Would that there were words to this composition," Buckley
whispered to Colleen, letting her feel the tip of his tongue
against her ear. "Perhaps you could set lyrics to Mr. Paxton's
music."

Colleen said nothing in reply. *Dear God,* she prayed silently,
give me courage; give me strength.

"If you ask me," Miranda said loudly, "it's not even music.
It's barnyard clucking."

If other members of the audience shared Miranda's opinion
of the first movement, the second quickly won them over. It
was here where Jason paid homage to his European training.
In the tightly mannered structure of his phrasing, he reflected
the courtly demeanor of old-world Europe. In a series of charming minuets, the influence of Haydn and Mozart was most
apparent. In the delectably pleasing melodies, Piero could hear
the sonorous echoes of the great Italian operatic masters. Jason
had applied all the aesthetically satisfying symmetry of, say, a
French formal garden to this section, and the audience—even
the major himself—was not only charmed, but impressed with
the musician's technical ability both as writer and performer.
At the movement's end—a flourish of sixteenth notes rippling
up and down the keyboard—there was even a smattering of
spontaneous applause, though it was apparent that the piece
was not yet complete.

Again, a brief pause, as Jason looked at Colleen, his eyes
saying, "Be strong, my love." Amazingly, he had the heart to
go on.

Watching the exchange between her brother and Colleen,
Joy couldn't help but turn around to seek out Peter's eyes. He
nodded to her, as if to confirm Jason's sentiments.

The final movement was bizarre and dissonant. It began
with a literal bang, and from then on Jason launched what
sounded like a musical attack. His body jerked back and forth
and his curls shook violently upon his head as he seemed to
be expressing the turbulence of his homeland in war. The sec-

tion was played in a radically minor mode, with no attempt to please the ear. As he stomped through the instrument's lower register, one could hear the thud of horses' hooves and the thunder of night. The rhythm was uneven, reminiscent of a frantic swamp chase. Colleen understood that this was the emerging spirit of Will-o'-the-Wisp. In fact, she detected a distinct anger at the music itself, as if Jason were expressing his frustration with mannered art in the face of life-and-death issues. Music, he was saying, was useless, ineffectual. If in the second movement he had charmed his audience with the soothing syncopations of a distinguished and mature civilization, he suddenly turned the tables. *Fortissimo* was the volume, unrelenting in its pace and improbable ear-splitting chords, one more grating than another. Guests turned to one another in puzzlement. "Rubbish," said Miranda in a voice that traveled at least a dozen rows back. It wouldn't be proper under the circumstances, but many were on the verge of walking out. Still, Jason played on, running his thumb down the keyboard, banging his fists on a block of notes, doing virtual battle with the instrument.

Colleen understood, as did Peter, as did Piero and Robin. His hair wildly askew, his face beaded with sweat, his fingers beet-red, he was playing out his heart, his fears, and his determination. Louder the music grew, and louder still, until, at the very end of this firestorm of crashing notes, a simple single-line melody emerged like a sweet baby duck emerging from a devastating flood. It was "Yankee Doodle" that Jason played, much as a child would play it, and while he played, he hummed along. After striking the final, plaintive note, Jason lowered his head, which all the while had been filled with desperate schemes to escape this trap. He had thought of nothing. He was prepared to die the death of a rebel—with dignity and defiance to the end—but he was still not prepared to watch Colleen die beside him.

Embleton slowly arose from his chair and, with Jason still seated on the bench before the pianoforte—the bewildered audience could offer him only the most meager applause at the end of his performance—the major cleared his throat.

"I have in my hand," he said, "another original composition that I'm also pleased to present to you for the first time. Much shorter than Mr. Paxton's work, it expresses some of the same bold sentiments. You'll be gratified to know that its distinguished author is with us tonight."

Holding the parchment in front of him, the officer read with a mock heroic tone:

> The summer of 1780, so bloodstained and long—
> Finds Fishing Creek and Camden in foreign hands.
> Yet in the hearts of fighters for truth
> These months are but grains of shifting sand.
>
> Our will is steady, our resolution strong,
> And like the sun rising o'er the swampy mist
> Freedom will shine on this American soil,
> Tilled by the spirit of our Will-o'-the-Wisp.

"The signature," Embleton continued, switching to his normal voice, "is marked 'The Sandpiper,' a name with which we're all quite familiar."

The major walked over toward Colleen and stared at her intensely. "Yes," he said. "Our poetess, no less gifted than the fabled Sappho herself, has kindly accepted the Crown's invitation to be here tonight. I welcome this opportunity, Miss McClagan, to publicly acknowledge your cultural contributions."

There was a gasp from the audience. The friends desperately searched their minds for a course of action, but each of them—Colleen, Joy, Rianne, Robin, Piero, Peter, Jason—felt maddeningly impotent. Buckley beamed, relishing the moment. Joy's head reeled with shock and confusion. Peter felt as if his pounding heart would burst through his chest. The guards against the wall took several steps forward. A side door opened and the dozen soldiers who had been stationed outside suddenly marched in and lined up against the front wall, behind the pianoforte.

"Indeed, this is a double pleasure," Embleton continued, "for not only do we have the Sandpiper in our midst, but her illusive friend as well, for, you see, her romantic counterpart in this city's seditious activities for the past several months has been none other than . . . our distinguished composer . . . Mr. Jason Paxton, who prefers to call himself Will-o'-the-Wisp."

The audience of British officers and Loyalists couldn't be contained. They bolted from their chairs, pointing to Colleen and Jason, whose composition had just brought them such displeasure.

"Traitors!" they shouted.

"Rebel scum!"

"Spies!"

"Hang 'em!" Buckley Somerset screamed.

"Tonight! We'll see them dead this very night!" his mother joined in.

The major calmly lifted his hand. "Please, please. I understand your vexation and share it entirely. But as I promised you earlier, the evening's entertainment is only half over. You see, for weeks I've known about these two. I've let them have their fun so that we might learn as much about their devilish plans as possible. Patiently—oh, so patiently—I've set this little trap so that everyone in this fair city can see for himself the result of these brilliant rebel schemes. Even as I speak, my men are rousing the citizenry of Charles Town to congregate in front of the Old Customs Exchange, where gallows have already been constructed. . . ."

A lusty cheer went up, Miranda standing and waving both her hands, shouting, "Yes, yes, I knew it all along! To the gallows! To the gallows!"

The rest of the gathering joined in, having metamorphized from a polite audience to a bloodthirsty mob.

"These gallows will accommodate not only our poetess and musician, but his entire crew of assistants—Miss Rianne McClagan"—Embleton sternly pointed to each one—"Miss Joy Exceeding Paxton, and the honorable Piero Sebastiano Ponti and Robin Courtenay. Now that the musical party is over, you're each invited to a hanging party. In the name of King George the Third, we will march together and see to it that our devious Sandpiper and her vile Will-o'-the-Wisp meet the end they so richly deserve."

With that, the major put his hand inside the crook of Jason's elbow and jerked him up from the bench. With his other hand, he did the same to Colleen as he prepared to lead them both to certain death.

❧ *Chapter 12* ❧

Two hours had passed when Ethan decided it was safe to come out of hiding. It had been a long while since he'd heard the sound of the raiding Tories, though the crackle and smell of burning wood hadn't died.

"Are you all right?" he cautiously whispered to Roy.

"A little weak, but still breathing."

He took the physician by the arm and led him back up the stairs, opening the trapdoor. The sight made Ethan sick to his stomach. He fought back an urge to vomit. Beams had fallen, walls had collapsed, windows were smashed, and furniture lay in mere piles of ash. Slowly, Paxton and McClagan walked along what had been the hallway. Ethan swallowed hard, reflecting how he'd built this now useless structure with his own hands. Outside, the corpses of his people—his helpers, his servants, his friends—were strewn about like so much refuse.

"I can't leave them here," Ethan said, standing in front of his house, smoke rising around him, the night misty and humid, the foul stench of human flesh and burned particles of every sort floating upon the polluted air.

"I'll help you bury them," Roy said in a whisper.

Paxton found an old shovel in a shed out back. Despite the doctor's offer to assist, Ethan dug the half dozen graves himself. He allowed McClagan to help him dump in the bodies. When

317

Ethan was through covering them with dirt, Roy said a prayer.

"Dear God Almighty, we know Your ways are beyond human comprehension. We know the suffering we see has purpose and meaning we cannot hope to understand. We beseech Thee for patience, Heavenly Father. If our faith is weakened, strengthen our resolve. If we are afraid, assuage our fears, as we lay these, Your children, to rest. In the name of our Savior, Christ Jesus, Amen."

In acknowledgment of his sentiments, Ethan placed his hand upon Roy's shoulder.

"What now?" asked the doctor.

"We should try to get to your place. They've slaughtered my animals, but somewhere in Brandborough I'll find us a horse, even if I have to steal one."

Roy nodded in agreement.

Creeping along Brandborough's dirt streets, ducking into alleys and crawling behind the backs of low-level buildings, the men saw that every rebel home in the city had been burned. It was midnight before Ethan was able to gain entrance quietly to the stable of a Tory banker and sneak out his prized gray stallion. Bareback, with Roy's arms around Ethan's waist, the two men rode out of Brandborough in the dead of night, avoiding the coastal road and heading through the swamps. They were halfway to the McClagan farm, a mile and a half away, when they saw the red night sky. Roy knew. The closer they came, the brighter the light—the fearful yellow and orange glow, the radiant flames. Out of the swamps, into a clearing, Ethan brought the horse to a halt. From the bottom of the hill, with the sound of dark ocean waves rolling to the shore from the east—they were but a quarter of a mile from sea—their view was uncluttered: dozens of Tories setting the McClagan house afire with burning torches, dancing flames everywhere, the deep-throated boom of musket fire piercing the air.

"Before we march with you to the Old Customs Exchange"—Buckley suddenly stood and began to speak, his ego bruised for not being recognized before by Embleton—"as commander of the Continental Tory Militia, I want to announce that while these infamous rebels are being dealt with in the city of Charles Town, in my own territory, on this very evening, I have seen to it that these two renegades' fathers—themselves traitors to the king—have met the same end that faces their children."

Joy gasped. Rianne, rife with rage and grief, went to Colleen's side. Jason brought up his elbow in an attempt to free himself of Embleton's grasp, but the major squeezed harder, shouting, "Guards, put this row of people under arrest!"

"You do, and you'll be sentenced for treason along with Embleton!" Captain Peter Tregoning spoke up in a voice ringing with assurance and clarity. From the foyer, he had walked down the aisle and stopped in front Embleton, Colleen, and Jason.

For a moment, the soldiers froze.

"Arrest this man as well," Embleton ordered as he pointed to Peter.

"This whole affair is a hoax," the captain explained to the astounded audience. "Just as it's now widely known that the American officer Benedict Arnold has sold his secrets to our army, so has Major Randall Embleton been working for the rebels. This evening's extravaganza is but a clever ploy to conceal this man's vile treachery."

"What! . . . why . . ." Embleton tried to interrupt, but Peter carried on.

"Yes," he said, pointing right between the major's eyes, "he knows the identity of Will-o'-the-Wisp—in fact, he has worked hand in hand with him. You officers have seen him there, time and again, conferring in Embleton's office in the Old Customs Exchange. You, Buckley Somerset—you're the secret rebel. And your mother—she's the one who's been writing those slanderous verses. You've paid the major hundreds of pounds; you've promised him a plantation of his own after the war. Shame, I say! What nonsense to lay the blame on a mere musician and schoolgirl. What a sham! General Cornwallis himself instructed me to follow Embleton's every move, knowing the man for what he is. In fact, the general and his men were to have been here by now to make the arrest themselves, but apparently they've been delayed. Therefore, in the name of justice, I must make the arrest myself. Fellow officers, fellow soldiers, fellow servants of the king, arrest this traitor before he escapes into the night like a common thief!"

"You'll hang with your friend Paxton, Tregoning," the major sneered.

"To the gallows!" Miranda screamed.

"Now!" Buckley insisted, sensing a confusion among the soldiers.

The guards did not move until Embleton gave the order again. "Arrest Tregoning!"

The soldiers hesitated. The group of officers who had been seated in the second row were standing. At first, Peter's argument seemed ridiculous to them, but so did the entire evening. A musician, who in reality was a spy, performing under the sponsorship of the major before his identity was revealed? It was all wildly unorthodox, especially contrary to the British sense of logic and order. Embleton's biting sarcasm and superior demeanor had made him a favorite with no one, but a traitor? Hardly. And why should they believe Tregoning?

"Yes," said one of officers, backing up Embleton, "arrest Tregoning."

Peter knew his options had run out. In a flash, he reached beneath his blouse and brought forth a pistol, already loaded and cocked, holding it inches from the major's head.

"Call them off, Embleton," he said coldly, "or so help me God, you'll hear no more music on this earth."

The major was forced to balance the fear of death with the fury of seeing his plans disintegrating before his eyes. "You wouldn't," he said to Tregoning. "You're an officer of the Crown . . . you're . . ."

"Quick, Jason," Peter said, holding the pistol steadily against the skin of Embleton's temple. "Get them all out of here. Hurry!"

Colleen and Jason broke free of Embleton's grasp as they, Rianne, Joy, Robin, and Piero turned and began to run up the center aisle. Seeing what was happening, Buckley Somerset lost control. He reached out to grab Jason, calling for Windrow and Simkins. "Jack! Sam! Shoot 'em! Shoot 'em all!"

More confused than ever, the soldiers made a move toward Peter, who saw he no longer had any choice. He squeezed the trigger.

An ear-splitting explosion. A groan. The major crumbled. Blood splattered everywhere—on Miranda's gown, in Rianne's eyes, on Colleen's blouse. Screams. Pieces of flesh, sections of ear, hair, brain matter, bone, and cartilage. Embleton's all-white uniform was stained with huge blotches of dark, dripping red. The horror of witnessing the head of their commanding officer blown to smithereens paralyzed the soldiers and officers—at least for a second. In that second, Jason decided on another escape route, leading his people into the garden. As they ran, pandemonium broke loose. From the foyer, Sam Simkins took out a gun, loaded it, and was ready to fire on the escaping band when Billy Hollcork plunged a knife into his heart. Simkins fell, gasping his last breaths. Seeing what had happened, Jack Windrow turned on the tanner with a knife of his own, but Billy was too fast for him, cutting him in the muscle of his left arm. Writhing in pain, the albino fell into his dead colleague's pool of fresh blood. Hollcork stormed down the aisle as he saw a group of soldiers, along with Buckley, pursuing the fugitives into the garden. Suddenly from the rear of the foyer, one-eyed Jeth Darney announced his arrival with a bloodcurling "Yoooeeeeeeeeeee!"

A gun in each hand, he opened his coat to expose a holster that extended from his left shoulder to his right hip and housed another half dozen pistols. "All right, you rebels!" he shouted behind him to an imaginary band of men. "Start shooting and aim straight! Make those Red-coated hearts bleed, for Christ's sake!"

With both guns blazing, Darney shot an officer in the eye and another guard in the gut, all the while looking for Frederic Pall, who had managed to slip away. Jeth's call to his make-believe comrades had the Redcoats taking cover. An army of extreme discipline, the English military reacted poorly to chaotic situations. This makeshift mayhem had them baffled. Miranda grabbed Buckley and forced him down under a seat, afraid there'd be shots from the rear. Thinking that in this instance Mother did indeed know best, he crouched down next to her. In the meantime, Billy had reached the others in the garden, where he and Jason climbed atop the short wall and helped everyone over onto the street. Rianne's petticoat got caught on a brick and ripped. Piero's supply of snuff fell from his waistcoat. Darney and Peter kept the rest of the room at bay.

"Go with them," Tregoning ordered Jeth, amazed to find himself fighting on the side of a pirate. "They'll need you."

Jeth did so, dashing into the garden and leaping over the wall, still looking for Pall. Oh, how he wanted that man's neck! By then Hollcork had run after his wagon and brought it back to the street side of the wall. Lifting them as if they were sacks of potatoes, he practically threw Rianne, Joy, Colleen, Robin, and Piero into the rig supported by two large wheels and driven by Billy's two trusty duns.

"Hurry, Jase!" Colleen cried, squeezed between her aunt and his sister.

"Peter! Tell Peter to come!" Joy begged her brother.

"Go with them, Darney," Jason ordered. "They'll need you."

"What about you?" Jeth asked as he joined Billy on the riding board behind the horses.

Still standing atop the brick wall, Jason glanced back into the room where the soldiers had positioned themselves behind the pianoforte, beneath furniture, aiming their muskets at non-existent rebels. "Come on, Peter!" he shouted.

Seeing that Jason had safely gotten everyone over the wall, Peter headed for the garden just as the white flame of gunfire chipped his right ankle. He fell. Before the attacking soldier could reload and shoot again, though, Jason took a knife Jeth had slipped him and, even from that great distance—through the open doors of the gardens into the parlor—threw the blade with dead accuracy, piercing the Redcoat's Adam's apple.

In a split-second, Jason had to decide whether to leap over the wall and escape with Colleen and the others, or to go back for Peter.

"Go on!" Jason shouted to Billy and Jeth as he spotted another group of soldiers running down the street toward the wagon. "You can't wait any longer! Go now!"

"No, Jase . . . not without you!" Colleen cried.

"Peter . . . where's Peter?" Joy wept.

Seeing the Redcoats, Billy let his horses feel the reigns against their broad backs. "Whoa!" he yelled, but not before Jeth, who had been reloading his weapons while his good eye continued to search for Frederic Pall, threw Jason two ready-to-fire pistols.

Jason took one last glance at Colleen standing in the wagon, her arm extended toward him, as she was surrounded by her aunt, his sister, and his patrons. With Darney and Hollcork riding up front, they vanished into the night. Would he ever see his friends or his Colleen alive again? With no time to reflect, Jason leaped from the wall and was back in the parlor, his eyes darting everywhere, the cocked guns held out in front of him. As the sound of Darney's gunfire rang from the street, the Redcoats, with the mangled corpse of their leader in plain view, still imagined themselves under seige. The non-military guests scurried for cover, screaming bloody murder. Jason reached Peter and grabbed him around the waist, dragging him toward the foyer while shooting the musket out of the hands of a Redcoat who was prepared to fire from under a portrait of King George III. Hoisting Peter upon his back, stooped over, dodging bullets, his blazing pistols clearing a path to the front door, Jason was somehow able to escape the confused melee.

Outside the chaos was perhaps even more intense. Even during the recital itself, interested citizens had gathered by the front door to catch the music as it wafted through the open windows. Once the gunfire erupted, though, hundreds of people had appeared, taking cover behind horses and houses. With the hysterical guests and baffled soldiers streaming out the door of the late major's residence, no one knew who was who. With Peter still on his back, Jason was able to locate Robin and Piero's carriage, though the driver had run off. He placed his English friend inside.

"'Tis madness, Jason. This whole bloody business is madness," Peter said as his ankle throbbed with pain.

"You were magnificent," Jason replied, his eyes filled with admiration. "Give me a little time to get out of here and I'll see to your wound. You've the courage of a lion."

"Wouldn't you think it'd be a good idea to exchange clothing?" Peter asked.

"Yes, let's do it in a hurry."

Undressing in such close quarters was tricky—bringing Peter's trousers over his swollen ankle was especially difficult—but they were able trade outfits. In the uniform of an English captain, Jason leaped onto the wooden board from which he drove the two horses through the back roads of a city where, in taverns and homes alike, word of Embleton's assassination and the revelation of the Sandpiper and Will-o'-the-Wisp spread like wildfire, exciting the rebels into a revelry of amazement and hope.

~ *Chapter 13* ~

In the tiny dressing room of the Dock Street Theater, Frederic Pall adjusted the petticoats, gown, and great gray wig atop his head. He checked his purse; the twenty pounds was there. He whitened his clean-shaven face with powder and applied a goodly quantity of rouge to his cheeks and artificial coloring to his lips. The long sleeves and frilly high-neck blouse covered his hairy arms and chest. With his makeup freshly applied and his bodice stuffed with crumpled advertisements for future theater productions, Pall took his leave. As he walked through the streets, his outfit afforded him a measure of comfort and security, even given the fact that citizens, still unsure of what had happened on this wild night, were milling about, nervously exchanging gossip and news.

The fact that during the melee outside the theater he had killed a woman by plunging an ice pick through her heart bothered Pall not in the least. In urgent need of another disguise, he had covered her mouth with his hand, dragged her back into an alley, murdered her, put her clothes over his own, and easily made his escape as he noticed Jeth Darney and Billy Hollcork riding away with a cartload of important personages. Such observations, he understood, were of inestimable value. He congratulated himself for having the presence of mind to stay close to Embleton's house, for just a few moments later he wondered what an English captain would be doing riding atop—

and not inside—a gentleman's carriage. Given the circumstances of the evening, everyone else was far too agitated to
notice. But as a master of subterfuge, it didn't take Pall more
than a second to recognize the musician's face under the British
tricorn, just as the actor also caught sight of Peter inside the
carriage.

Having observed the recital from a secluded position in the
entryway behind a large palmetto plant, Frederic was intrigued
by this man who had betrayed his country. Betrayal was something Pall understood. He admired Tregoning's tactic—the impassioned speech and accusation of Embleton and Buckley had
been a neatly improvised trick. But what were the man's motives? Certainly not money. The rebels were as poor as church
mice. They hadn't an extra shilling to pay truly professional
spies—at least Frederic hadn't been able to get a cent out of
them. No, this Englishman's sentiments lay elsewhere, in the
area of pure sentiment. Such a notion seemed not only silly to
Pall, but disturbing as well. There was something about this
entire rebel gang—the musician, the silly girl, the aunt, the
English captain, the two fops—that Frederic found repugnant.
Their self-righteousness was despicably cloying. He wanted to
see the whole lot of them dead.

With the certain knowledge that his talents were undoubtedly
worth more than ever, Pall sashayed his way to the Old Customs
Exchange, relishing his feminine role. The actor recalled that
the middle-aged woman to whom these fragrant clothes had
belonged wasn't especially attractive, but at least she had superb taste in perfume. Attaining French cologne during times
such as these was no easy task, and Pall appreciated her efforts.

It took him a while to gain entrance into the Old Customs
Exchange, but with a series of hysterical shrills and shouts
about how "she" had information about the escaped rebels, Pall
was finally admitted into the building and then forced his way
into the office that had belonged to Embleton.

As expected, Buckley Somerset was there, accompanied by
Jack Windrow; his arm had been bandaged and he had changed
out of his blood-soaked clothes. Also present was a group of
high-ranking English officers, all hovered over a map illuminated by two long candles. Miranda sat in the corner, compulsively playing with the ribbons on her wig. It was nearly
midnight.

"Who allowed this woman in here?" Buckley snapped.

"Well, sir," explained the aide who had shown Pall inside, "she insists that she . . ."

Miranda suddenly arose from her chair and pointed a finger at Frederic. "'Tis no woman. There's a man beneath that gown. Take heed, Buckley! He's here to harm you!"

Somerset quickly drew his sword, but Frederic just as quickly doffed his wig and shook loose his hair. "'And yet, believe me, good as well as ill,'" the actor recited in an hypnotically singsong voice, "'woman's at best a contradiction still.'"

"Pall?" Buckley asked suspiciously.

"Alexander Pope," Frederic replied, nodding his head toward Miranda, "from his illuminating *Moral Essays.*"

"This is the man," Somerset explained to the British officers, "who gave Randy and myself the information about Paxton and McClagan."

"Yes, of course," said one of the Englishmen, lifting his eyebrow, "the infamous Frederic Pall. He's been selling us information here in the South for the past two years."

"For sums, I might remind you," the actor added, "far below true market worth. Such, though, is the price of loyalty."

"What are you doing dressed as a woman?" asked Buckley, whose fierce gun-metal-gray eyes appeared crazed with frustrated energy.

"Many are the disguises of the Loyalist and thespian," he explained. "Moving around this troubled city grows more perilous hour by hour."

"You have information to sell?"

"And hour by hour it grows more valuable, Mr. Somerset."

"Then state your case and be gone with you. We've important work tonight."

"I don't trust this man, Buckley," Miranda said.

"Quiet, Mother."

"If Mr. Somerset's suggestions had been adopted by Embleton, the major would be alive this very moment," Pall informed the officers while ignoring the woman's accusations. "You see, he wanted Paxton and the girl arrested at once—in fact, the very moment I revealed their identities. He was right. It was your leader, I'm afraid, who favored the theatrics that led to his downfall."

"That's correct," Buckley confirmed, no longer quite so

anxious to be rid of Pall. "And it's paramount that we use every available man to catch them—which is exactly what I've been arguing."

"We've done all we can," said one of the officers. "Every road in and out of Charles Town is blocked. They'll not escape. But given the crazed spirit of the city, we can't sacrifice a large number of men to go chasing after a small party of rebels. Besides, until word comes from General Cornwallis as to who's to take this command, we simply have no choice but to wait."

"And simply let them slip from under your fingers," Pall said, aiming his remarks at Buckley.

"No!" the Carolinian exploded. "I'll not have it! They must hang, every last one of them!"

"Then you'll be interested to learn that they've divided into two groups—the tanner and the one-eyed pirate have all three women and the two womanly men," said the actor as he straightened his gown, "while Paxton and the captain have escaped in the carriage of the musician's mentors."

"How do you know this?" Somerset asked excitedly.

"My eyes do not lie. Besides, what motive have I for fabrication?"

"Where did they go? Where are they hiding?" Buckley wanted to know.

"They've no choice but to employ the resources of that surreptitious connection that binds the rebels throughout this colony. Even if they don't get through the lines, there are dozens of places they could be hiding within the city. And if they've managed to escape, there are only a certain number of places to which they'd flee—Patriots known by Darney and Paxton."

"We have those names," Buckley said. "My Tory Militia has been assaulting rebel bands with deadly accuracy."

"You have the *obvious* names. You've burned out those rebels silly enough to have made their sentiments known. But Darney and Paxton will no doubt seek refuge in the underground, with people not unlike myself, whose identities are known to no one save the true believers."

"Then you'll give me those names," Buckley insisted.

"You'll need more than the names," Pall explained as he sat down and crossed his legs, revealing his petticoats. "If you're going to dispatch your Tory Militia after Paxton and his people without the assistance of the Redcoats . . . and apparently they're not willing to help"—Frederic paused to nod at the

English officers—"then you'll require my aid and advice on a daily basis. Given my deep knowledge of the rebels' complex web of contacts, we could catch your fugitives as early as tonight or tomorrow."

"Or I might well catch them without you."

"I invite you to try, kind sir," Pall said as he placed the gray wig upon his head and prepared to exit.

"Wait. What would you charge?"

"I've thought of nothing else for the past several hours and have concluded that there's but one equitable system of payment. Twenty pounds a day is my price, beginning today— that is, if you're willing to start the hunt tonight."

"I am. My men are already combing..."

"You might as well call your men off. They've no idea where to look. This chase requires a distinct artistry, a finesse which..."

"How do I know that you won't protract the hunt in order to up your earnings?"

"Because I've other work that could be just as profitable, and, besides, if after a fortnight you haven't captured both your Wisp and Sandpiper, I'll refund all you've paid me."

"That seems most reasonable. You're that confident, are you?"

"The man's a liar and a thief!" Miranda leaped up and pointed her finger at Pall's bulging paper bodice. "Trust him not, I say. He'll lead you nowhere save to your own destruction. I'll lead you to the rebels."

"I've warned you before, Mother..."

"I'll not sit idly by and see you taken in by this charlatan!" she screamed.

"Jack, have a couple of your men escort Mother back to Marble Manor tonight. Father needs her."

"Father needs only the warmth of the coffin to lend him the comfort he so pitifully seeks. The man is worse than dead; he's half alive. I'll not go back and..."

"You'll do as I say."

Within a few seconds, two greencoats came in and forcibly led a struggling Miranda out the door. "You'll regret this," she said to her son, "and you'll see that I'm right, just as I've always been right. Besides, without me here, you'll start eating the corpses of dead animals again and..."

Once Miranda was forced outside the office, Buckley

slammed the door in her face and sighed in relief. "We were discussing fees, Mr. Pall."

"You put twenty pounds sterling upon the table and I'll lead you to your friends," the actor promised.

"Fourteen days," Buckley ruminated as he looked over the calendar hanging on the wall, "takes us to October Seventh. If by then you haven't succeeded, you'll give me more than the small fortune back that I will have paid you; you'll give me your life."

Pall smiled, not in the least put off by the threat. "I understand that these fugitives have been somewhat of an embarrassment to you, Mr. Somerset, and I've no doubt that with my cunning and your resources—your tenacious Tory Militia—we'll achieve our common aim. But there's no reason to carry this conversation any further if you're not willing to show me your silver, sir."

Much to the amazement of the English officers, who had been listening to the exchange with fascinated interest, Buckley reached into a hidden section of the wide leather belt supporting his green woolen scarlet-edged breeches and fished out a handful of British coins, dropping them on the table before him.

"Good," Pall said, counting the money with his eyes. "Now you can hear the plan I've formulated for going after them . . . this very night!"

Ethan Paxton and Roy McClagan arrived at Solitary just as dawn was breaking. The great green meadow rose out of the swamps like a magical island sprinkled with the fresh dew of morning. The slightly hazy sky—now gray, now purple, now faded blue—suffused the land with a mysterious and misty light. To both men, whose heads were filled with the images of brutal murder and the stench of burning death, Solitary appeared before them like some lost and innocent dream.

After waiting for the Tories to leave McClagan's house, which lay in ruins, they had paused for a few moments. The doctor's most precious holdings—his records, his library, his daughter's belongings—were all gone. His fields were devastated, crops burned, animals either slaughtered or driven off by the fire. Numb from the trauma of so much shared tragedy in so short a period of time, the men felt a growing bond between each other, like two travelers going through hell. Would another human being ever have believed what they'd witnessed? How could they have explained the suffering they'd seen? Such scenes were more than enough to have driven sane men mad. Were it not for the company of the other man, Ethan and Roy might have cracked. Together, they somehow had kept going, riding through the night, duplicating the journey they had made once before, through the woods and the swamps until, both riding bareback on the single horse, they had reached Ethan's hidden oasis. Without a tent or a supply of food, they stopped in the midst of a grove of oak trees.

"We're safe here," Ethan said. "This land hasn't been plotted on any map. There are enough berries, nuts, and fruits to keep us alive—at least for a while."

Ethan had stolen some rope and a few blankets from the Tory stable. He tied the horse and spread the coarse woolen blankets on the ground. As the sun inched its way up into the hazy sky, the men lay upon the blankets only a few feet apart from one another. Despite their tremendous fatigue, they were unable to sleep—at least not right away—for all the aching grief in their hearts and thoughts of their children whom they couldn't dare hope to see alive again.

Chapter 14

Piero Sebastiano Ponti had never seen so many pigs in his life—hundreds of pigs, baby pigs, mama pigs, papa pigs—pigs in their pens, pigs running loose around the yard, pigs inside the old farmhouse wandering about as if they owned the place. Their snouts and squeals and grunts and curly tails, their constant search for food scraps or garbage, their pungent piggy smell, their swollen bellies and squinty eyes—Piero was nearly beside himself. He loathed the little beasts. Yet there was absolutely no escaping them. Out in the barn, for the few hours that Piero, Robin, Colleen, Joy, Jeth, Rianne, and Billy Hollcork had slept in the hayloft last night, they had been joined by pigs. This morning at the breakfast table, the pigs were underfoot. In fact, the proprietors of the pig farm, Happy Coltin and his wife, Pamela, themselves bore a resemblance to the animals. Short, obese, and red-faced, the jovial couple seemed to have taken on the characteristics of the creatures with which they lived. In fact, Happy's nose was slightly upturned and pressed against his face. He even spoke with something of a grunt.

Shaky from the trip out of Charleston during which he and the others hid in the wagon beneath a blanket as Jeth and Billy blasted their way through two different roadblocks, Piero's head still reverberated with the sound of ringing gunfire. His nerves were shot as he tried to eat the porridge set before him. He was further upset by the realization that he'd lost his supply of snuff during the escape. His nose hungered for his special mixture. How could he get through this ordeal without his snuff?

No matter. They were alive—he and Robin and the women, conducted here by Hollcork and Jeth, who said he'd known these people for years as true if somewhat reticent rebels, people whose farm five miles outside the city would be beyond suspicion. They had been quick to put them up last night and ready in the morning to help them any way they could. They knew of Ethan Paxton, were happy to meet his daughter Joy, and thrilled to learn that her brother was Will-o'-the-Wisp, whose exploits they had secretly applauded for months. Colleen was proud to learn—and acknowledge—that it was her verses that had first informed them of the Wisp.

As everyone picked at their porridge, the silent questions around the table were nearly loud enough to be heard, though no one wished to articulate them: Robin, Piero, and Colleen prayed that Jason had been able to escape, though there was no evidence that he was alive or dead. Joy fought back images of his fellow soldiers murdering Peter as he tried to escape. Both she and Colleen wanted to believe their fathers hadn't been killed, but in the light of what Buckley had said at the recital, weren't they just fooling themselves? How and when could they know? Robin and Piero presumed that by now their house and all its priceless contents—the instruments, the paintings, the tapestries, the rare furniture, and the fabulous library—had all gone up in smoke. Rianne presumed the same about her shop. They were left with the clothes on their backs and an army on their trail. Where were they to go? How long could they hide here?

"I realize," Robin Courtenay said in his calm and dignified manner, "that this is not the time to panic. Each of us feels an enormous debt to you, Mr. Darney, to you, Mr. Hollcork, for your daring and bravery in saving our lives."

Piero, who was sitting next to the one-eyed sea cook, couldn't have agreed more, though never had he encountered a man with such strong breath and body odor.

"If I therefore question you gentlemen," Robin continued, "about our future plans, I hope you won't think me either unappreciative or naïve. I realize our options are limited."

"That they are," Jeth said. "We did some double turns and back-trailing that might have thrown them off our path, but one way or another they'll be out here. Happy's been good enough to post a man down the road to give us some warning, but, believe me, they're a-coming just as sure as I'm sitting here."

"I've places to hide you," Happy said in his bass-bottom voice.

"You're a good man, Happy," Jeth replied, "but they'll have ways to find us."

"Returning to my question, then, Mr. Darney..." Robin interjected.

"I'm thinking. I've been thinking every minute. A place where they wouldn't find us . . . a place that the bloody bastards wouldn't even know about."

"I may know of such a place," said a faint-hearted Joy, thinking of Solitary.

"Ain't necessary," Pamela Coltin said. "We'll provide for you, we will. Why, we've had rebels stay here for months without a soul knowing. Ain't that right, Happy? How long was that Pall fella around?"

The guests froze. Piero dropped his spoon, splashing porridge on his shirt, trousers, and shoes. From under his chair a pig started licking him before he shooed the beast away.

"Frederic Pall?" Jeth asked.

"That's the man," Happy said. "He works as an actor, I believe, but he's a true Patriot. When he stayed with us, he discussed many a plan to undercut the British in Charleston."

Darney bolted out of his chair. "We've got to get out of here, and we've got to go now!"

"What's wrong?" Happy asked.

"Pall talks out of both sides of his mouth. He's the one who set us up last night."

"Are you sure?" the pig farmer asked.

"As sure as I am that snakes crawl. The man's poison. When he comes, you'll say you've neither seen nor heard of us."

"Where will you go?"

"We'll find our way," Billy Hollcork said bravely, holding Rianne's hand.

"Solitary will be safe," Joy said.

"Will you take a bigger wagon?" Happy asked. "At least

the five of you riding in the back will be able to breathe."

"And provisions. You'll need food," Pamela said. "I'll get something ready right now."

"Would you have any fabric?" Rianne asked. "No matter how coarse. And a needle and thread? Our gowns and fancy suits are hardly made for traveling through the swamps. As we go, the girls and I will put together something a bit more commodious."

"Aye, you'll get what you need," Pamela informed her, "that and blankets as well."

"Just hurry!" Jeth urged, his one good eye looking outside.

"We'll prevail, my friend," Robin said to a frazzled Piero, putting his arm around him, a gesture of affection they had never before publicly shared.

"That we will," Rianne echoed as she rose from her chair, holding her tall frame perfectly erect.

Sweet Peter, Joy cried silently to herself, *if only we could find one another again; if only we could escape this world of misery and misunderstanding. Find me, Peter, and keep my brother safe.*

Dear God, prayed Colleen, *protect my Jason. Return my Jason to my arms.* All during their hurried preparations to depart, Colleen held the image of her one true love constant in her mind. *Jason,* she said to herself, over and again, *how I love you! Oh, how I will always love you!"*

"Does the name Happy Coltin mean anything to you?"

"No."

"Didn't think it would."

"Then why in hell are you asking?"

"'Ask,' says the good book, 'and it shall be given you; seek, and ye shall find; knock, and it shall be opened unto you.'"

"Ask all you like," said an irritated Buckley Somerset. "You wasted half the night leading us on a wild-goose chase."

"Wild indeed," Pall replied, delighted again to be dressed as a man and enjoying breakfast in the splendor of Somerset Hall. Only in Europe had he seen a structure of such palatial proportions. Ah, the comfort of fighting on the winning side! "The night," Frederic continued, "was of no small value. We know the route they took out of the city and the general direction in which they're headed. There are but a few places in the nearby countryside where they might have stopped—farms owned by people not suspected of being rebels."

"Where are these farms?" Buckley asked impatiently.

"Would you be good enough to ask your boy to bring me a drop more juice?"

With one sudden movement of his arm, Somerset swept Pall's juice glass from the table. It smashed against the wall, juice splattering on the actor's clean white blouse, which he had borrowed from Buckley.

"'Tis a shame," Frederic said calmly as he wet his cloth napkin with water and dabbed gently at the juice stains. "Such fine silk. I do hope the damage can be repaired."

"Damn the damage, you insufferable clown!" Buckley screamed, his eyes aflame as he grabbed the actor by the collar. "Take me to those blasted rebel hideaways—now!"

"My dear Mr. Somerset, if you'll grant me the courtesy of removing your hands from my throat—my skin's most delicate and irritates easily—and place twenty pounds sterling upon this magnificent mahogany table, I shall be more than willing to describe the course of action that I suggest you and your brave men may want to pursue today."

"You're a blackmailer, Frederic Pall, and a black-hearted thief to boot. I'd just as soon cut your delicate throat as look at you."

"Cutting my throat will not get you your beloved Colleen and her devoted musician."

Reluctantly, Buckley reached into his waistcoat and threw the money on the table. Instinctively touching the bone of his broken nose, he watched Pall silently count the coins.

"Splendid," the actor said, smiling. "As soon as you provide me with a fresh blouse and full glass of orange juice, we can leave straightaway on our rebel hunt."

It was a risky gamble, but it worked. Jason had driven the carriage back to the stables behind his mentor's home, reasoning that it would be the last place in the world the Redcoats and Tories would look. He suspected that the elegant town house would be pillaged and burned, but not this night. They'd be too busy chasing after him, Darney and the others in every quarter of the city. Therefore, he was able to tend to Peter's ankle, wrapping it in a nine-tailed bandage. A bullet hadn't lodged in the skin and the wound was superficial.

The men slept for a few hours, and in the morning, after

Jason warned the servants and sent them on their way with as much money as he could spare, he put on one of Robin's wigs and cloaks and set out for the Fierce Lion Inn. There he was able to convince Dan Greenely, the tavern's rebel owner, of his true identity.

"My situation's desperate," Jason said. "I presume you know Jeth Darney."

"As well as my own father."

"Well, I've got to find him. Where would he have gone?"

Having heard the news of last night's free-for-all and excited to be approached by the real Will-o'-the-Wisp, Greenely scratched his head and thought long and hard.

"We've a good friend a bit out in the country. A pig farmer. Darney may have called on him."

After receiving directions, Jason went back to Robin's, where, with sundry headbands and work clothes, he did his best to disguise Peter, whose longing for Joy was matched by a sickening feeling in his stomach of acute self-loathing.

"I've conducted my entire life according to the code of the British Crown. Do you understand what it means to desert that code? There's no facing my father or my uncles. There's no returning home."

"What you did, Peter, is of higher purpose than any code. You followed the dictates of your heart. You've seen that this is a country founded by people whose very moral obligation is to break a code. To break one and establish another—all in the sacred name of freedom. Whether you accept the fact or not, Peter, you've become an American."

By the time Jason had dressed himself and Peter, they both had the look of farmers or frontiersmen—coarse trousers, torn shirts, animal fur hats that Piero had collected as amusements. Jason loaded a large square cart with food, blankets, two rifles that Robin had owned for years and never used, and a supply of ammunition. In addition, he had three other pistols—Peter's and two of Jeth's. He tied the cart to Robin's two strongest horses and buried his friend beneath the supplies, giving him just enough air to breathe. With a great deal of makeup changing the complexion of his face and a coonskin hat lowered over his head, an unrecognizable Jason breathed deeply before setting out through the streets of Charleston. Ducking into alleys at the sight of any sentry, he managed to weave a circuitous course and make it to the outskirts of the city where a patrol of four greencoats blocked the road. Still several hundred yards away, he whispered to Peter without turning his head, "You're going to have to take the two on your left. I'll contend with the right side. Start loading. I'll cough and you'll shoot first."

From the back, Peter surreptitiously scrutinized his targets. He loaded both rifles, having already experimented with the accurate American weapons. They resembled a Swiss-made variety with which Tregoning was familiar. He fired at the sound of the cough. One man fell. The other started to run away, but Peter's second shot caught him from behind. With that, Jason whipped the horses and charged close enough so that, within pistol's range, he took out both his men, one in the groin, the second directly through the stomach. He silently thanked his father for years of training.

A while later, they knew, from the sounds of squealing pigs, that the Coltin farm was just around the bend. Their pulses quickened. Hope entered their hearts. But when they made the turn, it was the mad scramble of animals running wild that first hinted at disaster. A little farther up the road, smoke entered their nostrils, then a putrid stench. The farmhouse had been burned, the roof collapsed, the walls fallen in. Inside, bodies of men, women, and beasts were strewn about, charred beyond recognition. Obviously, they hadn't been able to get out. Neither man could bare to look. They put cloths over their noses. Breathing was painful. The only objects at all recognizable were a few scattered remnants of what appeared to have been gowns. Jason remembered Colleen's pale blue fabric, just as the hobbling Peter recalled Joy's muted pink and flowery lace. For a few seconds, the men stood there, choked, unable to move, too stunned to cry. They couldn't—wouldn't—accept the fact that their women were dead.

Jason realized how much Colleen meant to him—all her contradictions, her charms, her beauty, her poetry, her soft and fragrant skin, her courageous soul. He saw his life as empty and futile without her. No, she wasn't gone . . . it wasn't possible. His heart was overflowing with his love for this woman. He wanted to scream, to cry, to bring her back somehow. Yet, in spite of the painful emotions racing through him, he knew that he and Peter had to keep on moving, and that there was only one place left to go.

∽ *Chapter 15* ∽

All day they had slept restlessly, troubled by one graphic nightmare after another. A light drizzle falling upon their faces gently awoke them. They opened their eyes to a remarkably various and streaked sky. A simultaneous sun-shower and sunset had created a triple rainbow of such beauty and magnitude that, for several seconds, both men weren't sure whether they were awake or dreaming. If paradise existed, surely it could be no more spectacular than the sight before them. Suddenly all the horror they had seen, the mutilation and death, was overshadowed by this radiance of natural wonder. Blue and pink, orange and gold, lavender and yellow—rainbows to end all rainbows, glowing and wide, a thousand times more vivid than colored oils painted on a canvas, a thousand times grander than any church, basilica, temple, or shrine. The arcs seemed as if they were but a mile away. So fabulous were the formations that Ethan and Roy actually forgot their condition—that they were without food or supplies, cut off from civilization, hunted by an army of ruthless plunderers. What difference did it make in the light of such beauty? Neither man could speak. They merely sat up and gazed upon God's immense creations like worshippers in a cathedral. Their hearts were lifted, their souls refreshed. There was no doubt they were witnessing a miracle.

Suddenly through the center of the three rainbows, directly beneath the highest point, they saw two horses pulling what seemed to be a wagonload of passengers heading toward them. Amazingly enough, the men weren't alarmed. Ethan didn't grab his gun. Roy didn't start to run. They assumed that this, too, was part of the miracle. They may have wondered again whether they were indeed hallucinating, and for a second they looked toward one another to confirm the fact that they weren't seeing things. They weren't. They stood up as the glowing colors of the rainbows intensified, dominating the sky, and waited as the wagon drew closer and closer. They could almost feel something from its passengers—a longing, a sadness, a hunger, a love.

Closer and closer came the cart. Faces came into focus, and Ethan and Roy again silently questioned their senses. Could they be staring into the faces of their daughters? Had the men been murdered in their sleep and were they joining their children in another sphere? No, this was Solitary, Ethan understood, and there, only a few feet from him, among the others, was his Joy Exceeding. Helped down from the cart by Robin and Piero, she ran into her father's arms and together they held one another for dear life, weeping. Never before had she seen her father weep—not even when her mother had died.

Seconds later, Rianne and Colleen stepped down. The seamstress allowed her niece to greet her father first. Colleen and Roy embraced with an intensity strong enough to defeat whole battalions of men. Then Rianne also hugged her brother with considerable might, whispering the words, "Miracle, miracle . . . 'tis a blessed miracle."

The fact that the women, their long hair free of wigs, were dressed in smocklike robes of coarse cotton gave them a strangely angelic appearance, adding to the sacred mystery of the moment.

Jeth and Hollcork alighted from the riding board and strolled off to allow the relatives a private reunion. They, too, were touched by the spirit in the air, the sweet moisture of the rain, the dazzling rainbows. As soon as they had spotted the old men, they had taken up their guns, but were told by the women not to shoot. Even before Colleen and Joy had seen their fathers' faces, they'd felt their presence.

Respectfully, Robin and Piero, dressed in makeshift monklike robes, walked their own way, disappearing for a moment into a dense grove of oak trees. As they gazed upon the wondrous arcs and silently thanked the forces of good for this precious moment of holy respite, Piero's arm nestled into the crook of Robin's elbow.

It was another fifteen minutes before the rainbows faded, fifteen minutes before any of these extraordinary human beings—Colleen or Roy, Rianne or Billy, Jeth or Robin or Piero—could say a word. All together now, they found they were each touching one another, as if to confirm their own fleshly existence.

Blankets were spread upon the ground as night descended. Realizing how important it was to conserve, Jeth distributed a small bit of food, doling out substantially larger portions to Roy and Ethan, who had forgotten the last time they'd eaten. Robin and Piero had not met Roy before, but they were well acquainted with Ethan Paxton. Their previous encounters had not been pleasant. This time, though, it was as if they were meeting another man—someone whose humanity had deepened immeasurably.

Roy's memories of the time Jeth had lived with them were vivid and warm. He had always been fond of the infamous sea cook. Billy Hollcork was known to neither Ethan nor the doctor, but they immediately took to the big tanner's straightforward and openhearted demeanor.

The drizzle had stopped, the night cooled considerably, dry wood was found, and after a small fire was built they all sat around the burning twigs—Joy's head against her forgiving father's shoulder, Colleen next to Roy, Rianne and Billy hand in hand, Robin sitting close to Piero, and Jeth poking the flames. One by one, they had stories to tell, like the cave dwellers of old, of what they had seen and done.

While holding Joy's hand, Ethan told of the death of her twin sister, Hope, and her brother-in-law, Allan, the death of the rebel band, and the bravery of Roy McClagan in trying to save them. He explained that their house in Brandborough was gone, many of his help murdered. Joy sobbed uncontrollably.

As Colleen wept, Roy told of the burning of their farm, of how Ethan had saved him by bringing him to the hidden cellar.

It took Joy many long minutes to recover from the news of Hope. Finally, through a flood of tears, she found the strength to tell her father the story of his son, Jason, and his great bravery. "Were it not for the help of his fearless friends, Robin and Piero," Joy said, "he could have accomplished none of this."

Thunderstruck, Ethan got up and walked away for a few minutes while the others remained silent. They watched as he wandered off by himself, his mind racing with a thousand thoughts. A proud man, he was nonetheless pained by the realization of his own shortcomings. The silent questions assaulted him like gunfire: *How could I have so misjudged by own son? What kind of father have I been? How could I have been so wrong? How could I have known Jase so superficially?* He fought back the tears, the torrent of self-loathing. When he returned to the group, it was with one burning question for Joy.

"But does he live?" Ethan asked, his heart hammering against his chest, swollen with remorse. "How do I know if my son is alive?"

"We can only hope so," said a soft-spoken Robin, who went on to tell Ethan the story of Peter Tregoning. "He is the man," said the instrument maker, "who saved us from the gallows."

Rianne described the exploits of the Sandpiper, detailing her heroic adventures, her artistry, and her courage. "Such is the stuff of which your daughter is made, my brother."

Roy squeezed his daughter's hand—with fear for what might have been, with love and with new respect.

In his rough and colorful way, Jeth Darney gave a full explanation of the treachery of Frederic Pall, bringing them up to date. "From what we've learned from rebels on the long road today," he told Ethan and Roy, "I figure there's no safe place left in all of South Carolina. I was hoping that we could make it to the border. Rumor has it that those wild Scot and Irish mountainmen have had enough of Ferguson. They say rebel support is building in the vicinity of King's Mountain. That's the region where all the Patriots seem to be heading. Truth of the matter is that's where we were heading till your Joy, Mr. Paxton, showed us the way here."

"Joy was right," Ethan said, "you'll be safe here."

"But for how long, sir?" Billy Hollcork asked. "They're all over this territory."

"You saw for yourself," Ethan continued, "how hard it is to find this place."

"Well, we're certainly here for the night," Robin chimed in with his comforting and sagacious voice. "In the morning there'll be time to discuss our options in greater detail. I'm certain we can find a consensus of opinion. For the time being, our heads are overflowing with so many things—such glad tidings, such revelations of tragic loss—that we'd all do well to sleep."

There was no disputing Robin, who was doing his best to calm the still nervous and high-strung Piero. A half hour later, with the blankets huddled around the dwindling fire, its embers still aglow, they and the rest of the party closed their eyes and tried to rest their minds, although Joy cried for Peter, just as Colleen consoled herself by silently writing poems to her Jason:

> Accused of treachery and courageous crimes,
> The risks and dangers chill our minds.
> Yet despite cruel separation and cold, dark fears,
> The light of our love shines bright and clear.

"Eeeeeeoooooooooooooeeeeeeeee!"

The screech in the middle of the night startled everyone. Jeth, Ethan, and Billy grabbed their weapons. Perhaps Ethan's confidence about Solitary's seclusion had put them all off guard, for they'd been sleeping soundly. In any event, no one had heard the approach and now it was too late.

"There!" Ethan pointed. "From that grove of trees."

A thick cloak of fog had darkened and covered the night. Visibility was practically nil. Having been spotted, and certainly surrounded, they realized they were trapped. Each of them felt the hot fear of death in their throats and stomachs; each of them knew the end was near.

"Spread out," Ethan advised them. "Go off in pairs so we're not just a sitting target."

"Eeeeeeoooooooooooooeeeeeeeee!"

The awful screech again and suddenly racing through the fog two or three horses, perhaps more, it was hard to tell, and a voice screaming, "I knew it! I told him! The women know! They always know!"

"Miranda Somerset!" Rianne yelled. "It's her! Shoot her! Give me a rifle and I'll shoot the witch myself!"

But she and her comrades—were those other women astride the horses?—disappeared back into the fog, with only the sound of her voice ringing out: "Found! I found them! I knew I would, and I did! Oh, blessed victory! The cads have been found!"

The men knew that shooting into the fog would be little more than a waste of bullets. Going after them would be just as futile an exercise. They were already long gone. Relieved and grateful that they apparently had no guns—or at least

hadn't taken any shots—Ethan also realized that the damage
had been done.

"The woman's gone completely mad," Rianne said.

"Yes, but she's found us," Roy added.

"And her son will soon be back," Jeth speculated.

"We've no choice now," Robin said and sighed.

"Back on the run," Piero reflected, still dreaming of a snort
of snuff.

"We'll find Jason, I know we will," Colleen said to Ethan.

"Good-bye, Solitary," Joy whispered under her breath.

Having heard her, Ethan added, "But the Paxtons will be
back here . . . and when we return, it'll be to stay."

"Not even Joan of Arc herself led such a raid, such an
audacious act of bravery and cunning!" Miranda Somerset announced as she arrived back at Marble Manor at sunrise, still
astride her horse, dressed in a filthy, muddy riding habit, while
her son and Frederic Pall scrutinized her with amazement from
the front porch. That she and three other *white* women—servants who had worked for her for years—had been missing for
hours had been reported to Buckley by Jack Windrow. They
had slipped out on horseback sometime during the night.

"You've completely lost your mind, Mother, and never again
will you be allowed to leave this house."

"Knowing you'd say so, I brought witnesses. We've been
practicing in the fields and woods for months. Oh, but we're
a brave quartet. Ceilia, as good a horsewoman as she is a cook.
Like your grandfather, her father was also a sonless soldier
who passed his lessons on to her. She's as sturdy in the saddle
as any man. She followed me out through the swamps. Tell
them, Ceilia."

The tall, lanky woman, thrilled by the ride of her life, spoke
up: "She's right, Mr. Somerset. We saw them ourselves. We
snuck up on them and they were there."

"Who, for God's sake?" Buckley asked.

"Who in Hades are you looking for?" asked his wild-eyed
and wigless mother, her gray hair twisted sloppily into two
long braids.

"You found them? Where?"

"Surely she's seeing things," Frederic said, frustrated by
the fact that yesterday morning they'd just missed them at the
pig farm.

"The McClagan women were there," Miranda declared. "And the doctor himself. Plus Ethan Paxton. We saw him with our own eyes, didn't we, girls?"

Nelly Lills and Beulah Reed, athletic women themselves who worked the gardens and also tended to odd jobs around the house—painting and repairs usually reserved for men—attested to the truth of what Mrs. Somerset had said. They, too, had been trained for months under Miranda.

"Where?" her son kept asking.

"In a most solitary place, an enormous meadow surrounded by a swamp that I've known about ever since my father brought us here from England. Time and again I've mentioned it to your father, even to you, but you both claimed it was too isolated and remote. Men! Oh, this is the proof of the strength of sturdy green vegetables! My scent led me on. My hunting instincts. Fearless we were, my ladies and I. Snakes, wild cats, savages—we were frightened of nothing. Onward we went, through the woods and swamps, a trip I've made by myself when you've gone off to Charles Town or Brandborough and left me here for months at a time. I've done for you, my son, what you couldn't do for yourself, what your so-called friend here promised and was unable to fulfill. Let me ride with you, Buckley. Let me lead your army. Tell your men they're to obey my every command! Victory, I say! The enemies have been spotted and they're ours!"

"Was Jason Paxton among them?" asked an astounded Buckley.

"I didn't see him, but could he be far behind?"

"You saw them," Frederic said, "but did nothing else? You could have shot them, but you carried no weapons. Why? You could have set free their horses...."

"Listen to this man!" Miranda shouted, jumping from her horse with the energy of a teen-ager as she pointed to Pall's slender nose. "What does he want from a band of women? Was it not enough to spot them for you? Were we to go in with rifles and ropes, kill them, tie them up, and drag them back for you? Are you men capable of absolutely nothing? Shame! Now you've only to round them up, like helpless sheep. The hard work's been done—by us."

"But they saw you," Somerset said. "By now they're gone."

"I've made it something of a sport. Didn't my father always say that there'd be no hunt were the fox not given a head start?

This means we must leave Marble Manor immediately. Now you can't possibly consider leaving me behind. I'll go inside, change my clothes, and give you time to ready that small army you have camped around our property. Rouse your men, Buckley, and be a man yourself! Mother will point you in the right direction. There's no failing now!"

Chapter 16

Shortly after Miranda returned to Marble Manor, Peter and Jason made their way through the swamp surrounding Solitary. Emerging from the tall reeds, the immense stretch of green, even under the gray morning sky, emanated a mystical translucence. The moisture from the ground smelled fragrant and fresh. The fog, which had delayed their trip by hours, had lifted, and the view that greeted the men was breathtaking. For a while, they drove the two horses back and forth over the huge expanse of land, pulling their supply-packed cart behind them, as they looked for signs of human life.

"It's here where my father's always dreamed of building a home, separate and apart," Jason said.

"My God, there's room enough for a mighty plantation," remarked Peter, whose ankle, though still painful and swollen, showed signs of healing.

"Nothing mighty. No, my father envisioned fields of cotton and of corn, a comfortable house, a place where generation after generation of Paxtons could live securely, caring and loving this land, and yielding the harvest of its rich soil." Jason paused to breathe in the aroma of grass, tree, and sky. "Somewhere in my heart, Peter, I was praying that he and Colleen . . ."

". . . and Joy . . ."

"A dream," Jason said. "We know they're gone, so why do we plague ourselves with these dreams?"

"My heart says they're not gone, Jase."

"Our eyes can see. Our hearts deceive."

"In England my father said I was always too much the dreamer. He accurately predicted that it would get me into trouble. As I remember, didn't your father say the same thing?"

"Strange, but I realize that for all his practicality, my father's always been a dreamer himself. I just wish he knew me, Peter."

"If my own father could see me now, dressed as a woodsman and fighting against the English Army into which I was born, he'd claim not to know me at all."

"Yet if he'd seen what you saw, if he'd been through what you've been through, would he have acted any differently?" Jason asked.

"He always said to me, 'You know, Peter, you've too much the rebel in you to be a true Englishman. It's your mother's Irish blood. That red hair of yours, son, is entirely too red.'"

For the first time in days, they were able to laugh—if only for a brief moment. Riding over the magnificent land, their banter helped take their minds off their lost women, though not for long. They stopped beneath a grove of trees and watched a flock of spotted great-winged birds take flight.

Sighing, Peter began to speak reflectively. "You knew me in London, and you saw the way in which I enjoyed women. The easier the better; the lustier the liaison, the lovelier for me. If you had asked me about the nature of love, I'd have told you to go read a sonnet by Sir Thomas Wyatt or gaze upon some silly portrait of Cupid. Yet in my first hours upon these shores, being with Joy at that picnic, Jase, I finally understood what had inspired so many poets and painters."

"During that same time, my friend, my heart was experiencing the same revelation."

"And it changes us, does it not? Love changes the way we perceive the world. Look at those violet wildflowers on the horizon. Before meeting Joy, I'd never have noticed them. Now I see her face wherever I look. But knowing they've been killed, perhaps even . . ."

"Let's not enrage ourselves with thoughts of what *might* have happened," said the musician, who saw a mental picture of Colleen. "Having seen Jeth Darney and Rianne's tanner in action, we've at least some reason to hope that they all may have escaped. These are strong women, Peter, stronger than I had ever imagined. Were it not for Colleen, I would never have found the strength this summer to do what I've done. My manly pride prevented me from saying that to her, but now that she's gone, I know it for a fact: she was my inspiration. She showed me the path to courage. It was Colleen, Peter, my sweet Colleen, who led the way."

For several long minutes, the men remained silent, the images of their loves filling their minds and hearts.

Finally, Peter declared, "Well, we'd better stop daydreaming, my friend, and move forward. There's no looking back. But tell me, Jase—those rebels we met on the road yesterday . . . did you trust them? Did you believe what they said?"

"They had no reason to deceive us. They seemed sincere, and, besides, this news confirmed what you'd been hearing around the Old Customs Exchange. I'd be surprised if Jeth and Billy didn't have the same information. We need to head northwest, toward the Appalachian Mountains of North Carolina. Even if we weren't being pursued by Somerset, we'd follow the same course. Darney must be thinking like us. It's a simple matter of survival. The strongest rebel force in these parts— perhaps the last rebel force with any hope to resist the Tories— are the mountain men. They're intimidated by no one, and they will not be chased from their homes without a bloody battle, the likes of which neither of us can truly imagine. For Major Patrick Ferguson, operating under Cornwallis, is no coward. He'll do his best to destroy them."

"Strange Scotsman that he is," Peter said. "I met him once in Charleston two months back. An angry man, to put it mildly. Angry that his rapid-fire rifle has never been accepted by the Crown's military command, and angry that he still hasn't made his name. Ambition seemed to race through his nervous body like a raging fever. Recently other officers have told me that he resents safeguarding Cornwallis's flank while the general remains in Charlotte. Not only that, but he's not overjoyed with the command of a Loyalist militia. 'Tis a commission more suitable for a Tory like Buckley Somerset, not an English officer. Still, Ferguson's a servant of the king, and he'll fight like a man possessed. With a thousand or so greencoats at his disposal, he'll be ruthless, knowing that to destroy the last remnants of resistance in the South is to demonstrate to these Patriots once and for all that the Crown is invincible. I know men of his ilk. In his mind, he sees that under his personal charge this entire war might be won . . ."

". . . or lost," Jason added.

"Either way, if my memory serves me well, we've some one hundred fifty miles to travel before reaching those mountains."

"Slightly more. It won't be an easy trip."

"I imagine you know the route, Jase."

"You've studied the maps and know it as well as I. There's but one sensible way. We'll follow the rivers. The Congaree will lead to the Broad, which flows to the foot of the great mountains. Let's ride!" Jason shouted, striking the horses into action as, with one last forlorn sigh, he allowed his eye to roam over the extraordinary land that had so touched the heart of his father, his sisters, and himself.

With Miranda riding on his right and Jack Windrow and Frederic Pall on his left, Buckley Somerset, in a custom-made forest-green uniform, his polished black boots reflecting a gray overcast sky, led a cavalry of two dozen crack Tory soldiers out of Solitary. As expected, he had found no one there, was unable to pick up a trail, and thus began heading northwest. He suspected that the fugitives would follow the rivers to the border and try to hide among the rebels in the hills. He'd catch them; he knew he would. In his mind, he was convinced of his force's invincibility. The price of victory no longer mattered. He'd put up with anything to catch Paxton and the girl—even Pall's daily ransom of twenty pounds, even his mother's constant harassment. Informing his soldiers that their swift pace would allow little time to rest, he paid them inflated salaries in addition to what they'd normally receive as militiamen, and he promised them bonuses if the culprits were caught. "There's to be no discussion, no questions, no mercy. If you spot any of them"—he had described each member of the rebel band in exact detail—"shoot on sight. For the man who brings me the corpses of Colleen McClagan and Jason Paxton, there's an extra forty pounds on each head."

The vast sums of money astounded the men. Bounties of such proportions were unheard of, but Buckley was determined to motivate his men by any means possible. He was beyond caring that this foray was taking a decidedly personal turn. He'd chase this band of rebels into the flaming gates of hell if need be. The men themselves could see in Somerset's eyes the gleam of a man possessed. His front-line riding companions were bizarre—his mother, the albino, the quixotic actor—but all was tolerated in the interest of money. As they stormed out of Solitary, the hooves of their horses raising a great cloud of dust, the image of the mutilated bodies of Colleen and Jason never left Buckley's mind. He wanted them dead, all right, although the idea of slowly torturing them haunted Buckley's imagination like an endless dream.

She was pregnant and in the throes of her final contractions, alone in the green fields of Solitary under a sunless sky, screaming and frightened, with armies attacking from all sides, when she awoke. In the dream, Jason had been by her side. She still felt the strength of his loving presence as she slowly opened her eyes, relieved that the armies had been imagined, but dismayed that Jason no longer held her in his arms.

How long had Colleen been asleep as the wagon rattled on, bouncing and shaking, the dust from the road in her face and mouth? Robin and Piero were seated on the floor of the wagon, their cotton robes covering their legs and feet. Seated next to them was Rianne, looking out over the passing river, with the head of a sleeping Joy nestled in her lap. Up front, on the riding board, were Roy, Jeth, and Billy. Ethan Paxton, his eyes searching in every direction, listening for every sound coming from the woods, rode his stolen horse alongside them.

Squeezed in a corner of the wagon, Colleen remembered her dream and felt her stomach. For four days, ever since the arduous trip had begun, she had occasionally dozed off into the same dream—always involving Solitary, always involving Jason. Sometimes the images were frightening—burning brush and murderous assaults. Sometimes they were gentle—she and Jason living in a large, comfortable house, the doting parents of sweet, smiling infants. She understood that she, like the others, used sleep to escape the cruel and frightening reality that surrounded them. Covering ten—sometimes twelve or even fifteen—miles a day was grueling. So far they'd been lucky. Through the combined cunning of Jeth, Ethan, and Billy, they had averted one Tory position and encountered a band of rebels who advised them that the river course was indeed the safest. They knew they were on the right track, but they could also feel the hot breath of Buckley behind them. All the while, Colleen held the image of her love steadfast in her mind's eye.

At night they'd travel into the thick of the woods, maneuvering the wagon as best they could. There they'd camp and eat their meager supply of food, picking berries and fruits along the way. Jeth shot several rabbits, whose meat gave them welcome sustenance. Billy skinned the animals, and the doctor helped his sister cook. Rianne and Roy worked well together, and for the first time in years they actually enjoyed one another's company. Having whittled a piece of wood into a recorder, Robin played soft, lilting melodies as Piero sang along. Ethan sat next to Joy, his arm around her shoulder, a gesture of affection he'd never before extended. On the morning of the fifth day out, with only one eye open, Colleen saw Rianne and Billy adjusting their clothing as they returned to the campsite.

Without wigs or gowns, without perfumes or jewelry, Robin and Piero—with their bearded faces—and the three women began to take on the appearance of improbable pioneers. The circumstances brought out their fundamental character. Piero was still terribly frightened, but less so as the journey went forward. Jeth, Billy, and Ethan exuded a feeling of strong self-confidence, and having a doctor along made Piero feel that much safer. For the most part, the weather had been benign—especially cool for early October. The cloud-covered skies made the going easier, and by the sixth day out, having traveled nearly eighty miles, Piero began telling fantastical stories of his European journeys, an imaginative mixture of fact and fiction as, with flamboyant detail, he described exotic backdrops of castles, palaces, and courtly kingdoms. Accompanied by Robin's magical music, his tales proved to be as comforting to the group as Roy's medical expertise or Ethan's sharp-eyed surveillance.

As they rode on, everyone assumed—just as Jeth's rebel contacts along the way confirmed—that they were moving in the right direction, out of the colony, toward the rebel-held Appalachians. Still, the question that no one wanted to ask—or answer—was: What then? Their lives in shambles, their houses pillaged or burned, they felt themselves in the cold hands of fate, hoping that around each bend of the dirt road they would not find an army of murderous Tories.

They prayed in their own ways, silently, sometimes aloud, growing more stoic as the hours and days went by. Colleen wrote verses inside her head, memorized the lines, and, at night, shared her hopeful spirit with the others. Before falling asleep, though, her unspoken poetry focused on Jason as, closing her eyes, she saw the curls atop his head, his wistful smile, and the gentleness of his loving eyes:

> I prayed you'd return, and return you did,
> A different man, a deeper soul
> While the storms of our passion brought us closer
> Till two halves were forged into a whole.
>
> Now the mystery of night has us searching
> As time and distance keep us apart,
> But, oh, my love, my faith is boundless,
> As strong and true as your loving heart.

⟡ *Chapter 17* ⟡

Jason and Peter peeked over the great boulder and looked down upon the river road below. They counted twenty-four green coated cavalrymen, each armed with a musket. The soldiers were resting, watering their horses and talking among themselves. A few feet farther ahead, Miranda, Frederic Pall, Jack Windrow, and Buckley Somerset were speaking to a family of rebels—a young father, mother, and a blond ten-year-old girl— who had just advised Jason and Peter that they, too, were heading toward North Carolina after having been burned out by the Tories. Their worldly possessions tied atop a small canvas-covered wagon, they'd invited the musician and red-haired Englishman—who, not wanting to alarm the family with his accent, hadn't said a word—to join them on their journey. Jason had thanked them but had said they needed to rest for an hour or so before pushing on, and would probably meet them farther up the road.

Soon after, Jason and a hobbling Peter led their horses up the little hill where, behind a boulder, they sought shelter and a bit of sleep. Minutes later, the thundering hooves of Buckley's band turned their heads back toward the road below.

They struggled to hear, but were too far away. Frederic was questioning the family closely. Miranda was apparently interfering. It looked as if Buckley was trying to keep his mother quiet. The rebel father was obviously shaken and nervous, and

the more Pall spoke, the more frightened the family appeared.
Someone must have said something, because Pall pointed his
finger at the rebel. Buckley grabbed the man by his throat and
started shaking him. Suddenly, out of control, the rebel slammed
his fist into Buckley's face. At that point, Jack Windrow, his
left arm still bandaged, stuck his knife in the man's heart, and
blood gushed forth in thick spurts. The girl screamed, the wife
lunged for Somerset, there was confusion and a gunshot—
from Buckley's smoldering pistol. The mother fell dead and
the terrified child ran ahead. Another shot from Buckley and
the girl collapsed, a circle of red forming on her back. Miranda's shouts, villifying her son, rang through the air. Pall seemed
to be laughing while the albino calmly cleaned the blood from
his knife. Many of the cavalrymen witnessed the slaughter,
their faces filled with horror.

Peter and Jason were numb. To have taken their rifles and
tried to save the family by shooting Somerset or Windrow
would have meant their own deaths; Buckley's brigade would
have captured them in a matter of minutes. It had all happened
too quickly; there hadn't been time to stop the killings. Still,
Jason and Peter were overwhelmed with frustration, outrage,
and grief. They had witnessed cowardly men murder innocent
people in cold blood. Only Somerset's half-mad mother had
issued any protest. No matter how intense their feelings, they
were forced to lay low until Buckley moved on. Instead of
being slightly ahead of their pursuers, they'd have to stay slightly
behind.

An hour after the Tories had gone, they descended the hill
and returned to the road along the river. Renewed by a sense
of fury and purpose, loss and determination, they realized that,
no matter what, they had to go on, toward their destination,
their destiny—King's Mountain, on the border of the Carolinas.

On the thirteenth day out, Frederic Pall was increasingly
wary of the behavior of the ill-tempered Somerset. Buckley
never tired of reminding Pall that the actor hadn't yet turned
up the fugitives. Thus, to free himself temporarily of Somerset
and the nagging Miranda, and to see what could be learned,
Frederic managed to sneak six miles ahead while the company
was resting. Arriving in a small rural community, he came
across a notice nailed to the door of a small general store.

Gentlemen:

Unless you wish to be eaten up by an inundation of barbarians, who have begun by murdering an unarmed son before the aged father, and afterward lopped off his arms, and who by their shocking cruelties and irregularities give the best proof of their cowardice and want of discipline; I say, if you wish to be pinioned, robbed, and murdered, and see your wives and daughters abused by the dregs of mankind—in short, if you wish or deserve to live and bear the name of men, grasp your arms in a moment and run to camp.

If you choose to be pissed upon forever and ever by a set of mongrels, say so at once and let your women turn their backs upon you, and look out for real men to protect them.

Pat Ferguson, Major, 71st Regiment

Pall's eye moved from the notice to the scene around him. In the distance he saw the foothills of the Appalachians. The battle lines were being drawn. This was Ferguson's call to rally the Tories against the mountain men. It had been five days since Buckley had paid him a single pound. Pall knew that his credibility shrank with each passing hour. Somerset kept him around only on the faint hope that his contacts would somehow help them locate the rebels. Frederic had no illusions. He remembered Buckley's original threat: If, after two weeks, the couple hadn't been found, Pall's life wasn't worth a counterfeit shilling. The two weeks would be up the next day, October 7.

What sense was there in returning to Somerset's cavalry? None. *Pat Ferguson*—Pall mulled over the name in his mind. There was a man with ambition, a man in need of help. Having made a few inquiries in the general store, he rode his horse off toward the woods, in the opposite direction of Buckley's band. Pall's instincts were leading him in an entirely different direction, and his instincts were wrong.

Piero fell sick with a fever on the thirteenth day, but with Roy at his side, treating him with words of encouragement rather than medicine, the Italian—his skin perspiring, his hands shaking—fought gallantly for a quick recovery. They had maintained a rapid pace that had surprised even Ethan, who pushed them on with steady persistence. Perhaps Rianne, fearless and determined, was the most tireless traveler of all. With the foothills in sight and word throughout the countryside of the ensuing battle, they camped in the woods in early afternoon to gain their bearings. Jeth had gone ahead to scout and found a small rebel encampment. He returned to tell Ethan and Billy the eagerly awaited news. The others were napping.

Darney pointed ahead. "Over that group of pine trees. That's what they call King's Mountain Ridge. That's where they say Ferguson's gonna make his stand. Right there on top."

"Doesn't look that big," Billy commented.

"'Bout six hundred feet up the slope. More a hill than a mountain," Ethan said, observing its strangely flat top five hundred yards long and seventy-five yards wide, broadening to one hundred twenty yards at the northeast end. "But where are the mountain men?"

"Should be moving in from Cowpens any time now," Jeth said. "Least that's what they say. Tomorrow may be the day."

Still awake, Colleen overheard the talk and felt a shudder of fear pass down her spine. Had they arrived at their place of destiny? She closed her eyes and, for a few brief seconds, prayed to God, asking for His blessings upon her family, her traveling companions, and the one man she loved with all her heart. When she opened her eyes, she felt great relief. Ethan, Jeth, and Billy had wandered off while the others slept close by.

Silently, she got up and walked and stretched. The fear hadn't gone—the fear of death, the fear of never seeing Jason again—and the sight of the flat top of the distant hill, King's Mountain Ridge, filled her with an awesome anticipation. She felt the monumentous nature of the moment, the fact that the world seemed to be turning in this very place, at this very time. She realized that for nearly two weeks they had traveled to arrive at this one specific point. Almost to relieve herself from the overpowering feeling of expectancy, she turned her back on the mountain range and walked deeper into the woods.

Her mind far away, she walked and walked, farther than she had intended, until she almost tripped on a sudden lower elevation in the land. Behind a growth of wild shrubs she discovered a ravine—a secret ravine!—much like the one she had shared with Jason six months earlier. She descended, looked around in wonder, and ultimately reclined her body flat against the ground. Oh, Jason! Oh, the memories! Above her, the pearl sky appeared the color of gray silk. The forest smelled of minty new growth. The images came back—the look on his face, the strength in his loins, the short-lived pain, the moisture, the endless ecstasy. *Jase, Jase, Jase!* her heart cried. *If only you could hear! If only you could know that I've found another ravine! For you and me, my Jason! Can you hear me? Can you feel my love?*

For a long while, her heart spoke silently until her mind finally settled, her eyes closed, and she found, in the quietude of the afternoon and the comfort of this sylvan seclusion, a pleasant sleep. The dream, like all her dreams, was centered around Jason. He had found her; he had carried her into the forest; they had returned to the ravine. So intense, so graphic, so real was the dream that Colleen, still asleep, was convinced it was all true. And when she awoke and felt the presence of another human in the ravine with her, in the split-second it took for her to open her eyes, she believed Jason had actually come to her side. Instead, she saw a grinning Frederic Pall holding a hunting knife inches from her left breast as he suddenly slapped the palm of his hand over her mouth to keep her from screaming.

From afar, Jason and Peter watched a thousand mountain men roar into Cowpens, South Carolina, like a herd of thundering buffalo. The warriors wore the skins of animals on their backs and heads. Angry, burly, boot-stomping hunters, they gathered their long hair into ponytails beneath their wide-brimmed hats. Some walked, some rode horses, some wore shirts of vegetable-dyed cloth and breeches of weathered buckskin. Many blonds and redheads among them, their leather-skinned faces reflected a lifetime of battling the elements. The English were only their most recent threat; it was the Indians whom they'd been fighting for over a generation. Carrying knapsacks and blankets, the mountain men clutched their trusty long rifles, capable of firing great distances with astounding accuracy.

The greencoats camped atop King's Mountain Ridge were dependent upon their muskets, far less accurate than the rifles and not at all effective for long-distance shooting. The fact that the Tories were equipped with bayonets, though, instilled them with confidence: cold steel against flesh had been one of the Crown's most successful weapons since the beginning of the war.

Before joining the mountain men, Peter and Jason discussed their own situation.

"Would we be giving up the search?" Jason asked his friend.

"It just seems as if all movement is toward this battle, Jase. These men know exactly where they're going, and we don't. We've been lost in the dark long enough. Here at last is some firm direction, a fight that needs to be won."

"Then you're game?"

"I am," Peter said. "Do you have doubts?"

"I don't doubt the purposefulness or courage of these men—not for a minute. Yet, I'm still plagued by the thought of whether Colleen, Joy, Robin, Piero, and the others are themselves lost and in need of . . ."

"Such thoughts will drive us mad. I don't have to tell you that we're in the midst of a war, Jase, and wars are waged to be won."

Thus, they joined the boldly masculine aggregation. The mountain men, looking for all the extra support they could muster, were glad to accept them among their ranks. Jason and Peter couldn't help but catch the fever of the fight. There was a camaraderie, an engaging spirit, an infectious and irresistible pride of purpose. They felt their hearts beating rapidly as they listened to the Reverend Mr. Doak deliver a stirring sermon to the troops. He spoke with Old Testament thunder as he reminded the men of Gideon's attack upon the Midianites. "Gideon prevailed with a wrathful God on his side, and tomorrow so will you! Remember—the sword of the Lord! The sword of Gideon!"

A thousand rough, deep-bottomed voices shouted back in earth-shattering unison, "The sword of the Lord! The sword of Gideon!"

For months, Pat Ferguson had provoked these proud men with his plundering raids. Now the Scotsman had positioned his one thousand men upon the ridge, as if to say, "Come get me if you can." The mountain men understood his plan—to cut them down as they made their way up. But these were not frightened men. They brimmed with confidence. They relished the challenge to defend their homes with their lives. They welcomed the opportunity to go after Pat Ferguson and his turncoat Tories. And the sooner the better.

All night their frantic search through the woods was hindered by a chilling and steady rain.

Each had set off on his own. Ethan showed a sturdy Robin and a far less steady Piero how to look for signposts along the way—a distinctive tree, a boulder—so they could retrace their paths. Jeth and Billy and Rianne were indefatigable. Roy, half crazed by his daughter's absence, searched with the greatest intensity of all. Joy accompanied her father. And all the while the downpour worsened. Their eyes blinded by rain, they could do little more than poke around. Still, against all odds and without sleep, not one among them could stop searching, stumbling his way through the forest, over one path and down another, feeling into shrubs, kicking through high grass, hoping, praying, calling her name. "Colleen!" they cried. "Colleen!"

Atop King's Mountain Ridge, Buckley Somerset and his mother sat in the tent of Captain Pat Ferguson as rain fell outside. For all of his reputation as a ladies' man, the Scotsman was surprisingly short and fragile of build, with huge saucer eyes staring out of a smallish and serious face.

He greeted Buckley warmly. The notion of another twenty-five able-bodied men on horseback gave him a much needed measure of confidence. An impulsive man by nature, he had a few nagging doubts about the military position he'd taken.

Somerset reassured him. After a shot of powerful whiskey, Buckley also told him the story of the Sandpiper and Will-o'-the-Wisp. The captain was only half interested. His obsession was to rid himself of these bothersome mountain men once and for all. He knew he could do it, though if the English generals had only adopted his breech-loading rifle, he'd be absolutely positive. What a stubborn bunch of fools! How could they not understand the importance of rapid fire? How could they be so stuck in their old-fashioned ways? *Ancient history,* Ferguson thought to himself. *We're up here; they're down there. As soon as they start coming, we'll bayonet their guts out.*

"I think not," Miranda chirped in after the captain had explained his battle plan.

"Mother!" Buckley tried to quiet her.

"Let your mother speak, please," Ferguson interceded, respectful of any independent mind. "Where do you fault the plan, madam?"

"First, I must say that I've mapped out quite a few campaigns in my time. My son can tell you how I led him here. I knew we were heading for the right territory and told him every bend of the road to follow. I've been planning secret attacks for years, one more brilliant than another. Are you a meat eater, Captain?"

"Mother!"

"I am."

"That might explain your lack of insight in this instance. You see, the long-range rifle is perfect at picking off standing targets. That, I'm afraid, is the stage you've set for yourself."

"'Tis more complex than that, madam, I can assure you," said Ferguson, his heart beating fast as he recognized the logic in the woman's thinking. Nonetheless, he argued with her by describing his plan in greater detail. "There'll be a series of musket attacks that will not only surprise, but..."

"Say what you will," Miranda interrupted. "If I were your general, I'd relieve you of your command."

Ferguson tried to laugh at the obviously touched woman, but his lips refused to smile.

Outside Ferguson's tent, Buckley and Miranda walked with blankets covering their heads as they hurried through the rain back to their encampment upon the ridge when they were suddenly stopped in their tracks by Frederic Pall. Buckley spat on the man's boots.

"Out of my way, charlatan!"

"You'll want to hear what I have to say!" Pall screamed, the wind howling across the high plain.

"You're lucky I haven't killed you. If it'd make any difference, I would. But why kill an ant?"

"I have her."

"Who?"

"Colleen."

"Don't believe him," Miranda warned.

Buckley's eyes caught fire. "Where?"

"Five hundred pounds."

Somerset grabbed Pall by his throat, torrents of rain slapping them in the face. "You're a lying bastard!"

"Take my pistol," Pall said, putting the gun in Buckley's hand. "If she's not there, shoot me through the head and take back every pound you gave me. If she is, I'll keep the five hundred you're going to give me as soon as we get to your tent."

"No! I forbid you!" Miranda demanded.

"When can you bring me to her?" Somerset asked.

"The moment you put the money in my pocket."

Colleen was still in the ravine, her ankles and hands tied, her mouth gagged, the material from her dress matted against her skin, her hair, her every pore soaked. She had maintained her sanity only by turning her thoughts to Jason, by concentrating on him and only him. *Jase!* her heart had cried out. *Our love will never die . . . our love will survive even this. . . .*

Now she shivered and shook at the sight of a smiling Buckley Somerset looking down upon her, his legs spread wide. Her eyes went wide, wild with hatred.

"Well, well, you did find her after all," Buckley observed, inspecting the way her taut nipples were so evident beneath the rain-drenched garment. "I must say, my dear man, you prove to be a gentleman after all." With that, he pulled an already cocked pistol from his waistband and shot Frederic Pall once through the chest, and his body slumped against the side of the ravine.

With his life slowly draining from his blood-soaked body, the actor managed a small grin as he faced his murderer. "I'd only wish . . ."—he gasped, never losing the theatrical dignity of his speech—". . . to hear those words spoken to me . . . those same words that Horatio spoke to Hamlet: 'Flights of angels sing to thy rest.' The rest is silence, Mr. Buckley Somerset . . . for I've no more breath to tell where I hid your five hundred pounds . . . as we rode here . . . somewhere in the forest . . . you'll never find your coins. . . ."

"Damn you, you greedy bastard!" Buckley shouted before shooting him again, this time straight through the heart. With a final spasm, Pall fell dead.

Somerset blew the smoke from the pistol, reloaded, and aimed it at Colleen, smiling into her eyes. "Shall I?" he asked. "Perhaps not, perhaps not right now. 'Twould be a shame to ruin the fun this soon. Besides, I'll have my pleasure with you tonight. No, no . . . love should never culminate too early in the evening."

He untied her legs and, with her hands still bound, led her back to his horse. Avoiding the rebel encampments by retracing Pall's route, he rode back through the rain up to the mountaintop, his prize catch riding in front of him, bouncing against his crotch.

~ *Chapter 18* ~

Smoke from scattered campfires atop King's Mountain Ridge rose through the dewy morning air. The rain had stopped and the day was moist, the air refreshed, the countryside hushed. For hours, the red-coated Loyalists had been in position, waiting. They knew it was only a matter of time before the mountain men made their charge.

Buckley Somerset, at the northwest corner of the ridge, had yet to emerge from his tent. Never before had he felt more frustrated or enraged. The problem was that there was no one—least of all his mother—in whom he could confide. Perhaps it was the way in which the chilling rain had soaked through both his outer and inner garments, freezing his hands, fingers, and legs while rendering inoperative—at least that was his reasoning—the one organ that had been waiting for this moment for years. Never before had this happened to him. He had been with wenches and the wives of diplomats, all with smashing success. It had to be the fault of the rains or, he was less likely to admit, the fact that this prize had been so long awaited. Either way, after he'd warmed her by the fire, dried her skin and hair and studied her naked body as the light from the small fire's flames caught her delicate curves and angles, he could no longer deny the sad, soft truth. Infuriated, he began slapping her, aware that violence was his only hope of satisfaction. One fist to her jaw had nearly knocked her out. But she would be no fun unconscious. Discipline, he told himself, was the road to pleasure, and he was proud of the way he had restrained himself during the night—an occasional lash of a whip against her naked backside, the sight of the red strip of skin giving him almost, but not quite, enough delight to raise his limp spirit.

Several times he had toyed with the idea of murdering her, but always the notion seemed too rash. He still wanted to play. Besides, he didn't believe her claim that she knew nothing of Jason's whereabouts. No, these two had been in cahoots too long not to have anticipated a meeting place. He didn't trust her for a second. Holdig on to the Sandpiper—keeping her alive—would undoubtedly bring forth Will-o'-the-Wisp. And in that regard, her life still held value for Buckley Somerset.

Colleen hadn't lost faith. Humiliated and beaten, she nonetheless thanked God for Buckley's inability to take her. She would have laughed and spit in his face if she hadn't feared his gun and sword. She had understood that her slim chance for survival had rested in being quiet and reacting not at all. Somerset was a madman, and all she could hope to do was not agitate him. Covered with bruises, aching with pain, terrified, Colleen still clung to a thread of hope, calling up a reserve of strength she never knew was there. *Jason!* she silently repeated over and again. *Oh, my Jason!*

"The battle's about to begin," Miranda announced as she burst into the tent. Buckley had instructed Jack Windrow to keep his mother from his tent the past night, and this was the first time Miranda had seen Colleen, whom her son had put in a bright red velvet robe—the same robe Miranda had given him for Christmas.

"My God!" Miranda said, regarding Colleen with shock and disgust.

"When I parade her around the battlefield," Buckley explained defensively, half apologizing for letting her wear the robe, "I want to make sure the Wisp sees her. She's taking me to Paxton."

"She's taking you to hell!" Miranda screamed before turning and running from the tent. "You're doomed, my son . . . doomed . . ." Her voice rang out in the damp morning air.

"Shout like hell and fight like devils!"

The mountain men, who had been the target of savage Indian

attacks, began their assault by borrowing a tactic from their red-skinned enemies. They announced their presence from behind trees and brush situated up and down the hill by screaming war whoops and provoking the Loyalists from their positions atop the ridge. The rebels aimed their flintlock pieces, shot, and charged—from here, from there, from everywhere, with no apparent organization or scheme.

Ferguson had correctly guessed their crude strategy. He was ready. In retaliation, he had his men chase them down with their Brown Bess muskets, stabbing them in the back as they ran to recharge. *Let them feel the icy chill of British resolve,* the Scotsman told himself; *let them charge again.*

The rebel band—Roy, Ethan, Rianne, Billy, Jeth, Piero, Joy and Robin—steadily made their way through the fields to the base of the King's Mountain Ridge, where they joined up with more than a thousand mountain men just as the first shots of the battle began exploding like fireworks. The Irish and Scotish zealots were happy for the help and greeted the group with grateful encouragement.

Roy arrived at this point only with great trepidation. Part of him felt as if he were leaving his daughter behind. But what else could he do? They had searched the woods all night, and he reasoned that there was at least some chance that she'd be at the battle. He thought of how brave she'd been, a tribute to his family, to the very blood that flowed through her veins. A month ago, the notion of charging into battle would have paralyzed him with fear. But on this day, the crack of gunfire ringing in his ears, Roy went forward, not with the fury of Ethan, Billy, or Jeth, but with a steady tenacity, a resignation that he had already seen the worst and faced his fears. Grief-stricken by the loss of his daughter, he was nonetheless inspired by her own courageous example.

The fact that they were facing a Scotsman in Pat Ferguson gave Dr. McClagan even more pause for reflection. That his countryman had chosen to fight his own people—the Scots who had come here and settled this land—was a point of sharp and painful irony. For the first time since the war began, Roy felt a rising sense of patriotism. Along with his old doubts, his equivocation dissipated. This was his land, this was American land, and there came a time when a person took a stand. A time when one fought.

"You'll stay with Joy," Paxton had suggested to Robin and Piero, who, in spite of the search through the woods, had successfully fought off his fever and was feeling better, although he still suffered with a wildly nervous stomach.

"I'm going with you, Father," Joy had insisted. "I can reload the guns and care for the wounded," she said bravely, not willing to stay back while her heart told her that Peter would be there on this day of destiny.

"We're not expert shots, but if there's one thing we've learned on this journey, it's how to load a rifle," Robin had said. "It's a task we will be honored to carry out."

"We will?" Piero had asked, his voice cracking with the question. After a few seconds of reflection, he added, "Yes, of course we will." Robin was right. They hadn't come this far to hide. A lover of theater, Piero saw the enormous drama in this situation. They had reached the climax of the play, and he wanted to be there for the most dramatic moment. The courage was contagious.

While hiding in the swamps, Rianne had sewn crude clothes—coarse shirts and pants for Roy, Ethan, Jeth, Billy, Piero, and Robin; she had fashioned tent dresses for herself, Joy, and Colleen. She had assured Billy that'd she be there during the fight, reloading his gun. And so she was.

Their thoughts filled with fears for the missing Colleen, the group threw themselves into the heat of battle, forgetting their fatigue, mixing in with the rugged mountain men, moving up from the base of the hill as shrieking war cries pierced the air. The fight raged on.

On horseback, Ferguson circled around the top of the horseshoe-shaped ridge, shouting encouragement to his men. For all the vigor in his voice, however, he didn't like what he saw. The battle was chaotic, and the chaos was growing. The mountain men's helter-skelter charges were maddening. English-trained through and through, the Scottish captain disliked disorderly combat. So did his men. Battles were battles, not brawls. In any event, the rebels would be thrown back. It would simply take more time than Ferguson had anticipated. "Chase 'em down, boys!" he exhorted. "Let 'em feel your blades! Huzza, brave boys, the day is our own!"

* * *

Hidden in a grove of trees, Jeth, Billy, and Ethan burst out into the clearing, kneeling, aiming their rifles at the Tories on top, firing and then racing to the next cluster of trees, a bit farther up the hill where Joy, Rianne, Robin, and Piero had managed to crawl, offering them rifles and pistols that were already loaded. Their plan was that in between volleys, the gun loaders would try to stay a few feet ahead by scurrying up the hill, protected by the brush.

For all his panic, Piero couldn't help but feel exhilarated by the phenomenon. People shooting one another—actually shooting!—these fearless men charging their way up and onward, always onward, in spite of the downpour of bullets. Coughing, he never before realized the density of smoke caused by gunfire that covered the hill and ridge, blocking visibility and bringing burning tears to his eyes.

"They might as well throw mud rather than fire those blasted muskets!" he heard one ruffian rebel shout. "They can't hit the side of the trees with those things."

Feeling more confident as Ethan, Jeth, and Billy burst out into the clearing for still another charge, crouching as they ran, Piero, along with Rianne, Joy, and Robin, raced toward a cluster of trees, higher on the hill, twenty yards or so away. Robin, the heaviest among them, ran with great difficulty. Naturally quicker, Piero nonetheless stayed by his friend's side. The boom and crack of gunfire shot over their heads. In the chaos of this unfocused battle, Piero felt strangely safe. In fact, when Robin fell, the Italian was certain that his companion had simply tripped. It was only when Piero hurriedly bent down to help him up that he saw the circle of blood on Robin's blouse.

"No!" Piero screamed, bending over Robin, watching his eyes slowly close, listening to his gasping breaths. "No! Get up, Robin!" He tried lifting his friend while, with no thought for his own safety, Joy and Rianne rejoined Piero, unprotected by shrubs or trees. As they all huddled over Robin, Rianne spotted a Tory charging them on horseback, his bayonet pointing their way. She raised the loaded rifle she was carrying, aimed, and shot the man directly in the head. He fell, his horse reared, then ran back up the hill where, for the first time, Rianne caught a quick glimpse of Miranda, her gray hair blowing in the breeze, shouting orders to men who seemed to be paying her no mind. If the rifle had been loaded, the seamstress would have shot the madwoman. As it was, Robin demanded her attention.

Yet there was nothing to do. Cradled in Piero's arms, the instrument maker thanked those who surrounded him for their loving attention and then struggled to speak further, as if his last words were the most important message of his life. "Beauty . . ." he whispered as Piero wiped his perspiring brow with a cloth, ". . . beauty . . ." Robin repeated, "goes on forever . . . here on earth, so much beauty . . . be brave, my Piero . . ." —he reached up and touched the Italian's cheek—". . . there are other worlds . . . worlds without end . . ."

His hand fell; his life expired.

"Hurry!" Rianne urged Piero. "Those trees over there— quickly now."

"I can't leave him."

"He's gone. You must."

Seeing that words would do her no good, Rianne took a weeping Piero by the arm and pulled him to safety. "He's gone!" the Italian cried. "Robin's gone!"

Buckley stuck Colleen, her hands tied, in front of him on his horse as he rode back and forth along the ridge, hoping that Paxton would go for this red-robed bait. Having her in front of him allowed him to trot about in the midst of the battle with a distinct feeling of protection. If any rifleman's bullet headed in his direction, he was shielded. Confidently, then, he raced around the ridge's edge, pistol in hand, searching below for his lifelong nemesis.

For a moment, with bullets whistling around her, Colleen fought her unspeakable terror as she gazed upon the scrambling and fallen fighters below—their limbs torn, their cries of anguished pain. She asked herself how fate could have brought her to this point. Why was she being inflicted with such punishment? At any moment, a bullet could pierce her heart and extinguish her life. Only the thought of Jason kept her from begging Buckley for mercy; only that same faith that had endured for five long years—the faith in their eternal love—kept her from going stark raving mad. Again she looked below, searching the field for her lover, her friend, her man. All she saw were the blurred images of rebels and Tories, running, shooting, falling, bleeding, crying, dying. *Jason!* her silent heart screamed. *Dear God, where is Jason?*

"Enjoying the view?" asked Buckley, who continued to comb the territory below, looking for the man whom he wanted with every bit as much passion as Colleen.

Ethan Paxton, catching his breath and reloading his gun, was nearly two-thirds of the way up the ridge when he thought he saw his son. His heart beat madly. *Jason! Could it be Jason?* The thick smoke cover impaired Ethan's vision, though, and seconds later the image vanished as quickly as it had appeared—behind a shrub, out of sight.

Was he hallucinating, or had he really seen Jason? There was no time to think, no time to look for him. Firing at a Tory who stood at the very edge of the ridge, Ethan found his mark. The greencoat fell, tumbling down the hill as Ethan reloaded expertly, moving a few more feet up the ridge, searching for another target.

Miranda Somerset, coughing from the smoke of battle, pulled her horse next to Pat Ferguson.

"The day is theirs, Captain," she said. "As I expected, it's a rout. Surrender and cut our losses. If not, they'll slaughter us like cattle. These are angry men. The Brown Bess is no match for their rifles. You've eaten too much meat, you've lost your perspective, you've . . ."

"Quiet, woman, or I'll have you shot for treason! Away!" Ferguson barked as he rode off, still trying to rally his troops and deny the deteriorating situation the madwoman had analyzed with such accuracy.

Near the top of the ridge, Joy's heart stopped beating—at least for an instant. She saw Peter—alive! It was Peter! He was positioned behind a small boulder just thirty feet ahead of her. She cried out his name.

Peter immediately recognized her voice. He turned and stood, forgetting about the battle for a split-second. There she was! A miracle! She wasn't dead!

She ran from the bush, leaving Rianne and Piero. Her love! Her life! Her Peter!

"Down! down!" he cried, his heart pounding inside his chest. She couldn't contain herself, and as Peter caught her in his arms and tried to throw her down to the ground, a Tory charged from out of nowhere, his bayonet aimed at the Englishman's chest. Joy screamed as Peter's pistol shot the greencoat at the very last second. Lifelessly, the Tory fell to the ground. His horse bolted and ran wild.

More shots were fired. Gunfire flew from every direction. Peter grabbed Joy just out of harm's way, leading her to the safety of a grove of small trees. There the jubilant lovers embraced, but only for seconds, for the battle was not yet over. The fighting flared, fiercer than ever.

Up the final few feet to the top of the ridge, the battlefield an arena of slaughter, screams of exaltation—"the sword of the Lord!... the sword of Gideon!"—hand-to-hand combat, the rebels having trapped the now frightened Tories, who saw their ground disappearing from beneath them. A valiant Jason breathed deeply, fighting alone, having lost Peter somewhere along the way.

Inches from the top of King's Mountain Ridge, crawling on his belly, the taste of dirt and blood in his mouth, Jason looked up and saw the feet of Somerset's horse. He stretched his neck. There was Colleen, in a red robe, exposed to the rifle fire of a thousand men, with Buckley behind her.

At first Jason didn't believe it was her. It seemed incredible. It seemed impossible. But there was no mistake. His Colleen! His love? Alive! The woman was alive! All his prayers, all his hopes, all his faith had led him here! But there was no time to waste. She was a target. She could be struck at any second.

Crawling quickly, silently, maneuvering himself behind the horse, Jason sprang like a cat, leaving his rifle on the ground— not willing to risk a shot that might hit Colleen—and landed on the animal directly behind the saddle. Buckley instinctively leaped from his horse, out of Jason's grasp. With both feet on the ground, Somerset held in his right hand a pistol aimed at Jason's forehead; in his left hand, his saber was pointed at Jason's heart.

An astonished Colleen turned and witnessed the combat, but she was not completely surprised that Jason was here, no more surprised than she had been on that day back in May when he had returned from England. She had felt his presence all along. She had never lost faith. She watched as an unarmed

Jason jumped from the horse and, in one sweeping motion, kicked the pistol from Buckley's hand. Somerset tried running his saber through Jason's heart, but Jason was too quick. The blade caught only Jason's right hand, which began bleeding profusely. Colleen cried out, and the distraction was enough for Buckley to lose his advantage. With his good hand, Jason knocked Somerset's saber to the ground. The two men faced one another, moving cautiously in a small circle, Jason's hand still bleeding.

Buckley made the first move, his clenched right hand grazing Jason's cheek. Jason's full-fisted left-handed blow to Somerset's stomach, though, took the aristocrat's breath away. Spitting in Jason's face didn't deter the musician, who countered with a straight jab, smashing Buckley's teeth, knocking him to the ground. Out of control, filled with fury, mad with his own strength, blood still dripping from his right hand, Jason found an extra measure of power, beating Buckley to the ground, encircling his fingers around his neck, and squeezing, squeezing, choking the man until the distorted sound of Somerset's final gasps—"she was right . . . Mother was right . . ."—dissipated into the air along with the other dying noises as the day's brutal battle came to a conclusion. The mountain men had taken the ridge.

No time passed before Colleen ran into Jason's arms, embraced him, kissed his mouth and his eyes, kissed his forehead and his chin, bathed him with tear-stained kisses, then tore a section of the battle dress Rianne had fashioned into a bandage that she tied around her lover's hand. Again they embraced, then stayed locked for a long while in one another's arms until a voice—an old familiar voice—called out his name.

"Jason," the voice beckoned.

Jason turned and looked at his father. Ethan stood but a few feet away, his clothes torn, his face covered with mud and dust, his arms crisscrossed with bruises, his eyes filled with remorse.

What was there to do?

What was there to say?

Still embarrassed, still ashamed, the proud elder Paxton hesitated before he approached his son. He was at a loss for words.

Finally, two words fell from his mouth.

"Forgive me," he said to Jason.

Jason, who had been clinging to Colleen, didn't hesitate before opening his arms to his father. Slowly, Ethan moved to form a circle, embracing Colleen, embracing his son—oh, how good it felt to embrace his son!—whispering the words one last time.

"Forgive me."

Chapter 19

The mountain men were leaving. The battle was over. The tear-stained reunions had taken place. Standing atop King's Mountain Ridge, Jason and Colleen stayed back as the others began slowly to descend the hill. Peter, his arm around Joy's waist, turned to ask, "Aren't you coming down?"

"In a very short while," Jason answered, waving to his friend and sister, who disappeared down the side of the ridge.

Facing one another, Jason placed his right hand gently upon Colleen's cheek and sighed, a sigh of enormous relief after a wild and fearful storm. Hanging low in the west, the golden rays of a softly setting sun were filtered through the clouds of smoke that hung low over the dusty battlefield. Below, the once-beautiful fields and woods were burned, darkened and scarred by the fires of battle.

"So much suffering," said Colleen, "so much destruction."

"Sometimes in this strange world," Jason replied compassionately, "it's necessary to tear down before building up again. For the English, it's the begining of the end. For America, it's a brave new beginning."

"And for us?" Colleen asked, looking into her lover's eyes.

His eyes answered her with a sweet, tender smile. Without saying a word, he took a medallion that hung on a gold chain around his neck and slipped it over his head. He held the Paxton family amulet in his hand, cleaning off the dirt with his fingers so that the image was clear: a tall, strong tree triumphantly rising from a thicket of brambles and bushes. Then, as the high-pitched chirping of a distant robin blended with the rustle of a fresh early evening breeze, Jason placed the sacred memento around Colleen's slender neck, kissing her soft lips and saying the words, "I love you, my darling. Now and forever."

Atop King's Mountain, the Tories fell—
'Twas a painful revelation
For the Crown to face the rifles of
A free and newborn nation.

Yet the blood we shed, the lives we lost,
The sacrifices young and old;
Oh, the agony of this tortuous war
Will always haunt our souls. . . .

—Colleen McClagan Paxton

Turn back the pages of history...
and discover

Romance

as it once was!